SOUL OF FLAME

THE IMDALIND SERIES, BOOK FOUR

REBECCA ETHINGTON

IMDALIND PRESS

Published by Imdalind Press

Copyediting by
Production Management by Imdalind Press

ISBN (print) 978-1-949725-03-2
ISBN (e-book) 978-0-9914313-4-2
Printed in USA
This Edition, February 2014

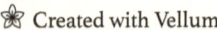 Created with Vellum

THE IMDALIND SERIES

CONTENTS

To My Dad
Who use to record my stories. Scared they would be lost forever.

1

_____

I HAD NEVER KISSED someone before. Yes, I had been kissed, but to make that last move—the final step before lips pressed against lips and warmth and wet blended together in an orchestra of emotions, need and magic—I had never done that before.

I had never wanted it so much that I would fight against my own insecurities to do it.

I had never been brave enough.

Not until Ilyan.

His hand was a soft pressure through the blanket on my leg, his magic a strong presence through the Štít in my chest. I felt the connection, felt the warmth as I ran my fingers over his face, tracing the canyons of his laughs and the valleys of his sorrows.

We sat on the cold stone of the balcony outside our room as he asked me what was beyond my anger. Except all I felt was anger; all I felt was the mad desire to hunt Ryland down and make him pay for what he had done to me, for every bone he had broken. Even through my exhaustion from healing Wyn minutes before, the anger still consumed me. I didn't want to let go of my rage. It was all I had after the hell Ilyan had saved me from, and I wasn't quite sure what was on the other side. I wasn't sure what would be left of me if I released it.

That was wrong, however. I knew what was on the other side. I could feel it in the pressure of Ilyan's hand against my leg. I could feel it in the warmth of his magic as it comforted me.

"Ilyan." His name flowed off my tongue, heavy and strong. It felt so right to utter his name, to hear my voice without a stutter. His eyes opened as I spoke, my fingers frozen against his lips. "You are behind my anger."

The lights of the fireflies that surrounded us erupted as I spoke the words, the truth of them rocking through me. I knew beyond anything that he was there, hidden behind the madness that consumed me, just as I had been for him. He was my rock, and he somehow made everything clear.

I looked up to him, my breath catching at the look he was giving me. The tenderness in his face calmed me while the ocean of his eyes devoured the last of my nerves and insecurities. I let myself get lost in him, and for the first time in months, I felt like me.

Just Joclyn Despain. Not the girl who had lost everything. Not the girl who had been hunted and tortured and broken. Just me.

My nerves loosened like an iron band had been shattered, and my magic stretched away from me; the power that my anger had restrained flooded the world like a tsunami. I had never felt so much strength. The force of it scared me; the normalcy of it terrified me. I could feel everything, the strong waves of Ilyan's emotions as well as the gentle tug of his thoughts. I could feel the nervous magic of the earth as it trembled in fear. I could feel where everyone stood within the old stone walls of the abbey that provided our security for the moment. Wyn was sleeping in her bed, Sain and Thom were tucked away with Ryland, and even though I could feel him, I no longer wanted to hurt him. Ilyan had somehow taken that away.

If only for a moment.

I understood everything.

Everything that had happened, that was going to happen. It all stretched before me like a welcome mat to what could be. In the golden-flecked blue of Ilyan's eyes, I could see every good, every bad, and in that look I knew I wanted it. Every bit of it.

I wanted him.

"I always will be," he whispered, his breath tepid against my fingers, the warmth surging through me. My muscles tensed. My heart beat faster.

He was right; he always would be. I had seen it. I just hadn't accepted it, but now, feeling my emotions so strong and clear for the first time, I knew. My own emotions mirrored his, my heart slowed to beat in time with his, and I couldn't help it, I kissed him.

I leaned forward and pressed my lips to his, the skin hot and moist as we connected. I could never have prepared myself for the strength of my connection with Ilyan. My heart beat faster at the touch, my magic heating as it rushed through me, wild and uncontrollable. I would have fought for control. I would have calmed. But I couldn't focus beyond the feel of Ilyan's lips against mine, the way everything inside me burned. I waited for the earth-shattering explosion that had come when Ryland had kissed me, and while the flash never came, everything else around us seemed to glow.

The earth's magic surged as if someone had awakened it,

the green glow of the fireflies twinkling around us in excitement. Tiny pops of jewel-bright color joined in, the sparks of Ilyan's magic mixing with my own and igniting in the air like a million Christmas lights.

Ilyan didn't even seem to notice. He wound his arm around my waist as he pulled me off the cold stone of the balcony and onto his lap, pressing me against him. He held me there, his lips moving with mine in a fevered heat. He held me as if he were afraid I would disappear, as if this wasn't real. In a way, it didn't feel real, and I was thankful for the pressure, the promise that this wasn't all a dream. The certainty that Ilyan was here and he was kissing me back.

He pressed his lips against mine roughly, moving in perfect harmony as he deepened the kiss, as he moved into me, became part of me. The deep connection rocked through me again as his magic reacted, flaring in a white hot spark of passion.

Passion.

It was different, so much different than before.

My magic pushed through me, right to the point where my hands made contact with Ilyan's skin. It bubbled and grew in a turbulent movement that shook my nerves. It flowed through me like Ilyan was calling it home, and I realized that, in a way, he was.

He groaned at the sensation, his fingers clawing at my shirt as I felt the conflict rise up in him, and he pulled away, his magic withdrawing from me. Everything swirled in a dizzying heat as his magic left me, the world spinning while I fought the need to call out for him and his magic. He held me against him, his breath panting over the long strands of my black hair as he fought the same desire.

"Stop, my love. I can't bond myself to you, not yet," he

gasped as he pressed his cheek against mine, his winded words soft in my ear.

Is that what was about to happen? I was certain it was. Without a doubt, I knew.

I had felt the same wild need and desperate possessiveness when Ryland had bonded himself to me before, though nothing on this level. Before, it was something that I had thought was real. Feeling this now, however... feeling Ilyan's magic flow through me while his arms cradled me, his lips held me, and his magic protected me—feeling his passion, his commitment, his selfless love— I knew how wrong I had been. *This* was home. *This* was love.

This was *real*.

"I want this," I sighed into him; my voice was soft, each word formed perfectly. My fingers trailed over the small hairs on the back of his neck, causing him to tremble underneath me. I couldn't help smiling at his reaction.

"Joclyn," he moaned, and I could hear his deep regret as he tried to convince himself he was doing the right thing even though his desire to lose himself in me almost won over.

Ilyan kept his hold on me as he moved away just enough to look at me, his face so close I would only have to lean forward to connect with him again. My breath faltered at the thought, the energy of my magic picking up. Ilyan smiled, obviously sensing the activity for himself, his eyes dancing in joy.

"*I* want this," he whispered, soft and intimate. His eyes dug into mine as his hand moved away from my back to caress the side of my face. The scarred skin of his palm was strangely soft and comforting. "I want to bond myself to you and be with you for as long as we walk the earth, but this is your choice to make, and I will never take that away. I want to know you are making this choice for you. Not in fear or anger. Not when things may change and other emotions may return. I want you to make this choice in love, and I will wait for that. It is so soon after my father severed your bond with Ryland. I don't want..."

I jumped at the mention of his name, causing Ilyan to stop mid-sentence. Hearing his name spoken aloud brought back the horrors, and my body quaked as my vision faded, creating red walls and destroyed floors in my imagination.

"Shh, my love," Ilyan soothed as his thumb ran over my cheekbone, his gentle touch and the warmth of his magic spreading through me in an attempt to take away the fearful edge of the hallucinations that lacerated me.

I tried to focus on him, but it was no use. I had heard the implication behind what he'd said, and my shoulders knit together as I tried to find the pressure that my battered subconscious craved.

"I d-do n-not l-l-love Ryland-d," I hissed, my voice shaking as I stuttered.

"Jos, we cannot be sure of that..." Ilyan began, but my fear and anger overpowered him. My voice erupted in his head much louder than I intended, and he flinched.

I do not love him, not like I once did. My face burned with painful tears, Ilyan's warm hands against my cheeks catching them as they fell. *I close my eyes and I see blood. I think his name and I feel pain. I can't make that go away. I can't make my fear, my need to attack him, leave. I cannot love someone, I cannot be with someone I only feel hatred for. Who I am scared of.*

"Those are not your true emotions, Joclyn. They are what my father has infected you with. They will fade with time," Ilyan whispered, his pain at seeing me so scared, so sad, tumbling through me. I ignored it, clinging to the last bits of sanity I had left as I tried to get the words out, to help him understand.

They are my emotions now, Ilyan. Cail made sure of that. I stared into him, my jaw clenched as I fought the tirade that bubbled to the surface. I stared at him, pleading with him to understand me while my nerves jumped. I could feel his thoughts as they swirled through him: his regret, anger, love... and finally, understanding.

He pulled me into him, his nose rubbing against my jawbone as he moved to whisper in my ear. The soft touch sent a jolt up my spine. "I'm sorry, Joclyn. I am sorry I didn't get there in time." I could only nod my head in acceptance. He ran his hands over my arms as he kept me enclosed on his lap, his palms trailing over my skin. "You will become bigger than it, my love. I know you will, and then anything you desire will be yours."

I listened to Ilyan's words, the truth of what he said sinking in. His choice to wait wasn't about the relationship I had with Ryland or any feelings I may still have for him. This was about me and helping me move past what had been done to me before I made the choice to move forward. Ilyan would never take away my choice, not in the way that Ryland had. I fought the tremor as his name came to mind, my arms twitching whether or not I wanted them to.

What if that never comes? I sent the words into Ilyan's mind as I exhaled shakily, my fear still fighting its way past the calming current that Ilyan had wound through me.

"It will come. It may take time, but it will come. I will be here to help you find yourself again." He whispered the words into the crisp night air around us, the promise sounding more like a guarantee.

I knew it was.

"Ilyan," I breathed out, my voice pleading as I whispered

into the night. I clenched my fingers around his shirt as I pressed myself against him.

"It is not my time, my love," he whispered as he caught my meaning, the pain at the words that I wasn't sure he agreed with taking his voice away.

It is your time, Ilyan, I spoke into his mind as I pressed my lips against his neck, keeping my skin against his as his breathing caught. *It always was. It always will be. I was just too dumb to see it.*

His arms tightened around me as he fought against his resolve. Our hearts beat in unison as the chilled night breeze pulled at my hair. The strong wave of his affection flowed into me so quickly that it caught me off guard and I gasped shakily as his emotion grew, triggering my own.

"I have waited eight hundred years to hear you say such things. I thought I had understood the love I felt for you before, but until now, I didn't fully know how amazing it was. I didn't know how unworthy I would feel of it. I am lost to you," Ilyan whispered, his voice breaking as tears threatened.

My breath caught in my chest. My soul was overcome by the strength of the love that my body absorbed from him. I just wished it was enough, enough for him to bond himself to me, to know that I felt it was right. It wasn't though; not yet.

I wanted to tell Ilyan how being near him made me feel. I wanted him to know how clear my mind was. I just couldn't find the words. I couldn't form the thought to push it into his mind. My soul teetered on the edge of nothing as I waited for the words to come, as I tried to put voice to them.

"Say something," he pleaded, his thumb gently caressing my cheek.

I love you, Ilyan, I whispered into his mind as I leaned

against him, his arms coming up to wrap around me and keep me close.

"Say it aloud," he whispered, his breath moving through my hair, the warmth sending a shiver down my spine.

"I love you, Ilyan," I said, my voice strong and steady.

I had never felt so much certainty behind my words, so much honesty. I did more than just speak the words. I *felt* them.

I felt them down to the very tips of my toes. I felt them course through me. In many ways, the truth of them scared me, yet in others, they made me comfortable because they made me aware of who I was and what I was meant to do. They made me feel normal and loved.

They *were* love.

"I have waited my entire life to hold you in my arms in this way, to feel your lips against mine." The whisper of his voice faltered as he moved away to look into me. "And now that you are here... I will hold you every night," he vowed as he placed his lips against my forehead, his touch soft and hesitant, "and I will protect you every day," his mouth ran over my skin, down the bridge of my nose, "in hopes that the day will come that I can bond myself to you and call you mine."

His voice was so soft, it almost wasn't there. I wasn't even certain I had heard it before he kissed me again.

2

"He's fanning out."

"At least the north side is still clear. We could make it to this cave in only hours if we went that way."

The voices were loud in my ears as they pulled me out of the deep sleep I had been in seconds before. Anxiety tensed my shoulders together as I listened to the voices that were so close, alerting me to the danger I was in. My mind begged me to run from them, sure I was back in Cail's tortured nightmares. But I lay still, trying to make sense of the voices enough to understand why they were here.

My hands wound around the soft warmth of the blankets that lay against my skin, the fabric pulling my mind away from the horrors. I had never had blankets in the Tŏuha that Cail had trapped me in. If only for that reason, I knew I was safe inside my own reality. I begged myself to believe it. Even with that knowledge, however, I couldn't stop the panic from continuing to seep through me, rocking through my muscles until I shook.

I hated the way the terrors ran through me, the way they controlled me, became bigger than me. They hadn't been this big last night when Ilyan had kissed me. They hadn't ruled over me then. When *I* had kissed *him.*

I worked to regulate my breathing and brought the vivid memories of last night to mind, letting them swirl and flow through me as I fought against the agitation in order to become bigger than the fear Cail had instilled in me. I focused on the memories of Ilyan's hands against my arms, the heat of his breath against my skin. The residual fears rippled through my muscles as the pleasant imagery chased them away, the sensation comfortable in my heavy, over-tired body.

I couldn't have been asleep that long. My mind was still fuzzy; my lips still tinged with the sweet taste of Ilyan's kiss. I could still feel the warmth of the bed where Ilyan had lain behind me, the heat fading from the fabric of the sheets as it evaporated into the cool, fall air.

"Yes, but if we have missed this one, then how many others are out there?" The rough edges of a vaguely familiar voice snapped me out of my revelry, threatening to pull my fears back into my already shredded nerve endings.

"Did you see any more? Were there any sights of what is to come?" Ilyan asked, his voice a powerful force as he commanded over the others in the room.

My body calmed at the sound of his voice. I wanted so much to open my eyes and see him standing just across from me—to let his presence take away the last of my agitation—but I was afraid. Afraid of who else was there; of seeing blood-soaked walls instead of smooth stone ones. So I kept my eyes closed, focusing on the pressure of the blanket as I tried to understand what was going on.

"No, My Lord." Another voice, this one different from the first, cut through the night. My mind tried to place it while fighting the fear its unfamiliarity caused me.

"We have to be missing something!" Ilyan's voice was hard, as a loud bang echoed in my ears, triggering a million memories of clanging pipes and haunting footsteps.

The nightmare jumped through my nerves and my body crinkled together like balled paper. My hands moved to claw into my shoulders as my knees came into my chest. I fought the panic, pushing away the gasps that tried to snake from my lips as I forced away the anxiety.

I tried to keep my breathing level as I kept the fears at bay, pleading with myself that I could open my eyes, that I was brave enough to face my fears. I exhaled a stuttered breath and opened my eyes, waiting to see the blood-stained walls, only to be met by darkness.

My eyes adjusted to the dimly lit room, the heavy darkness of night seeping through the open windows and covering the room in shadows that my mind distorted all on its own. The only light came from a small lantern and several small, colorful orbs that had nestled into the ceiling. The colorful rays cut through the long, dark shadows of night. Everything was as it had been for the last few days— the wall of open archways that led to the balcony, the large ornate furnishings. It was just our room, no nightmares.

Ilyan stood in the dome of dim light, his hands stretched over a table that had been pushed against the wall. He looked intently on the wooden top below him with his hands balled into fists against the wood, making it clear where the loud sound had come from.

The two other men stood across from him; one with long, dirty blond dreads that hung over a leather jacket in stripes of monochrome. Their backs were to me as they, too, hovered over the large table. The other man hunched next to the first, as if he were about to fall asleep. Everything about this man, from his clothes to his posture, was worn and disheveled, as if he had just been caught shoplifting. Hair the color of pitch tangled around his ears and stuck to the back of his neck, making it look like he hadn't combed it recently, if ever.

Thom and Sain.

Their magic flowed through the air around me, alerting me to the security that the height of my anxiety had hidden.

It was foolish to have gotten so worked up; it scared me that it took so little to trigger the demons Cail had infected me with. However, it had only been hours since Ilyan had rescued me from that prison. There would be no quick recovery from my insanity.

I wanted to be patient; I just didn't know if I could be.

"One group would not move so far away. Trpaslíks are too cowardly for that." The lines in Ilyan's face deepened as he took a few steps around the table, his fingers trailing over the surface as he focused on it.

I watched him move as I tried to figure out what the three of them were doing in the first place, the strength of Ilyan's determination almost answering the question for me. The odd connection we now shared sparked. Flashes of his memory, flickers of their arrival, flitted over to me as he focused on the table.

The two men had arrived at our room minutes before, where Ilyan, in his frustration, had ushered them in. He hadn't even considered that I had been sleeping in the bed. No surprises there. His mind had been solely focused on what Sain and Thom had come to tell him, his need to solve the problem, and on protecting his people.

What was left of them, anyway.

I tried to understand what they were talking about, but it was like they were speaking in code. I could ask the question into Ilyan's mind, but something about the way he was focused on the table set my hackles up, making me question whether I wanted to know in the first place.

"Chances are high that there are more between them, My Lord," Sain said, the unfamiliar voice I had heard before now making sense. Sain shifted toward Ilyan, his body still leaning over the table as if he couldn't stand straight on his own.

"Are there any camps here?" Ilyan asked, pointing to a spot on the table as he moved back to his original place.

"There is one here, My Lord," my father answered, his fingers pressing into a spot not far from the one Ilyan had indicated.

"How many?" Thom asked, the familiar agitation in his voice rippling through me.

"I don't know," Sain admitted, his voice somehow dejected, like he had failed.

I stared at the back of Sain's head, his hair as unkempt as it had been in that nightmare so long ago. I wanted him to turn around so I could look at him with my own eyes for the first time since I was five. I wanted to see his smile; I wanted to hear him laugh.

His magic flared abruptly as I looked at him. His signature was so different than the others, deep and calming with an underlying violence and pain that scared me. My desire to reconnect with him vanished as my shoulders tightened.

"Existují zde?" Ilyan asked in Czech as his finger slid over the table to stop at another point on the flat surface.

"Unless they are really good at pretending to be trees," Thom said, his gruff voice low as he leaned over to look at the place on the table Ilyan had indicated.

Ilyan's lip twitched at Thom's comment while his hand moved over the table, one piece of the picture suddenly making sense. They were looking at a map, their attention on the placement of Trpaslík that surrounded us.

It made me uneasy. I could still feel the angry waves of the Trpaslíks' magic from where they hid among the trees, waiting for us. Why they were there was something I was already sure I didn't want to know.

I shifted in the bed as I watched Ilyan pace before the table. His handsome features deepened in the shadows. He looked powerful, the energy of his magic rippling off him in a wave that shook me. I hadn't seen him so focused since Santa Fe.

"What are you playing at, sister?" Ilyan growled. "You do not lead without a stronger force behind you." He spoke like he was talking directly to her, his voice a groan of disappointment through the tense silence of the room.

"You don't think he is here already?" Thom asked, the deep scoff of his irritation almost completely swallowed by his panic.

"No," Ilyan rumbled, his head tilting up toward his brother. "I would feel him if he were. Besides, enough time has not yet passed. I only sent Ovailia away from the abbey last night. She will wait for him."

I cringed at the thought of the night before; it felt like so long ago. The terror as Ryland had barged into my room, and the screams as Ovailia had tried to kill Wyn. I reached my hand up to my face, my fingers gentle as I pressed them into my cheek where Ryland had struck me. Although I was aware that my magic had healed me, I still expected the pain from a new bruise; I expected the sting. Nothing came, however, except the flash in my memory of his black eyes as he had hit me. I cringed at the reflection of the pain, pulling the blanket into me as I blocked it out.

"So that gives us what? Eight hours?" Thom asked, his

panic heightening into anger, leaving his voice hard and derogatory as he questioned Ilyan.

"I am hoping it will be closer to forty," Ilyan replied sternly, his eyes digging into his brother as he tried to control Thom's impending outburst. "He needs to place his pawns after all, and we are beginning to see the early stages of that."

"Forty hours until Edmund arrives and the final battle begins. Sounds reasonable to me. I am sure we will be ready in time." Thom's simple statement put everything into place.

I couldn't stop the panic that rolled over me as true understanding hit me. As much as I tried to fight it, the awful truth triggered the horrors that I was beginning to think I would never be free of.

"Can I leave now? I would love to get back to Wyn," Thom said, but I barely heard him.

The realization of what they had been talking about stabbed through me, my muscles seizing in anxiety as my breathing picked up. I had known they were talking about the Trpaslíks, about whatever attack they had planned, but it was so much more than that.

Edmund was coming; Edmund was attacking.

They were getting ready to start a battle.

The last battle.

The battle that I had seen in the sight Ilyan had received of me, the sight my father had given. The battle I was expected to defeat Edmund in. The battle that had been prophesized about all those years ago. The battle I could not stop.

The thought ran through me like a flame, blazing into every inch of me. I didn't know if I was ready to face Edmund. I had seen the sight and knew what was expected of me, but I couldn't. I wouldn't be able to defeat him. Not after everything Edmund and Cail had done to me. Not after what Ryland had done to me.

The thoughts swirled as my anxiety reached a peak I hadn't felt since before Ilyan had released me from Cail's prison.

My body shook as the sound of my breathing grew into sobs and screams that pushed away the frantic voices I heard shouting through the air. Fear gripped me, flinging Ilyan's magic away as it flared in an attempt to calm me.

"You are stronger than the demons, Joclyn," Ilyan whispered as he pressed his hand against my cheek. I jumped at the touch until I registered the familiarity of his warmth, my eyes flashing open to see him kneeling right in front of me.

"You can fight it," he whispered. "Focus on the good."

I stared wide-eyed at him as I focused on the color of his eyes, the golden light pulling me away from the edge of insanity as the soft tones of our song began to fill his mind. I heard them as they trailed from him in silence, where only I could hear. The calm the melody brought wrapped me in warmth. My voice was no more than a whisper amid the silence of the room as I began to sing along, as I let the words give me the strength I had somehow lost along the way.

Ilyan smiled as I sang, the song ending as my breathing slowed, my hand unwinding from the comforter I had clenched.

"Good, mi lasko, good," he soothed as his hand moved to run through the long strands of my hair. I focused on the gentle feel of his touch as everything melted away.

I wanted the calm I felt to stay forever, but I knew it couldn't—because I had to ask. I had to hear it from Ilyan and know exactly what I was facing.

I bit my lips as I looked at him, knowing I couldn't wait. *Is Edmund coming?*

My heart rate sped up at the thought, the icy steel of his eyes clouding the blue as he nodded.

"Yes." That one word pounded through me, threatening to collapse the fragile calm that I had found.

For the final battle? For what was in our sight? I asked, even though there was no need. I had heard what had been said, and my blood heated as it promised me the truth of what was racing forward.

"Yes," he said again, his voice strong, even though I could see the sadness in his eyes, hear his worry over how it would end.

Not like there was anything we could do about it. We already knew.

You will protect her, but you will fail. The one bred to change the world of magic, the one bred to die.

Die.

I could hear the words of the sight run through me. The image of Ilyan holding my blood-covered body was sharp against my heart.

"I'm n-not read-dy," I gasped out, my voice quaking through me.

"You are stronger than any, my love. I know you will overcome what has been done to you. I promise you, I will help you to see it happen," he whispered low enough that only I could hear.

I let out a shaky breath as my stomach tightened. I was scared. I felt weak, but I knew that wasn't who I was. If I wanted to find who I was again, I knew what I needed to do.

I needed to face it.

I pushed away the agitation as I reached through the blankets to wind my hand around his neck, the soft pads of my fingers pressing against his skin as I pulled him closer, pressing his cheek against mine.

"I need to see," I whispered to him, a calm rush moving through me at the clarity of my words.

Ilyan nodded once against my cheek before he pulled away, his hands moving to pull the warm blankets off me.

"St-stay with me," I whispered to him, grateful when only a small stutter found its way into my voice.

"Always."

I shivered as the cold air hit my skin, wishing we had found something thicker than Ilyan's lounge pants to use as pajamas. I sat on the side of the bed as I slid my feet into the small, red leather shoes Ilyan had made for me.

Ilyan wrapped his hands around mine as he pulled me up and right into him, molding me against him. The warm pressure of his hands pressed into me as we walked toward Thom and Sain, who watched us with wide eyes. I cringed at the look they gave me at the same time that the steady beating of Ilyan's heart echoed through me, calming my own frantic beat while the harmony of the sounds rang in my ears.

My father moved toward me in eager anticipation, his wide, green eyes staring at me in wonder. I couldn't stop myself; I stared into him, desperate to see the father who had become more of a myth to me.

His gaze saw through me, even more than when Dramin looked at me.

When Dramin looked at me, I felt naked, my life and soul x-rayed and open to view. When my father looked at me, I felt like I had been cut open with a blunt knife, and even the secrets I tried to hide were open game.

I could barely see the shadow of the man I'd held on to behind the unkempt hair and the shallow scars on his face. I could see the man that still lived in my memories, the man who had knelt before me in the middle of the clearing during the nightmare Cail had controlled.

Even though I could see him, there was something else I couldn't see. My father.

I didn't know who this man was. I'd had an entire life without him; he had centuries of one without me. I didn't know where he fit, where I fit, and with the way his gaze made me feel I wasn't sure I wanted to find out.

I wanted to tell him to look away, to leave me alone, although part of me—the part that had clung so desperately to that tiny, black backpack all those months ago—couldn't help screaming that this was my father. That he hadn't abandoned me after all.

"You are stronger than it," Ilyan reminded me as we stopped before the table. His hands ran over my arm before they were gone, leaving me standing alone while Sain and Thom stared at me. I wasn't really sure if I wanted to look up again, so instead I kept my focus on the massive map that covered the top of the table.

The map was huge, much bigger than I had originally thought it to be. The large abbey that we were hidden in was the size of a matchbook in the center; the forest that we were surrounded by stretched out on the yellowing parchment with small cartoon circles randomly popping up as if to remind us of the trees.

I didn't need Ilyan to tell me what the red circles that littered the surface of the map were. The black chicken-scratch numbers written next to each one had made it obvious. It was the army that Edmund had sent after us. I could easily add the numbers up to well over two hundred, but I knew deep down inside that something was wrong with that number. Yesterday, the hostile magic around us had throbbed in a violent wall that felt like more than only two hundred men.

"We will wait until Edmund arrives, and then I believe we should start the attack here," Ilyan said as he placed his finger against the map near a large circle of camps.

My whole body jumped at the word "attack," bringing my focus off the map and back to Ilyan, whose deep voice rumbled as he instructed the two other men. "We can flush them out from this side while Wyn and Thom pick off the second wave from the middle—"

"I'm sorry," Thom interrupted, his voice somewhat hysterical. "Attack? Wyn... fighting? Ilyan, you can't be serious."

"It is what the sight has shown, Thom, and we must stand by that. It is not our way to disregard the sights of the Drak's," Ilyan practically snapped.

Sain nodded in agreement, even though he didn't seem to be able to look away from me yet. I caught a glimpse of his intense stare before I looked away, the glaze in his eyes making me feel as though I was food, not his long-lost daughter.

"And who, exactly, do you think will be able to aide in this attack, brother?" Thom snapped back angrily as he leaned over the table toward Ilyan, his dreads swinging over his face and darkening the already angered expression.

Ilyan turned toward Thom at his challenge, his face hard. I cringed the same way Thom wilted under the look in his eyes.

"We may only be six, but I know how to lead us in battle," Ilyan said, his voice deep and menacing as he looked into Thom.

I had never seen this side of Ilyan before, this imposing presence that demanded respect. It was different than when his voice had told of his place and power, when by just looking at him you knew who he was. This was Ilyan when his power—his regality—ruled him. It was awe-inspiring.

"Yes, if we were six whole-bodied individuals, but we are not," Thom countered, his voice light and mocking with his usual irritation as he defied Ilyan's reprimand. "Wyn has only just been removed from the zánik curse; she hasn't been awake for more than a few minutes from when the Silnỳ healed her six hours ago. Ryland is locked in Sain's bathroom as we speak, rocking back and forth, mumbling about death and traitors. The Silnỳ is cowering, right in front of me, scared of her own shadows. And Dramin..." Thom's voice faded and broke at the mention of Dramin's situation.

I wanted to say that Thom was wrong about me—about everyone—but I could still feel the anxiety that just hearing Ryland's name had given me. I could feel Wyn from where she slept, her body still weak from all that she had gone through. I knew he was right. We were only six and most of us were broken. Fighting was impossible.

"We cannot attack, My Lord, not now. Our only chance to live is to escape." Sain's voice was deeper than it had been before, the tone strangely flat and monotone. My ears perked at the familiarity of the sound of a sight, which weaved his normal words with the deeper tones of his ability. My blood prickled as my own Drak magic heightened, yet his eyes never darkened and his own magic never flared.

"But what of the sight, Sain?" Ilyan asked, my focus darting back to him as he ran his hand through the short strands of blond hair, his frustrations flowing into me. "The sight clearly showed a battle within the walls of Rioseco."

"A battle with you and the Silnỳ only," Sain said, his

calm voice rumbling. "If you think back, it showed no others involved in the last battle."

"Then we should get everyone else out in the morning," Thom said without hesitation, his strong voice blocking out the rebuttal I had been trying so hard to form. "I need to get them out of here. *I* need to get out of here." Thom's patience snapped with his last words, the mad look in his eyes taking over. My nerves unraveled at the insanity behind his eyes. I understood that look because I felt the same need to run, to get everyone away from the danger that surrounded us.

"Impossible. Joclyn will not be ready to aide in your escape by tomorrow." Ilyan didn't even look at Thom as he spoke; he kept his eyes down on the map, his thoughts only on what was ahead of us.

"She looks ready."

I cringed at Thom's tactless statement, at the thought of being pressed into some form of battle right then. I could already feel my fears push against me, my magic surge so uncontrollably it scared me.

"No," I said softly, not sure my voice was loud enough for anyone to hear.

No one moved.

Ilyan leaned toward Thom over the table, his eyes hard and threatening as he looked into him. "I pulled her from Cail's mind three days ago, Thom. Three. For most of that she has slept. She needs time." Ilyan's voice was a hammer meant to put Thom in his place, however his hot head only fumed more, his anger growing underneath Ilyan's displeasure.

"We don't have time; Edmund is coming," Thom snapped, his magic sparking in his fury. It rushed against me and I cringed, the alarm on his face scaring me.

"You don't think I know this? I do!" Ilyan roared, his

voice so loud the furniture in the room began to shake. "It is my responsibility to keep my subjects safe, and I will do this the way it needs to be done. The way the sight has shown me. You will follow, Thomas."

The silence that followed Ilyan's power shocked through me. I felt the need to bow before him just as Thom and Sain had moved to do with mumbled apologies, the tension in Ilyan's back leaving as they did.

Ilyan's eyes narrowed at the submissive curve of Thom's back before he turned away from him, his own posture tall and straight. Ilyan's fingers trailed over the surface of the map in contemplation before his lips turned up in the smirk I had grown to love, his eyes darting over to me.

"I will fight with Joclyn by my side," Ilyan said, his focus unwavering from me. The hard lines of before had gone, leaving everything about him soft and warm as he looked into me. His hand covered mine as he promised me of my strength in silence, his thoughts screaming of his confidence in me; his confidence building mine.

"What if Ovailia attacks before Wyn heals enough to move?" Thom asked in desperate panic that broke the spell Ilyan had wrapped me in. "I will need her help to move Dramin and Ryland. I need to get them out of here alive."

"She won't," Ilyan said sternly as his focus moved back down to the map.

"But what—"

"Ovailia is more talk than action." Ilyan put a stop to Thom's insistence quickly, the depth of his voice demanding respect. "She won't do anything without someone backing her up. She will not attack until our father is here, and I don't sense him yet.

"When will Wyn be ready to move?" Ilyan asked, his voice floating over the table toward no one in particular.

"I don't know; it's been hours since Joclyn healed her," Thom growled.

"It will be tomorrow," I said, my magic wrapping around her from across the abbey. I felt the steadiness of her heartbeat along with the continual strengthening of her mind and magic. I didn't look at anyone as I spoke. I only focused on Wyn and on the last of Talon's magic that swirled inside of her.

"Good," Ilyan sighed. "Then, unless anything else happens, we will move as soon as Joclyn is ready. It will be nice to have Wyn on my side again. I have to admit, I have missed her this past century."

My focus shot toward Ilyan at his words, my eyebrows arching in confusion, but he didn't even seem to notice. I must have misheard. She had been married to his best friend for the last century. I wasn't sure how that constituted missing someone. I opened my mouth to question him, only to be cut off by Sain, his comments only adding to my bewilderment.

"You are not the only one, My Lord," my father said, his voice resonating in a peculiar, happy tone. It filled the room in an incompatible way, the words seeming false against the stress I still felt. "I think she is even glad to be back. A little confused at times, but she is coping well enough," Sain continued, a deep vein of pride in his voice, like a father to a particularly disobedient child.

"What do you mean she's confused?" I asked, my eyes darting toward my father for the first time since I had moved to stand beside him.

My father, however, only smiled and looked toward his mug, diverting his attention to whatever was happening in the bottom and not in answering my question. I sighed and looked toward Thom, my eyes digging into him. The anger that had fueled him for the last few minutes faded as he looked away from me, obviously uncomfortable.

"Can we move on, please?" Thom interrupted, unwilling to answer my stare. I pursed my lips at his little outburst, knowing I should be mad, yet his reaction was too much like him for it to matter.

"We have at least twenty camps, that we know of, and at least a hundred Trpaslíks surrounding us on the east side of the abbey. That does not account for any that we may not have seen on the west or north sides where this camp is." Thom's voice was loud as he rattled off the information. He spoke with an authoritative tone that I had never heard from him before. I hadn't thought Thom had that in him.

"Thank you for the recap, Thomas," my father said, the smile on his face evident.

"Well, if you would stay on track..." Thom's voice rose more, the command gone, only to be replaced by a somewhat hysterical anger.

"I stay on track as well as you win at gin rummy," Sain said, unable to hide his laughter now.

"Gin rummy is an old man's game." I wasn't sure if Thom was still angry or if the banter was habitual. It seemed so natural, yet I had the feeling that they could still break out into a fight at the tiniest prodding.

"Remind me how old you are again, son?" All laughter was gone from Sain's voice now.

"Don't call me that, grandpa. I could wipe the floor with you."

I took in nothing from their repartee. All I saw were the crimson circles that littered the surface of the map, the glistening numbers right beside.

I had thought the numbers were wrong before, but I

hadn't questioned it much. Now I could feel it. While thunder rolled over us, shaking the abbey as it grew louder, my magic surged through the darkened grounds and sensed them.

All of them.

"Wipe the floor?" Sain asked.

"You are too old to understand," Thom said, his own laugh sounding hollow in my ears as my mind remained focused through the miles of forest that surrounded us.

"Enough," Ilyan interrupted, his voice caught between a laugh and a yell, and I jumped. "I had forgotten how bad you two were together. Even my parents never bickered as much."

Everyone laughed around me as I felt the first swells of the Trpaslík hatred and anger, their violent magic surging as they milled around the edges of the protective barrier that Ilyan had placed around the abbey.

My magic began to paint the image of their camps in my mind, giving me a second sight as I watched them drink and sleep around magical fires. I stretched until the magic of the Trpaslíks changed to one of a different nature—one that I couldn't place—moving around them. The hatred in this unknown power was even stronger than Edmund's men. I moved away from the foreign magic, unwilling to feel more of it, and let my mind embrace what I knew, creating my own map inside my head.

They were everywhere, surrounding us, and what was more, there were much more than had been placed on the map. I gritted my teeth together and kept my eyes closed. I needed to tell him.

Forty-two camps to the east, totaling two hundred and twenty Trpaslík and a few whose magic I have never felt before. Ovailia is by them, near the back. I looked toward him as I sent the message, his eyes widening as he registered what I was saying.

He locked eyes with me, a small smirk playing around his lips before he ducked down and began writing on the large map on the table.

"Forty-two camps?" Thom asked as he read the number Ilyan had written, the confusion clear in his voice. "There cannot be nearly that many, Ilyan. The highest we have counted was twenty-eight."

"And to the North?" Ilyan asked as he ignored Thom's question. He looked up at me in expectation, his eyes dancing as his emotions surged in pride.

My magic spread away from me again and back into the forest around us as I counted the camps one by one. My heart beat heavily as I realized how much trouble we were in. They hadn't thought there was anyone on that side of the abbey. It was the way they had hoped we would be able to get away, but there wasn't any chance of that happening now.

Twenty-one camps, at least ninety Trpaslík. There is more of that odd magic over there. I am not sure what it is, I replied internally, and Ilyan's hand moved to add the number to the map.

"Twenty-one? What in Buddha's pants are you playing at, brother?" Thom interjected. He was practically yelling now, his confusion increasing.

"Are you sure, mi lasko?" Ilyan asked, his head still bowed as he ignored Thom's outburst.

"Yes," I whispered, not willing to elaborate to the two men who were now staring openly at me. Sain looked like he was getting ready to sacrifice a calf in my name.

"Where else are they, Jos?" Ilyan whispered. He raised his head to look at me, his eyes digging into mine. I just stared at him, not quite sure how to tell him all that I felt, not entirely certain how he would react.

"I need to know where they are, mi lasko. As accurately as you can." His regality was broken for a moment when everything about him softened as he looked into me.

I nodded my head once before I scanned over the map, looking at the dozens of red marks that they had carefully drawn to mark each of the Trpaslík camps which they had found. Most of them were very precise, but so many of them were wrong, too far in the wrong direction, not enough members accounted for. I looked from circle to circle until my eyes stopped, focusing on a blank space, the old paper bare and yellowed, but I knew that was wrong.

I reached my hand forward, unsurprised to see my fingers shake as I crawled them along the smooth paper until I reached the spot I had seen clearly in my mind. I could see them, the stocky men gathered around the fire, the weapons piled to the side, the want of blood that pulsed through their magic.

Eight are here, I sent to Ilyan, his hand flying forward as he drew a large number eight right where I had indicated.

The ink dried as I looked over the paper, my magic stretching away from me as it recalled what I had felt only minutes before. I moved from one bare place to another, my fingers crawling over the paper as I pointed out camp after camp. Ilyan followed with me, his pen working fast as I gave him the information they had been so desperately in need of.

The numbers grew as I worked, the circles increasing until it became clear that Edmund had effectively trapped us inside the ancient, stone walls of the abbey. I didn't know what battle they had planned, but looking at these numbers now, I didn't see how we could get away or even survive a fight. I cringed at the thought, pushing the imagery away as Ilyan's magic flowed through me, soothing my joints that had knit themselves together in anxious fear.

Twelve, I said as I gave him the last number.

"We are trapped," I whispered as Ilyan's arm snaked around my waist, pulling me against him. I could feel the heavy pulse of his heart, the maniacal need to fight conflicting with his need to protect me as well as to keep everyone alive.

"Not necessarily," Ilyan announced as he pointed toward a large camp right in front of where Ovailia was currently stationed. "If you and I begin our battle here, we might be able to clear enough Trpaslíks out of this area to give everyone else a chance to escape."

"Will that work?" Thom asked, his voice sounding hopeful for the first time.

"It should." Ilyan's small smile played through his eyes. "If Joclyn and I can create enough destruction, then the others won't be able to stay away."

I could see the brilliance of the plan, the simple logic probably just enough that it would be overlooked. The only variable was me.

"When?" Thom asked eagerly.

"If we coordinate it right with Edmund's arrival, we should catch them off guard," Ilyan said. The tone of his words made this all sound strangely final, as if tomorrow morning we would wake up and stroll into the forest, expecting to come out again in one piece. Ilyan maybe, but the sight had shown me something other than that for myself.

"Joclyn," Ilyan whispered, his voice only for me, even though I was sure everyone else could hear him. "I will need your help to track their movements and pinpoint my father's arrival. Can you do that?"

I nodded at his question, knowing that even if I wasn't yet ready to fight, that at least was something I could do.

"Then I will need you two to continue watching over the abbey from the tower. Thom, I also need you to watch over Wyn and Dramin. I would like to know the second we can move them." Ilyan's voice rumbled through me as he spoke.

"Why don't I knit you a new Christmas sweater while I am at it?" Thom grumbled under his breath.

"Thomas."

"Yes, My Lord," Thom relented, nodding once in acceptance, even though I could tell he was upset over having to do so much.

I had expected to see the same acceptance of the plan on Sain's face, but instead, he stared right at me, his green eyes as wide as saucers.

I cringed as the knife of his eyes cut into me, moving closer to Ilyan on habit.

Why is he looking at me like that? I asked into Ilyan's mind, my confusion growing.

I heard Ilyan's heart rate pick up in my ears before his hand moved to stroke the side of my face. His fingers grazed over the skin as his emotions shifted, his thoughts moving right along with them when his own confusion gave way to a gentle pride.

"He is amazed by you, as am I." His voice was a whisper as he spoke to me.

"It is more than amazement, Ilyan," Sain said, his tone matching the awe that his face had held before. I almost jumped at his voice, shocked that he had been paying attention at all.

"What do you mean, Sain?" Ilyan asked, the muscles in

his arms tensing as he held me against him protectively, the action flaring my nerves.

"She has been speaking into your mind," Sain said as an answer, the words almost sounding like a revered song.

"Yes," Ilyan's deep voice rumbled through his chest, making it clear he didn't want to elaborate.

"I had my suspicions before when I saw the burn of the Black Water on your hand, but I thought you were just pacifying an old man..." Sain whispered softly.

My fingers clung to Ilyan's shirt as I waited for the news that was sure to come.

"You have fused your souls."

3

"F-f-us-sed-d?" The word was out before I could stop it, the stutter worse than right after Ilyan had pulled me from the nightmare, when I huddled against the toilet. I couldn't help it, though; I couldn't make sense of the confusing mess my father had just divulged.

"That is only lore, Sain." Ilyan's voice rumbled in disbelief, his emotions moving through me as his thoughts tumbled over each other.

"Is it?" Sain asked, his awe fading into amusement. "Then tell me, how does my child speak into your mind? There is no magical ability that can accomplish such things. I am sure there are others anomalies that connect you two. Things that cannot be explained."

I looked away from Ilyan's shocked expression to my father, my pulse quickening at being referred to as his child. The surprise at such an intimate title wore off as his words sank in, though.

There were other things that connected us.

I had felt them in the way I could feel Ilyan's emotions, the way I could understand his thoughts before he put words to them. I had thought those were supposed to be normal magical abilities, which had come to me when my full powers had awakened. They felt normal to me. My magic, my mind just knew what to do—how to find Ilyan when he wasn't near me, how to feel his emotions.

Then why was it only with Ilyan? Why could I not hear my father's thoughts or feel Wyn's emotions from across the abbey? The only time I had felt something similar was with Ryland, but we had been bonded then.

Is it a Zělství? I asked as I turned in Ilyan's arms, my hands soft against his chest as I looked up to him. I could see my shock looking back at me through him, my silver eyes wide as I tried to understand.

It was the only thing that made sense, out of the limited knowledge I had of magic. I felt like I was sifting through sand in search of a diamond as I tried to understand what Sain had been talking about.

"No, my love," Ilyan whispered to me, his hand running down my face as he moved my hair out of my eyes. I could hear his thoughts as they trickled down to me; the promise to never bind himself to me until I was ready still strong.

"Then what is it?" I asked, my stomach tightly wound in fear.

"I am not sure. It is lore. If it is true, I can tell you that it is so much more than a Zělství ..." He said nothing more as he held me against him, our eyes closing in harmony as our magic met, moving together. I could hear Ilyan's thoughts trickle down to me, his mind tripping around thoughts and words and languages until it was a jumbled mess that got lost in the air between us.

"Ilyan?" my father asked, his voice soft as he interrupted us. "May I see your hand?"

Ilyan eyed him skeptically before he moved away from

me. His steps were slow as he removed the heavy bandages he kept around the burn, allowing my father to see. I stood still against the table as Thom also came forward to see the dark red marks that Ilyan had given himself.

Ugly divots of black and blood red covered Ilyan's entire palm, the burn stretched along the backs of his fingers and up his wrist. The angry, red skin was still glossy as it worked to heal itself, the burn not more than a day or two old. I had seen it last night, and even then I had been aware that it would never heal, not in the way the marks on his chest had. He would wear these painful scars forever.

"That would be why I despise that poison," Thom said, his voice crinkling in disgust. He looked like he wanted to move away, but he held still, almost as if he couldn't help himself from looking at the burns. It was the same look he had given me when Dramin had first given me the water, like it had offended him.

The problem was that his look was offending me. Ilyan's hand looked terrible, but without that sacrifice and without the water, I wouldn't be here.

"That poison saved me," I said, the anger rippling through me. Thom lifted his eyes to meet mine, though he only rolled them and looked away, mumbling something about Dramin that I couldn't hear. Ilyan's back stiffened at his comment, but he said nothing, his muscles rippling under the dark cotton t-shirt he wore.

"This is very deep. I don't think I have even seen one this deep before," Sain whispered, his fingers prodding the sore skin, which caused Ilyan to jerk in pain. I jumped as Ilyan did, my fist reaching up to wind its way around the fabric of his shirt.

"Are all your burns tied to Joclyn in some way?" Sain

glanced at Ilyan, his bushy eyebrows disappearing into his unkempt hair.

"Yes," Ilyan replied through his teeth, his pain pulsing stronger the longer Sain touched the burns.

I didn't like the way his muscles twitched as he restrained his agony. When I stepped up to him, wrapping my arms around his chest, his muscles tensed under me, the shadow of his pain flowing through me from the Štít. I buried my face into Ilyan's chest as my magic worked to calm him, the scent of his shirt full of his magic.

"You are not privileged enough to touch the Black Water so frequently," Sain said, his eyes not lifting from Ilyan's hand.

Even I didn't miss the slight disgust in Sain's voice over Ilyan's supposed disgrace of what Sain viewed as holy. To me, Black Water was still just food.

"I do not think this is a matter of privilege, Sain," Ilyan said as he took his hand back from my father. "And not all hold your views of the Water. You would do well to remember that."

Ilyan's fingers were tense and stiff before he placed the burned skin of his hand against my arm, his magic surging alongside mine at the contact. His body calmed as my touch took away the pain that had fired through his blood, my skin almost acting like Novocain to him.

"You are not a Drak, Ilyan," Sain countered, his voice full of scolding.

Ilyan tensed against me at Sain's foolish comment. Even Thom backed up, shaking his head at Sain's pride.

Ilyan was King, though I wasn't sure if that title applied to my father. My father was one of the first of all magic. For all I knew, Ilyan should bow to him, but judging by the reactions of those around me, I guessed not.

"The water reacts differently to you than it does to my kind," Sain plowed on, oblivious to Ilyan's wrath that was about to release. "The water is part of me, fused with me body and soul, as it is with Joclyn."

I stifled the gasp that tried to fight its way out of me; I had never thought of the Black Water being part of me that way. Although, in some ways, I had felt it; I had felt how my blood pulled at me, how it warmed after sights. The tone in Sain's voice made it sound much more ominous, though, like it controlled me, instead of the other way around.

"When one who is not a Drak touches the Black Water, it infects their soul, like a poison. That is what enables us to give you sight. To peek into your future or your past, but you purposefully burned yourself to save her, and the Water moved into your soul in an attempt to infect it, to give you sight. Your body cannot handle such a change, so instead, it clung to your soul as you poured the water into Joclyn. Then, in its attempt to recreate you, the water sought out the magic of a Drak and your souls were fused together. Permanently."

Permanently? I asked in silence, the word not frightening me as much as I knew it should.

Ilyan looked away from my father at my question, his eyes catching mine as he unwound his arms from me. The flow of his magic spiked in a wave of warmth.

"He means, my love, that this... this connection between us can never be undone." Ilyan's hand moved away from my shoulder as he spoke, his burned fingers soft against my skin as they ran over my neck toward my mark.

I know what permanently means, Ilyan, I said into his mind. He smiled at my comment.

My lip twitched, my own grin trying to sneak past my nerves.

37

"Do you resent my choice?" Ilyan asked, his touch gentle as his hands moved down my arm to clasp my hand.

"No, Ilyan, never," I said, my words calm and controlled. *Do you regret it?*

"For you, I regret nothing," Ilyan breathed as he pressed his forehead against mine.

I pulled his magic into me in the stolen moment before Ilyan straightened, his back returning to its regal pose as he turned to face my father. "Sain, tell me. What I feel for your daughter, what I hope she feels for me—"

"Do I have time to leave?" Thom interrupted, obviously sensing where the conversation was going. I smiled at his outburst, but didn't look away from the depth of Ilyan's eyes that had captured me. I didn't want to.

"How much has this connection influenced that?" Ilyan asked, his voice calm and strong, even though I could feel the worry behind it. My own apprehension grew, the question I hadn't even thought to ask clenching my heart.

I felt so comfortable with Ilyan; everything felt so right. I didn't want to think of that being a forced reaction from our woven souls, that it wasn't real.

I *knew* I had felt the connection before. I had first recognized it when he lay unconscious in the cave, but it had grown since then. That alone promised me how real this was.

"It is your souls that are fused, Ilyan. Not your hearts," Sain said, his face breaking into a wide grin that flashed a million childhood memories into my eyes. "Your future together may be defined—your essence combined—but your emotions? Your love? That was there before any seal took place. Without love, you wouldn't have willingly sacrificed yourself for her. Without love, her heart wouldn't have called to you and given you a way to find her. It was always there. It always will be."

My heart relaxed as Ilyan's did—mine in gratitude, his in eager anticipation.

"What will this do when we perform the bonding ceremony? What might happen to us?" Ilyan asked smoothly, his choice of words a lightning bolt through my nerves.

When.

Ilyan spoke of something akin to marriage, and I fought the blush that threatened to cover my face.

Sain bounced on his heels in eager anticipation, the bright-eyed look making me uncomfortable.

"When?" Thom spat, his irritation growing as the same word gave him a completely different reaction. "Surely not right now. You'll at least give me time to leave, right?" Thom growled, his scowl growing before he turned away to focus on the map in an obvious attempt to drown us out. I was surprised he had stuck around all this time.

"I do not know, My Lord. As you said, this was only lore until now. *You* were lore, my dear child," he said, his eyes darting to me as his voice echoed. "The treasured sight of a child who would come forth and save us all from the destruction that Edmund has brought."

"You should be more worried about what your fused souls are going to do to the sight," Thom said loudly as he smacked the table in frustration, causing me to jump at the sound. "The Silný will still be able to fight, right?"

His desperate panic moved back into him again as he walked over to us, his hands deep in the pockets of his jeans. I had never seen him look so haggard, as though he was going to snap any minute.

"I'm right here," I mumbled, trying not to let my

frustration bristle at being referred to like a dog that had been taught tricks.

No one seemed to hear my quiet voice. Thom didn't even look at me before Ilyan's arm tightened me against him, his voice raising as he faced his brother.

"The sight has shown she will fight, so she will fight. I believe in her ability to do so," Ilyan said as he held me against him protectively.

"Yeah, but did the sight say Ilyan was going to go off and fuse his soul to hers?" Thom asked as his hands jumped from his pockets, the movement so quick that I jerked in the expectation of being hit.

I flinched like a wounded dog, the action making Thom's eyes glare into me more. The fear that lived in him turned into disgust that made me feel worse, made my anxiety jolt.

"No!" Thom snapped, his tirade continuing on as if he hadn't noticed the way his action had affected me. Or maybe he had. "We have no idea how this is going to change her magic, her ability. She may be useless to us now."

"Useless?" I spat, a strong, jagged edge of anger running through me. Right then, he only saw me as a thing, a pawn.

"It has made my magic stronger, Thom," I said, my voice shaking even though I had tried to push the strength of the anger into it.

Thom only looked at me with the same disbelief he had held before.

"She will rise to the path the sight has chosen for her. I expect nothing less from her," Sain said, his voice deep and mellow.

His words promised his confidence in me, but he did not look into me with the pride my mother always had. He looked at me with a reverent awe, almost as if I was untouchable.

Like I was a god to him.

The thought made me sick to my stomach.

"I would hope not, considering that now we are surrounded by hundreds of blood-thirsty Trpaslíks. You ready to face that, Silnỳ?" Thom turned to me with the same hard look in his eyes, the plea for an answer digging through me.

I wanted to tell him yes. I wanted to say I was strong enough—that I was ready—but I knew it would be a lie, so I held still, my arms clinging to Ilyan even though I was aware it made me look weak. I needed the rock of him underneath me.

Thom's eyes narrowed at my lack of response, the fear in my eyes giving him all he needed to know.

"Didn't think so," he growled before he turned away, his back crouching dejectedly.

"*You must find your strength to protect her, to be near her, for it is only by your side that she can find her true purpose, that she will find the strength to kill those that would end the magic of the world.*" Ilyan's words flowed from him, the air rippling with the power that they held as my blood warmed. The second the last word left him, thunder rumbled around us, the sky opening up as if the earth felt the power as well.

"The words of the sight, Thom," Ilyan continued. His voice lowered as the air continued to crackle with an electric charge. "You should know better than to doubt them. Joclyn has been given this path, and this power, for a reason. Without them, Wynifred would have never survived the zánik curse."

Something that Ilyan said had hit a live wire in Thom. He spun around to face us, his dreads swinging as the fire in him turned into a torrent. "And Dramin would be standing next to us, not dying in his room."

I cringed at the snap of Thom's voice. My anxiety flared in warning, the unwanted fears breaking through as he glared into me.

"D-dying?" I stuttered out, unable to look away from Thom, even though I knew I should look anywhere other than at the face that was fueling my fear.

I couldn't. Because, even though I could feel his anger, all I could see was the pain. It wasn't the fearful looks I had been given in the Tòuha. No, it was the same raw fear, the same heart-breaking anger that I had felt every time the demons of the Tòuha had come after me. It made it so I could almost understand him. I *heard* the pain that seeing Dramin injured had caused him, the fear of losing someone so close to him.

My eyes widened as Thom came undone right before me.

"Yes, Silnỳ," Thom snapped. "When you attacked him, you killed his magic. Ilyan has been able to revive it, but it never stays, his magic keeps fading to nothing. He's an ancient. How long do you think his mortal body will last without his magic?"

"I-I didn't... I th-thought..." I stuttered out, not knowing what to say to take away his pain. How to explain the regret I had felt after the attack had left my hands days ago, the fear that rocked through me now.

"You tried to kill him!" Thom yelled, the blue of his eyes glossing over as his face turned red.

"Thomas Krul!" Ilyan roared as he stepped toward his brother, blocking me from Thom's rage. His magic flared while Thom cowered before him. Ilyan's muscles rippled as he stood protectively in front of me, his arms spread wide as he shielded me.

I should have been grateful for the protection, for Ilyan's

willingness to stand up to him right then, but I couldn't. I was too focused on Dramin's sleeping body in his room across the abbey; on the gentle lull from all that was left of his magic, on the way he didn't move. Thom had spoken as if Dramin was moments away from death, and now I could feel that in him.

He couldn't die, though.

I wouldn't let him.

4

My sanity was slipping away, just like it had last night when I had run to Wyn.

I had run from the others without thinking, my feet pounding down the halls toward the weak spark of Dramin's magic that called to me from the other side of the abbey. I tried to ignore the way the walls that surrounded me crumbled and warped in my subconscious, but it was no use. Thom's anger echoed through my mind as I moved, flaring my fears, and the horrors of my insanity followed me even though I could still see reality clearly through my eyes. It had all become two parallel universes working against each other in an attempt to drive me mad.

I clenched my teeth as my heartbeat quickened, my hands running along the walls as I struggled to stay standing. I turned the last corner at full speed, my magic opening the door in front of me to a large, dark room less than a quarter of the size of Ilyan's. The blue light of night seeped in through one of the large windows, casting everything in shadows. The room was a cluttered mess with piles of books, stacks of paper, and shelves that lined his walls. Each shelf was full of the earthen brown mugs from Imdalind, each full of Black Water. In the middle of it all, Dramin lay still on a small, white bed, the blankets pulled up to his chest.

He lay completely motionless, a ribbon of moonlight laying over him, enhancing the dark purple rings which hung like dirty hammocks under his eyes, his skin an ashen grey that matched the ancient stone of the walls. Someone had placed his hands one over the other on his chest; the same way my great-grandmother's had been at her funeral, as I am sure my mother's had been when they buried her. It was as if whoever had placed him there had thought him dead.

Except he wasn't dead; I could see him breathe, feel the weak pulse of his magic that was buried deep inside him.

I had known that I had attacked him—that he was weak —but somehow, seeing him like this made it all the more real. The thoughts of coming battles and the war I was expected to win vanished in a wisp of smoke. They didn't mean anything anymore, not as much as what I had done to Dramin.

My body folded into itself as a violent surge of regret wound through me, tensing my muscles. Ilyan's arm wrapped around me as he came up behind me, pulling me into him. I felt Thom and Sain step into the room, but I didn't turn to acknowledge any of them. I couldn't look away from the steady rise and fall of Dramin's chest, my heart pounding against my ribs until they hurt.

I did this, I hissed into Ilyan's mind, my anger igniting the words viciously.

"You had reason," Ilyan whispered, his voice calm despite the worry I felt run through him.

"I had-d no reas-son to at-tack my b-brother," I stuttered,

the acknowledgment that he was my brother an iron barb in my heart.

The world broke around me as I felt the hard stone floor slam against my knees. The impact ricocheted through my bones, my shame breaking free in a wail of agony and fear.

"Joclyn?" my father asked, his confused question drowned out by my howl.

"I d-d-did this. I k-killed h-him!" I cried into the floor, my voice as broken and strained as when I had been trapped, when I couldn't remember anything. I stared at the floor, the creases between the stone turning red with blood that was not there.

"No, my love," Ilyan whispered against me, his arms wrapping around me as he kneeled down beside me.

"I h-had-d n-no re-reason." Tears flowed from my eyes as I tried to pull away, his arms loosening just enough so I could look at him.

"You did not mean to attack him, but you had a reason for what you did. You know you did." Ilyan looked at me, his love and worry projecting through the deep blue of his eyes, but I didn't see that. I only saw Dramin's eyes when my magic had hit him, the sadness as he bid the world farewell. I only saw the magic as it flew from my hands, the last of Cail's mind disintegrating around me.

I clenched my hands into tight fists, my long nails pushing into the skin of my palms as regret and anger filled me.

Ilyan must have felt my panic because he clutched me to him, his lips pressing against the mark on my neck as he held me. The aggressive shock wound through me in a surge of energy that took away just enough of my anxiety to give me a chance to control it.

"You are strong, my love. You can fight it," Ilyan reminded me, his voice a whisper.

Emotions and memories ran through my mind as I fought the torment, desperate to regain the strength I knew was still hiding within me. At the same time, I danced with the urge to disappear into the insanity that had opened its arms to me.

"Teď tiše, moje malá. Upokoj se, buď klidná. S novým úsvitem se svět změní. A když se změní, uvidíš, jaký bychom měli být, ty a já." Ilyan whispered the words of our song to me, the meaning clear even without the tune behind it. His words broke through just enough to give me a jolt of strength, allowing me to banish the fears from my body.

The pain and horrors scattered like light in the dark. I raised my head to my brother, my stiff body uncoiling as I moved to step toward him. I could feel the apprehension try to return, but I pushed it away, my need to see him compelling me forward.

I reached out shakily to touch Dramin's arms, his skin clammy under my fingers. With my skin against his I could feel what I had done. I had destroyed his magic, just as Thom had said.

Just as I had feared.

I hadn't been able to stop it; the attack had controlled me.

It was just as I had seen in the cave in Italy as I hovered over the pool of Black Water. When I had seen Dramin's death.

My body collapsed onto Dramin's, my hands clinging to him as my regret and pain swelled and grew until a howl broke from my lips.

Ilyan was next to me in a second, our song a whisper on

his lips as he gave me something to focus on, something to chase away my terrors.

"I s-saw this," I sobbed as he held me, his song fading as I spoke. I let my magic flow into Dramin as I clung to him, his body feeling cold and lifeless against the heat from my power. *In my first sight, I saw Dramin's death. I saw the flow of magic, the way the life left his eyes...*

I just didn't know it was me who would kill him, I said to myself, the words trapped where I wasn't sure I would ever let them escape.

"Show me," Ilyan whispered, his breath hot against my skin.

I closed my eyes, the vision coming to the front of my mind as I pushed it into Ilyan the same way I spoke to him.

My vision came like a reel from a movie, flashes of white before the images of the sight came. I saw everything as he did, my body still as I was trapped in Cail's mind, the yelling as I woke, and then the fire and the screaming. I showed Ilyan the stream of magic that I now knew had come from my hands, the slow fall of Dramin's body. I showed him the way Dramin was tightly wrapped in white cotton, his face covered in a red handkerchief. My chest tightened as together, we saw the hole in the ground, the frozen dirt covered with snow. I wished I could look away as the next image came, the sight of me standing alone in an ancient cemetery, my face streaked with tears, the imagery fading to black as the sight ended.

I gasped as the sight left, Ilyan's footsteps moving away from me as I collapsed against Dramin.

"He knew? You knew?" Ilyan asked, the betrayal in his voice generating a bitter taste in my mouth. My regret became a pain as Ilyan's thoughts filled me—all the years he had hidden him from Edmund, and all of it had been for nothing.

I didn't know what to do, I moaned in agony, hoping Ilyan would hear me through his own regrets, that he would understand what I was really saying. That he would hear my fears.

"What is going on, Ilyan?" Sain asked, the stress in his voice flaring my own.

"Dramin... he was..." Ilyan tripped over his words as he questioned having to tell Sain the truth.

That his son, my brother, would die.

My father stood before me, his soul rent in fear of what he would be told. Yet, only minutes before, he had relished the idea of my part in the sight, the sight that would end in my death. Had he ever cried for me? It was a foolish thought and I knew it, one caused by years of abandonment and resentment. I batted it away, my regret at telling him the truth vanishing as the words spewed from my lips like poison.

"I saw him die," I said, cringing at the shake in my voice, the memory replaying itself in the blacks of my eyes.

Sain stiffened at my words, his magic angry and violent in the air before it receded.

"Did you see it in sight?" my father asked, his voice wavering as he moved toward me. I looked up from where I still clung to Dramin's body, my hair falling over my face in long, black strands that blocked my vision.

I could see him standing on the other side of the dark room, his eyes widening toward me in desperation to know more, to feel hope. I couldn't give him that; I couldn't lie. I tightened my lips as I pushed the desperate look in his eyes from my mind, and I nodded once in agreement.

That one gentle head bob sealed Dramin's death, and

Sain's face fell, his jaw slack as his breathing lengthened. Sain's silence stretched through the room, throbbing like the knell of death in my ears.

I couldn't look at the pain in his eyes anymore. I didn't want to feel the agony of regret over what I had done to him. I lowered my head, my ear pressing against Dramin's chest, to the dull throbbing pulse of his heart.

I listened to the rhythm of his pulse, the heat of my magic moving through him, pulling at me in gentle tugs and jolts as it guided me through him. The pressure built in me as my magic swelled, the feeling similar to last night when I had healed Wyn.

Then, I had heard her cries and my magic knew what to do, my mind showing me the way as my Drak blood flared within me. Just like it was doing now.

I raised my head to the three men who stood around me. Thom, standing right in front of me as he wrung his hands in worry. His thick dreads had come loose from his ponytail, his eyes red and swollen. He was haggard and broken. I had felt his desperation before, but now I saw it, and I knew I would do anything to help him.

I had only ever been told to accept the fate that sights had given me, that there was nothing that could be done to change them. Feeling Dramin's cold skin, the gentle rise and fall of his chest, I didn't think I could just walk away from that; I couldn't let him die.

"I can save him," I moaned.

Thom's eyes widened as Ilyan's hand froze on my back, his surprise at my commitment rocking through me.

"No!" Sain yelled the moment I had spoken. Everyone jumped at my father's outburst, and I cringed at the intensity of his yell. The venom he had awakened coursed through my veins.

Thom turned toward him as his eyes seemed to catch fire. "You will let your son die?"

"I will let the future be as it should be," Sain said, his words directed toward Thom even though he moved closer to me. His calm nature made his movements slow, and my agitation increased.

"But I can save him!" I yelled at Sain. His face only spelled regret and pain as he stood in silence. I knew he was suffering—that he wanted his son to live—but he wouldn't admit it, and he wouldn't fight for it. He just stood there, silently accepting fate.

He was walking away from Dramin the same way he had walked away from me.

Pain and anger flashed through me with more animosity than I had ever felt, it rippled over my body, blacking out my vision in spots of obsidian. Everything in me screamed, everything threatened to explode.

"Why won't you save your children? Why don't you love us? Love me?" I pressed against Ilyan's arms as he held me in an attempt to calm me. I could hear him whisper against me, but the anger flowed as clearly as the words did, years of pain spilling out of me. The mugs of Black Water that lined the walls began to shake as my power surged.

"This has nothing to do with love. I love him, as I do you," he said, his voice a mellow calm that only infuriated me more.

"Then let me save him!" I shouted, the words clear and concise as I continued to fight against Ilyan's arms, against the rage.

"You saw him die, Joclyn," Sain said, his voice mellow as he stood still, his body calm even as the room seemed to pulsate under my anger. "You cannot defy a sight. There is nothing that can be done."

I ground my teeth, my body writhing as I fought my anger and the truth of what he said. I wanted to accept the truth of my sight. I knew I needed to, but I couldn't bring myself to do it.

I reached toward Dramin, my fingers long and desperate, as if I was saving him from the slaughter. "I have lost s-so m-much." I cringed as my stutter began to surge through me, the heat of my emotions unleashing my instability. "M-my m-mother was mur-dered... M-my b-brother-r... I-I j-j-just b-barely f-found-d h-him..." I stopped talking, the stutter so bad I knew it was foolish to go on.

I glared at Sain, breathing deeply as I tried so desperately to control the stutter. Ilyan's magic consumed me as he finally broke through to calm me, the warmth so normal to me now that I almost felt bare without it.

"It doesn't matter about the sight; sights can change. They cannot be set in stone. They can't be. I can save him. I will save him," I pleaded with him as I leaned across my brother with my magic surging angrily at the words I knew to be false.

I stretched my magic into Dramin, willing it to do what it wanted, to bring my brother back. I had begun to feel the warm tendrils of Dramin's magic awaken when Sain rushed me, his hands rough against mine as he pushed me away from my brother. The force sent me tumbling into Ilyan, his muscles tense as his magic flared in agitation.

I looked at the black of his eyes in shock, only to see the color fade back to bright green before the black replaced it again. The color shifted as his magic ignited, his own demons bringing themselves right to the surface, his carefully crafted calm shattering into ice and glass.

"You know nothing of our kind!" Sain bellowed at me as his

eyes continued to flash so that I wasn't sure what color they were. I cringed away from the sound of his voice, my muscles seizing as he sped on, his words bouncing over each other in their rage. "The blood of a Drak flows through your veins, yet you know nothing! You know nothing of my kind or our rules and laws. You are as foolish as a child and as dumb as a mortal."

"How can I know anything when you weren't there to teach me? You abandoned me!" I screamed at him. The words that had fueled me for the last few minutes tumbled through me as my body threatened to collapse, my cheeks burning as the tears came.

"I didn't abandon you." His cold eyes glinted as if walking out of his five-year-old child's life was nothing more than walking out a door, simple and meaningless. It wasn't nothing, though—not to me. It never had been. That one action had dictated my entire life until Ilyan had saved me and I had become more. Now, the man whose actions had defined me sat before me, denying what he had done, denying me.

"You left!" I screamed, my anger rushing out at the lack of responsibility he was taking, the real reason for my anger breaking free.

"I didn't leave, Joclyn." His soft voice was so irritating I could barely stand it. "Jeffery Despain left, and I am not Jeffery Despain."

There it was, the reason I would never be able to view this man as my father. The reason I would never understand the decisions he had made and the reverences he felt toward what he was, what we both were.

Jeffery Despain was my father. And this man was not Jeffery Despain.

I stared at the stranger in front of me as ice ran through

my veins, unable to find the right words to say. I only felt numb. Broken.

"Is that why you won't teach me? Because I am not your daughter?"

Thom's eyes widened as the words burst out of me, his jaw clenching in anger and pain that I didn't understand. I pushed away from Ilyan's hold as I spoke, taking the few steps to face my father from over Dramin's body.

"I shouldn't have to teach you; you are a Drak, Silnỳ. It is in your blood. You should know to follow sights, to respect the visions your magic gives you. But to question them? That is not what a Drak, what my daughter, should do." His voice was calm even though his magic seemed to be on fire.

"You are *not* my father," I hissed, my anger settling into a low rumble as I faced him, my fists balled at my side. "You left that when you left me."

"Step away from my son, Silnỳ. If he is meant to die, then I will see it happen, and anything you do to hinder that is heresy to my kind."

"Enough!" Ilyan roared as he pulled me away from Sain and back into the comforting rock of his chest.

I tried to fight the anger that still pressed against my heart, the pain that filled me as the hope I had clung to for so many years evaporated into the stifling air that surrounded us.

"She hasn't been taught, Sain," Thom said from across the room, his rough voice loud as he pleaded with his friend. "How can she know something that has not been fully explained to her?"

"That is not my fault." Sain stood next to Dramin as he spoke, the already broken fragments of my heart lodging themselves painfully through my chest at the sight of Sain's hand wrapped around his son's.

"I know you are in pain; I know you are mourning. But Dramin is not your only child," Ilyan said, his speech elevated to the level of a command. His magic sparked as his agitation rose and I cringed against it, pressing myself into his chest to listen to the rumble of his voice.

"I do not know—"

"You are better than this, Sain." Ilyan interrupted him, his words echoing through me as they vibrated his chest.

"As is she, Ilyan." Sain's statement faded into the air, the harsh words taking the air out of my lungs.

The muscles in Ilyan's back stiffened under my touch, his anger at words I was sure I didn't fully understand a drowning pool in my heart. I looked up to him in expectation, yet his eyes didn't move from the hard stare he had trained on Sain.

"If you will excuse us," Ilyan began, his voice a deep boom in the tense silence around us.

He didn't wait for a response before sweeping us out of the room, his pace quick as he practically carried me down the dimly lit hall. The bracketed torches that were set in the grey wall looked more like blurs as we moved, the light leaving as he closeted us in a small alcove that was hidden amongst the smooth stone.

My pulse quickened at the dark enclosed space. The tightness of the walls made it feel as though they were going to close around me. It was as though I was trapped, like I was cornered in the pit of Cail's mind, just waiting for Ryland to find me.

"I am here, mi lasko," Ilyan soothed. His arms came around me, his lips soft as he spoke against my forehead.

Ilyan's magic ran through me until I felt it inside every inch of my body. I moved my head, careful not to let too much of myself become exposed. Even though I knew this wasn't a trap, I couldn't ignore the learned responses that were still ingrained in my mind.

"Are you all right?"

"I don't understand, Ilyan. I can heal him. I need to save him," I whispered into the dark.

"You know why you cannot, Joclyn," he said, his fingers running down my face as he pressed his lips into a tight line. "The Drak believe their sight to be infallible. I know Dramin has told you this, my love. You cannot change a sight." Ilyan soothed me, his voice low as my heartbeat slowed to match his.

"I know, but I can't just let him die, Ilyan."

"You have to. We cannot let it become one of the zlomený," he whispered, his lips pressing into a tight line.

Yes. But, Ilyan, the zlomený are sights which have never come... This has come.

I knew I was pleading, but I didn't care. A man was dying only feet from me, and no one would let me save him. I didn't care about the sight, about my magic showing me what was to come. Right then, I only cared about saving Dramin.

"Not in its whole, and by healing him, you would be changing the future of a sight thus *creating* a zlomený."

I cringed at his words as well as the truth behind them. He was right; there had been no burial, so the sight was not completed. But I couldn't imagine him dead like the rest of the Drak; all of his children, his grandchildren, and his mate. My chest seized at the thought of Dramin being placed in the cold ground, only to be covered by dirt and snow.

"That doesn't make any sense. If I can change it, why wouldn't I? Change it, create a better future," I said aloud, pleading with him to understand me.

"It is the way of the Drak. Dramin would want it this way as well."

I gasped at the words I didn't want to hear, their utterance sharp and poisonous.

"You sound like my father."

"It has to be this way, my love. Whether or not you or I agree, it is the way of the Drak—of your father—and, as Dramin's father, you have to respect Sain's wishes."

I wanted so much to say Ilyan was right—that this choice was right—but I couldn't. I couldn't accept that Dramin wanted to die. He wouldn't have fought for life for so long only to give in. I had seen the sadness in his eyes when I had foreseen his death. He had been accepting of it, but he hadn't wanted it, not really.

Dramin's plea for me not to tell anyone suddenly made sense. It wasn't out of worry for others. He didn't want anyone to change it; he didn't want me to change it, and he had known that I would try.

I wasn't sure I still wouldn't.

If I can't change the sights... what does that mean for me, Ilyan?

Ilyan's thoughts stopped abruptly at my question. The image of him screaming in agony as he held my body surged through me. The sight's promise of what was coming for me loomed heavy and unwanted. His eyes burrowed into me, so bright I could almost see into him. Into his soul. His movement was slow as his hand came up to cradle my face, the soft skin hot.

"It means I stand by your side," Ilyan whispered, his thumb softly tracing the line of my lips. "*For you were born and you were bred to only protect her.*" His voice deepened as he quoted the sight, my heart seizing even under his delicate touch.

It wasn't the words that he had said that had affected me so; it was the words that came after.

The ones that told of my death.

It was those words that made me doubt the truth of the sights at all.

Because if I didn't, if all the sights were set in stone, then my life was coming to an end just as Dramin's was. And I wasn't ready to give up yet.

5
_____

DARK-BLUE CLOUDS ROLLED over the forest that surrounded me from where I sat on the ancient balcony in Ilyan's room. They blocked out the stars and cast a dull grey shadow over everything. I knew it was well past midnight—it had to be after the night we'd had—but with the storm, there was no way of being certain. The dark blanket of clouds lit up before the distant rumble sounded, warning us of the storm that, when I had been awakened by Ilyan's war meeting, had been off in the distance. The storm that was now right over us.

I took another drink from the earthen mug I held, the Black Water keeping me nice and warm against the chilled air that caught on the thin cotton pants I wore.

The smell of rain that saturated the air mixed with the scent of eucalyptus that wafted off my hair, making everything around me smell warm and heady. My body was relaxed and my mind clear, thanks to Ilyan.

He had insisted on drawing me a bath when we had returned from Dramin's room because I couldn't calm down. I was fuming over my father's decision and his pigheaded belief in magic that he had so thoughtfully told me I didn't understand. I had felt broken and beaten by those words and the way he resented me. My soul had screamed at what my future held, fighting against it. Everything had been frayed and broken, making my agitation increase.

So, Ilyan had placed masses of flowers in a hot bath, hung twigs from the ceiling, and placed hot stones on every surface he could find. The whole effect was different from what he had done in Santa Fe, and at first, I thought he had lost it. Then the steam came, the aroma loosening the prison of emotion that trapped me, and I could have hugged him. Though it felt like hours, I was sure I hadn't spent more than a few minutes in there.

Minutes that had taken off months of stress.

I smiled at the thought just as I heard the bathroom door open behind me, my nerves cinching together at the sound before I felt Ilyan approach me, bringing with him the powerful floral smell he had created.

I drained my mug as Ilyan walked up beside me, his bare back to me as he leaned against the balcony, watching the thunderheads. His skin glistened with the last of the shower water, his dark-blue pajama pants clinging to his hips.

I saw the tension in his back, and for the first time, I began to wonder if he could feel what I could. The anger and sadness of the earth. It came on the wind as the earth mourned the coming battle, and it seeped through the ground from the army that surrounded us, ready to strike. Everything was on edge, the very core of my magic trembling with the oppressive force that threatened to cave me in.

The earth is crying. I knew the phrasing sounded like a child's comment, however Ilyan understood and nodded once, his gaze still focused off in the distance.

"She can feel the anger that surrounds us. She can feel what is coming," he whispered reverently.

I could only nod, understanding what he meant. It was more than just the earth that trembled. I could sense the Trpaslíks' anger in the trees. I could feel the strength of the weird magic off in the distance. I could see the tiny, magical lights flare just beyond the tree line as the Trpaslíks began to wake and light their fires. They were close, so close we could see them and they could see us.

There was a promise of battle in the air; the same promise which drowned my hope that nothing would happen until Edmund himself arrived. To know he was coming, that we expected him, and that I would have to fight him—perhaps when the next sun rose—was terrifying.

"I don't know if I will be ready in time," I reiterated my fear aloud, my eyes pulling away from the dangerous depths of the forest and back to the mug I held in my hands.

"You will be," Ilyan said, his focus still on the bright lightning strikes that covered the sky. "I have seen it."

"I am beginning to doubt if the sights are true at all, if I want them to be."

"I am not talking about the sight, mi lasko. I am talking about you," Ilyan said as he turned to face me, his body towering over me.

I looked up to him in confusion as he slid down onto the stone floor of the balcony, his back pressing into the stone pillars. He leaned forward and placed his hand on my face, the warm current of his magic flowing into me at the touch. His skin was soft as his eyes poured into me, giving me no other place to look, no other place I wanted to look.

"I have seen your strength when you protected me in the snowstorm, when you stood up to Cail in every nightmare, and when you fought Ryland in Santa Fe. I have seen it. I know how strong you are, how confident you are. You are the Silný, and you will be ready."

"I don't feel like the Silný. To me it is still just a nickname," I confessed, my voice little more than a whisper.

"You will," Ilyan promised, his magic slowly leaving until all I felt was that heavy relaxation the bath had given me.

"Well, maybe I will if you keep drugging me like this." I sighed as I refilled my mug with the warm amber fluid. The sweet honey smell of the Black Water mixed nicely with the fragrance already surrounding me.

"I did no such thing." Ilyan laughed as his hand dropped from my face. "I only cleared your mind."

Well, it worked.

"I am glad." Ilyan smiled at me from where he sat, his short hair glistening with water. He leaned against the banister, one arm draped over his lifted knee as he studied me, giving me an open shot of his bare torso.

I looked away, not really wanting to be caught staring at his chest again. Sometimes I wished he would just put on a shirt. It wasn't like he looked terrible or anything. His figure was almost perfect; it was just distracting. Of course, I knew why he did it. I could feel the shadows of pain that drifted over from him, the way his chest burned when fabric rubbed against the scars.

My magic flowed through the Štít as I moved to take away the pain, surging comfortably as I trailed the burn of Black Water and numbed it. It was something I was sure only I could do—equalize the painful burn of the water flowing through him. His thoughts tumbled over to me as the sting left, a million thank yous swelling his gratitude. They all rushed through me at once and I smiled.

You're welcome, Ilyan. You owe me nothing, I answered his

thanks before he was able to put words to them. His eyes widened in surprise as I did so, the movement ever so brief before his smile returned.

"I knew you could hear me," he said, his accent deep as he leaned toward me, his fingers weaving through mine as he grabbed my hand. "I knew it wasn't just me when you sang with me earlier, your voice in perfect time with mine. I knew you could hear me as well."

I could feel his love surge before his thoughts started flooding mine—images, questions, memories, emotions, they all blended together as they drowned me in a suffocating mass that pushed away the peace I had captured. The apprehension that had been kept at bay crept in, my shoulders knitting together as my heart started pounding in my chest, a groan escaping my lips.

I fought the need to curl into myself as the flow of Ilyan's consciousness continued, my chest constricting until I couldn't breathe under the pressure. I crumpled beneath the weight until every muscle in my body was ironclad. A torrent of pain pressed against me and I began to rock back and forth, my hands moving to claw against the tender skin above the Štít.

Ilyan moved closer to me as my frantic movements increased, his arm pulling me into his chest as the flow of his thoughts evaporated.

"Fight it, my love," he soothed as he ran his other hand over my damp hair that hung down my back, his magic flowing into me as he calmed me, giving me enough relief so that I could push some of the tension away. I could smell the strong scent of the flora on his skin, the scent mixed with the familiar smell of his magic, and I breathed it in, letting it take away the last of my anxiety.

"I am sorry, Joclyn. I didn't know it would do that." His

voice rumbled through my ear as I lay against his chest, my hand moving up to run against the smooth, white lines of the thin scars that peppered his warm skin.

"It's okay," I whispered as he shivered under my touch. *Just don't get so excited next time,* I spoke into his mind, the feeling of his excitement still pulsing through me.

His eyebrows rose a bit, that familiar smirk of his pulling at his lips. His enthusiasm surged as he tried to understand what I could hear from him, what I felt from him.

"I can't hear you word for word," I explained, answering his unasked question again. "I only hear pieces of your thoughts and feel pulses of your emotions."

"My emotions?" he asked, his voice even more surprised as his mind ran over similarities that I didn't understand.

"Yes," I whispered.

"So tell me..." Ilyan's wide hand moved over my hair, his fingers gentle as they pulled through the strands. "What am I feeling right now?"

My stomach tangled around itself as I heard the answer. It was something that I had felt a million times before, something that I had even told him. For some reason, though, this time it felt weird to sense the emotion so strongly from him, knowing he wanted me to experience it and to tell him what he felt for me. The heavy sound of his heartbeat echoed in my ear as my own matched his beat for beat, the comfort of our heartbeats taking away my embarrassment.

Love. I sent the word into his mind, my breath catching as his emotion swelled.

"Not quite..." He chuckled, my nerves heightening again. "It is more than love; it is astounding, all-encompassing love." He sighed into me, the last of my stress leaving as he pulled me away from his chest, his hands warm on my shoulders as he looked at me.

The chilled air swirled around us as I gazed into his eyes, and the deep pulse of his passion moved through me. I had no desire to look anywhere else.

What is going to happen to us, Ilyan? I asked as I placed my hand over his heart, thunder rumbling at the contact as if the earth were reacting to the feel of my skin against his.

Ilyan placed his hand over my heart as I had his, the warmth spreading over my collarbone. He didn't look at me, he only looked at his hand against me before closing his eyes.

I focused on the pulse of his heart against my hand, our breathing the only sound in my ears as I waited for an answer. Ilyan finally looked up at me, his hand lifting to glide over the side of my face before he moved to sit behind me. My heartbeat surged at feeling him there, at feeling his chest against my back while he held me from behind. Even when he had braided my hair in the hotel near Isola Santa he had never sat this close, close enough I could feel the beat of his heart. A ripple of calm moved up my spine before he leaned away, his hands moving up to weave through the damp strands of my hair once more.

Ilyan ran his fingers over the crown of my head and through the long waves in a gentle rhythm that sent goosebumps down my spine. The pressure of his hands was soft as he moved my hair away from my face and into a low ponytail, the soft tips of his fingers fluttering across the back of my neck before grazing the mark behind my ear, and I gasped, my magic jumpstarting at the contact.

I sighed as the sensation left, Ilyan's joy and misplaced worry mixing together as heavy Czech words I didn't understand drifted over to me. His fingers continued to move through my hair, deftly separating it before he began to twist and pull it into a braid.

"I was ten when my father first taught me how to braid."

"Your father taught you how to braid? Isn't that kind of girly?" I asked, unable to hide the smile from my voice, or picture Edmund himself knowing how to braid for that matter. I had always assumed Ilyan had taught himself, a necessity of having long hair.

"To you, perhaps, but to my kind, braiding is the way to care for and to show your affection to the people you love." His words were a revered softness that ignited my soul, the real meaning as to what he was doing not lost on me. "As a Skřítek, it is the man's responsibility to braid his hair as well as his wife's and his children's."

"I love it when you braid my hair," I said without thinking, my heart rate pounding in sudden embarrassment. "I mean... I have never really done much with it," I continued in a quick attempt to cover up my blunder.

"I know," he whispered, the side of his hand pressing against my face before he went back to his gentle movements.

"For thousands of years before my birth, and centuries after, braiding was one of the most cherished traditions of the Skříteks. It was the way to convey moments in your life to others, to show stature and accomplishments in battle. Each braid was infused with magic of good blessings, of strength, of love. It was revered, and in many ways it still is."

I had thought his father teaching him how to braid was silly. However, now I almost felt bad for having mocked it. I had poked fun at more than just a boy braiding hair; it was his culture, a tradition, just as it had been with my father. My eyes pinched together at the unwanted connection and I pushed it away. I could tell by the tone in Ilyan's voice that the braiding meant more to him than he was putting on. I felt terrible for having laughed at him, yet the emotion vanished at the sensation of his fingers in my hair, relaxing me. He was braiding my hair, but I knew at once that he wasn't just braiding it.

He was weaving the hair of someone he loved.

"Is that what you are doing now?" I asked, my voice shaking in nerves as I trembled under his touch, my eyes trained on a bolt of lightning that lit up the sky.

"He began first with the child's braid." Ilyan ignored my question as he continued his story. "The simple three-strand crown the girls wore, the long plait the boys wore. He made me braid the hair of every child in Prague. Parents even brought their children to line up for a chance to have the little prince braid their hair."

They lined up? I asked into his mind, my voice probably too loud in my surprise.

"Yes," Ilyan chuckled as his fingers gently pulled and prodded, my head still under his ministrations. "I sat in the square before the main cathedral as the Skřiteks brought their children out. I am sure the mortals looked at us like we were conducting some sort of exercise. I even had a few come up and ask me what I was giving away."

He chuckled again and I couldn't help smiling right along with him. The images from his thoughts flowed into me, painting a picture of what had happened. I could almost see the small, redheaded boy approach Ilyan. I could see the golden sleeve of Ilyan's clothing as his tiny hands moved.

"I bet you were a pro after that," I probed, careful to keep my head still as he worked.

"My knuckles were sore for weeks afterwards, but I

mastered it." I could feel his pride at the success he felt, even after all these years.

"After that one, he taught me every other braid in succession. The braids for council, for war, for new life, for mothers, for loss. When I was old enough, my mother taught me the sacred marriage braid; the twelve-strand, double-layered braid that is performed by a woman's mate during the ceremony for the Zělství. That braid is only known by the king and is taught to the man the night before the ceremony is to take place. My mother spent years spying on my father, breaking tradition in order to learn it and pass it on to me, terrified it would be lost forever if she didn't. I believe my mother knew of the darkness in my father's heart before anyone else."

I placed my hand on Ilyan's knee as I pushed away my nerves over the braid he spoke about, my magic surging alongside his deep sadness at the memory of his mother teaching it to him.

I am glad she taught you, I said, relieved when his sadness dissipated. I squeezed his knee, leaving my hand there against the soft cotton of his pants.

"So am I," he whispered. My heart beat heavily at the way his soft voice flowed over my skin. "It is the most complicated of all the braids that our kind uses, and the one I have done the most. I have sat for thousands of sleepless nights as I taught my friends, my subjects, how to braid the hair of their mates for the one ceremony that would forever change their lives."

His fingers brushed against my neck as he continued to work, each touch of his skin against mine sending electric pulses of magic into me. I smiled at the sensation and lowered my head a bit, giving him easier access to the long lengths that fell down my back.

"It was why I cut my hair the first time," he said, the tone of his voice changing to that deep pull that brought my attention back to his story. "I was the first one to do so, hundreds of years before it became the fashion of the mortals, and I cannot tell you how many elders scorned me for my choice, but to me, I had no other. I would grow my hair out for council or for battle. For the most part, I kept it short, however, unwilling to place the braids that in many ways seemed almost a painful mockery to me. Then I received the sight, which told me of your existence, and I grew my hair out naturally and wore my hair longer more often, knowing someday I would finally get the chance to braid your hair, that you would braid mine…"

My chest constricted as what he said seeped into me, the warmth of his fingers as they moved along my neck sparking my concerns. I wasn't sure if I was excited or terrified. It wasn't like a bonding wasn't something we had talked about —okay, had almost done. It was how he spoke about it in that moment that was different.

"Ilyan?" I said, my voice barely above a whisper; my heart seemed to have stopped beating. Ilyan's words burned into me, blending with his thoughts in a cacophony of emotions and desires.

I don't know why I had never understood it before. Beyond waiting for me, beyond keeping me safe, Ilyan had wanted nothing more than to have that which he had seen others have. What the sight had told that he could only have with me. I knew—I could feel it in the way he pushed away the flare of his emotions—that he would never fully admit that. Even to himself.

Ilyan lightly pulled on my hair as he secured the band. His weight shifted as he turned to face me, his legs stretched out on either side of me.

"I do not know what this connection of our souls means, mi lasko," he whispered as he finally answered my question, his hands enclosing around mine. "It affects us in ways I never thought possible, and while I am not sure how that may affect our future, I can tell you this: it changes nothing between us."

They were words that hours ago I would have loved to hear, and I did. For some reason, though, my stomach had turned into butterflies and my heart had taken on a stutter all its own.

So you are still my kick-butt trainer with bad taste in clothes? I spoke into his mind, trying desperately to ease my nerves, but it didn't work. Even my subconscious voice trembled.

"Something like that," Ilyan said with a smile, his hand squeezing mine before reaching up and running his finger over my hairline. I smiled at the touch, my muscles tightening all on their own as a snake of pleasure ran through me.

"So... what braid is this?" I asked as I lifted my hand behind my head, the tips of my fingers trembling against the perfect silken strands that Ilyan had just woven.

My nerves jumpstarted in apprehension as Ilyan captured my hand, his own unease surprising me. I had never expected Ilyan to be so nervous, yet I could hear the frantic pulse of his heart, the trembling of his emotions.

"The braid of true love," he whispered as he released my hand, his eyes unwavering from mine. "It is normally braided by the man after the woman consents to be his mate. The sign that she is taken. The woman receives this braid, while a man will let his hair hang free for the first time in his life, showing he is waiting for her to braid it after the bond is complete." His eyes never even deviated a millimeter from mine as he spoke. I was sure I looked like I had been hit by a truck.

Ilyan? I asked, my nerves melding into a form of eager panic that I wasn't sure made sense. Heck. Nothing made sense. Was Ilyan asking me to bond myself to him? Now?

"Hmmm," Ilyan sighed as his hand moved to press against my mark, his touch soft as the jolt wound through me, his fingers continuing to run over the raised skin.

"I hold by my original choice, Joclyn. You are not ready to make a decision like that yet. I chose this braid because of how our bond has formed between us, how our hearts beat in time, how you speak to me, and how you can feel the thoughts in my heart. You see, in every transition of the hair, small hearts form, making a trail over your head and down your back..." Ilyan led my hand over the braid as he spoke, his fingers moving mine over each of the hearts that he had formed into my hair.

"One heart for every beat of mine that you own. Every single one," he whispered as he pulled me close, his soft lips brushing against mine gently as he held me against him. I gasped, my breath trapped in my chest as I waited for more to come. His mouth moved over my cheek to my jawbone before turning to my lips, the touch as soft as a feather.

My heart pulsed faster in expectation, my hands moving to cling to his elbows in a frantic need to have him closer. I could feel his heart beat against me, the heavy bass drum of it thumping against my chest as he held me, his skin flush with my body.

He didn't move any closer. He stayed still, his lips a soft whisper against mine.

"Kiss me," I begged in a soft, breathless voice.

Ilyan's breath drifted over my skin as he laughed, his fingers caressing my mark as a small surge wound its way over my spine before he pulled me into him. His lips pressed into mine as his hand wrapped around my waist, holding me against him.

My hands trailed from his elbows to his back, the feeling of his bare skin shocking. I clung to him as he kissed me, as I kissed him. My chest heaved as he pulled away, his hands still tight against my clothing, keeping me against him with his cheek pressed to mine.

I breathed deeply while the sky lit up around us, the rumble of thunder loud as it rolled through the air, the magic of the earth a raw and powerful jolt that weaved its way within me.

"Do you feel that?" Ilyan asked, his voice a whisper in my ear. "The power from the earth?"

"Yes."

"Then I am no longer alone," Ilyan said, his voice deep and relaxed.

The thoughts of all the time he had been ostracized because of his power filled me—the feeling when he killed his friend, as well as when he had been too scared to help those around him. The thoughts took away my breath and I clung to him, my fingers pressing into the skin of his back as I held him.

"You never were," I breathed against his skin, my fingers running over his hairline before I kissed him.

Never.

6

————

THE RAIN HAD STOPPED FALLING sometime before dawn, the long streaks of water vanishing into the air as a chilled breeze took their place. I had watched for hours as the lightning struck, the abbey rumbling with every thunder clap as the storm came closer. The wind had come after the rain left, the powerful gusts driving against the barrier that Ilyan had placed over the open window frames. I almost wished it would break through.

I wanted the wind and the rain to splash against my face and to feel the magic they carried move into me. I wanted to stand still in the midst of the storm as it raged around me. I would have removed the barrier, but I didn't want to wake Ilyan. He slept so soundly as he held me against him, his breathing calm and shallow as he dreamed, his arm a comforting weight around my waist.

I had tried to sleep, to take advantage of the calm I felt, but it wasn't taking. So I had lain still, breathing into Ilyan's chest while our song flowed from his lips until he had drifted away, his words fading into nothing.

I wished I could sleep, but I wasn't tired. The Drak blood

ran through me stronger than it had before, the promise that Dramin had given me of less sleep and no food ringing clear. I guess the no sleep part had finally kicked in.

I smiled at the memory of Dramin giving me the mug on that very first day, his kind eyes and the sound of his laugh. My smile faded as quickly as it had come, the image of my jovial "uncle" replaced with one of my dying brother. Just the thought of Dramin brought a bad taste to my mouth. My brother, dying in the other room with nothing I could do to save him.

No, that was wrong.

Sain wouldn't let me save him.

I gritted my teeth at the thought, my blood boiling at my father's stubborn and ancient mindset. I still didn't understand why they wouldn't let me save him, why they were so adamant that they follow the sight.

No matter how many snow-filled graves I saw in my sights, I couldn't let someone die. My mother hadn't raised me that way. I should be able to help someone who needs me.

What was to say that the future wouldn't come about another way?

I wish my father had told me something, anything, about *why* it was so important to follow the sights. More reason than a culture I didn't understand, more than the nameless sights of the zlomený, or unknown factors with no real consequence. I needed a reason. The fact that he hadn't given me one almost worried me more.

I knew I should be as protective of the sights as my father was. I had sensed their power and the promise of truth they held as the visions had unfolded before me. I knew that what I had seen would come to pass; I knew it because the magic told me so.

I just wished that were enough for me.

I could feel Dramin across the abbey, alone in his room where he lay with his magic dead inside of him. My magic prickled through me as I felt him, and a thought I almost didn't want to let in came over me. Everyone was sleeping—everyone except Sain, who stood guard in the bell tower.

I could save my brother.

I didn't care what the repercussions were; right then, it didn't matter. It was my choice, and I wouldn't let him die. With my breath trapped in my chest, I turned my head toward Ilyan, his body relaxed in sleep. If one thing was certain when it came to Ilyan, he didn't wake up easily, and when he did eventually awaken, it always took him a minute to understand what was going on. I could use that to my benefit.

I didn't dare breathe as I shimmied away from him, his arm falling like a dead fish against the white sheets. The coldness of the stone floor quivered up my legs as my bare feet pressed against the smooth surface, the breath I held burning to escape at the chill. I stayed still as I waited for Ilyan to react to my movement, but he didn't even move.

"Forgive me, love," I whispered without knowing why. I had felt Ilyan's own frustration when Sain had expressed his desire. His role as king had dictated his decision to let Dramin die, not his better nature. It was my better nature that I wouldn't let lay quiet.

I uncoiled my body before slipping my feet into my red shoes and moved across the room, shuffling my feet in an attempt to be as silent as possible. The large wooden door opened noiselessly as my magic pushed into it, the gentle tap of the wood as it closed behind me sounding like a battering ram in my ears. My muscles tensed at the sound, but I pushed the anxiety away as my hands pressed against the door, waiting for a sign that Ilyan was waking up.

I stretched my magic toward him as I closed my eyes, my mind pulsing with the image of the room that came into view. Ilyan slept soundly, his arm still stretched out over the warm sheets I had just vacated. The image almost made me want to curl up next to him again. He looked so calm, so beautiful. I only wished he would understand my choice in what I was about to do.

I ignored the small flame of guilt that was trying to build inside of me and ran my hand over the edges of the door. My magic fired as I sealed the door with a heavy barrier that I hoped would keep him in place, in silence, and oblivious to my departure. I just needed enough time to get to Dramin and heal him before Ilyan woke up. It wouldn't take him much to break through the barrier, no matter how powerful I was.

I faced the door as the excitement at healing Dramin began to grow, the guilt falling away with the knowledge that I was doing the right thing. That was, of course, before I turned, ready to make my way toward Dramin's door that called to me through the dark.

With one look at the long, dark hallway, my ironclad cage of security slipped, releasing the demons. Muscle spasms rippled through me and my arms moved to circle around me in a desperate attempt to hold myself together.

"It's j-just a hallway," I reminded myself in a whisper. An ancient passageway made of stone, lined with fire-burning sconces. *Just a hallway.* I tried to hold on to what should have been a simple fact, but it didn't look like just a hallway anymore. It looked like a nightmare.

My eyes widened as the walls of the passage moved in and out as they breathed, red lines trailing down the stones as they bled. My breathing picked up as I watched, my anxiety peaking as the floor seemed to shift beneath me. A small gasp escaped my lips as I clung to the door, my hands pressing into the wood as I waited for the unstable movement to stop.

My eyes snapped shut as I looked away from the horrors I faced, trying to push away my irrational fears. I kept my mind trained on the rough ridges of the ancient wood that stretched underneath my fingertips. The shadow of Ilyan's magic bolted through the Štít as he slept, the familiarity like a warm blanket, the strength just enough for me to push away the panic and find control over it.

The floor stabilized as my breathing settled, the rhythm matching the pulse of my heart as I focused on the black behind my eyelids.

My eyes opened to the pure grey stone of the hallway, the shadows wavering in the light that flickered from the sconces. There was nothing else, not anymore. No monsters, no demons. Just me and a clear path to Dramin.

"You are bigger than it," I said to myself, my voice a stable whisper in the dimly lit hall. I smiled at the thought and put one foot forward, almost expecting the floor to shift at the step, but everything stayed as steady as my heartbeat. My lips twitched into a smile as I let my fingers run over the smooth, cold stone of the wall as I walked forward. My steps slow as magic pulled me toward the dying man.

The corridors stretched on forever as I moved, the flickering of the lights chipping away at my sanity. I turned one corner after another while the nightmare threatened to invade, the quick return scaring me. I had only just pushed away the fear, and to have it come back to me so soon made me doubt the progress I had thought I had made.

My heart thumped as the volatile tension wavered

through me. The door came into view as I turned the last corner, the tall, wooden slab stretching high above me.

I took the last step and pressed my hand against the door, the tension in my neck growing as I paused. I was here. I could feel my magic beg me to move forward, yet I was scared. Scared I would be caught; scared I would fail. I didn't know which fear was stronger.

I let out a shaky breath as I pushed the door open, my fingertips grazing over the smooth wood as I let it swing away from me. The door opened with a low creak that caused me to catch my breath. My eyes darted over the halls as if Ilyan would walk around the corner, but I knew it was foolish. I was too far away for him to hear me now.

I turned back to the pitch-black room where Dramin slept, fear knitting up my spine until I worried I would snap. Light filled the room as I stepped in, scaring me that I had been caught already, that someone was here, but I was alone. It was only the old torches that had lit with my arrival, my magic awakening them and filling the room with a dim, flickering light.

The light gave life to shadows that rose up like a forest. Dark fingers reached toward the ceiling, the skeletal ridges clawing at the joists and threatening to collapse the room. The frayed edges of my panic increased, my muscles overwrought.

I fought the need to fold into myself, pushing away the monsters as I turned to Dramin, focusing on the gentle rise and fall of his chest. He still remained in the same place, in the same position, and in the same clothes that he had from hours before. Nothing had changed.

I let out a shaky breath as I moved into the room, the powerful waves of my magic bathing the room with warmth in their mad attempt to reach him. It was the same as it had been with Wyn. My magic knew what to do, and it was desperate to begin.

"Hello, Uncle," I whispered as I came up beside him, that familiar phrase sounding strangely out of place. "I'm sorry I hurt you, but I'm here to fix it."

My voice trembled as I pleaded with the mostly lifeless man in front of me, asking him to forgive me. I took the last two steps, my fingers shaking as they reached toward the grey, clammy skin of his hands.

My magic reacted as my hands wrapped around his, the thin strands of my power flowing into him in eager anticipation. I let it flow, hoping it would warm him and take away the deathly hue in his skin.

Hoping it would bring Dramin back.

I exhaled as it filled him, my breath shuddering and crackling through the silence of the room. My nerves had almost completely gone, my mind so focused on what I was doing that there wasn't any room for my insecurities or for doubt. It was only me and the magic that flowed through my fingers.

I let it move into him like a slow drip from a fountain, waves of power settling through him like thin layers of paper. I was sure it was too much; I could already feel his kidney giving out under the pressure. His heart beat so wildly, I was afraid it was going to put him into cardiac arrest. For the first time, I actually wished I had chosen to take biology instead of chemistry last year. I probably shouldn't have used so much magic; I knew too much would kill him, but something told me I needed to, and I didn't question it.

Tiny beads of sweat began to form underneath the braid that lay against my neck as I searched for the injury as Thom had taught me. The colorful swirls of the watercolor paint that my mind created shifted as I searched through him, the abstract images dancing while my magic moved. My shoulders tensed as I watched the bright colors within Dramin begin to dim, the black streaks of death that lived deep inside of him taking shape. The lines in my forehead wrinkled as I looked into the poison that was trying to kill him.

The wispy strands of his magic had curled and died into ash that settled in the pit of his heart. I needed to give back what I had taken from him. Even if he never woke up, even if he really passed away, I would make sure he left this world whole and with the most important thing.

His magic.

Everything in me felt tense as I worked to re-spark the tiny flame of magic that still lived inside of him, the light smothered by the dark soot. I coaxed and swelled my magic around that spark, but nothing happened. Dramin stayed still, the tiny flame doing nothing more than flicker inside of him.

My fingers wound themselves tightly through Dramin's. I clung to him, my heart pulsing painfully as my magic did, the weakening strain in Dramin's heart heating.

I jumped as a flash of silvery light shot through the darkness, the white heat of lightning catching the ground just beyond the window. The air crackled in an explosion that shook through me, electrifying the stagnant air. My magic jumped in fear that caused a bolt of energy to run into Dramin. I fought the scream of fright as the magic filled him, terror wrapping around me at what I had done.

The jolt was enough to kill him.

I waited in agony to hear Dramin's last heartbeat, to feel his final breath against my skin, but instead, I felt the spark of his magic jump and flare under the surge, then nothing more.

His heart still beat strong under my fingertips.

I didn't question how he had survived the surge as I gritted my teeth together, my magic flaring into his in a pulse of fire, coaxing his growing flame to find life. I tried to keep the yell restrained in my throat as my magic tired, my body heaving in exertion.

Dramin's magic continued to grow and flare until it was almost what it had been before: a powerful torrent of ability and determination. It was more than that though: it was alive.

I had saved him.

I could feel the full torrent of his ability inside of him, his magic alive and well. My soul seemed to soar as I felt it, pulling away the layers of my magic from the now powerful flame of his ability, only to feel his magic flicker and die.

"No," I gasped as a weight collapsed over me.

I felt his magic return to the ash it had been. It hadn't been enough. Healing him wasn't as easy as I had assumed it to be, no matter how strong I felt, no matter how my magic had guided me. My attempts hadn't been enough.

I needed a jumpstart, like an EKG machine or a car battery. The pulse had been an accident before, but now I needed to try. My lips pressed together in a tight line at the thought. Doing this was going to be dangerous. Too much magic and I would kill him, too little and it wouldn't work. There weren't any more excuses; I had to try.

I needed more power, more magic.

Before, I had taken it from Ilyan. I knew I still could, I could feel the gentle hum of his magic through the Štít, but I couldn't risk waking him, not when I was so close to succeeding.

A low rumble of thunder bled through the dark room, my head jerking up to the sound.

I hadn't only taken magic from Ilyan before.

I smiled toward the dark storm that swirled through the window, the surge of the earth's magic ticking over my chilled skin as it rode on the wind, relaxing me, energizing me.

My breath came in staccato spurts as I pulled the earth's magic from the air, my own swelling as it came in contact with it. My body ached the more I pulled, the more I worked. The exhaustion that weighed on me was almost enough to topple me over. I might have if it wasn't for the deep strains of earth magic. The powerful waves moved through me like a soothing balm. The pure power was intoxicating.

My body acted like a filter as I pressed my magic into Dramin, the dangerous power of the earth's magic trapped inside of me, while the powerful strains moved softly into him. I layered the magic as I had before, the strong blankets moving one after another over Dramin's heart, over the dying flame of his magic.

I wanted to believe this would be easy, that only one jolt would be necessary, but I could already feel my hands beginning to shake at what I was about to do. Afraid I would succeed at killing him this time.

I shook my head as the bitter taste of guilt filled my mouth, as I tried to focus on the way my magic felt inside of him. I could do this.

I let my magic surge once more, the pulse strong, but I could tell at once that my nerves had depleted the strength. It wasn't enough.

"Come on, Jos, don't be a wuss," I scolded myself as I closed my eyes, ready to try again.

Only to have another form of magic stop me in my tracks.

Every nerve in my spine jolted in fear as magic the color of ice, and just as cold, struck my body.

The wet chill of the unfamiliar magic wound down my spine as my heart shuddered in my chest. I gasped and tensed, my power surging as my magic bolted through my brother in a torrent of force. It should have been enough to end his life, but instead it did what I had been trying to do all along. Dramin's magic ignited at the potent surge, his magic catching fire as the pulse of power spread through his body.

I glanced at the dark room around me, expecting to find the source of the icy magic. Nothing was there, nothing but the heat of Dramin's magic. I ran my magic through him, checking for injury, failing organs, anything. I felt nothing other than his magic as it coursed through him.

I only hoped it would stay that way this time.

I bit my lip as I stood, my hands unwinding from Dramin's warming fingers. My breath remained captive in the expectation that his magic would flicker and die with the lost contact, but it stayed strong as I released him, the heavy flow warm and welcoming in the air around me. A powerful pulse of life now wound through him.

I had done it; I had healed him.

I didn't dare move as I waited for him to wake and be whole, but he didn't move; his magic didn't flare. He just lay as still as stone, the same deathly sheen on his face.

I clenched my hands together as I stared at him, not wanting to accept that after everything, I had failed, that even though his magic was alive, Dramin was still destined to die.

I could feel my magic buzz through my fingers as

thunder rumbled around me—desperate to try again—when the same icy magic I had felt minutes before shot through me again, the touch cold and painful.

My magic surged in an attempt to find where the terrifying jolt had come from, to find out who was coming, but as quickly as the magic had come, it left.

I stood still in the room, trying to steady my breathing as I scanned the dark, my magic soaring down dark hallways as I searched, only to find no one. I stretched out to the very edges of the abbey, but still, I felt nothing. No sign of the ice that had washed over me.

Until it came again.

Then the familiarity of the magic made sense. It was the feeling I had always gotten before Cail had come, cold like ice.

My breathing picked up into frantic pants as the thought raged through me, my insanity trying its hardest to drag me back down to the nightmare that haunted me. I fought against the pull, against the fear, Ilyan's song coming right to mind in a desperate attempt to cling to the good memories and not let the blood that ran down the walls take over.

Still, I couldn't stop my brain from screaming that Cail was here, that he had found me. Even though I knew he was dead.

I needed to get out of here.

My shoes slipped as I ran from Dramin in a desperate attempt to get away, to run from the nightmare that was so willing to drag me down. My feet sounded like bass drums against the stone walls, the heavy slaps of my shoes echoing in my ears. I opened the door and closed it without looking, not caring if it made a sound. My focus was only on making it back to my room, on getting away from Cail.

I didn't even get the chance.

The cold magic flared again at the same time that something deep inside of me screamed in desperation. I fell against the wall right outside of Dramin's door, my whole body seizing as footsteps even softer than mine made their way toward me, the familiar sound of his gait freezing me in place.

Except it wasn't Cail, and the knowledge of who it really was gave me no chance to escape.

Ryland had found me.

7

"Jos!" Ryland's voice erupted behind me, loud and unmistakably happy. I wished I could feel the joy that I had felt so long ago, but all I felt was the cold dread that I had lived with for months.

I dug the soft pads of my fingers into the stone I leaned against in my desperation to escape, the sound of my heartbeat a bass drum that a normal human wouldn't have been able to live through. It banged painfully against my chest as my voice ripped into a scream of panic that burst through the darkness around me, even though I knew my yell would do nothing.

He had found me.

He would hurt me.

I could hear him walk toward me, his steps slow as the nightmares began to infiltrate my soul, my scream fading into a whimper. The cold, painful surge of what I now knew to be his magic flared next to me again, and I pushed myself into the wall as if it would give way and let me meld into it.

Let me get away.

"No, no-no-no-no-no," I moaned, my fingers moving from the wall to knot through my hair. My chest pulsed angrily as it prepared for the bruises to come, for the bones to break.

"Jos, baby," Ryland said from over me, my mind distorting the sound into a menacing laugh, into the drip of blood.

His footsteps echoed in my ears and I jumped, my fingers pulling at my hair with hard, little tugs that part of me hoped would wake me from this nightmare, convince me I was still safe. I pulled until I could barely handle the pain, until the soft touch of his hand against the skin of my arm made my magic explode.

I jerked as the icy touch reacted with my magic in an explosion of white light and wind that rocked the ancient stone on which I sat. Strands of hair that I had pulled from my braid lashed around my face as I screamed in fear. Ryland's angry yell was drowned by the crash of stone as the explosion pushed him through the wall across from me.

I screamed at the sound, my voice breaking in sobs as my stomach knotted in fear. I moved forward on my hands and knees, desperate to get away from the yells, the explosions. To get away from Ryland, to get back to Ilyan.

"You don't need to be scared of me, baby." His voice was rancid honey as it echoed through the hallway from behind me.

I crawled faster, my frightened sobs covering the sound of his steps as he advanced on me. I wasn't fast enough to escape him, though; I never could be.

I screamed as I felt his fingers wrap around my ankle, my nails digging into the floor as he pulled me back, the fragile slivers of bone cracking under the pressure.

"Help!" I screamed as hand over hand he pulled me toward him. My scream drowned into blackness as Ryland laughed deep and loud. He pulled me around to face him as his eyes flashed blue, his lips stretching into a smile. I tried to move away, to fight against him, but I was trapped; trapped underneath Ryland with nothing but my sobs.

My mind spun at having him so close, my vision swaying and whirling as I continued to scream. I knew at once that it was not only fear that was making the world turn. I could feel my Drak blood flare in preparation.

"No, no, no." I gasped as blackness blurred the edges of my vision, part of me willing the red burn that preceded my sight to take me away from the horror I faced. I saw the tinge of scarlet in a flash of flame before the warm sting of Ryland's hand against my cheek pulled me from the sight. I inhaled sharply at the pain, at the lost vision, when Ryland's now disgusted face swam back into view. The knowledge of what I had done, of what Ryland now knew, sliced like a hot knife to the gut.

"You're nothing but a pathetic Drak!" he screamed as he moved away from me in disgust, leaving me clutching my swelling jaw in the dark. "All the power in the world and you waste it on that. It's disgusting!"

A sob broke from my lips as he yelled, the weak sound drowned by the repulsion in his voice, hearing what he thought of me. It was something that I had come to treasure about myself, and to hear it spoken about with such hostility —the words tore me apart, bit by bit.

"Disgusting!" He screamed again, a sob ripping from my chest as I stretched my shaking fingers away from me, dragging myself away from him.

"That's okay." The revulsion in his voice lessoned like he had flicked a switch, his hands pulling me back from what little progress I had made in my escape. "I can make you strong again."

His nails dug into my arms as he held me beneath him. The boy I had once loved glared down into me with more hatred, more disgust, than I had ever seen while his hand moved to press against the mark on my neck. Ice shot through me at the contact, the sensation painful and caustic as my magic rebelled against me, his hand jerking away as he felt the same reaction.

"What did you do?" he roared, the ebony hatred of his eyes snaking up my spine, and I cringed, fighting for a desperate escape, even though I couldn't move an inch.

"I did nothing other than what you begged me to do!" I screamed, my magic flaring in distress, sending one strong pulse into Ryland, knocking him off his feet and to the ground right next to me.

I turned and crawled away as fast as I could, my sweaty hands slipping against the stone before I was able to stumble to my feet and run away from him, find someplace to hide.

"Jos, don't leave me," Ryland pleaded through the dark, his voice sounding so normal that I almost turned back. Almost, if it hadn't been for the clanging of the pipes that filled my ears; if it hadn't been for the memory of each and every one of his attacks. "Don't leave me... don't leave me... leave me. Leave me."

His words echoed through the halls that had become a labyrinth to me, his voice breaking in tears before his agonizing screams reverberated through the dark. I jumped at the noise, the fading sound replaced by the frantic pulse of my heart, by the agitated breaths that thundered from my chest.

My hands guided me down the crumbling halls as I tried

to fight the fears of the haunted torments that I had been infused with, but they were too strong. I could no longer find the line of reality, the line of what was safe and what was not. The world I had so recently escaped became the only world I knew, the hallucination taking over.

"Joclyn! I will find you!" His voice again echoed around the stone, making it impossible to be certain where he was.

My eyes darted through the darkened hallways as I ran, trying to figure out where to hide, my feet stumbling as I tried to find my toilet, find the room with the books.

They were nowhere.

I stretched my hand forward to pull me around the corner, only to fall back in fear at the slick surface that met my touch, the cool wetness that covered the stone. Blood dripped down the stone wall in front of me, my body tensing in horror at glistening patches of red that covered the pads of my fingers.

"I-i-t-t's... al-l i-in-n... y-yoooour h-head-d." My stutter took over as I stared at my trembling fingers, the stammer so bad I could barely make out my own words.

I backed away from the wall in raw fear, tripping through unfamiliar corridors, only to be met with a wide hand that tightened around my neck, the skin pulsing hot as his magic crippled me. The strong grasp coarse like sandpaper as he burned me.

I tried to scream at the contact, but no sound came out, only my strangled cry as Ryland's hand cut off my air supply. A sharp pain swelled against my skull as he smashed me into the wall, my lungs gasping as an ache inflated inside of me, my head swimming. My broken nails clawed at his hand and my lungs began to burn, my legs flailing as I kicked wildly in an attempt to get away.

His hold increased as his smile did, the darkness behind his eyes blazing, his voice a low growl of rage in my ears. "Ilyan thinks he can keep you from me. Well, he's wrong. You are mine and everything about you belongs to me.

"You are mine! Mine... mine... mine!" He moaned again, his voice growing louder with each word as his instability increased. His eyes darted around the room as he mumbled the same word over and over.

My jaw opened as I gasped for breath, my fingers continuing to dig into his hand as I tried to pry it away, to give my body the oxygen it screamed for, little stars of white popping in my vision. I fought the tears as I fought Ryland, my fear swelling in pain as my lungs burned.

"Mine, mine..." His chant had turned into a sob when his hand finally released me from the wall, his arms gathering me into him as he held me against his chest.

I wanted to scream at the contact, at his cold touch against my skin, but I couldn't move. I could only lean against him weakly as I gasped in air, the pain that had swelled through my body trying to lessen with each breath I took.

The burn in my chest left as his magic rushed into me in an angry torrent that ignited my fears. The painful cold of his magic provoked my own, sending a powerful spark out of my hands, right into his abdomen. I screamed as the magic left, the fear rumbling down my spine as the dark hallways filled with the sound of his scream. The flame hit him with a flash of light that shook the walls around us, sending him away from me and through one of the many wooden doors that lined the corridor.

I watched where he had landed, my breath held in the hope that he had gone, that I was safe. But I knew better.

My soul screamed in horror as he pulled himself to standing, his chest heaving as he faced me. A prickle of panic ran across my neck at the black in his eyes. I felt the fear, the panic, but this time I felt something more, a wave of emotion that ripped through me. Anger.

"I d-do... n-not bel-long... t-to y-you!" I yelled as I rose to face him, a line of fire surging toward him, only to have him snap his fingers and turn the weapon into harmless smoke.

"You are bonded to me! I own you! I can kill you... love you... kill you." His voice rumbled as he walked toward me, his hands clenching through his curls. His icy eyes bored into me, the look exactly what I remembered from before.

I didn't care what Ilyan said. It was him. It had always been him. It was Ryland who had always attacked me. And now he was going to pay.

"Not-t anymore!" My teeth ground together as I sent a rush of wind at him in an effort to drive him away, but he didn't so much as flinch from the power. He only smiled as he rushed me, his wide gait closing the last few steps as he backed me against the wall.

"You are mine, always mine. I won't lose you," Ryland whispered, his voice hard and possessive as his hand wrapped around my waist.

Not anymore.

"I-I do not b-belong to you!" I yelled as I grabbed his hair, my fingers knotting through the long strands before I pulled him past me into the wall. My magic surged with strength as I bashed Ryland's head into the old stones, the ancient masonry cracking under the pressure.

I waited for him to scream, to call out in pain, but he stayed still, his breathing absent until his chest heaved in a low, menacing laugh that caught in my chest and ignited my fears. Fear as black as ice ran over me as he turned to face me, a thick stream of blood flowed from his hairline. The look in his eyes froze me in place for a moment too long. His blood-tinged teeth flashed in a smile right before a stream of red light surged from him, the red-hot burn flaring through my chest.

Fire burned through me as I soared away from him, the agony growing as I blindly reached for anything to grab onto, to stop what was coming. I found nothing. My body hit against the rubble of the now destroyed hallway with a violent jolt. The snap of my body against stone echoed in my ears, and I cried out, an acidic burn moving through me as my back stiffened, my spine arching in agony.

I drove away the burn of pain as my magic rushed to the aches that rippled through my body, healing the bones and tendons that I was sure had fractured. My arms shook as I moved to fight back—ready to face him—when Ryland's footsteps echoed in my ears. His steps were slow as he moved closer until he towered over me from where I lay on the ground.

"Do you think you belong to Ilyan then?" Ryland asked, his desperation growing as a deep mania rumbled through his voice. "Is that what you think? Lies... lies... lies..." He growled at the same time his fingers pulled violently at his sagging curls, the words coming over and over. "He lies and you believe him—"

"Ilyan d-doesn't lie to m-me!" I screamed in anger as I stood before him. The rocks around me shook and shattered with the waves of my rage.

Ryland's eyes widened at my exclamation, his jaw clenching as anger moved into his face.

"He lies to everyone!" Ryland roared, his magic throwing me into the air like a ragdoll. I felt the hard impact as my body hit the ceiling, only to feel the air rush through my hair as I dropped like a dead weight back to the floor.

My fingers grasped at nothing as I fell, the descent too quick to even have a chance to stop it. Fire rippled through my bones as one after another they snapped and broke with the impact. My magic throbbed toward the painful shards of the breaks as it took the pain away, as it tried to heal me. I needed to face him—to make him pay—but the broken bits of my body had turned me into a rag doll, leaving me panting and gasping in the middle of a rubble heap.

I opened my eyes as my body twisted and writhed, only to find Ryland above me, his legs straddling me as they locked me in place. My chest tightened in fear at seeing him there, everything tensing as I fought the pain, fought the fear. Even if I could move, I had nowhere to go.

"He told me he would keep you safe for me, that I could have you back!" Ryland whimpered as he clawed at his hair, his voice broken in tears while his body rocked in the air above me. I writhed in pain below him as he lowered himself to lie beside me, his body pressing against mine as his hand extended to rest against the skin on my face.

"I can have you back. Ilyan said, Ilyan said, he said..." Ryland's words were a painful promise that sliced through my heart. Even though I knew it was a lie, it was the same as it had been on the rooftop when he had looked at me with those black eyes and told me Ilyan loved me for the first time. I could feel the doubt burrowing into me, through the anger and fear that had wound its way up my spine. I didn't believe him, even though—deep down—I knew.

"He wouldn't say that," I said as I tried to push away from his touch, my voice a grunt through my clenched teeth, willing the words to be true.

"He did. He did... he did. You belong to me. Mine...

mine... mine." His arm wrapped around me, pulling me against him like we were lovers, the movement of my body rippling through me in an ache of pain and fear.

He was lying. I knew it. It didn't matter if he was, though. His words meant nothing to me. I was not a piece of property.

"I belong to no one!" I spat as I threw Ryland off me and into the stone ceiling. The aggressive force of my power shifted in the air as I sent him into the opposite wall, driving him into the stone.

"I don't need anyone! Not to save me, not to own me! I can do this on my own!" My blood boiled as I scrambled back to standing, my hand swiping to the side repeatedly as I sliced through his shirt and cut through his skin with the heat of my power.

He screamed in pain as I did in anger, blood drizzling over the white of his shirt in rivers of the darkest red. Seeing the brightness of the blood—the color so vivid against the white—stopped me as a chill trailed down my spine, leaving my hand extended in front of me.

The anger that had clung to me left as he fell from the wall in a heap. I could only stare in horror at the red that drenched his back. I needed to leave, to get out of here. To run away from what I had done.

I backed up as I tried to remember how to walk—as I attempted to tear my eyes from him—only to see his pale face turn up to me, his fingers flexing as razor-sharp blades soared through the air, slicing across my face. I felt the heat as they cut through the skin, the painful burn as they gashed me open.

I stumbled back in pain as my hands flew to my face, the warm wetness of my own blood flooding over my skin.

"You are nothing without me," he yelled as he

approached me, "and even less with Ilyan. If you won't kill me, then I will gladly kill you. My father was right all along. You are nothing, and you deserve to be dead."

"I am NOT nothing!" My voice rumbled, my magic growing as I fired blindly through the rivers of my blood. In my attempt to fight back sparks of electricity and flame flashed through the smoke-filled air.

"Ilyan!" I shouted through the pain without knowing if I called the words into his head or aloud, not knowing if the barrier I had trapped him in would keep him from me.

The word escaped my lips just as Ryland pulled me back into him, his body hard against mine, his iron arm pressing me against him. I tried to fight the hold—to move away from the unwanted contact—but he only held on tighter, his face moving closer until I could taste his breath on my tongue.

"Why do you call for him if he doesn't own you? Why do you sleep with him? Why do you cling to him?" He hissed his words against me as he held me, my heart stuttering as it fought to beat.

I just glared into him in response, my eyes narrowed dangerously as his words seeped into me and joined with my anger.

"You are weak with him! But I can *make* you strong. I can make you strong enough to be the Silnỳ. Strong enough," he whispered, letting the pressure he held me with drop just enough that I gasped for air, "for me."

My breath was stuck in my chest as his hands ran over my face, the touch acid and ice as my magic fought against his. I gasped at the contact, but he only smiled as though he thought I enjoyed it. Could he not feel the burn, the way his magic raged through me? I could see in his smile that he couldn't. He believed in what he was saying, every word; that I belonged to him.

It was what was behind the words that scared me—the possessiveness, the control. I could see the danger in his eyes and hear the violence in his voice, and it boiled through me, hot and angry, as my magic moved to match it.

"I don't need you!" My words sounded more like the roar of a thunderstorm as my magic rocked through the air, pulsing in a wave of white light as Ryland stumbled away from me.

My feet left the ground as my magic picked me up, speeding me through the air only to land above him, straddling him as he had me.

"I can do this on my own! I was born to do this! I am the Silnỳ!" His hair whipped around his face as I yelled at him.

"Are you?" Ryland asked, his weak voice mocking from underneath me. "You have all the magic in the world and you can't conjure enough to kill me." He smiled again, his teeth red with his blood, his eyes dark and dangerous. "If you won't take me... kill me! Kill me! Kill me!"

It was enough. I felt the anger snap into a wave of loathing, the emotion so strong and hot that I willingly let it take over me. I let it rule over me. I wouldn't let him do this anymore.

"I won't let you hurt me!" The air around me rippled as the hurricane of my anger surged, pulling in the magic that surrounded me and sending it right into Ryland as I lifted him out from under me. I suspended him in the air, the whirlwind I had created circling closer and closer as it compressed against him.

"You *deserve* to die!"

The tanned skin of his face faded to white before the red of his lips painted blue. He clawed at his neck as an invisible force squeezed the life out of him. I only smiled as I watched him fight it, knowing it was pointless, knowing I wouldn't let him get away.

His hands stopped fighting as his eyes began to close, his body moments away from death. I wanted to watch him die. I wanted to see his legs stop kicking. I wanted to see the last tendrils of life leave him.

I was going to be the one to do it.

8

─────────

RYLAND'S EYES opened in horror, his mouth gaping as the last of his air left him, his body moments away from giving in. I was going to see his end; see the final breath of the boy who had haunted me and hurt me more times than I could count.

The boy I had loved once.

If only Ilyan hadn't barreled into my side, his arms wrapping around me as he knocked me to the ground. Ilyan's warm magic surrounded me in a rush, the flow only a futile attempt to calm me. I wouldn't let it. I just screamed louder, letting my magic surge as I blocked him, attempting to finish what I had started.

"Stop, Joclyn!" A rough surge of Ilyan's magic encapsulated around us as he yelled, breaking my connection to Ryland. The wind that had been a torrent in the room left, a loud slap of flesh against stone signaling Ryland's fall to the ground.

I fought against Ilyan's hold, desperate to get back to Ryland, to wrap my hands around his neck, to take his life another way. Ilyan only locked his hands tighter around me, keeping me in place.

"Let me go," I yelled again, my movements rough and volatile in my attempt to escape.

"No! Joclyn!" Ilyan yelled, but I couldn't hear him through my screams.

His hands held strong, his magic surging through me as he tried to calm me and my magic, but I wouldn't let him. I continued to thrash beside him until he moved over me, his hands on my forearms and his legs pinning mine down. He should have crushed me, but his hold was gentle with only enough pressure to keep me in place. He flared his magic harder against my skin as he tried to calm me, my magic still restricting him even though my heart—my very soul—begged me to accept him.

All I felt was anger and hatred and heartache, and before I knew it, I was fighting him again, his face crestfallen as I screamed at him in agony. I didn't want to let Ilyan in; I didn't want him to take away the rage that filled me. I liked the way the anger felt, the way it bubbled and grew and made me feel something besides jitters. I liked the way it made me feel alive.

I only wanted one thing, the thing that Ilyan had taken away from me.

"I want to kill him!" I growled through gritted teeth, my hands clenching and unclenching as I fought the need to attack Ilyan, something I knew would end in my defeat.

"No, Joclyn, you don't." His voice was calm as his thumbs ran over my forearms, something that should have calmed me only aggravating me more.

"I do!" I said between the tears, the dreaded things joining in my battle as my emotions swelled. "I don't want him to hurt me anymore! He deserves to die!"

"No, my love, no," Ilyan whispered while he lifted me off the ground, his grip strong as he began to pull me away.

I let my heels grind into the rubble-strewn floor as I tried to fight him, but it was no use; he only kept moving.

My body felt heavy in exhaustion, my overused emotions making my magic slow and sluggish. I couldn't fight my way out of Ilyan's hold if I tried.

I yelled out in outrage one last time before I caught sight of Ryland, folded over as he tried to regain breath, Sain wrapping his arms around him in comfort.

Sain.

My father had gone to Ryland first. He didn't even look at me as I screamed and writhed against Ilyan's hold. He only denied me yet again.

I stopped fighting, everything stiff in shock before my rage grew as Ilyan dragged me away from the rubble I had created, from the battle he would have me lose.

From the father that I would never truly have.

I continued to scream as Ilyan pulled me around the corner and away from them, his magic pressing against the Štít—against my skin—but I wouldn't let him in.

"Put me down!" I screamed as he plunged us through the halls, his pace quick in an attempt to put as much space as possible between Ryland and me.

"Let me do it!" The words ripped from my throat as the door closed behind us, the heavy wooden slab shutting us into our darkened room.

Lights flared through the space as Ilyan's magic sparked them, taking away the heavy clouds that hung over the oppressive darkness from what should have been a bright, dawn sky.

Ilyan said nothing; he only moved us farther into the

room until he released me, letting me fall onto my hands and knees on the hard, cold stone.

I could hear his labored breathing as he stood behind me, his strenuous huffs matching mine as his magic still pressed against me. My magic quivered in exhaustion as I fought him, as I forced his out of me, closing off the Štít and the connection we shared.

"Let me in, my love. Your soul will not be able to calm if you don't let me in." Ilyan's words were soft, but they had the opposite effect on me.

I turned toward him, my jaw tightening as Ryland's words came right back, whether I wanted them to or not.

I was weak, and Ilyan had exposed my instability.

My magic throbbed at the betrayal, causing the heavy alabaster chandelier that hung above the bed to tremor.

"Focus on what is behind your anger," Ilyan advised calmly, ignoring the glare I shot toward him, the feral animal that seemed to have taken control. His eyes smoldered as he once again attempted to push his magic into me while the angry barrier I had built kept him out. His face cringed at the realization, his hurt emotions swirling toward me. I pushed them away—not wanting to feel them—yet I couldn't keep them out, not entirely.

"Nothing is behind my anger! Not right now!" I screamed at his face, my body seeming to rebel against the lie. I hated how my heart clenched up, how the wrath ebbed and the guilt attempted to take its place. I knew what was behind my anger. I saw him standing right in front of me. I just didn't want to admit it.

I looked into his face before I cried out in confused agony, my fingers weaving through my hair and pulling out more of the braid Ilyan had worked so hard on.

"I want to kill him!" I moaned in anguish, letting the foremost desire take control.

"No, mi lasko." Ilyan's voice came from right above me as he hovered, attempting to protect me from myself. He wasn't going to leave me alone anytime soon, no matter how much I wanted him to.

I wanted him to leave me. I wanted to run back to Ryland and finish the job. I wanted to yell and scream and destroy things. Everything in me felt so tight, so angry. I needed to let the flames out.

My hands moved from the now-destroyed braid to knead and grind into the unforgiving stone below me, my magic sparking from the tips of my fingers as it tried to escape the flood of pain that had trapped me.

"Let me kill him. I want to kill him," I pleaded, my voice deep and menacing as I ground it between my teeth.

"No, my love, that is not true. You need to calm—"

"I don't want to calm down!" I erupted at Ilyan's serene voice, my body moving to stand in one swift movement as I turned to face him. I clamped my teeth as my fists writhed together, my neck muscles straining.

"You used me! You lied to me!"

Ilyan's eyes widened at my outburst; his normally stoic face shattered in confusion.

"I did nothing of the sort!"

"You are supposed to protect me and you didn't! You sold me to the wolves!"

"I cannot protect you when you leave in the middle of the night." Ilyan's accent amplified as the lines in his face began to deepen in displeasure. I should have been afraid—I should have backed off—but my feet stayed planted. My fists remained tied in tight little rocks.

"I tried to save Dramin! I tried to heal my brother. I

failed. And *he* found me. He hurt me! I want to kill him. That way you can never sell me to him."

"Sell you? Vat are you talking about?" His words were almost unrecognizable through his heightened accent, his final attempts to comfort me drifting away as his face darkened.

"You said that to him, didn't you?" I spat, my fists compressed at my sides as I tried to keep my magic restrained, to stop myself from hurting him. "You fell in love with some fantasy of me eight hundred years ago. Then, when you met me, you didn't like me. You don't want me. Even after the last few days. It was all a ploy, wasn't it? It was all a lie. You want me to die when the battle starts, just as the sight has shown."

I wasn't sure if I believed the words or not, but part of me knew that I did... Deep down, I did. Ryland's cruel words had only fueled that fire, revealing the deepest regret and worry that had hidden in the dark pit of my mind. It burned through me like a red-hot branding iron, the misery that my fears had held captive rolling over me.

I dug my nails into my palms and fought my tears, keeping my eyes trained on Ilyan.

"Joclyn, my love, that isn't true," he whispered, his hand moving forward to rest on my hip, but I pushed him away, not wanting to feel what I wasn't sure I could have anymore.

"You told him you were saving me for him," I interrupted him, the deep ripple of my words making my whisper sound like a rumble.

"Tak jsem to nemyslel.," Ilyan mumbled, his teeth clenched as his animosity grew. I felt his emotion rush into me through the wall I had forged against him, the jolt of pain that stabbed into my stomach almost taking my breath away.

I stared at him, waiting for him to translate, but he said nothing; he only stared straight ahead, away from me, as the muscles in his jaw clenched. I had seen that look before, the way he battled over himself, over what to say. Over who to be. Now that battle raged right before me, over what he had said about me.

I stood still as I waited for him to deny it, yet nothing came. His eyes dimmed as he finally met my intense stare, the regret and the unspoken apology as deep as an affirmation to me.

"You did?" I asked, flabbergasted that he had ever said such a thing, while he remained silent. My anger prickled again at the silent acknowledgment. "When?" I asked breathlessly, the words barely tumbling out in my agonized shock.

I couldn't move. I just waited, staring into the blue depths of his eyes, the color dark and as unforgiving as a shallow pool. I could already see the regret in them—the plea for forgiveness—but I didn't want to hear it, not anymore.

"After you awoke, after you attacked Ryland, I didn't know the full extent of what Edmund had done. I assumed it to be reversible—"

"You told him that he could have me?" I snapped, interrupting the lies he was trying to pass off as excuses.

"Yes." One word reignited the rage.

It burned through me, the next words surging with my fury until they hissed out of me, rumbling through the air.

"Like I was property."

"No, Joclyn. I never meant it in that way. It is not viewed as being that way among my kind," he pleaded, his voice deep as the royal strain that he had very rarely used toward me tried to take control. I flinched at the tone, at the implications behind it. Whether he meant it or not, he was speaking to me just like my father had, reminding me how little I knew.

"I don't believe you. You lied to me," I growled under my breath, trying to ignore the life-wrenching tension that pinched at my heart. "You kissed me, you held me, you slept beside me, you ran your fingers through my hair... and all the while you planned to hand me over to the man who has done nothing but try to kill me for the past few months. Like I was some unwanted pet."

My voice grew as I spoke, the deep rumble that had taken control before Ilyan had stopped me from killing Ryland coming back. My magic and hurt melded together until the room began to shake. The shields that Ilyan had placed over the windows vanished with the shattering pulse. With the barriers gone, the wind from outside flooded the room in a wave of swirling energy that surrounded us, the rain I had wanted to feel against my skin gone now.

"No, Joclyn, that was never my intention. I told him such things to calm him, but when I spoke to you, I realized that the love you two shared was gone, forever broken because of my father."

I stared into him. I wanted to believe him, desperately. I couldn't, though; I couldn't see beyond what Ilyan had told Ryland, not why or with what intention. Just the simple fact that he had said it. I was blinded by my heartbreak, letting it guide me, no matter how hard my better judgment cried for me to stop.

"Why did you kiss me?" I asked, careful to keep my breathing even.

"Because I am in love with you. You. I fell in love with you when I held you broken and screaming, when I dried your tears, and as I watched your strength grow. I kissed you because my soul, my heart, and every part of me is yours," Ilyan whispered, his hands stretching toward me as he tried to pull me into him the way he had always done.

My heart faltered at seeing his hands there—at the comfort I knew he could give me—knowing that I could just step into his arms and let them wrap around me; yet I couldn't move. As much as my soul berated me for being ridiculous, I couldn't see beyond the pain and the lies that my mind had formed.

"Because you own me!" I spat. My heart tightened, and I stepped away from him, not wanting to give in, to let him win. To let him think that what he had done was okay. "I am not property! I don't need to be owned. I don't need someone else to be strong. I am strong on my own."

"I know, my love. I see that more than any other." Ilyan's voice was soft, the serenity of it fueling the calm that swelled beneath my anger; but it wasn't enough to let it break through.

"Then why won't you leave me alone?"

"Because I am your protector. I was born to keep you safe, to help you find strength enough to fight the Trpaslíks that surround us."

"What if I don't want that?" I snapped, my fists clenching at my sides as I yelled at him. "I don't need someone to save me, to own me."

"No one owns you, mi lasko, least of all me. Ryland only thinks that way because of how he has been raised." Ilyan took another step toward me as he spoke, his eyes indulgent.

I stepped away farther, my arms coming up to wrap around my torso, my fists tangling around the fabric of my shirt in an attempt to keep them there. I clung to my shirt as I looked into him, the hair that had come loose from the braid fanning around my face in the wind that was now little more than a gentle breeze.

"You told Ryland he could have me, but all he does is hurt me."

"He cannot help it—the same way you cannot harness your desire to kill him. Edmund has seen to that. He has no more control of his emotions than you do at this very moment."

I could hear the truth in Ilyan's words, my own memories mixing with them until the anger that had stopped my heart lessened, leaving only a dull pain that crippled me. I couldn't help it—the tears came freely through the anger. I could feel the heat of them behind my eyes, the cold, wet trails against my nose.

I ignored them, my voice rising in desperation.

"He was in perfect control of his thoughts when he tried to cut me apart and when he punched me. That wasn't in Cail's mind, Ilyan!" I stepped closer, my voice rising as it broke and bled with my heartbreak.

"Joclyn, I need you to understand me," Ilyan said, his voice straining as he rushed me, his hands moving to clench around my biceps. I tried to step away, but he held me tightly, keeping me in place as his magic surged between our skin, his desperate need to calm me hot against my body. "It was not really Ryland inside of Cail's mind."

"Then who was it?" I asked, demanding the answer that I knew Ilyan wouldn't give me. "Because the Ryland you seem to trust just attacked me, the same as before."

Ilyan stared into me before he moved away from me, his hands dropping from my arms as he dragged his hand over his short hair in frustration. His steps took him away from me before he rushed back, the intensity of his eyes catching me off guard and causing me to flinch.

"You must listen to me, Joclyn," Ilyan demanded, in a tone he rarely used on me. "He can't control it, mi lasko. His heart and soul have been diced apart. His very essence has been separated in your name, in love, and by others who try to work against you. They have torn him apart, and he doesn't know what is right anymore. His father rent his soul in two in order to torture you, and before that, Ryland cut out a piece of his own heart in the hopes to protect you."

I listened to Ilyan's words, the familiarity of them scaring me. Ryland had said the same things in the nightmares. Cail had taunted me with them for months while he had tried to erase my mind. Hearing them repeated through Ilyan ran through me like cement, cold and unmoving. I didn't want to hear it. I didn't want to believe it.

"What are you saying?" I asked, my voice softer than I expected.

"The necklace he gave you, the one you wore for months, the one that bound you to him. The necklace that bridged you to him and opened up your Tŏuha. It isn't a ruby. It is a diamond with a shard of his heart. It is possibly the only untarnished piece that is left of him."

I heard him, I understood him, but I couldn't process it. Everything was ice and pain and cold and hard within me. Something like that, it couldn't be true. It couldn't. It was just another lie.

"You're lying!"

"I would never lie to you, my love. Never. I only ask that you understand why he is broken, why he sees you as an enemy." Ilyan came right up to me, his hand soft as he pushed the hair out of my face, the scarred palm warm against my skin before it made contact with my mark, making my body jump. I should have found joy in the jolt of the connection—the way he seemed to—but I couldn't. I couldn't let my heart feel the joy it wanted so desperately, no matter how much it begged for it.

"Are you on his side? Is that why you told him you didn't want me?" I snapped, shoving his hands away from me as I foolishly stood my ground. When the action heightened as my magic surged, he skidded across the floor away from me, his back hitting the wall with a giant jolt.

Ilyan squared his jaw and looked up at me, the anger and surprise flexing through his muscles. I clenched my teeth and returned the gaze, my body radiating with my outrage.

"To se nehodí, Joclyn. Nevím, kolikrát jsem ti řekl, co je v mém srdci a ty si mi nevěřila!" He screamed at me, and I jumped, the anger in his voice catching me off guard.

I knew I should have stood down. I could feel the waves of his magic surge through the air, his fury bubbling through them as they heated the air in warning.

"If you don't want me then just leave. Me. Alone!" I screamed at him, my voice cracking as I forced out the sound. I balled my fists against my pant legs as I screamed, my body leaning toward him with each heightened word.

"Do not speak to me in such a way, Joclyn!" Ilyan yelled, the deep strain of his royal blood taking over his voice as he walked toward me. He talked to me like I was nothing more than a servant or one of the subjects he had ruled over for years. The words cut through me, my mind screaming at me again to stand down—to apologize—but I couldn't make myself do it. He had never spoken to me that way before.

"Why? Because you are the king? King of no one—they are all dead. You are just a guy on a power trip!" The words came out of my mouth like vomit. My brain and heart disconnected from them as my shattered heart fueled them. I didn't know why I said them or where they had come from, but I couldn't stop them. The words were out as my anger grew, Ilyan's magic retreating from me as I pushed him away one last time.

"Joclyn!" Ilyan yelled, his attempt to berate me obvious, but he couldn't seem to get the words out. I didn't really give him a chance.

"I don't care about who you are. Who you used to be," I spat, my temper continuing to fuel my words. My heart clenched up as I said it, the pulse deep and rumbling as if it had somehow forgotten how to beat.

"Tímhle spůsobem se mnou mluvit nesmíš! Nemůžeš si to dovolit. Možná, že já jsem to udělal, ale ty nejsi mého rodu, Nedávam ti své svolení!" he yelled back, the words so quick that even if I understood them, I wasn't sure I would have been able to make anything out.

"Speak English!" My voice cracked as it broke and fizzled into nothing, the tears washing it away.

"Learn Czech!" Ilyan spat, his magic surging as a giant crack broke through the air. I jumped at the sound, turning toward the noise just as feathers began to fall over us, the last surviving remains of the bed that Ilyan's temper had just ripped to shreds.

I looked back to Ilyan as he pulled a silver chain from his pocket, the red ruby glinting in the dim light before he threw it to the ground, the soft tinkling of it against the stone echoing off the shards of what was left of my heart. I looked at it for a minute before turning back to Ilyan, his eyes glistening with his own tears, and my heart tightened.

I hadn't meant to hurt him. I hadn't meant what I had said. Any of it. I had said it in my anger, and afterwards the regret that it brought threatened to kill me.

I looked at his face and my heart shattered over the stone floor between us, a million shards of pain and regret. I opened my mouth to say something, to plead forgiveness, to take it all back. Nothing came, and Ilyan stormed out, the door slamming behind him as I flinched and fell to the ground.

The rage I had been so ignorantly holding onto left, an incomprehensible sadness taking its place. My arm twitched as my muscles constricted, a small sob escaping my lips. I didn't want to feel this. I preferred the anger that disguised the words that Ryland had ingrained into me.

My filthy hands wound around my hair as I tried to push the emotion away, as I attempted to stop the anxiety from taking over. I pushed at it, forcing it away, until my shoulders loosened and the crippling sadness took its place. The anger that had been so strong was now only a small spark within me.

I started to cry before I was aware of it, the strong fabric of my magic pushing away from me, through walls, through the Štít, in desperation to find him, to apologize, to calm him—anything.

I didn't find him. He had blocked me as effectively as I had blocked him. He had left me alone.

I didn't blame him.

9

I HELD COMPLETELY STILL after he left. I don't think I could have moved if I tried. Everything felt dead inside of me. I just stared at the door as the tears coursed down my face, my breathing working itself into a panic. I knew I should calm down; somewhere in the back of my mind my heart screamed at me to relax, to go after him, to do something.

I couldn't make myself do any of it.

So I stood still and stiff like a rail while the desperation constricted my muscles. The anxiety that my anger had taken away came back so fast that I gasped, my back tensing.

I didn't even try to fight the fear and desperation that Cail had ingrained in me. I let it infiltrate me like a virus; I let it destroy me. It seemed fitting, after all. I had just said the cruelest, most terrible things to someone who meant more to me than anyone else. I had hurt him. What was worse, I had known I was doing it, and I hadn't stopped myself.

The tears kept falling as my body began to shake, my breathing swelling until a deep wail rose from my throat, the tears turning to ugly sobs. I didn't even try to wipe them away; I just let them slide down my face, reflecting the agony that was ripping me apart.

From somewhere else in the abbey, a loud scream of heartbreak and loss echoed mine. The desperation of Ilyan's broken heart shook the walls around me. My heart tensed at the familiarity of the sound. The pain that mirrored my own. The loss, the agony.

I jumped at the deep growl that followed the crash of wood and stone, the floor rocking underneath me. Everything tightened as my anxiety began weaving its way up my spine, the tight bands of my insanity taking over. My arms moved around my stomach, my fingers clutching at my shirt as the wails that had been for Ilyan turned into my own cries of pain and sadness.

Another distant yell followed the others. Another rumble shook the abbey, and my body reacted, my feet dragging me to the only place where my fractured mind promised me I could find safety. Tears streaked down my face as I ran past the big, beautiful bed that Ilyan had destroyed and into the bathroom that had been my security so many times before.

I slid against the wall as I wedged myself between the toilet and the sink, almost sighing with relief as the furniture pressed against me, holding me in place. Holding me together.

The abbey continued to roll and groan with Ilyan's pain and anger as I gasped for air. I had heard warning of his temper for months, and in that moment I understood what everyone had meant. What I had done to him.

The residual aroma from the bath Ilyan had drawn for me was still infused in the tile and wood of the small space. The sweet and spicy smells filled me as I breathed, taking away the hard edge of the anxiety that was cutting through me.

It didn't help the heartbreak, however. It didn't help the tears that streamed endlessly over my face. Those kept coming, my heart clenching painfully as I wailed. The abbey rocked again as my head swam, the coming sight giving me the chance to get away and not to feel. This time I didn't fight it. I wanted the numbing escape the sight provided.

The sight came on quickly, my vision burning red before flashes of the future came so fast that I could barely distinguish them from one another. It was only after they began to slow down that I recognized them, the same images from the sight Sain had given Ilyan eight hundred years ago.

The images of Ilyan fighting alongside me flashed in my eyes, his hand around mine, my hair flying as we battled through the forest. I saw the tenderness of his kiss, the way he protected me.

I almost regretted letting the sight come as I watched those moments, grateful when they left to be replaced by images I had never seen before.

An old church I could only assume to be the abbey sat engulfed in fire; the shock at seeing something familiar was almost incapacitating. Another flash of fire, a flash of light, and then I was left with an image of Ilyan sitting behind me on the bed he had just destroyed, his fingers moving through my hair as he braided it, his lips moving rapidly with words I couldn't hear.

I still felt the heartbreak. I still felt the pain of loss. However, I looked into the future that my sight provided—into an image I knew I didn't fully understand—and my body calmed. My blood burned hot as my sight whispered to me of its importance, the part this would play bigger than I would ever understand.

I watched Ilyan reach toward a small, gold box that rested on the bed beside us, something golden glinting between his fingers as he removed it from the depths of the container.

The pressure in my head grew as I watched him continue to braid my hair, my mouth opening wide as my jaw extended on its own.

"*He will tear us apart. If you wish to see the end, give me your heart.*" My voice croaked out the deep lines of my sight, my heart seizing at the familiarity of them, even though I was sure I had never heard the words before.

I looked back at the images as they left me—the sight of Ilyan fighting by my side, of me using his magic as I battled. It was something that I wasn't sure would happen anymore.

My hands unwound from my sides to fist in the fabric of the shirt that rested over my heart—over the Štít—but everything felt cold and lifeless. Even the beat of my own heart felt dead. I pressed harder, pooling my magic around it—desperate to feel something—but I felt nothing. Not even a shadow of where Ilyan had protected me for so long.

The Štít was gone. He had left me alone more than just leaving the room.

For the first time in months, I didn't have the warmth of his magic within me. I didn't have the knowledge that he would protect me. I had pushed him away, and now I was alone.

I had wanted this; I had begged him to leave me, screamed at him. Now I wanted nothing more than to feel that warmth again.

I pressed my hand into my chest as the pain in my heart

grew. The tears that had streaked down my face increased along with my howls.

I had done this. I had opened my mouth and let my anger dictate my words—my feelings—and in turn, lashed out against someone who meant more to me than I had truly understood. I had acted like a fool. Worse, I had learned nothing. I had sat over Ilyan's unconscious body and talked to Thom about pride, about anger, about who I was and what I was expected to do. While I had learned so much, I still hadn't learned enough, and I had pushed away the one person who was supposed to help me through this.

The person who had been born to stand by my side.

The floor around me shook again, a loud crash sounding from somewhere off in the distance. My hands trembled as I pulled my legs into my chest, leaning against the side of the vanity as I curled into myself.

"I'm sorry, Ilyan," I wailed, knowing he couldn't hear me, knowing the words were not enough.

It didn't matter. I let my voice carry my pleas, the sound growing until it gave out, until I succumbed to the exhaustion just as the sun peeked out from behind the clouds.

My emotionally drained body slipped away, desperately claiming the sleep it needed. It was the first time I had slept alone since that first nightmare in Santa Fe, since waking up from the torment of Cail's mind. It was a miracle I slept at all.

I woke again just as the sun was preparing to set, the whole day having passed without me. The bedroom was bathed in the glow of the last of the day's sun, the light so bright that it almost seemed unwanted. The room was unwanted. It felt empty and cold without him here.

I splashed water over my face and unwound what was

left of the careful braid Ilyan had placed in my hair, my fingers aching as they pulled the long strands out from their bindings. My heart tensed as I removed something so precious—something that had such a good memory attached—but I didn't feel worthy to wear it anymore.

Not after what I had done to him.

My fingers froze at the thought. My mind almost expected the abbey to shake in Ilyan's anger, however nothing came. Only the silence of evening, the gentle sound of a few crickets who had beat the others to the night.

I stretched my magic away from me as I stood before the mirror, pulsing it over the abbey as I searched for him. I scanned through hallways, through rooms I had yet to see, and right to the very edge of the gardens, but he was nowhere.

I knew that couldn't be right. I didn't want to believe that he could just be gone, that he could have left us all alone.

I clenched my teeth and pulled out the last of the braid, leaving my hair to hang around my face as it had done for so many years.

I looked at myself in the mirror—the silver eyes, the dark sheet of hair. I should have looked the same as I had only months before, yet I wasn't the same, not anymore. My eyes seemed darker somehow, more grey than silver, and my hair didn't hang quite so heavily.

I ran my fingers over my face, my hands shaking as I tried to find the girl that I had been, but she wasn't there, not anymore. The girl I had been would never have said those things to someone she loved. She would never have tried to kill Ryland, even though he had tried to kill me.

Without thinking, I reached up and pulled the collar of my shirt down, letting the line of my scar shine through the mirror, the scar where Ryland had stabbed me. It had been months—almost a year—since that night, but the line was still white, a painful reminder of what we had become.

I pushed the thought away and grabbed the earthen mug by the sink and filled it, my magic heating and dancing through me as I took a drink of the Black Water. I exited the bathroom, only to come face to face with the destroyed bed. I hadn't looked at it last night; I hadn't wanted to see what I had driven Ilyan to do. I could see it now, however, and it wrung through me. The destroyed remains wound uncomfortably through my stomach. Everything had been sheared in two—comforter, feather mattress, and frame— right down the middle.

Just as we had been. Broken.

Ilyan had done this in his pain with only one thought. It made me worry for what he had done to the rest of the abbey, for why the building felt as if it were falling apart. I cringed and moved away from it, not really wanting to see what he had done.

Not wanting to see his pain.

I didn't know what to do. Should I track him down? Write him a formal apology letter? Hang a white flag from the balcony? I had never been in a situation like this before. One thing was clear; I needed to find him. I needed to apologize.

I took another drink and moved toward the balcony, hoping that I could perhaps see him from the stone outcropping, like Romeo and Juliet. I almost laughed at the thought, the ridiculousness of it catching me off guard.

I took two steps before I jumped back, Black Water splashing over my arms as my bare foot hit against something hard and cold that cut into the soft tissue of my heel.

"Ow!" I groaned as I rubbed the tender spot on my foot,

my magic pushing aside feathers until I found the red ruby glinting at me from within the blanket of white that covered the floor.

No, not a ruby, I reminded myself.

My heart seemed to beat faster, my hands clenched around the mug of Black Water as I glared at the necklace. My brow furrowed as if it had somehow offended me. I guess in a way it had. I could still vividly recall Ilyan throwing it to the ground in his anger. I could see the pain on his face when I told him I thought he was lying, that I didn't need him.

My shoulders knit together at the thought, my stomach twisting uncomfortably as the guilt bubbled up aggressively.

I drained my mug and tossed it on the massacred bed as I stared at the necklace, my fingers twitching as I moved the feathers out from around it to get a better look. Even the idea of touching it made me feel a bit uncomfortable. I didn't think it was the whole "heart enclosed in a piece of diamond" thing. It was just that it had come from Ryland.

The feathers flew through the air around me as I dropped to my knees just as the door opened. I jumped at the movement, my gaze flying toward it as my heart rate picked up. My hope at seeing Ilyan mixed with the fear of being attacked until someone who I wanted to see just as much walked into the feather-covered room.

"Gee, if you were going to have a pillow fight, you could have at least called me," Wyn said, the smile in her voice lighting up her face. I tried to return her smile, but the guilt that had been raging through me grew, and instead, I stared at her, frozen in place.

Wyn just looked at me as she leaned against the door, her body still weak as she relied on the slab of wood for support.

She looked different, and it was more than the odd, old-fashioned nightgown she wore, although the absence of bangles and a band shirt did make her look like a different person. The marks that had once lined her face and arm were now a shadow, like a marker that someone had attempted to wash away, though it didn't quite come all the way off. Even through the weakened sag in her spine, she stood taller, looked more confident, older.

I stared at her, trying to decide if I was imagining the changes or if they were really there. She had been through as much, if not more than me, and I was certain that I looked different to her as well. It had been so long since I had seen her; twice as long for me thanks to Cail's nightmare. Right then, however, I didn't care if there were changes or not.

"Wyn," I sighed as I bolted off the floor, my feet taking me to her in three giant strides before I fell into her arms, both of us falling into the wall behind her.

The feel of her arm wrapped around my back was all it took for those desperate emotions that I had been trying to ignore to come through. Regret, pain, anger. I was so emotionally drained from the last day that I couldn't stop them.

Wyn was here. It didn't make it all better—it didn't take away the desperation and the fear—but somehow, it made it all seem a little more manageable.

"W-w-w-yn," I stuttered out, my voice distorted by the staccato breathing that had taken over me.

"Geeze, girl, you under attack by Reavers or something?" Wyn asked with a laugh as I cried against her. I was aware that there was a joke there that I hadn't gotten, but I didn't care. I just clung to her as the ugly emotions spilled from me.

"Jos?" she asked, the light laugh dropping from her voice almost immediately. "You okay?"

Everything stopped in expectation of an answer, one that I knew I wouldn't be able to give. So I just clung, my fingers tangling around her nightgown as I internally pleaded with her to drop it, not to make me expand on something I was almost sure would end in a panic attack.

"Jos?" she asked again as she shut the door behind her, the heavy wood slab closing with a loud bang that echoed in my ears and flared the alarm that my weak emotions had let take over.

I jerked at the noise, my arms flying away from her as they moved to cover my ears. Wyn's eyes widened again at my reaction, which only made me shy away from her all the more. I didn't like being looked at like that, least of all by Wyn.

"Calm down, Jos. It's okay. It's okay," she soothed, her hand rubbing over my back. I tried to settle down—I really did—but I couldn't seem to get my body to cooperate.

"If you want, I can sing you a stupid Styx song," she offered, a wide, cheesy grin on her face. The absurdity of her suggestion wound through me in sweet familiarity, the joyful light in her eyes breaking through my anxiety enough that I could return the smile. Albeit, it was more chagrined than wide and cheesy.

"That's better. Let me get you some water."

I sank down to the ground as Wyn weakly walked away from me toward the bathroom, her hand clinging to different pieces of furniture in an attempt to keep herself steady.

I needed to pull myself together. It was only Wyn. My friend. She had been there from the beginning, and I didn't see that changing anytime soon.

My lungs ached as I breathed, my body protesting the surge of anxiety and emotion I was still trying to calm.

"You are lucky I was able to come," she said from the bathroom, her voice carrying to me as I kept my focus on the floor. "It's my first time out of bed since yesterday... since... well, you know..." Her voice trailed off as she rambled, the sounds so familiar I couldn't help smiling.

"Everyone wanted to keep me there, but I couldn't, not after today. So I kinda snuck out; hence the 1970s gown. I'm just glad it's not brown," she jabbered on as she came out of the bathroom, another large earthen mug in her hands. My fingers twitched as I wrapped them around the mug she extended toward me, my body seeming to relax from the magic that seeped from it.

"Th-thank-k... y-you," I said, my voice shaky as I brought the mug closer.

"Yeah, I really am sorry. I didn't think you were that bonkers... I mean, I didn't know how scared you would be... I mean, Thom told me, but I guess I just assumed he was full of it..."

I smiled at her. Her crazy banter was familiar, even though her voice was a little different. I brought the mug to my lips, grateful for an excuse not to answer her implied questions and assumptions.

I took a big gulp of the water in relief, only to gag when the tasteless mass hit my stomach. My body revolted, heaving as it tried to get the imposter out of me. I don't know why I hadn't checked, why I had assumed. Wyn hadn't given me Black Water; it was regular water. It tasted like sand and moldy bread against my tongue, and it felt the same in my stomach. I hadn't expected my body to have that kind of reaction, and I certainly wasn't ready for what came next. My stomach heaved, and I turned to the side, my body expelling the mass in a bubbly mix of water and stomach acid.

"God, Jos, are you okay?" Wyn exclaimed, her body jumping away in disgust.

"Th-that's wat-ter-r," I managed to get out before my body embarrassed me again, more yellow acid spreading away from me and over the feathers that covered the stone floor.

"Well, duh, I told you I was getting water," Wyn shrieked, her voice finally sounding like herself for once.

"I m-mean... it-t's w-wat-ter." I moved toward the wall, pressing my head against the cold stone in hope that the chill would stop my body from rebelling against me further. I wasn't sure it was going to get the message, though; everything still felt like I had eaten a live fish. At least the anxiety had lessened to a manageable level. My stomach hadn't reacted like that when I had forced down the mushrooms in Isola Santa. I wondered what the difference was.

"Yeah," Wyn said in oblivious confusion.

I lifted my eyes to her, my body suddenly feeling extraordinarily heavy in understanding.

She didn't know.

"Dude, is everything okay?" she asked again as her magic ran from her in a bright streak of red, the powerful surge burning away most of the mess I had just made.

I nodded at her and dumped the rest of the poisonous water over the smoldering remains of feathers and vomit, letting it run in long rivulets somewhere under the destroyed bed and away from us, thankfully taking the smell with it. I watched them run away as I placed my hand over the rim of the mug, the Black Water refilling immediately. I don't know why Wyn had given me regular water in a mug that was made for Black, but no harm done. Well, besides a little bit of vomit.

I took a long drink and let the water supercharge me, taking my crazed emotions and settling them, letting the stress melt away until I felt a little less like a mental patient.

I looked up to Wyn, expecting that same opened-mouth wonder that Ilyan had given me. But, she just shook her head, a small smile playing around her lips, almost as if she had expected it.

"I guess we both have our secrets, huh?" she said as her body folded to sit right in front of me.

"What?"

"Never mind," she sighed, her voice sounding oddly deep in my ears. "If I would have known it wasn't only Ilyan having a freak-out, I would have come sooner."

"Where is Ilyan? I need to see him; I need to apologize," I asked, my nerves prickling as I said his name.

I grabbed Wyn's hand as I stood, ready to beg her to take me, but she didn't even move. She only stared at me from where she sat, a giant smile plastered on her lips.

"You *do* love him," she sighed, her voice practically melting around the words. "Thom said so, but I didn't—"

"Wyn," I groaned in interruption, really not wanting to go into this right now. "I need to see him."

I looked down at her, my eyes pleading as I clung to her hand, desperate to go, and yet she still didn't move.

"He's not here, Jos," Wyn said, the love-struck, teenager look on her face melting away. "He left after his little fit; probably to go destroy something else after he collapsed the cathedral on the other side of the grounds."

"Destroy..." I began, unable to get out more than just the one word.

"Yeah, I thought it was weird. I mean, he helped to build

this place back in the eleventh century, and he has spent most of his time restoring it since he purchased it in the eighteen-twenties."

Guilt. Raw, violent, never-ending guilt slammed into me, taking my breath away. I just wanted to run away and cry and disappear, but I wasn't sure how that would help.

I slid down the wall. Specks of white fluff exploded into the air in a flurry of soft, warm snow at the abrupt movement, each feather feeling like a stab of pain in my chest. He had destroyed a chapel, and by the sound of it, it wasn't just any chapel; it had been a place that had meant something to Ilyan. It had been a treasured part of his past.

"What happened between you two?" Wyn asked as she sat down next to me, that same deeper strain still polluting her voice.

"We had a fight." I still wasn't sure how to categorize it.

"Oh, yes, that I heard. In fact, I think everyone heard. You went at it like a newlywed couple battling over toothpaste squeezing positions," Wyn said lightly. The comment was innocent enough, however I could hear the implications behind it, and I blushed.

We had fought like newlyweds, like lovers, like a couple. I guess in a way that was right. In oh so many ways it was what we had become; it was what we had always been meant to be. Maybe that's why it was only my anger, not my heart, that had said those things. That's why it hurt so much now that he was gone.

"Everyone heard?" I asked, my voice soft.

"Oh, yes," she said with a smile. "I wouldn't be too worried, though. You should have heard some of the fights Talon and I had after..." The perky tone of her voice left as her voice faded to nothing, the mention of his name setting my own heart into an overactive hyperdrive.

She didn't need to explain her pain, her loss; I could feel it. I could feel it in the way her magic sagged as she spoke his name. I could sense it in the heat of his magic that lived inside of her, deep down in her belly. I desperately wanted to tell her that Talon's magic was still with her, tell her how much I hurt for her, but I didn't know if I should.

"I'm sorry," I whispered, not knowing if it was the right thing to say or even if she wanted to hear it.

"I felt so lost after my mother was murdered..." I began, regretting the words almost instantly. I shouldn't have even said anything. I still didn't really want to talk about my loss, and I was sure Wyn felt the same.

I brought my knees into my chest, wrapping my arms around them as I tried to fight the pain of the loss, the memories still a blistering branding iron against my heart. We sat still, side by side, lost in our own misery as the feathers settled while the last of daylight left.

"Edmund kept us in the old prison in Prague," Wyn said suddenly, her words soft as she spoke toward her toes, her voice distanced as she became lost in thought. "Talon got sick... He just didn't make it out... It's okay, though. I killed my father for what he did to him. I will make Edmund pay for what he did to Talon, to Cail..."

I jumped at the sound of his name, my hands winding through my long strands of hair as the insanity battled for control.

"I'm sorry he did that to you, Jos. I wish I could have stopped it. I tried..." Her voice trailed off again as I turned to look at her. Her dark eyes widened as I looked into her pain, sure she could see the madness in mine.

Our eyes met in silence, neither knowing what to say before she broke the stare, her hands writhing in her lap, her thumb continually rubbing over a scar on her hand that I hadn't seen before.

"He hurt us, too, Jos," she whispered, as if that made it all better, yet it didn't. It only confused me more.

I thought I had understood all about turning the other cheek and being understanding and forgiving, though I had never assumed I could feel so much bitter hatred as I did for Cail.

"Then why do you want to avenge him? Because he was your brother?"

"It's complicated."

"I don't see what's complicated about it," I said, my voice hard and angry as I stared her down. "He trapped me in his mind, tried to kill me. I c-can't-t cl-lose my eyes w-with... with-out... without-t—"

I stopped abruptly, my nerves tingling at the memories as the insanity tried to take over. I pushed it away only to have my vision sway, the familiar swimming in my head rushing through me. My hands flew to my head as I pressed against my scalp, trying to block out the sight, my chest heaving as I tried to will some of the sweet-smelling fumes from the bathroom into my lungs.

I am bigger than it.

I breathed deep as Wyn placed her hand against my back, the warmth shocking as the heat of her magic warmed my skin. I gasped at the feeling, the difference from the icy cold I had felt before alarming.

"It's okay, Jos," Wyn soothed as she rubbed my back. I focused on the touch—on the memories of before—and felt the anxiety seep away into nothing. "I know. I know what he can do. I've known my whole life. He beat Talon and tortured Ryland until he broke while the only thing that kept Ryland together was Sain. I think Sain is the only thing that is still keeping him together."

I knew I shouldn't be surprised. I had seen the way my dad had comforted Ryland, the look of pity on his face as Ilyan dragged me away. I guess now I understood it. I had tried to kill his precious prince.

I gritted my teeth and looked away from Wyn, my eyes falling on the small sliver of glinting red that shone through the feathers. I wanted to take it and throw it against the wall, shatter it into a million pieces. I didn't need a piece of Ryland's heart anyway.

"Well, then maybe he can be Ryland's dad," I hissed the words out, the anger that I thought had left me coming back so fast I wasn't sure where it had been hiding.

"Jos?" Wyn asked, her voice so soft I barely heard her.

I clenched my teeth as I breathed in shakily, trying to control the anger, but once again, I wasn't sure if I wanted to. I closed my eyes as I pushed it away, only to have the image of Ilyan's face after I had snapped at him coming right to the surface. I gasped at the image, the anger leaving as a shard of my broken heart stabbed uncomfortably through my chest.

"I'm s-sorry... I sho-ouldn't have said-d that. It's j-just... after last night... when I tried to kill Ryland. He didn't help me. He went to Ryland," I said, my voice choking through the emotions.

"I know," she admitted, the response taking me off guard. I had almost expected her to erupt at my blatant admission of my attempt at Ryland's life. "I wanted to go help Sain calm him down after Ilyan dragged you off."

"You helped Sain?" I asked as I leaned toward her, the words accusatory and harsh, but I didn't try to hide it.

"Yeah, Jos, we are like bosom buddies now," she said as

she winked at me, her face breaking into a wide smile that I wasn't sure how to interpret. I narrowed my eyes at her in question, but she just sighed and leaned against the wall. "It's hard to keep Ryland calm after everything they did to him. Sain spent so much time with him, so he's the only one who can keep him calm..."

I looked away from her, my jaw tensing as I threw myself onto the hard floor, the feathers billowing around me instead of cushioning my fall as I had hoped.

I didn't want to hear what she had to say. It felt like I was in some kind of Ryland intervention, and she was getting out all the reasons why I should forgive him and go back to the way things were. I just didn't want to hear it. It wasn't like I didn't care because part of me still did. Part of me wanted him to be happy, just not in the way he wanted. I couldn't be with him, not anymore.

It was like when you had a reoccurring dream of falling. Every night for months you fell off the same building. You were screaming, and no one could stop you from the impact that would wake you up in a cold sweat, your chest heaving. It happened for years, and then, one day you would find yourself face to face with that building. You wouldn't go in. No one would.

Just like I couldn't look at Ryland the same way. Even for those brief moments when my mind was clear, I couldn't see beyond the nightmares that he had given me.

Sometimes you just fall out of love. Sometimes you can't be with someone who hurts you.

"Your dad loves you, you know," Wyn whispered into the silence.

I sighed at her words, but I didn't move from where I lay among the feathers.

"He has a funny way of showing it. The only thing he

has really said to me is that I am supposed to save the world."

I cringed at the thought, not liking the reminder of the fight that was knocking down our door. I could still feel the angry pulse of the Trpaslíks, reminding me that as soon as tomorrow, I could be forced into a battle I wasn't ready to fight. That I knew I would lose without Ilyan.

"That's the Drak in him talking." She said it like that made it all better, and I guess to her it did. Not to me.

To me, I was still harboring that image of my father that I had been clinging to from when I was five. The dad who would give me pony-back rides, chase bugs with me, and read me bedtime stories. I knew it wouldn't be the same, but I had at least expected him to care more about me than about my abusive ex-boyfriend.

"Yeah, well, I have Drak in me, too, but you don't see me telling Ilyan to bring me crumpets," I said, trying to ignore the guilt that mixed with the gentle swoop in my stomach as I said his name.

"Ah... so that's why he tore apart the chapel. Ilyan hates crumpets." Wyn laughed as she came to lie down next to me, her body pressing against mine as her movement sent feathers flying over me. I hacked and sputtered as they flew over my nose and tried to wiggle into my mouth.

Wyn laughed and pushed more toward me, but the attempt at playing was only halfhearted. My soul was too sore for me to focus on much else.

I gasped as the words came to mind, the realization almost so simple I felt stupid for not realizing it, and even more stupid for not having done something to stop it. Ilyan held part of my soul and I part of his.

No wonder everything hurt.

10

I LAY with Wyn among the feathers, the gentle breeze from the windows picking them up and swirling them over our heads in a blizzard of stars and cotton down.

We hadn't said a word for the last few minutes. We had merely lain in silence as I continually searched for Ilyan, my magic stretching as I sought out his magic, his soul. I searched for any sign that he was still alive, but I felt nothing. The thought only frightened me more, yet I kept it locked up, too scared to put words to my fears.

I exhaled deeply, my chest shaking with the threat of tears as the air left me. I had hoped the haze of sadness that lay over me would have gone, but I was still trapped underneath it.

"You are supposed to tell me this stuff, Jos," Wyn whispered into the silence, her hand moving to wrap around mine. "I'm your best friend; we are supposed to eat ice cream, watch movies that make us cry, and talk about how dumb boys are."

"There is no ice cream," I said sullenly, even though I knew I wouldn't be able to eat it if it were available.

"True, but I'm here, and I'm even better than ice cream."

"That's the weirdest thing you have ever said," I replied without looking at her, my lips turning up whether I wanted them to or not.

"Yes, but it's still true, so let's talk about boy problems," she said it as bright as day, but I could hear the pain behind her voice, my heart breaking at the thought that she wanted to help me with Ilyan while she had lost her mate only days before.

It didn't help that I could see her, staring at me, waiting for an answer.

I exhaled shakily, the pain in my chest seeming to grow with each breath.

"I upset him. I said things I shouldn't have said..." I purposefully whispered in the hope she wouldn't be able to hear me—that I wouldn't have to explain—but Wyn obviously wasn't going to let me get away with that.

"Everyone does things when they are scared," Wyn said, her voice breaking into a deep parental tone that I was not used to hearing from her. "It's normal. It's a defense mechanism, projecting your fears out in anger..."

I sighed and looked away from the ceiling to meet her head on, almost daring her to continue, but instead she stopped, her words trailing away to nothing.

"A defense mechanism? Who are you?" While it wouldn't be out of character for a two hundred year old immortal to say things like that, it was out of context for my nerd chic best friend. The whole thing caught me off guard.

"I've watched quite a few people over the years, Jos." She rolled her eyes up to the ceiling; obviously, it was her turn to avoid me.

"What? In the last six months?" I asked, prodding her

side with my finger, causing her to jump and move away at the contact.

"Everyone has fights," Wyn said as she carefully scooted back over to lie next to me. "It doesn't matter if you have been together for five months or five hundred years. No relationship is perfect, and expecting it to be is setting yourself up for disaster." Her voice rumbled through me, the sound low enough that it was more like a gentle hum in the silence of the room.

Even without the happily married parents as an example, I knew she was right; that everything was fixable. I didn't know if it was because it was the first time something like this had ever happened to me, or because Wyn had referred to me as being in a relationship with Ilyan, but her words caused my soul to ache and yearn in a deep need I had never felt.

"What did you say to him, anyway?" Wyn whispered, her apprehension at asking making me a bit uncomfortable. "That his hair was ugly? He smells like rotten fruit?"

I laughed at the absurdity of her suggestions, a momentary joy spreading through me as I lay next her, my body settling into the cold stone and feathers as well as the warmth that Wyn radiated. I knew I couldn't put it off; I knew I had to tell her what had happened. I had to let the words fly out into the air, let the pain and sadness go with them. At least that was my hope.

"Ilyan told Ryland that he was saving me for him, that Ry could have me. Like I'm a cow." I said it all very fast, my face beginning to burn in threat of tears the second that first word was out. I held the ugly tears in stubbornly, however. I didn't want to cry, not anymore. I wanted to fix what I had done, and I was fairly certain that crying wasn't going to do that.

"Did you really think that Ilyan would let a guy who keeps trying to kill you take you?"

"No."

"Then what are you so mad about?" Wyn asked, the smile on her face leaking through as she bounced her shoulder, playfully jostling my head around. I scowled and moved away to glare at her, wishing I could find the humor in the situation that she had, but it just wasn't there. She was obviously missing the biggest problem, the thing that ground at my stomach.

"I'm not property, Wyn. You can't buy and sell me."

"Did you let him explain?" Wyn propped herself up on her elbow as she looked down at me, her body hovering over me like a helicopter. I don't know if it was her dark eyes or the close proximity, but I suddenly felt like I was underneath a magnifying glass.

I hadn't let him explain; he had tried, but I hadn't let him get the words out, and even if I had, I knew that I wouldn't have listened. My stubborn anger was already begging me not to listen to Wyn.

I sighed and looked away from her, knowing that would be all the answer she needed.

"Můj majetek se proto rozšířila tento den dní, moje srdce roste v zemi a způsobu. Pozemky jsem chodil, se navždy, vázané na můj kamarád přede mnou." Her voice was a whisper of magic that prickled over my spine and I turned back toward her in a rush, my magic desperate to hear as much as I could.

She sat still, her face soft, her eyes closed as the words that were familiar and precious to her flowed off her tongue like a song. Her magic swelled as she spoke, the warmth of Talon's magic surging through her briefly before it settled back down.

"What does that mean?" I whispered, my magic still pulsing as the sky rumbled, disrupting the calm in the air that Wyn's words had brought.

"It's a line from the bonding ceremony, the part of the Zĕlství that Ryland conveniently skipped over, you know, after he forgot to ask you if you wanted to be bonded," Wyn said with an exaggerated eye roll. "Mates are supposed to braid each other's hair and bind their hands in oils. The Drak's share Black Water for whatever reason, and then those words are spoken. The first lines happen to be, 'My property has expanded this day of days.'"

Wyn sighed as she came to lie back down beside me, the uncomfortable twisting of my stomach increasing. "He doesn't view you as property. It's just the line—tradition. It means something else to us than it does to you. It's something that Ilyan, as King, has held dear for centuries."

"I'm a terrible person," I groaned as I rolled into Wyn, burying my face into her shoulder. The full weight of what I had done hit me, coming down on my chest like an anvil. I gasped for breath, the heaviness of my regret suddenly making it impossible to breathe.

"No, you're not," Wyn began, the lighthearted tone in her voice making it clear she didn't understand. "You are just overwhelmed, stuck in a new world with a dad who gets confused about his role in your life, a best friend who has a whole other life that she—..."

"No, I mean I am a terrible, bottom-of-the-rung, absolutely horrible human being," I interrupted.

Before I knew it, the hateful tears were falling down my face again. "I told him I didn't care who he was; he wasn't King anymore because everyone was dead..."

"No wonder he had a fit," Wyn whispered after my

words faded away, her dark tones making it clear how much of a mistake I had made.

I sat up, curling my legs into my chest as I hid my face in my knees. Piles of feathers billowed up into the air at my movement, a cloud of white surrounding me as I let the feathers fall on top of me. I had never wanted to disappear as much as I wanted to right then.

"Listen," Wyn whispered as she sat up next to me, her hand moving to rub over my back. "Ilyan may not take the formalities seriously all the time, but he can't help who he was raised to be. You undermined that. It didn't help that he lost his best friend, either. Talon was more than just his friend; he helped to keep Ilyan's temper in check."

Wyn's words trailed down my spine in a wicked prick of pain. I knew that what I had said was wrong, but hearing exactly why was a very broad slap to the face. I wished I knew where Ilyan was. I yearned to hug him and apologize. Even if I could, I wasn't sure of what the outcome would be anymore. I wasn't sure I deserved to be forgiven. The things I had said... The way I had behaved... It was inexcusable.

"What are you going to do?" she asked softly, her hand coming to a stop against the middle of my back.

"I don't know." I pushed the long strands of black hair out of my eyes as I turned to look at her. "Grovel at his feet and beg forgiveness." I tried to laugh as I spoke, but it didn't quite work, and so I pressed my forehead back into the hard joints of my knees.

"I'm sorry, Ilyan," I groaned, knowing he couldn't hear me. I couldn't even feel his presence near me enough that I could push the words into his mind. I was trapped in my room, with words that meant so much to me that I could hardly breathe, without a way to get the message to him.

"I'm sorry, too, Joclyn," his voice was a soothing balm

right to my soul. It cut through me and I jerked up, my breathing picking up to see him standing in the doorway.

His hair was longer than I had ever seen it, stretching to about halfway down his back and over his torn and filthy clothes. His blood-shot eyes were soft as they searched into me, pulling out the love and happiness that I had thought I had lost and bringing them right to the surface.

He stood still as I looked at him, the air heavy with expectation. I could hear the beating of my heart in my ears and feel the breeze as it blew the feathers over the floor like the waves of the sea, but nothing else existed beyond the two of us.

My heart pounded as I tried to find some footing, my mind desperately trying to figure out what to say while my core just begged me to run to him.

"Well, don't let me interrupt such a silent reunion," Wyn said as she moved past Ilyan toward the door, her hand on the doorknob before she spoke again. "Be nice to each other."

The door clicked shut and I ran to him blindly, well aware of the joyful tears that were flowing down my cheeks. He wrapped his arms around me as I made impact with his chest, his wide hands pressing me against him as I breathed deeply, the familiar scent of his magic moving into me.

I could hear the beat of his heart in his chest, my own frantic pulse moving to keep time with his. I buried my face into his neck as he held me, the warmth of his magic tucked away just under the surface of his skin. I pressed my hand to his neck, letting my magic flow into him, glad when he accepted it, my soul relaxing at the renewed contact. His warm breath moved over my cheek as he brought me closer to him. One hand tangling in my hair until it reached my neck, his magic soared into me at the skin contact. I sighed with the warmth that flooded into me, the anxiety and anger that had been plaguing me disappearing almost immediately.

I knew I didn't need him to take these emotions away for me anymore; I was perfectly aware that I could fight them on my own. Right then, however, I savored the feel of his skin against mine and the warmth of his magic. I cherished the feel of having him back, the pain in my heart that no amount of magic could take away leaving almost immediately.

Ilyan's hand slid over my neck until his fingers grazed the corner of my mark, the comforting touch soft and gentle against the raised skin. I felt the silky touch of the tips of his fingers before the jolt came, the sensation so strong and powerful that I gasped, my back arching as my magic supercharged. Ilyan supported my weight as my knees buckled, the torrent of magic flowing away from me in a gust of wind and energy that swirled around us, whipping hair and clothes, lifting the feathers that lined the floor.

The soft puffs of white swirled like a blizzard, enclosing us in them until everything was white. I held onto Ilyan, the colored sparks of magic erupting among the storm as our magic met and joined in the bright air around us. The lights flashed and twinkled until we were surrounded by them, spots of brilliant color among the white that made me feel like we were trapped in a cloud of light.

Ilyan's arms tightened around me as we watched our magic join together again, our souls rejoicing at finding their other halves, welcoming each other home. The flow of his thoughts came again at his touch, the joy of his emotions rushing into me.

"I'm sorry, Ilyan," I whispered. *I am so sorry.*

"As am I; I never should have made that promise to

Ryland," he whispered, the rate of his heart picking up slightly in regret.

"It's okay; I know why you did it. I shouldn't have gotten so angry. I'm sorry."

"I know, my love, I know. I apologize for having lost my temper," he whispered into my hair, the warmth of his breath running pleasurably over my skin. My heart beat faster at the greeting. The knowledge that he still thought of me that way soothed the pain in my heart.

"Never block me out again, all right?" Ilyan pulled away from me, his bright blue eyes pouring into mine as he looked at me, his hand soft as he moved my hair out of my face. "Your soul cannot survive without mine."

I nodded once, his words confirming what I already knew—what I had already felt. In my anger, I had blocked my soul from its other half, the act supercharging my loss and anger, injuring me. Never again. I never wanted to feel that pain that had controlled me for the past day again.

I smiled and pressed my face into his chest, the hollow of my ear pressing into his shirt as the heavy pounding of his heartbeat filled me.

Never, I said into his mind, relishing the return of our connection. *Never. Never.*

"Good, because I never want to feel like the world has broken in two."

"Like my heart was shattered," I finished the thought, my emotions having mirrored his own.

"I was so scared," I said, my voice a gasp of air from the tightness in my chest. Everything tensed at what I was about to say. "I never meant any of what I said, and after you had left, I couldn't find you. I couldn't feel you, even through the Štít—"

"The Štít is gone, Joclyn. When you pushed me away, my

love. I was so angry..." He stopped mid-sentence as his breath caught, his regret growing as I held him. "I broke it," he finished dully, the regret plaguing him.

It hadn't just been me who had pushed, who had let the anger win. Ilyan had, too.

I nodded once in understanding, my fingers moving over his collarbone as he shuddered beneath me.

"Can we fix it?" I asked. "Can you put it back?"

"Our magic is so closely connected that, if I attempted to do so, I believe your magic would bond to mine without us making any attempt."

Even though I would have gladly consented to such a thing, I could hear the echo of Ilyan's answer in his mind. He wanted to wait, wait until my mind was fully healed.

I had to respect that. Admire the respect he had for me.

"I'm scared, Ilyan, that without it there... how am I supposed to defeat Edmund?"

"You are worried that you won't be able to control your emotions; that you won't be able to fight?" His fingers trailed over my jaw at the question, the touch sending a comforting warmth up my spine as I shivered.

Yes. I kept my eyes averted as I spoke into his mind, trying to fight the blush that heated my face and neck at having reacted in such a way.

"That is exactly why I cannot replace the Štít. As much as I wish to protect you, as much as I wish to do everything for you, you know as well as I do that is not always a possibility. You must master your emotions on your own—master your power—so that things like this do not happen again."

"But what if Edmund comes tomorrow? I am not ready."

"You will be, my love. I will help you to be in any way that I can."

I nodded once in understanding before I moved into him, my arms wrapping around his wide torso while my head turned just enough that I could press my lips against his shirt. *I am sorry, Ilyan. I should have never said those things.*

"It is all right, my love. I forgive you. I can feel your regret in my soul. I taste your tears on my lips. We all say things that we do not mean, even to the ones we love, but it is because we love them that we can forgive them."

"I never want to lose you, Ilyan," I said, the hand that Ilyan still held against my neck pulling me back so he could look at me again.

I could see a million words in his eyes, hear a million things that he wanted to say in his thoughts. Nothing was solid, though, and so many of the words were in Czech that I wouldn't have been able to understand them even if I tried. So I stayed still, savoring every part of him, while the warmth of his hand seeped into my neck, his other keeping me tightly up against him.

"We are not made to fight, my love," he said, his voice soft and rumbling. "Our souls have been forever bound, both of us carrying each other's precious cargo. You take away a piece of your soul and you will only feel hatred and fear; your emotions can never be your own."

"Like Ryland?" I asked, my tongue tripping over the words as my heart constricted.

"Yes," he answered, his tone making it clear he had felt the brief pain that had moved through me.

"I don't want to feel that way ever again, Ilyan. Like I was broken. Like I would never be myself again. I had enough of that in Cail's mind, and I never want to feel it again."

"I never want you to feel it again."

"Ryland shouldn't feel that way, either," I said, my eyes pulling away as I ground my teeth against my bottom lip. "I don't know if I believe you that it wasn't Ryland in Cail's mind, but even if it was, he shouldn't have to feel broken."

The feathers swirled around my feet as I walked away from Ilyan toward the middle of the floor where the giant stone of the necklace stared up at me from within the feathers. I just stared at it as Ilyan came up behind me, his arm wrapping around my stomach as he pulled me against him. I said nothing to him, even though I could feel his confusion, my eyes trained on the sliver of red amongst the white.

I couldn't believe I was going to do this. Part of me begged myself not to—to let Ryland suffer—yet that part wasn't me; I could never be that cruel. I had felt the hopelessness at being apart from something that was integral to me. If Ilyan was right, if Ryland's heart was enclosed in this stone, then I knew that he was hurting. In his mind, the only way to make it better was to give him his heart back. To him, that was me. However, it wasn't, not anymore.

His heart was here, on the floor, just waiting to go home.

"I want to give him back his heart," I said softly, unable to look away from the snaking chain of the necklace that had meant so much to me just weeks before.

Ilyan's awe washed over me as he relaxed, his arms wrapping tightly around me from behind as he leaned forward to rest his chin against my shoulder.

"Are you sure?" his voice was heavy, his worry almost catching me off guard.

"I am," I sighed, knowing he needed more of an explanation than that. "I may not love him the way I did, but that does not mean that I don't care. Right now, he scares me, and I don't want to be around him. But I can't let him keep living with the pain of being broken in pieces, of not being able to control his emotions. I may not be able to give him back the piece of his soul that Edmund has stolen from him, but I can return this, and if it helps, then it is enough."

Ilyan said nothing as he held me, the awe I had felt growing before his head bowed down and he pressed his lips against the mark on my neck. I sighed at the contact, my heartbeat increasing as the touch supercharged the connection that lived between us.

"You amaze me, my Joclyn," he whispered into my skin as his lips pressed against my neck again before he turned me in his arms, the deep pit of his eyes swallowing me up again. "If this is what you wish, then I will see it happen."

"It is," I replied, my voice no more than a whisper.

Ilyan nodded once in understanding before pressing his lips against my forehead, the heat from the contact shooting through me. It was more than the heat that I felt, however. It was the steady stream of thoughts from Ilyan, his awe, his amazement.

For one brief moment, everything was right. Everything felt perfect. I knew it wouldn't last. How could it? For right in that moment, though, I would hold myself to it, and hold it dear.

Forever.

11

I SAT on the edge of the now-repaired bed. My legs were crossed under me as I looked at the necklace that sat in front of me, my back stiff as I leaned away from where the silver chain snaked through the folds of the thick feather comforter. The glinting red of the stone stared at me in the dim light of dusk. The color of it—the way it glinted in the light—was almost taunting, begging me to touch it.

But I couldn't.

I couldn't bring myself to stretch my fingers out and touch the surface that I had caressed so many times before. The stone that I had held when I was scared, that I had hidden under bulky clothing when I had only wanted to disappear. I didn't know why I was so scared to touch it. I knew what the stone would feel like: cold and unmoving, smooth as glass. It wouldn't be warm as it had been before. It wouldn't beat in time with Ryland's heart. It wouldn't open up a connection between us. Not anymore. Because everything had changed.

The connection was dead, and the necklace was the last thing I had that reminded me of how things used to be.

Maybe that's why I was scared to touch it—because I didn't want the reminders of how things used to be. I didn't want those memories, those fears. I didn't want the regret. Even if I didn't want them, though, I got them anyway. By just looking at it, my mind was filled with the distorted memories that both haunted and calmed me.

If I closed my eyes and really focused, I could see so much of my life before Ryland had tried to kiss me that first time. Before he had found my mark. I could see Ryland's joyful face and the way we joked and played. I could see my mother's smile, and taste her soup. How one little necklace could hold so many memories, however, I wasn't so sure. It was hard to recall those moments, though. It was the bad ones that came easily.

Most of the time all I had seen was Ryland's wicked glance as he hunted me, his evil sneer from inside of Cail's mind. I had been haunted by my mother's lifeless body on the kitchen floor of our tiny apartment. The good memories had been tarnished and in many ways forgotten.

All except this necklace.

Even then, I wasn't sure I wanted to keep the memories, not with the knowledge of what it had cost Ryland. What it had cost me, and Ilyan, and Wyn. What everyone had sacrificed, just to keep me safe.

The soft bed sagged as I shifted my weight, my shaking fingers stretching through the air as they moved toward the familiar red stone, my morbid curiosity guiding me forward. Just one touch, one moment of memories before I gave Ryland back his sanity. I almost felt like I needed that, as though I had earned it.

My fingers hovered over the stone as I hesitated, my heartbeat speeding up when Ryland's wicked laugh filled my head. My shoulders knit together as the shadow of his laugh faded, a loud, booming knock against the door taking its place. I jumped at the sound, my heartbeat stuttering as I looked to the door that stood directly across from me.

My magic peaked in expectation of Ryland walking through, of the exchange that was about to take place. My breath felt caught in my chest as my bubble of agitation grew, but I kept my magic restrained within me just as Ilyan had instructed. I knew who was on the other side of the door, and I didn't want to feel the icy chill that his magic gave me. I didn't want to feel the fear and hatred, not if this plan was going to work.

I pressed my back into the headboard as the knock sounded again, the door to the bathroom swinging open as Ilyan marched out, his damp hair shorter than it had been before, hanging only just above his shoulders now, the same way it had been when I first met him. He shook out his hair as he walked up to me, causing small droplets of water to fall over the room.

"Are you sure you are ready to do this?" He asked as he pulled a dark blue t-shirt over his head, the bed sagging as he moved to sit in front of me, the cold necklace between us.

I said nothing as I reached forward and wiped a small streak of shaving cream that he had missed off the side of his face. My fingers were soft as they ran over his chin, lingering against the warmth of his skin.

Our eyes met as his thoughts washed over me. The tenderness of his desire and the strength of his concern caught in my chest.

"I'm sure," I squeaked out, knowing it wouldn't be enough to calm his fears.

He nodded once as the knock sounded again, this time considerably louder and more impatient.

"I will be here, mi lasko," Ilyan sighed before leaning

forward and placing his lips against my forehead, the touch soft and gentle. My magic reacted to the connection, the flow warming as my stomach tightened in fear and love, the two emotions feeling rancid against each other.

I sighed as I pushed the last of my anxiety out, knowing it would return to plague me much sooner than I wanted. Ilyan's fingers lingered against mine until he pulled away, his steps slow and confident as he moved toward the door.

I watched him until the door began to swing open, my mind suddenly panicking at what was about to happen. I wanted to look away—I knew I needed to—but I couldn't. The frantic beating of my heart had frozen me in place. My eyes were glued to Ilyan's back as he talked in rapid Czech to whoever was on the other side. I could feel his own nerves peak before I pushed them away, trying not to focus on his emotions and thoughts that were hardwired into my brain.

The sound of chicken scratches hit the air as whoever he was talking to replied, their voice deep and staccato in the Slavic language.

Ilyan nodded once before exiting the room, the door shutting behind him without him even looking back toward me.

My arms wound tightly around my waist, my fear dripping over my back as I watched the door. The room seemed to grow colder the longer I was left alone, my tongue feeling like lead in my mouth.

I stared at the large wooden door as if it was going to change, a ridiculous part of me scared that it would somehow disappear. Even though I knew the fear was foolish, I couldn't seem to push it away, and the worry only grew the longer I waited.

My breath finally escaped my chest when the door clicked open again. Everything relaxed until my father stepped past the open frame, only to close the door right behind him.

I stiffened at seeing him there, at being alone with him. My shoulders knit together as my eyes narrowed dangerously. I wasn't sure what he was doing coming in here. I didn't want him here. He hadn't really shown much interest in me beyond planning for my ultimate demise and yelling at me over my lack of knowledge. It wasn't something I wanted to continue—not right now when everything felt so close to a meltdown.

I clenched my teeth as he came closer, my fingers knotting around the fabric of my shirt until they dug into my skin in my attempt to disappear into myself. To disappear from him.

"Hello, Joclyn." The words sounded more like the formal greeting you would give to someone you didn't really know, and in a way, I guess we didn't know each other.

I nodded once in silence, my eyes narrowing as I glared into him, hoping the look would be enough to scare him off, but I knew better.

He continued moving closer until he sat across from me, his body far enough away that I couldn't reach him, which was probably a good thing. I didn't want him to touch me, either.

I didn't trust myself enough to know what I would do if he did.

Sain didn't even look at me; he only smiled sadly at the necklace before reaching out and picking it up, his hand curving around it as he tested its weight. I cringed as he held it in his hand, my frustration swelling as I tried to ignore the surge of ownership that welled up inside of me. I didn't know where the selfish emotion had come from, but it scared me, the sensation unwelcome.

I had no ownership over what my father held in his hands. I didn't want any ownership of it, not anymore. Which only made my reaction all the more unwanted.

He looked at the necklace like he was proud of it, a look I was not sure he had ever given me as of yet. Awe, surprise, disgust, yes, but not pride. Not the look a father is supposed to give his daughter. I swallowed heavily and looked to him again, startled to find him peering at me, his eyes darker than they had been before.

"This is a good thing you are doing, Joclyn," he said, his voice so distant that I wouldn't have been sure he was really talking to me if he hadn't said my name. "It will be hard for him to accept this gift, but he needs to; he cannot be himself without it."

I knew what he was saying was meant to be a compliment, a show of acceptance from father to daughter, and the very thing I had been so desperate for. I didn't hear that, though. I only felt my anger swell at his words. I saw the flash of disapproval as he held Ryland's gasping body, my foolish mind pulling out a different meaning altogether, the same as I had done before.

He was happy I was doing this for Ryland; he was concerned for Ryland. I knew that wasn't what he meant— he meant that he was happy that I had made the choice I did. Still, I couldn't stop the jealous anger from swelling.

I cringed at the sensation, my breathing picking up as I tried to push the frustration away.

"Is that-t all you c...care about?" I stuttered out, my voice faltering through the emotion. "That Ryland is saved?"

Sain looked away from me, the action making my frustrations grow. I exhaled through my gritted teeth, hating the way my body was beginning to hurt.

I waited for him to look at me—to deny it—but he sat still, his focus on the forest outside of the windows.

"Is that what you think?" he asked toward the darkening sky. His tone was calm enough that I wasn't even sure he had heard me. Nevertheless, I knew he had, he just wouldn't rise to me. He wouldn't fight for me.

It wasn't the Drak way.

He dropped the necklace back onto the bed, the chain falling in a heap around the stone.

I fought the desire to reach out and lay it out nicely again, to berate him for treating it so haphazardly.

My anger only seemed to flare at seeing the pile of metal, at hearing his calm voice and before I could stop it, it exploded out of me again. "You only care for him!"

I didn't like feeling this way. I needed to control it before I did something stupid. I exhaled as I pushed my anger away, pulling the positive memories I had clung to right to the forefront of my mind. I relaxed a bit as the uncontrollable hatred that had been threatening a hostile takeover left until I could only feel the pain from my father's abandonment.

"Is this because I helped him last night?" Sain asked as he finally looked back at me, his weight shifting on the bed in his discomfort.

I didn't respond to him, I only gritted my teeth as my eyes shot fire and anger. I didn't trust myself to speak. I didn't want to yell, to fight. That was not what this moment was supposed to be about. I had waited for this since I was five, since the day he first left. I had seen him over the past few days, but I hadn't been able to ask the questions that had been burning a hole in my soul for the last twelve years.

Now that I could, I couldn't find the words to gain the

answers I so desperately needed. I just sat, staring at him, my pain growing until my heart began to ache.

"I helped him because he needed me, Joclyn. You almost killed him. I needed to help him." He shook his head like he was disappointed in me. The cold look in his eyes was a steady reminder of where I stood in his life.

"And not your own daughter?" I asked, my voice hard as the anger and pain tried to break through the calm I had found.

Sain's eyes widened at my words, as if I had offended him somehow.

"You are a Drak; you should be able to calm yourself." His harsh words cut through me like a knife and I winced, my heart burning and tensing.

It was the same as it had been before; he knew I was a Drak. Somehow, his perfect Drak blood had made me into something else, something more. Something beyond what I even understood, and he obviously expected more from me. What that more was, though, I wasn't sure. I didn't know if I could give him that.

"But I can't," I practically whispered, the pain in my chest making it hard to form words.

Sain closed his eyes and breathed deeply as he took control of his own emotions. Almost as if he was proving to me it could be done.

The look was one I had seen on his face before when he and my mother would fight, when he would calm himself. For a fleeting moment, he was that same man from my childhood; he was the same person I so desperately wanted him to be. That was before he opened his mouth and took all those memories away.

"You had Ilyan, Joclyn." His voice was the mellow calm it always was, the calm he expected from the Drak. I cringed against it, the sound grating on me as I fought the need to yell again.

Sain reached out as if he was going to comfort me, but I shied away, pushing myself into the headboard again.

I looked at that hand in disgust, the palm littered with at least a dozen scars, the small lines of raised skin lying one over another. They almost looked like the ones I had seen on Wyn's palm, but there were so many, they were almost unrecognizable.

"Ilyan left!" I spat, tearing my focus away from his scarred palm.

"I know."

"And still you didn't come." I sat stiffly against the headboard as I whispered in pain. The soft sound taking away my desperate attempt to get him to understand.

"Some things are guided for me, Joclyn. As they are for you. The Water told me where I was needed, and I stayed there." He spoke like I should understand, and I guess in a way he expected me to, but I couldn't. Because I didn't.

Ice ran though my blood, numbing me at the realization. My eyes drifted toward the wad of silver chain on the bed in my need to look anywhere other than at his loveless eyes.

I forced one stiff nod, the movement more of a dismissal than an acknowledgment of understanding.

"Thank you for this," Sain said as he pointed to the necklace, his voice a thousand miles away in my ears.

He patted my hand once before he stood—the bed bouncing as he left me—walking right back out the door, and in a way, out of my life again.

12

My chest felt tight as the door opened right after Sain had closed it, the painful heat in my face growing. I looked up in expectation, my heart jumping to see Ilyan speed-walking toward me. My magic expanded around him automatically, his moving to do the same, as our souls and magic met in the middle. While the connection I was seeking bound together, it wouldn't be as strong as I was used to without skin contact. Not anymore, not without the Štít.

I jumped up at the thought, my legs shaking underneath me as I took the two steps toward him, his arms wrapping around me as I met him.

"Are you all right?" he asked, the true meaning in his question not lost on me. "I heard yelling."

Yes. I sent the lie into his mind as he held me, his grip tightening as he sensed my discomfort. His thoughts pressed right into me, begging me to tell him the truth. His need to help me was sharp, but I wouldn't tell him. I was controlling it on my own. After all, I wasn't quite sure what to say. The hope that I had for a father had been dashed, leaving me only with distrust and a numb hole somewhere deep down.

I shook my head into Ilyan's chest and he sighed, his hands moving over my back as his magic flowed into me.

"It is all right, mi lasko," he whispered into my hair as his scarred hand ran over my neck, the touch a familiar, comforting calm. The tender edges of his scarred finger ran over me until they pressed into my mark, the contact warm and hot as the jolt moved through my body, my magic supercharging while Ilyan held me.

"We don't have much time," Ilyan whispered, his voice soft against me.

"Is he here?" I asked, my head moving away from Ilyan's chest just enough that I could make out the door behind us.

"Yes. And he is waiting for you."

Ilyan pulled away from me, his hands wrapping softly around mine.

"Are you sure you are ready to do this?" he asked for what I was sure was the twentieth time. I knew his concerns —I was probably just as concerned as he was—but there was nothing I could do about it.

When Ilyan had made the suggestion of returning the necklace to Ryland, Ry had flipped. He had insisted on speaking with me first, certain that Ilyan was lying. I had heard his yells echo through the abbey, full words drifting toward me as I heard the pain in Ryland's heart.

I wasn't sure what Ilyan had done to calm Ryland down, to make him safe enough to talk to, before he had finally agreed to a meeting with a few requirements. Both of our emotions needed to be numbed and there had to be a door between us; he didn't want us seeing the other. Not because he was going all 'I own you' control freak on me, but because he didn't want us to try to kill each other again.

Sadly, I knew he was right. Just the knowledge that Ryland was on the other side of the door prickled through me, my anger growing as my magic twitched in agitation.

I knew that if I saw Ryland right now, I would kill him on the spot. He wouldn't hesitate to do the same to me, either.

I exhaled shakily and shook my head, squeezing Ilyan's hands in mine as I answered his question. I could still feel Ilyan's doubt—his concern for whether I was making the right choice—but I wasn't backing down, not now.

Ilyan said nothing as he turned my hand over, placing the stone against my skin for the first time since before I had been trapped in the Tòuha.

I inhaled sharply as the stone touched my skin, my shoulders tensing together in expectation. Part of me wanted to feel the warmth of the stone as I had for so long, the pulse of Ryland's magic surrounding it. I had been so hesitant to touch it before, fearing the change, fearing the memories that I was sure would come along with it. However, nothing happened. The necklace was nothing except a cold, dead weight in my hand.

I stared at it before turning toward Ilyan, his focus still boring into me.

"I am going to numb your emotions with my magic, my love. You may feel nothing, or you may feel like I have drugged you. Everything should feel distanced, and you should not feel any anger." I nodded silently at his words as his magic flooded into me, the pleasant warmth spreading through me before it congregated, swelling in the base of my neck.

"I will be here the entire time, Joclyn, ready to help if needs be." I nodded again in understanding and then followed him to the door, his hand squeezing mine before his other made contact with the door, three hollow knocks sounding in my ears.

They were the toll of a bell, and I froze, suddenly doubting my decision, or even if I was going to be able to keep my head through this. In only a second I would hear his voice.

"I can't do this," I moaned as I turned into Ilyan, his arms holding me against him as I let the necklace fall to the ground.

Ilyan's tension flared as he held me, his thoughts rushing into me as his concern for me and for his brother took me off guard. Ilyan's silent admittance of how much Ryland needed this—needed his heart—shocked me.

I had barely registered Ilyan's thoughts before his magic flared, the warm pulse growing in my neck until the agitation left, leaving me feeling like I was floating in Ilyan's arms.

Like I was a bubble of nothing.

Ilyan had numbed my emotions, just as he had said it would. His arms left me drifting just as a calm, loving voice I don't think I had heard in years seeped through the door, the sound somewhat muffled by the large, wooden slab.

"Jos?"

It was Ry.

Ry.

Not the monster who had hunted me, not the boy that I had watched break apart in the Tǒuha. His voice was soft and kind, like it had come from a memory and not from his lips.

I turned in shock, the familiarity of his voice taking away my blissful ignorance all at once. Millions of memories washed over me at the sound, the feeling initially pleasant until the bad ones tried to take their place.

"He sounds the same. Like he used to," I said, my voice almost a whisper as I stared at the darkened door in expectation.

"I took away his emotions and many of his memories that fuel his hatred toward you," Ilyan said. "The bind is not permanent, at his request, and it will only last a few minutes. But with both your emotions bound, it will give you time to talk to him as you used to."

I barely heard Ilyan. I only stepped forward, my free hand pressing against the door as I waited for Ryland to speak again, my heart beating heavily in needy expectation.

"Jos?" he asked again, and I inhaled sharply, my heart warming at the sound. "Are you there?"

"I'm here," I gasped out, the sound strangled from the tension in my chest, and from the tears I hadn't realized I was shedding.

"Are you okay?" he asked, his voice deep as he pressed his face against the wood, probably hoping to hear better I realized and took a step closer.

"I'm fine," I said, almost feeling like it was true and not just a forced serenity. I could still feel the pressure of Ilyan's magic in my neck, the soft touch of his hand against mine. His magic made everything feel light, making it hard to distinguish what my real emotions were. Even though I knew the peace I felt was all forced, I didn't care.

"I'm so sorry," he moaned, his voice pained.

"Ry?" I asked, something in me flaring at the sound of desperation in his voice. I knew I needed to respond—to say something—but I wasn't sure what. I was having trouble thinking through the warmth that seemed to be taking over my body. I pressed my forehead into the wood, my eyes closing at the rough and coarse texture that ground against me.

"I'm sorry I was selfish," he said, his voice loud and rumbling through the wood. "I am sorry that I hurt you. I'm sorry I wasn't strong enough to protect you. I don't want to lose you, Jos,"

The deep pleading of his voice caught me off guard, turning the momentary comfort into vapor. My hand pressed into Ilyan's as my spine stiffened, a small spike of fear winding its way through Ilyan's oppressive magic. I heard Ryland; I understood what he was saying, but there was one very important piece of the puzzle that I wasn't quite sure he was comprehending, one that I had almost forgotten.

Even though we were numb, even though for these few precious moments everything felt fine, it didn't change everything. I wanted my best friend back as well, but I was afraid we were both too broken for that to ever happen.

Even though Ryland sounded the same right then, he wasn't the same as he had been, and the person he was now still terrified me. I clawed my fingers into the wood as the muscles tensed in my back. Ilyan's magic responded immediately to soothe the tautness away.

"I don't want to lose who you were, Ryland," I admitted, "but I can't trust who you are... I mean..." My throat closed up as words failed me, my chest tightening. Part of me was still terrified about how he would react to what I had to say.

I waited in the silence, Ilyan's hand leaving mine to run over the skin of my arm, the gentle contact soothing me further, but it wasn't quite enough.

I lifted my other hand to the door, almost wishing I could open it and speak to him face to face. I knew that was impossible, but just the thought brought the image of Ryland gasping for breath to mind, something deep inside rejoicing at the memory and calling for blood.

"I know what you mean. Part of me still loves you, Jos. Part of me is desperate for you, but then I close my eyes and that you vanishes. I'm only left with the nightmares my father gave me," Ryland said, his voice soft as he repeated the words that had just gone through my mind.

It wasn't just me; it was Ryland, too. He was trapped in the same middle-ground hell that his father had created for us with the sole purpose of keeping us apart in the hopes that, sooner or later, one would kill the other and break the sight apart. It had almost happened, too.

"It's not fair," I moaned, trying to ignore the stinging in my eyes, the guilt at what I had tried to do, and the anger at what Edmund had done to us.

"Jos... if you weren't scared of me, if you didn't want to fight me so bad... do you think... I mean... could we..." The tension in me grew the longer Ryland spoke, the intentions of what he was saying bringing back the tidal wave of fear. No matter how much Ilyan tried to work against it, it kept coming.

"What? Be together? Replace the bond?" I spat, disgusted. The idea was almost laughable even in my numbed state. I knew it wouldn't work, and even if it did, those feelings that I had for him had been killed over the months that I had run from him. Whether I was trapped in reality or not, the love I had once felt was gone, and I didn't think there was any way to get it back.

"No, Jos," he said as the small amount of tension that had escaped Ilyan's hold vanished. "I wasn't lying when I said that I loved you and would do anything for you, but I don't think I can anymore. I loved you once, but I can't deny that part of me that wants to kill you. I'm trying to fight it, but it will always be there. I don't want to risk hurting you. I need to let you go. You need to let me go, so that we can both heal."

My hands dropped from the door at his words, shock wrapping around me at what he was saying. I supposed I should have been more upset—my heart should have broken—yet it wasn't. Because I was free. Free from a relationship that had only caused me pain.

"Besides, I don't think my intentions of being with you were the most honorable," he said, his voice fading away as he turned from me.

"Did Ilyan tell you to say that?" I said, the laugh in my voice sounding a bit more accusatory than I intended it to be.

"What? No. I still have a hard time with it, but Ilyan is good. Really good. He makes me feel like I am actually part of a family who loves me."

My eyes opened in shock at his words, my head turning to Ilyan, but he wasn't looking at me. He was focused on the door, his lips in a tight line as relief radiated off him, as he tried to lock his joy inside. His thoughts flew through me, memories of all the siblings he had helped, and all the ones he had failed, mixing with his fear that the same would happen to Ryland. However, Ryland had dashed all of that and had given Ilyan joy. Joy that Ryland was calming, and that Ilyan was going to be able to help him, that he may not lose him.

I pulled my hand away from the door and wrapped it around Ilyan's, my groggy magic flowing into him. We stood in silence like that, Ilyan's relief mixing with the numb bliss he had already given me until I felt like I could float away.

"I miss my best friend." Ryland's voice came from the door after a few minutes, and I turned toward it, the drugged feeling swimming through me with the quick movement. "I miss laughing and joking. I miss you."

"I miss you, too, Ry," I whispered, not sure he could hear me. "But I don't think I can—"

"I know," he interrupted, his voice just as soft as mine.

I could hear the desperation in his voice, the gentle longing so powerful that I couldn't help but agree. I nodded quietly, knowing he couldn't see, but unable to put into words the fears and hopes that plagued my own mind. Right then, it was my chance to make things better, possibly the only one I would get.

I looked down at the necklace on the floor, my heart beating wildly in my chest. Maybe we weren't quite as broken as I thought.

Ilyan followed me as I sunk down to the floor, my back pressing against the door frame as I sat on the stone floor, my fingers curling around the fine silver chain.

"I have something for you, Ry. Something that might help." I raised my voice to make sure he could hear, and moved the necklace under the crack in the door, careful to keep my fingers on my side.

"Jos? What?" Ryland asked, his voice rising in confusion. Even though he knew why he was here, I was sure he couldn't see it.

"It's your necklace, on the floor."

"I can't take this back, Jos. It's a piece of me, remember." I cringed at his voice, the memory of that day slapping me in the face.

This was exactly what I had been afraid of. I was scared of the good memories, the ones that would bring regret. The ones that weren't tainted. Part of me wanted to keep them hidden, keep them safe from the horrors that I was sure were just waiting to destroy them forever.

"I know," I said, my voice breaking as I fought back the tears that burned behind my eyes. "But I need you to. I need you to take your heart back, Ry. It doesn't belong to me anymore."

"Did Ilyan tell you to say that?" he spat, his angry voice causing me to jump, the same voice that had haunted me coming back so fast that the anxiety increased, my panic rushing right to the surface.

My breathing picked up as my magic swirled, the joints in my jaw stiffening. I was one quick move away from rushing the door when Ilyan pressed his hand against my face, his magic rushing into me as he smothered the fear and anger that rose up in me. I focused on Ilyan's eyes as his warmth filled me, knowing how dangerous I was right then. I knew that with only one surge of my magic the door would fly right off its hinges.

I exhaled deeply at feeling the numbing blanket of Ilyan's magic take over, my mind coming back to myself. I could hear whispering on the other side of the door as Sain did the same to Ryland, Ry's voice spouting out in anger every few minutes.

"The memory bind is slipping; we don't have much time left," Ilyan whispered to me as I focused on him, and the last of my anxiety melted away. "You need to hurry."

"Ry," I said loudly, even though I could hear whispering on the other side of the door. The whispering stopped almost immediately, and the door jerked against my back as Ryland pressed himself against it.

I closed my eyes as I tried to focus, not sure if what I was about to say was going to help or not.

"I want you to have your heart back, not because I don't love you, but because I do, just not in that way." I stopped midsentence as my heart compressed inside my chest, the pressure so much I wasn't sure if it was still beating. I swallowed hard and continued on, knowing I needed to say this. I needed him to understand. "I want you to have your heart back because I don't want you to hurt anymore. I want you to feel like yourself."

I exhaled deeply when I finished, my eyes focused on the door as I waited for him to respond. The seconds dragged on, my fingers pressing into the door as I waited, as I silently pleaded for him to accept the necklace, to take back the piece of him.

"When I made this, I had no idea who you really were," he said out of the blue, my pressured grip against the door loosening almost instantly. "I wanted you to have it, forever, because I knew I would never see you again. I was going to run away and try to disappear. Anything to keep from what Edmund had planned for me. My father had been training me for years to hunt Ilyan. I wasn't even going to school. He was going to send Cail and me on a kamikaze trip to kill my brother. I guess, in some ways, that still happened."

My eyes widened at his words, Ilyan's surprise joining my own as this new bit of information was revealed to us.

"And then, when I found your kiss, and I knew I could use you against my dad, to make him hurt the way he had made me hurt. Hurt. Hurt," Ryland continued, his voice a snap that shot through me, the tone deep and angry. I shrunk away from the door at the sound, glad when Ilyan wrapped his arm around me, bringing me into him protectively.

"Sain?" Ilyan spoke up from beside me, his voice tense and worried as his grip on me increased.

"We are close," Sain said before his voice deteriorated into frantic whispers on the other side of the door.

I held still against Ilyan, not sure what was happening. I

could hear the whispers from the other side, soft whimpers that made my heart ache.

"Will you keep the necklace, Jos?" Ryland said through the silence, his request freezing me in place.

"I can't..."

"No, not my heart. Just the necklace. A promise that maybe we can try to be friends again." The plea on his voice cut through me, my breath catching in my chest. I didn't want the necklace back, but I couldn't deny him this.

"Of course," I whispered as I lay against Ilyan's chest.

The whispering on the other side of the door picked up, the frantic nature of it building until it stopped, followed by a loud grunt echoing in my ears. I moved closer to the door, Ilyan's arms dropping from me as I pressed myself against it, desperate to hear something that would clue me into what had happened.

"It looks just like your eyes," Ryland said, his voice so strained I barely heard it. "Wear it always."

Ryland's voice cut out, a scraping sound catching my attention as he pushed the necklace back under the door. I dropped to my knees as I saw it, the now clear diamond streaked with his blood. It rested on his fingertips as he pushed it toward me, the red smudges on his hand as bright as the sun.

I reached down, the tips of my fingers pressing against the cold skin of his hand as I covered the necklace. I kept my hand there, my skin pressed against the only part of him I could see. I held my breath, waiting for the connection—for something to happen—but all I felt was the iron chill of his skin and the rough texture of his hands. His fingers moved to wrap around mine, his hand twisting to drop the necklace into my hand, the stone as cold as his skin.

The necklace fell into my hand before he withdrew,

taking the last of our connection with him. I looked at the necklace in my palm, the silvery diamond, the color of my eyes, just as he had said.

My face heated and burned as I stared blankly into my hand, my body feeling numb as Ilyan's barrier wore off. I barely registered his fingers as they carefully removed the necklace from my hand, his touch soft against my hair as he moved it out of the way.

Silence stretched between us as Ilyan placed the necklace around my neck, the cold stone falling just below my collar bone.

I may have lost my first love, but I wasn't going to let Edmund take away my best friend, too, even if it took years to trust him again. I would give my heart to try.

"Always," I gasped, even though I knew he had gone. My fingers reached up to wrap around the stone that was now nothing but a diamond.

13

I KNEW I WAS DREAMING, like really dreaming. Not the controlled nightmares Cail had cursed me with, but the disconnected visions of my own subconscious. Although I wasn't sure that was any better.

It had been so long since I'd had an actual dream that I had almost forgotten what they felt like. I had forgotten the way everything felt disconnected and wobbly, as if I was trapped underwater.

I stood still in our room as I watched the storm rage beyond the balcony, flashing in angry light as it came closer. Thunderheads rumbled as the lightning flashed, the aggression so quick I was afraid the storm would move right into the room, and the lightning would take us away.

Ilyan stood on the balcony, framed by the flashes of white. His back was tense under his shirt as he watched the storm, both of us frozen in fear before he turned around. I saw his mouth move as he yelled at me, his face panicked. I jumped in place at Ilyan's reaction before I began to run around the room, following instructions that I couldn't hear. I collected items as Ilyan continued to yell, most of which I had never seen before. Candles and clothing mixed together with weird twigs, leather-bound books, and a golden box with bears embossed on the top. I kept running, the pile growing higher and higher until I was sure I had grabbed everything.

I turned to face Ilyan, his back still to me as lightning erupted just beyond the balcony, so close he could almost stretch out and touch it. So close, that I wanted him to try.

One after another the bolts hit the ground until the room was so full of light I had nowhere else to look than at the raging storm, and the dark-haired man who stood where Ilyan had been only moments before.

Everything in me seized up at the sight of Ilyan's father, his oppressive size holding me in place. I knew I was screaming. I could feel the terror ring clear as my heart rate increased. However, I heard nothing until he turned around, the wicked hunger in his eyes cutting through my soul.

The sneer on Edmund's lips turned into a laugh as he approached me. The silence left as my ears filled with the gut-wrenching laugh, the sound louder than it should have been, feeling like tar against my heart.

I knew I was screaming louder, even though I couldn't hear the noise—I only heard Edmund's laugh. I only saw the nightmare. I fought against the dream, my conscious mind begging me to wake up, but I only stood, glued in the icicles of Edmund's eyes as he walked closer. Step by step he came until he was right in front of me... his hand reaching toward me, his laugh echoing in my ears.

The laugh stopped as the dream ended, a loud gasp escaping my lips as I sat straight up in bed, Ilyan's arm falling off me.

My chest shook as I gasped in large ragged breaths that followed me from the dream. My magic felt raw and ripped as I sat heaving, my muscles tensing uncomfortably in my fear. I pushed it away, pushed away the deep pulse of anger and hatred that flooded over me from the forest, but the raw edges of my magic seemed to be pulling it into me. I tried to calm myself, to loosen the pressure that had bound itself in my muscles, my eyes wide as I stared into the pitch dark of our room.

"It was all a dream," I said aloud, begging myself to believe it. "Just a dream."

I took in another quaking breath as I pushed my fear into nothing, turning toward the balcony that looked over the forest.

I knew I shouldn't look; I knew it was foolish, but I couldn't stop myself. I turned as the darkness of the cloud-covered sky met my eyes, a fork of lightning cutting through the dark and I jumped, only to be met with the empty balcony.

I took one cleansing breath before there was a loud knock on the door, the sound echoing through the silence of the night.

Fear tensed through my back as I pulled the blanket up to my chin, my fingers knitting through the soft cotton. My mind screamed for me to hide, to run. I stayed still, though, my body crippled in fear as my mind fought the panic that the ragged remains of the nightmare only seemed to heighten.

I peered through the darkness that surrounded me as the knock came again, this sound more persistent, almost fearful. I looked toward Ilyan, ready to wake him up when a muffled noise came from the other side, and the anxiety that had wound its way through my spine loosened.

"Open up," Wyn pleaded, her voice low and strained.

My eyes widened at her voice, my magic flying away

from me until I felt the warm strength that surrounded her hit me. I should have felt the familiar pulse of her magic before, but the heightened aggression from the forest had smothered it, my own panic forgetting to check.

It *was* her.

I navigated my way through the darkness that felt heavy and forbidding, opening the door to Wyn to find the hallway lit with shadows of black and light from the orb of orange light that hovered above her hands. She was dressed in dark washed jeans and a black leather jacket that looked vaguely familiar, the dark colors making her blend into the pitch of the hallway.

"Took you long enough," she said as I opened the door, her voice strained. I had been so happy to hear her voice, but that joy slipped into the darkness as I caught sight of the deep worry that lined her face, my own anxieties trying to flare again.

"Is Ilyan awake?" she asked, the panicked edge growing more persistent.

"No." I shook my head. "Is everything okay?"

I asked the question, even though I could see the answer in her eyes.

Wyn sighed and looked past me into the darkened room, her brows knit together as she tried to decide what to do. I just stood still as I waited, not knowing if I should let her in or not. I wasn't exactly sure of the protocol in a situation like this. I couldn't exactly say, 'Please come in and wake up your shirtless king. I'm sure he won't mind,' and be met with happy smiles. Ilyan didn't wake up easily. Besides, I was sure that he would mind a lot more than Wyn would assume. So I stayed still, my shoulders tense as I blocked her path, waiting for her to explain why she was here.

"I'm not sure yet. I was on guard and... something has

changed. I want Ilyan's opinion," she whispered as her eyes darted back to me, even though it was obvious I wasn't the one she wanted to be talking to.

It didn't matter. I knew what she was talking about because I had felt it. I had felt the swell of anger when I had woken up. I could still feel it now, prickling through the air, no matter how much I tried to ignore it.

"Is it about the anger in the camps?" I asked.

"You feel it, too?" she asked, the awe in her eyes taking me off guard. I looked at her for a minute before nodding once, not sure how else to respond to her.

"I don't know what it is," Wyn said, the deep alarm in her voice growing. "We haven't had a bigger swell of them from what I can tell, but something is different."

Wyn shuffled her feet as she spoke, making it clear that there was something she wasn't telling me. Something was wrong, something must be coming. If something was coming... I swallowed heavily, pushing the thought from my mind. Just knowing that something was wrong felt like a contagion against my heart. We needed Ilyan.

"You better come in," I said before stepping aside and closing the door behind her. I didn't know if Ilyan would approve of this decision, but I had a feeling this was something he needed to know right away.

The light Wyn held in her hands suddenly flew away from her and nestled in the large wooden rafters of the ceiling only to cast weird fingers of light over the room. It flickered in elongated shapes that brought some of the horrors of my dream back. I looked toward the window, almost expecting to see Edmund there, but it was empty.

"It is so weird that you two sleep together," she said from right behind me, obviously seeing the rumpled sheets that I had jumped out of a moment before.

Embarrassment wiggled through my stomach at her observation. I suddenly felt very uncomfortable having her here, like she was seeing something that was meant for me and Ilyan only. I folded my arms around my torso, wishing I had made her wait outside, wishing I could ask her to leave.

"I have nightmares," I said, the attempt to defend my choice coming off flat. Not like it made any difference, especially since I hadn't had any of those nightmares in months, weeks for everyone else.

"Yes, Thom told me," she said casually, and I narrowed my eyes at her. She had mentioned him more than once the few times that I had seen her, making it sound like Thom had somehow become her confidante in two days flat. I wanted to ask, but she wasn't even looking at me anymore; her focus was out the large windows as she chewed on her lip.

I was suddenly glad that Wyn wasn't watching me as I draped my arm over Ilyan, leaning over him as I ran the tips of my fingers over the scars on his chest. I pushed the warm pressure of my magic into the thin white lines as I traced them, the small surges forcing him awake.

Ilyan. I sent the whisper into his mind, knowing he could hear me even if he wasn't fully alert. *I need you to wake up.*

His alarm peaked at my statement, his fear for me heightening in apprehension. His arms wrapped around me without warning, pulling me into him before I could get away, my feet leaving the floor as he rolled me on top of him.

"Jste all right, mi lasko?" His lips brushed against my jaw as he mumbled, his accent thick as he transitioned between English and Czech.

I'm fine, I said as I tried to fight the blush that moved up my cheeks from being in this position with him in front of someone else. "Wyn is here."

"What do you mean Wyn is here?" he asked, his usual morning impatience invading his voice like the snap of a whip.

"She means I am standing next to you, watching this horrible display," Wyn's voice was a sugar smack that I didn't think I had heard from her before. "So, if you wouldn't mind putting a shirt on..."

I wasn't sure if Wyn was being snotty or trying to be funny, but either way, I couldn't ignore the way her presence made me feel guilty, or the way Ilyan's hackles went up while the joy at having me in his arms vanished into frustration.

I looked up at her and narrowed my eyes, confusion setting in. I did not understand where this snappy attitude was coming from, or even why she was talking to him like this. Wyn had always been so polite, so formal, to Ilyan. She had even told me on several occasions that they didn't get along because she was scared of him.

I looked to her, almost shocked to see her standing differently, her face a little more ruffled than fun loving. The change caught me off guard, almost like I was looking at someone else. I stretched my magic toward her, suddenly worried that it wasn't her, but the magic was the same—if not a little warmer than it had been a few minutes before.

"Wynifred," Ilyan said, his voice shifting into the deep, commanding tone he usually kept hidden. "What are you doing in my chamber?"

"I have something I need to talk to you about."

"By invading my quarters before dawn? You should know better. We have a meeting scheduled for noon; it can wait until then, I am sure." Ilyan's voice was hard, the disappointment startling me. I had never heard him speak to someone so harshly before.

Ilyan sat up swiftly, his arms still tight around me as he kept me in his lap, obviously intent to keep me there. "I had no idea you and I were already back on such loose terms."

"You know you missed me, My Lord," she cooed, the honey in her voice increasing, if that was possible. "You can blame Jos for letting me in."

I looked up at her and narrowed my eyes at her, thoroughly lost now. I had thought it weird before, but this behavior was downright alarming. I held onto Ilyan tighter, hating how her voice made me feel almost possessive of him. My eyes narrowed at her as I demanded an explanation in silence. Her eyes met mine, and she wilted, her face changing as our eyes met, the lines softening as she looked at me with the same fear she had a minute before.

The Wyn I knew came to life before me, just as I felt Talon's magic flare inside of her. My heart clenched at the realization, the understanding of what was going on. She was talking to Ilyan, her mate's best friend, someone who must be reminding her of what she had lost. I could understand that pain; perhaps not to that extent, but I understood. The heartbreak was fueling her frustrations, her pain.

"It is not Joclyn that I am speaking to; it is you, and you would do well to remember the respect that I demand." His voice was stiff as his arms tightened around me. His grip was firm, as if he was afraid I was going to leave, and judging by the amount of embarrassment in my body, it was a good presumption.

"Yes, My Lord," Wyn said, her voice stiff and uncomfortable as she curtseyed.

"Good, but for now, why don't you wait outside for me."

"We don't have time for that," Wyn said, the sass that had lined her voice before vanishing into a deep desperation, "I think Edmund has arrived."

Before, I could tell she wasn't being honest with me, and now I knew why. The simple admission was like a slap to the face. The air left my chest as the fear that I had been ignoring engulfed me in a painful pressure that fought its way out. Ilyan became rigid beneath me, the tension in his arms growing as he reacted to the news of his father's possible arrival.

Ilyan's sudden tension over Edmund shocked me. I had watched Ilyan mock his father as well as fight him in Santa Fe, yet the feeling that moved from him to me now was anything but eagerness to continue that fight.

It wasn't because he was scared of fighting him, however. It was because he was scared of losing me.

I didn't need the flash of Ilyan's memory to see that heart-breaking moment of the sight, my limp body in Ilyan's arms. I pushed it away as he did, his muscles tightening.

"How do you know?" Ilyan's voice was a tight line, his eyes narrowing toward her. Even though I had felt his fear, I saw no sign of it, only the powerful determination he always had.

"The magic has changed, My Lord; the strength of it has grown. Although, I can't pinpoint why."

Ilyan pressed me against him once, his lips moving against my hair—unseen by Wyn—before he stood, the strength of our connection slipping as our skin lost contact.

"Where?" His voice rumbled as he pulled a shirt out of the bureau next to the bed, the muscles in his back rippling as he pulled it on, the tension in his body growing.

"To the east, mostly, but it's spreading," Wyn said, her

voice confident until Ilyan turned around to face her, her usual apprehension around him returning.

"How fast?" Ilyan took a step forward as he spoke, his tall frame towering over Wyn's small one, and she recoiled, stepping back a bit.

"Fast."

Ilyan left Wyn cowering in the middle of the room as he moved toward the large map that still sat on the table near the window. He glanced at it briefly before looking up to me, his eyes seeming to glow as his thoughts flowed through the weak connection between us. I cringed as they hurtled into my mind, the distorted worries and fears mixing together until they came through.

You want me to find Cail? Cail is dead. Isn't he? I almost screamed the words into his mind, my agitation almost blinding me.

That thought had sent my emotions tumbling into the deep abyss, my fingers clenched into the bed. My body began to shake as I stared at him, trying to focus on him, but it didn't help. The walls that surrounded Ilyan had already begun to bleed red, and my breathing picked up as it clouded my vision.

"Yes, he is passed," Ilyan said softly, his eyes still intently focused on me as he watched me battle my demons. "But the magic will be similar; someone will be stronger than everyone else. That is who we are looking for."

I swallowed at the idea, my throat constricting and making it hard to breathe. I gasped as I tried to push the fear away, to bring the song and the memories to my mind and stay in the here and now. It wasn't helping, just the idea of feeling Cail's magic against me again was crippling.

"You are bigger than it," Ilyan soothed, his voice soft and familiar. I turned from the bleeding walls to look at him, my eyes wide as I tried to fight the feeling, as my magic pushed the fear away.

"You can do it, Joclyn," he whispered as he moved to kneel before me in his attempt to soothe me. "You can do it," he whispered, his voice wearing down the edges of the fear that plagued me.

Ilyan reached up with his free hand and placed it against my cheek, the skin warm as he looked into me, his mind filled with a kiss he couldn't give me right now. The thought pushed the last of the fear away, and my body relaxed as I looked at him, blocking out the blood-covered walls, stopping my fear.

I *could* do this.

I nodded once before I closed my eyes, my magic flying away from me as I searched the forest that surrounded us. I felt my way through trees and the anger of the camps that were closest, pushing harder and faster until I was surrounded, the anger almost painful to me. My face squished together as I focused. Ilyan's hand was a warm pressure around mine as his magic plunged into me, his power strengthening mine. I pulled at his magic, brought it into me and used it, allowing myself to search wider, faster.

I searched through the hordes of Trpaslíks, my magic skimming over more of that weird, un-definable magic I had felt before. My heart clenched at the uncomfortable feeling it gave me—the knowledge that I couldn't place it disheartening—but I moved on, my desperate need to find what Ilyan sought only growing.

I gasped when I found it, pure anger pulsing through the air, stronger than all the others. It was ice and hot and acid all at the same time, the feeling so much like what I had felt inside of Cail's mind.

It felt just like him, but it wasn't Cail.

And there wasn't just one.

I stifled the fear that tried to incapacitate me and let my magic jump from Trpaslík to Trpaslík as I registered the pulse, each one connected. What was more, the magic that I was feeling didn't belong to them, either.

My eyes flashed open at the realization, Ilyan's stony face greeting me as his worries washed over me.

"There are six of them."

"And their magic is all the same?" Ilyan asked, his magic pulsing in excitement. I cringed at the feeling, the way his mind relished the idea of the coming battle, and I pressed my hand further into his.

Yes.

"It is the forward guard," Ilyan said as he stood to face Wyn, her jaw tensing at his words.

I didn't quite understand why the tension grew; after all, it wasn't Edmund himself. On the other hand, Cail had been the forward guard. It was just like when I was trapped in Cail's mind; Cail always came first. Except this time, Cail was dead, and Edmund had sent others to clear the way.

"If he has sent six, then he will be here soon. If I can get closer, I could tell who it is, what their attack plan is—"

"You are not strong enough to fight yet, Wynifred," Ilyan interrupted her wild excitement, his order heavy as he moved back to the map. "I will not allow you to take that risk."

"Yes, My Lord," she said in obvious irritation, her hands writhing against the dark wash of her jeans.

"I need you to wake everyone, Wynifred," Ilyan said, the deep base of his imposing voice rumbling over the room as he kept his focus on the large paper. "Tell them to strengthen their portion of the shield and inform them that we will be meeting in the dining hall at ten."

"Ten? Why so late? If he is coming, we don't have time..." Wyn began as she hastily moved toward Ilyan. Her movement was stopped by one sharp glare from him. His eyes were like ice as he stared into her, the message clear. Do not defy him. I swallowed heavily at the cold steel in his eyes, the heartless color unfamiliar to me.

"I need *everyone* there, Wynifred, and I will need to prepare Joclyn to meet Ryland face to face. Please tell Sain to do the same." Ilyan's frosty eyes bored into her, his tone making it clear that there would be no more discussion.

"Yes, My Lord." Wyn nodded once before she curtsied, her eyes still downcast when she turned to leave the room. She only looked back at me when she turned to close the door, a wide smile on her face. It was the first sign in the last few minutes that she was still my best friend.

I just stared at her, unsure of what to say, until the door closed, and I could feel her magic scurry away as she ran to do what Ilyan had demanded.

I watched the door long after she had left, trying to ignore the discomfort that was winding up my spine. I didn't belong here. I only felt out of place.

Lately, I had always felt comfortable with Ilyan; everything between us felt so natural. However, hearing him command Wyn in a tone so different from any other time, the look in his eyes—a defiant glare that had almost sacred me—I felt like a lowly servant who had stolen kisses from the king.

Which was essentially what had happened.

I looked toward the bathroom, seeing nothing as I listened to Ilyan work behind me. I was content to look anywhere other than at Ilyan until I could figure out what had just occurred.

"My love," Ilyan said from behind me, the tenderness in

his voice almost catching me off guard. "I need you to show me where they are."

I sat still for a minute before sliding off the bed, knowing I couldn't ignore him for long while truly dreading being ordered to do anything by someone I had viewed so tenderly.

The stones were cold on my bare toes as I walked toward him, my eyes focused on my feet as my heart pounded in my chest. I walked right up to the map, my eyes scanning over the surface before I pointed to the spot way off to the east where I had felt the guard.

"Here." My voice was barely above a whisper.

I kept my focus on the map, even though I knew Ilyan was no longer looking at it. I could feel his eyes on me—feel him move closer to me—but I held still, my head hanging low.

He came up right beside me, the soft pads of his fingers trailing over my jaw as his magic surged into me, mine swirling comfortably in greeting. I closed my eyes at the touch, happy when he didn't try to calm me, leaving me only with the comfort of his magic, like a hot water bottle against a chill.

With the softest of touch, he pulled my chin up to face him. I opened my eyes, unsure of what I would see, only to be met with eyes different from what I had seen before, the color almost calming.

"What is wrong, my love?" he asked, his concern taking my breath away.

I bit my lip at his question, knowing he would need an answer, though I didn't feel even remotely able to give him one. I wasn't even sure how to explain the odd cyclone of discomfort and pleasure I was feeling.

"Ilyan... I mean..." I stopped abruptly and looked away

from him, my throat feeling swollen and uncomfortable with what I was about to say.

You are the King. I sent the words to him as I swallowed, my eyes still focused away from him.

"It took you this long to realize that? I thought I told you months ago," he laughed as he spoke, his words obviously meant to break the tension, but instead they made me more uncomfortable.

Yes, I had known he was King. I had seen him dispense orders, and I had seen him with a crown on his head. I knew he was King. Though, somehow, over the past few months I had forgotten what that meant. I had forgotten that I was kissing a king; that I lay next to a king when I slept. Seeing him with Wyn right then had been a devastating reminder, something that had made me feel lowly and unworthy to be around him. I shouldn't be here.

Ilyan's hand trailed over my skin as he cupped my jaw, the rough pad of his thumb gliding over my cheek as he caressed me. His magic flowed into me as the strength of his love surged. I sighed at the feeling, the hot water bottle sensation growing as my eyes drifted back to meet with the soft blue of his, the expressive orbs an inch away from me.

I could feel his breath against my lips as he spoke, the warmth of his body so close, somehow taking away the worries that I had let infest me.

"I may be King to Wynifred, to Sain, to Thom, but to you, I am your Protector first. I could never rule over you," he whispered, his voice soft as his fingers moved over the skin surrounding my mark, the touch a stark reminder of what would happen if he touched the raised brand, of what he really meant to me. That he was more than my Protector.

The touch was meant as a reminder of how different I was to him; a promise of what I meant to him, and why I didn't need to worry. While my stomach still knit together in embarrassment, the nerves didn't seem quite so important anymore. Because they weren't. Even though the touch of his fingers against me set me on fire, Ilyan meant more to me than that. And I to him.

"I just want you to be Ilyan," I whispered, sure I had stopped breathing.

"Always. For you, my love, I will always be that."

14

"I NEED YOU TO FOCUS, JOCLYN," Ilyan said, his voice a cross between humor and that strict tone he always had when he was training me, which was essentially what he was doing—training me to keep the anxiety out of my mind even when I came face to face with my horrors.

Or in this case, Ryland.

We had about an hour until everyone was to gather in the kitchen and make the final plans for escape; for battle. Ilyan needed everyone to be there, which meant Ryland and I would be in the same room. Face to face. While last night had gone fairly well, Ilyan had essentially been controlling both of our emotions, and with a battle coming, my emotions couldn't be numbed all the time. I needed to be able to move beyond the fear and anger and try not to kill him every time we saw each other.

Which meant I needed to be able to control my emotions more quickly. Which meant training.

I tried to remind myself that it was only training.

Except this felt like anything other than training.

When he calmed me from the nightmares or held me

while I slept, he had never held me this way. This was different.

I stood still on the stone floor of our room, a lightweight blanket wrapped around me while Ilyan's arm enveloped me, his wide hand fanned out on my stomach as he pressed me against him. I couldn't feel the touch from his skin through the thin blanket he had wrapped me in, however, I could feel his warmth radiating through the thin fabric as it tried to reach me.

I rested my head back against his chest as he had instructed, my ear pressed against the soft cotton of his shirt as the sound of his heartbeat echoed into me. I focused on the sound as he ran his fingers over the skin of my face, down my neck, and across the lines of my collar bone. The touch felt slow and steady, the burn on his fingers comforting against my skin. Everywhere he touched left fire behind, igniting me even though he kept his magic restrained within him.

He ran his fingers over my lips again and my heart rate jumpstarted, the pulse heavy against my chest.

"Joclyn," he scolded again, and I couldn't help but smile.

"It's really hard for me to focus when you are doing that," I whispered, not trusting my voice to get louder than that without faltering.

"That is good, my love, because I want you to focus on me *and* what I am doing." He continued to run his fingers over my face as he whispered, his accent deepening his voice.

"Mmmhmm," I moaned as I looked out on the Spanish countryside that stretched beyond the windows in front of us, the low thunderheads kissing the tops of the trees as the lightning fired off in the distance. My breath caught again at

Ilyan's soft touch, my magic flaring in time with a bolt of lightning.

"Keep your eyes closed."

I didn't dare question him. I closed my eyes and leaned into him, letting the beat of his heart fill me. I focused on it, focused on the feel of his touch, the flow of his thoughts. I shuddered as I felt the need he tried to keep hidden, his joy so overpowering that my knees wobbled underneath me. Ilyan's grip against me increased as my legs shook. He held me against him until I calmed myself, and stood still. His fingers ran down my jawbone as my breath caught the smallest bit of his thoughts that were pouring through me.

"Salsa dancing," I whispered, my words sticking to his fingers as he ran them over my lips.

"Good," he whispered so low it was more air than sound, his breathing faltering before returning to the heavy rhythm that he wanted me to focus on. "Focus on the memory, Joclyn. On the way we danced, on the sound of the music. Focus on the bridge that moment has between us. Focus on the beat of my heart."

I didn't answer; I just held still against him as his fingers trailed down my neck, the tip of his index finger pressing into my mark like a button. With the touch, my magic shot through me like a live wire and I gasped, Ilyan's magic erupting right alongside mine. Together they grew into a torrent of power, the twinkling stars of our combined magic filling the air around us in a thousand lights. Our magic danced and swirled as the lights sparked, surrounding us with our own brand of fireworks.

"Make it snow," he whispered in my ear, his breathing labored.

Ilyan had spoken the words before the flow of his magic changed, the power infusing the air with the clanging of pipes, the creaking of wood, and the screams that Ilyan had borrowed from inside my mind. I knew he was controlling it, but I couldn't stop the fear or the way the heavy vein of my terror waited to take over. I tried to focus on what Ilyan had asked, but nothing was working.

"You are stronger than it," Ilyan whispered through the terrifying sounds that echoed around us.

Still, the fears ruled me.

"Focus on my heartbeat." His hand pressed against my head, holding me against him until all I could feel was the steady rhythm of his heart.

I could still hear the clanging, the screams; they didn't go away, not like when I pushed my fears away. These were not part of me and only continued to fill the air around us, requiring me to be strong while they echoed in my ears. I had to convince myself that I was safe even though I was surrounded by my fears.

It would be the same with Ryland, standing in front of him, knowing he would attack me, though also knowing that I was safe. The two had to exist in harmony from now on.

I had to find a way to make that happen. It was my only hope to defeat my demons, to embrace them.

This was the only chance for me to make that happen; for me to find stable footing while still living with my terrors.

I let the sound of the pipes move through me as Ilyan's heartbeat did, the two sounds cancelling each other out until I could control the anxiety; until I could feel it enough to push it away.

"Make it snow," he repeated, his voice low and rumbling as it vibrated through me.

I focused on the beat of his heart as I brought the snow,

the cold air traveling on the back of my magic. The icy breeze tugged at the thin blanket I was covered with as small, wet droplets came in through the window to fall over my face.

"Good. Focus, Joclyn. Listen to the beat of my heart. Focus on the flow of your magic." I cringed at Ilyan's words; no matter how soft and gentle he made them, I knew what was coming. He was going to step away and leave me standing alone as the pipes clanged, the wood creaked, and the screams filled the air. My soul seized at the thought, the fear of the pain that would come filling me up and turning the soft flakes of snow to freezing rain almost instantly.

"Calm, Joclyn," Ilyan soothed, his emotions raging through me as his thoughts echoed his words, the strain deep as he replayed the memory he had chosen to be my anchor. But it wasn't an anchor anymore, and the rain stayed, the storm growing into a torrent wind and freezing rain. It soaked the blanket and my hair until it hung limply against me and I began to shiver.

The memory of salsa dancing left as Ilyan quieted the haunting sounds, leaving me standing in only the sound of the wind. Ilyan's hand ran over my skin, the heat of his touch warming me until I calmed and the rain stopped, leaving us drenched as we clung to each other.

We just stood there, damp and cold, our arms wrapped around each other as I waited for Ilyan to point out what I needed to work on. The scolding never came, however, which only worried me more.

I wanted to master this—I needed to—we were running out of time, but it wasn't working. Every time he moved to pull away, my anxiety moved in. The horrors that haunted my subconscious ran rampant through me, the sounds Ilyan's magic produced only heightening my fears.

I shuddered as the last of my tortures ran through my mind, unsure if the chill came more from the horrifying memories, or from the cold water that dripped down my spine. Ilyan's grip increased as his magic surged, drying and warming me.

"I have an idea, Joclyn, although I am not sure if it is going to work," Ilyan whispered, his apprehension a steady thrum through the air.

"Nothing has worked so far, Ilyan. At this point, I'll try tight rope walking if you think it will help."

Ilyan chuckled, the sound rich in my ear as it vibrated through his chest.

"This will work," he said as he pulled me away from him, his hand steady when he unwrapped the soaking wet blanket from around me.

I bit my lip as the chilled morning air hit the skin on my arms, the breeze tugging at the thin fabric of the pajama pants I still wore. Ilyan didn't seem to notice, however. He only stripped off his shirt, revealing the dozens of criss-crossed scars on his chest. I held my breath as I attempted to focus on his eyes, fighting the need to run my fingers over the scars.

"Ilyan?" I asked, still waiting for him to provide me with the insights into this idea, yet none came. He only smiled and pulled me back into him, his arms wrapping around me like I was as fragile as glass, the heat from his chest and hands shooting into me. I could feel the raised skin of his scars against my face, my soul seeming to move closer to him, to connect to the places where the Black Water had burned him. My magic moved into him on instinct, his doing the same, as if the increased skin connection gave them permission to mingle where they hadn't been allowed to before.

"Focus on me, Joclyn," he instructed, his voice tense, making me wonder what I was missing.

Aren't you going to tell me this mysterious plan? I asked into his mind as I pulled away to look at him, my eyebrow raising. He didn't seem too interested in filling in the gaps of whatever crazy idea had sprouted in his mind; he just smiled in that coy way of his before leaning down and kissing my forehead, sending a little jolt of pleasure through my spine.

"Focus on me, Joclyn."

I heard the thrum of his heart as I leaned against his bare chest, my own a pulse that moved in perfect time with his. I focused on the steady beat, the sound filling me as his hands moved over my skin, leaving a trail of ice and fire behind it. The touch mingled with his magic, warming me, comforting me. It wasn't like before. It wasn't distracting; it was perfect.

I exhaled in bliss as I floated away in Ilyan's arms, the sounds of my haunted nightmares coming again without warning. I expected the anxiety that would come with them. I cringed in expectation of the fear. Both wound around my spine, threatening to break through the calm I had so recently found

"Do not be afraid," he whispered to me, his voice as soft as the breeze in my ears.

I closed my eyes as Ilyan's emotions began to flood me, the need replaced by dedication; the love and passion only increasing. I felt them flow through me as my own emotions matched in time, his thoughts following close behind.

It wasn't like before, when I saw snippets of his memories and portions of his thoughts. Everything was clear as it played inside of my mind. I saw the new memory as he did, heard every word as he thought it.

Except it wasn't a memory.

It was a dream.

The dream that Ilyan had imagined from that very first day he held me in his arms eight hundred years ago. A day of bonding.

Our bonding.

The whispers of pipes and screams faded into nothing as I focused on the image Ilyan lent me, the vision so strong it was all I could focus on.

We sat together in a darkened room. His hands were soft as he held me in front of him, the touch of his lips soft against mine. I wore a long dress of gold, he in one of those medieval outfits I had seen in his closet so long ago. My breath felt caught between reality and fantasy as I watched him braid long ribbons into my hair, his touch gentle as he worked tirelessly on the intricate weaving. He was so focused as he worked.

He spoke in rapid Czech before I returned the phrase, the unknown Czech words sounding odd in my voice, the vow spoken before he wrapped me in his arms and fused his magic to mine. I could almost feel the way that would feel, the power of it rocking through me, taking my breath away.

I gasped as the emotion filled me, the clarity of the dream departing as I was left in the swirling winter air. I could feel the snow I had brought dance on the breeze, the flakes soft against my skin as they made their way to the ground. I lifted my fingers to my lips as the dream faded, my calm overtaking me, even though he had gone.

Ilyan had gone.

My fear spiked at the loss of his warmth, the loud moan of a pipe that wasn't really there cutting through my calm. I cringed as I heard it, my magic wavering as the fear threatened to move into me.

"Focus, my love," Ilyan whispered from somewhere behind me, his voice barely louder than the haunted whimpering that came from somewhere before me.

I cringed at the sound—at the fear it held—before Ilyan's thoughts repeated the future he had shared with me and I could move beyond it.

I exhaled shakily as I pushed the fear away, grabbing the dream and bringing it into me as the air around me warmed. The once cold winter breeze became as gentle and warm as a spring rain. I focused on Ilyan's dream as the terrifying sounds continued to play, but my emotions remained steady, my fears now locked away.

I stretched my arms away from me, my back straightening as I reached to touch the snow that danced around me, the breeze running through my fingers like a silky ribbon. I stretched my body out, extending everything further than it had for months. Since before I had been trapped; from before I had been beaten.

I could feel my joints creak as my body straightened, everything in me feeling more human, more alive.

The soft flakes ran over my face as I inhaled the crisp air, the sound of thunder filling my ears as it took the place of the now silent horrors. Everything felt so light, so free, and I couldn't help smiling.

"Open your eyes," Ilyan whispered in my ear, his hands gentle as he pulled me back into the heat of his chest. My magic bubbled at the contact, the clarity in my mind making the surge that much stronger. I smiled at the sensation, my eyes fluttering open to the white world before me, and I gasped.

It wasn't snow.

I extended my hand out as a soft, white rose petal floated into my hand, the perfect petal resting in my palm as thousands more floated through the air around us. I could see them as they floated from the stormy sky and drifted over the forest. They covered the ground in a bed of silky white, filling the air with the desirable aroma of life and love.

I looked at the rose-covered world, my stomach tightening in awe at the miracle that I was surrounded by.

"How is this possible?" I asked, my question hanging in the air as my hands extended again, the rose petals floating over my skin as they danced to the ground.

"You are doing this, Joclyn. Your magic. Your heart." Ilyan's breath grazed the skin of my ear as he spoke, his lips brushing against my neck. "I gave you my most cherished dream, the one thing that I have held onto since I first laid eyes on you. I shared it with you to help heal you. And you created this."

"*I* created it?" I stammered, my eyes still scanning the beautiful image in front of us.

Ilyan chuckled as his hand interlaced with mine, leading me through piles of petals that covered the floor. We moved them aside like a fragrant snow drift as Ilyan led me onto the balcony, the air filling with their perfume as we moved.

The petals were a blizzard that covered the world, creating beauty that minutes ago I had forgotten could exist. Despite what my walking terrors would have me believe, the world was not always blood-soaked walls and torture chambers. The world was not all anger and hatred as Edmund had hoped. The world was beautiful.

I don't know how long I watched the petals fall, my body standing straight and strong, my mind clear. I leaned my head back against Ilyan's chest, and his arm wrapped around me as he kept me close to him.

"It's beautiful," I finally whispered, knowing the word wasn't enough to describe what I saw before me.

Ilyan's hand slid over my arm as he turned me to face him, my eyes tearing away from the white-covered world to focus on him.

"You are stronger than any, my love. Your power stretches into the very core of the world, your heart dictating all that you are. I know you feel broken, but this... This is proof that you are not. You are perfect and stronger than anything that my father has imprinted you with. You will always rise up above it. And if you stumble? I will be here to pick you up, to help you bring beauty back to the world."

Ilyan looked at me with all the love in his heart, his eyes a lighter blue than I had ever seen them. I couldn't help but smile at him, my hand stretching to cover the scarred skin over his heart, the rhythmic thump of his pulse heavy under my fingertips.

"Miluju tě, Joclyn. Ty jsi moje navždy. Můj začátek a můj konec." He whispered the words like a prayer, and although I understood nothing, I understood everything. I could hear his thoughts as he spoke, his heart translating for me what my mind could not understand.

"You are my forever. My beginning and my end," I whispered back to him in English.

His eyes shined as his fingertips ran over my face before moving down, careful to avoid the raised brand behind my ear. He kept his hand there, his fingers soft against my skin before he brought me closer, so close I could see the facets of golden light in the blue of his eyes, the shining color dancing before his lids closed, his lips pressing against mine.

I wrapped my arms around his shoulders as I kissed him

back, my fingers trailing along his hair line as I felt the soft pressure of his kiss, his warm breath moving into me as he held me against him. His lips then moved off mine to graze over my cheeks, my eyes. He littered the sweet touch over me while we stood, wrapped in each other's arms, rose petals falling around us in a blizzard of white.

I sighed as Ilyan pressed his lips against my jawbone, the touch slow before he raised back up, his eyes more gold than blue in the dim light.

"Ty jsi moje navždy. Můj začátek a můj konec," I repeated the words to him in Czech, not caring if my pronunciation was off. "I have no doubt. You have taken all of that away."

"And if it comes back, I will chase it away." His accent was so heavy I could barely understand him, yet I smiled nonetheless, the promise one that I wasn't sure I needed anymore.

Ilyan had lent me a dream, a piece of him that I could take with me always. I could feel his magic thrum through me, something I had grown so used to that I had almost forgotten what it really meant for us. Now I knew, though. Ilyan's dream had become my dream, and with that hope, I could overcome everything.

Even though the demons were just waiting to knock down the door.

15

———

RYLAND WAS WATCHING ME.

I could feel his eyes on me from where I stood, sandwiched between Thom and Ilyan around the large, raised table. My shoulders tensed in fear as I heard Sain whisper to Ryland every few minutes. The fear blended into anger as Ryland clung to my father's hand. Sain's voice was calm as he tried to stop Ryland from doing what my mind continually screamed at me to do to him. The desire that I was desperately fighting.

The need to attack.

I ground my teeth and pushed the craving away, careful to keep myself as close to Ilyan as I dared. Even though he had warned me not to touch him, not to get too close. Ryland's perception of me was still distorted, and getting to close to Ilyan could shatter the flimsy veil of sanity Ryland had found. If Ryland erupted, it would only be moments before my own sanity shattered.

So, instead of stepping closer to Ilyan as I wanted, I took a deep gulp from the mug of Black Water I held, letting the deep magic that it provided warm me, numb me, and settle my madness. Although it wasn't enough, it helped. I took another small sip before setting it back on the table we stood around, grateful for the residual calm it gave me.

I kept my eyes glued on the ancient parchment that Ilyan had brought from our room, the yellowed surface lined with streaks of colorful light from the numerous lanterns and orbs that lit the dusty room. I knew the sun was shining somewhere above the dark clouds that shrouded us, but all we received was darkness and the steady drum of thunder.

Ryland mumbled as the sky ripped open, and my breathing picked up, my shoulders tensing as Sain's murmurs became a dense white noise to Ilyan's commands. I moved a step toward Thom, but he only seemed to be concerned with Wyn, who stood opposite of him. Wyn, whose hand was wrapped around Ryland's.

"Hurt her!" Ryland suddenly erupted and I jumped, my eyes darting toward the sound. I knew at once it was a mistake.

My anger licked at my soul in a flame of heat and fear, the emotions screaming at me to lunge across the table at him. I clenched every muscle in an attempt to stay still, my joints aching as the raw anger attempted to bully its way past the wall I had built, threatening to take me down.

Just as I fought the madness, Ryland fought to maintain the calm he had built. I could see it in the way his shoulders tensed and sagged, the way his fingers compressed into tight, little fists.

Until now, Ryland had been calm. His voice mellow when he spoke, his emotions didn't seem quite so volatile. But he still wasn't whole; he still wasn't the boy he used to be, and the monster was threatening to come back.

I had hoped the return of his heart would have helped,

and while I could see the calm it had given him, it hadn't been enough.

I just wished I didn't feel so awkward wearing the now clear diamond around my neck. I don't know what it was, but the necklace almost felt like a war prize, something tainted that I should return. Or destroy.

I swallowed once and looked back down to the table top, knowing that one look into the depths of his eyes would unleash my nightmares. Knowing that part of me wanted it to. I could already hear the liquid thoughts of my anger begging me to attack, to slice him apart.

I grit my teeth and closed my eyes at the thought, not liking how my mind accepted the idea as rational. I pulled the vivid image of Ilyan's dream to mind, letting it settle my nerves for the hundredth time in half as many minutes.

The meeting had to almost be over; Ilyan had told me it would only be an hour, and I was sure that we had almost reached that. Although for all I knew, it had been only ten minutes. I let my focus wander from Ilyan's fingers as they traced over the map to the rows of tables we were surrounded by. Most of the wooden surfaces had been worn smooth over centuries of use while others looked like they had been hewn only recently.

I was sure it had to be a kitchen, either that or ancient monks needed a lot of fireplaces. The large, rounded stone alcoves were evenly spaced along the wall behind us, each ancient outcropping covered with ash and soot. So, a kitchen, although the lack of chairs seemed a little odd. Only two tables had chairs, and they were stacked...

"Joclyn," Ilyan said, making me jump, my attention pulling from my temporary distraction to look at him. "I need to know how many camps lie along this stretch here."

Ilyan asked the question with that same loud boom of

command that I had heard this morning, and I almost wanted to deny him and give my imprisoned anger some type of an outlet. However, the last thing I wanted was another fight, so I closed my eyes, swallowed my pride, and sent my magic away from me, my mind searching through trees as my magic gave me sight to what was miles away.

I let it pulse and surge until I had a clear enough understanding of the land. Then I opened my eyes, grabbed the pen from Ilyan's hand and wrote in the single camp that had been missing from the map.

"This might work," Ilyan said, letting his finger drag over the paper and leaving a glittering trail of red behind. "If they leave this space untouched, you," he glanced over at Thom, "and Wyn should be able to get Ryland and Dramin through here without much of a mishap. From there it is a straight shot home."

"Do you think there will be enough space there?" Thom asked, his finger tracing over the line that Ilyan had just made to stop at a small line of camps not far from their path. "All it would take is one Trpaslík to find us, and we would be toast."

"Excuse me," Wyn said loudly, her voice bubbling in agitation. "I can feel a Trpaslík if they come, and I am quite capable of protecting all of you, in case you have forgotten." Wyn smiled slyly at Thom in dissent, her hand dropping from Ryland's to flatten against the map as she leaned toward Thom.

I half expected him to take a step back from the wicked look that Wyn was giving him, but he held his ground, shaking his head and laughing, the sound almost uncharacteristic for him.

"I have not forgotten; I still have the scar, thank you. I just do not wish you to push yourself too far, so soon."

The sincerity of his tone caught me off guard. Thom had always been calm and soft spoken, but the way he spoke to her was different, kinder, more loving. My head snapped toward him and I looked into the long, thick strands of his dreads, feeling the soft waves of his magic whisper through the air. My eyebrows disappeared into my hairline as I tried to figure out what was going on, and what scar he was referring to. Hadn't they only met a few days ago?

Thom held still as he looked at her. Wyn's posture softened further as her face broke out into a wide, playful smile.

"I am fine, Thomas," she said, her eyes glimmering with her sass.

"I need all of you to travel with them," Ilyan continued as if the exchange hadn't happened, his deep voice attempting to pull everyone back on track. Almost everyone turned back to Ilyan, but I stared at Wyn until I caught her eyes.

Typical silent girl talk was not going to cut it; I could tell already. No matter how many times I heightened my eyebrows at her in question, she only got more flustered, the reaction increasing my confusion.

"I will need Wyn and Sain to help keep Ryland in check and, Thom, you will need to move Dramin." Ilyan's voice echoed off the stone as Wyn's head snapped back over to him, her eyes brightening in anticipation.

"That still doesn't answer how you will keep the mass amounts of Trpaslíks away from us? We can't possibly fight if we are carting invalids around," Thom said, his voice back to his hard scoff.

"Joclyn and I will draw them away..."

"So *she* gets to fight," Ryland interrupted Ilyan with a loud snap, his voice hard and accusatory. Ilyan withdrew his hand from the map as I cringed, the sound of Ryland's anger igniting the mania that I was trying so hard to control. "You are going to take a weak Drak and leave me behind, aren't you, brother?"

"You are not fit to fight yet, Ryland," Ilyan said in a deep rumble that I could tell he hoped would calm his brother, even through the ripples of anger that flowed off Ryland.

"I can fight! Let me kill him!" Ryland yelled, his anger ripping out of him before Wyn and Sain placed their hands against him, his face calming a bit.

Ryland's outburst was the breaking point for Ilyan. The calm he had projected evaporated as he rose up to his full height, towering over the table toward Ryland. The edges of his voice rumbled as his anger surged in an oppressive weight. "Not until you see us all as your allies. Including Joclyn."

"And she can do that? She tried to kill me!" Ryland countered, his eyes narrowing dangerously as he stared into Ilyan. Although he tried to stay strong under the power of Ilyan's aura, I could see his resolve lessen, his anger dampening as he curled away.

"She has been trained; she is strong. And the sight has shown us that she will be ready! I know she will be!" Ilyan roared, his confidence in me like a rolling balm over my skin. "Besides, they do not want you. They would rather see my head on a pike, and Joclyn's body in a pit. Would you like to be bait, Ryland?"

"She will never be fit to face our father; she is weak and will get us all killed," Ryland hissed through gritted teeth.

The two men stared malice into each other from over the table. My jaw clenched while Ilyan's muscles tensed in warning. I could feel Ilyan's anger move off him in waves as it intersected with mine. My pain and anger at Ryland's words grew until I couldn't control it, until it boiled out of me in a torrent that I couldn't help but release.

"I am not weak," I growled through the tight clench of my jaw, while my magic rippled and bubbled until I was all but willing to let it explode out of me.

Ilyan moved back to an upright position at the snap of my voice, his arm moving around my waist in an attempt to pull me into him, but I moved away from it. My anger and pain mixed together violently, and my breathing picked up. I knew I should accept Ilyan's comforting touch—that I should calm myself—yet I couldn't. I didn't think I needed it.

Right then—even through the anger, and the pain, and the fear—I could still feel myself. I could still feel Ilyan's dream. Somehow, I was controlling the waves of fear and anger, instead of letting them control me.

My thoughts remained, and when I looked up to Ryland, when my eyes met the blue of his for the first time since I had walked in this room, I didn't feel panic, and the walls didn't turn to blood.

I just looked at Ryland, letting all the things he had said to me over the past few days meld together into a furious conviction that took over every part of me. I could hear his disgust at discovering I was a Drak. I could feel his fist against my cheek, his taunt that I was nothing with Ilyan, nothing without him. That was wrong, though, because I was something.

I grit my teeth as my muscles rippled, the blinding rage dimming my vision.

"I do not need you, or anyone else to make me strong." I didn't take my eyes away from him as I spoke. I could see his own anger pulsing just under the surface, waiting to escape and attack me, no matter how hard Wyn and Sain tried to control it.

My magic flashed once, and I slammed my fist into the table, a powerful ripple of my magic resounding through the room in a tangible cloud. It moved through the others in a gust of wind that sent them off balance, their clothes and hair whipping around them in the torrent.

I could hear their yells of surprise as the wind grew, the roar of my magic a snap in their ears. My magic exploded into the paper under my hand as the power moved through the air, flying through the ancient fibers and into the space that surrounded us.

Like the ripples of a wave against smooth water, my magic surged again as I prompted it. The flux of energy saturated the map as the markings that dotted the surface wiggled and moved over the top. Ink spread over the paper as my magic did, thick black lines rising from the map like wisps of smoke, the grey vapor growing and multiplying as they moved and danced in the air above the aged paper.

I didn't look away from Ryland as my magic spread through the forest, focusing on everything that surrounded us. I saw the fine, red hairs of a Trpaslík's beard, and the glowing green rocks of a fire. I saw them in the shadows of my eyes as I looked through Ryland, the images becoming part of me. I brought them into me, pushing them into the inky tendrils that floated above the map, morphing them, changing them into a perfect replica of what we were surrounded by.

Trees sprouted from the paper, the black and white figures unfurling from the soot as if they were growing there. The wispy spirals of ink joined together as they formed tiny, two-inch tall shadows of each of the Trpaslíks who surrounded us. The small figures moved through camps and around fires, the same way their counterparts moved miles away from where we stood. Figure after figure took shape over the surface of the map; my magic rippled powerfully through me as tents, trees, cars, everything that the enemy had brought with them began to materialize.

"I am not weak," I growled at him again, trying desperately to ignore the look of amazement that lined everyone's faces.

Everyone but Ryland.

Ryland just looked at me, his face stony and callous as glowered down on me. My father was already mumbling in his ear as he took the fight out of him, something I would be lucky to keep at bay.

I scowled at Ryland as I leaned away from the table, grabbing my mug of Black Water, content that I had made my point even though I was sure he was immune to whatever I had just displayed to him.

I jumped a bit as Ilyan placed his hand against my bare arm, his magic flowing into me in one quick burst as my mind filled with his thoughts of awe and pride. I turned to him at the touch, the look on his face soft and gentle before he removed his hand, the weakened connection leaving me with only shadows of his thoughts. He turned back to the few of us who huddled around the map, his voice that deep rumble of royalty again.

"Here," Ilyan prodded through the ghostly shadows of ink as he displayed a new path, different than the one he had originally decided upon, this one further west, further from the main camp where Edmund's guards had settled.

His finger traced through the camps, a line of red glitter flying from the tip of his finger again as he left the trail for all to see. The red sparkled among the wispy smoke figures, trailing away from the center of the map.

A sure getaway.

Then why did it make me so uncomfortable? I heard everyone else agree, saw their heads bob in agreement out of the corner of my eye, but I couldn't look away from the end of the map where the beautiful line of Ilyan's magic stopped, where the swirls of my magic had not taken on a true shape, leaving only a patch of grey smoke that swirled through the air.

"The five of you will travel along this path here," Ilyan began as he indicated the red line, but his voice sounded tinny and distant, my mind pulling away from them.

I stared blankly at the swirls of grey above the map, my body weighed down as my magic stretched away from me. I pressed into the power as it moved, my heartbeat rising as I focused on the shapeless smoke, my desperate need for understanding only growing.

"Joclyn and I will begin an attack here, allowing for the section to clear out."

The world where Ilyan spoke was a million miles away as I focused on the bare patch of land miles from where we stood. Except it wasn't bare; I could clearly see the burlap tent that stood in the bare space, in the exact position on the map where the ink still danced through the air.

I stared at the tent in my mind's eye, the plain square shape feeling like an oppressive force even from this distance. The flap to the tent moved in the breeze as my magic stretched through the air, a gentle buzzing replacing Ilyan's voice as I focused, as I moved closer. The closer I got, the heavier my mind and magic grew, until I felt that same, weird feeling as before; the peculiar magic I had felt so many times before hitting me hard.

I had felt it first less than two days ago when I woke to Ilyan and Thom around the table, but it didn't have the same strength then as it did now. Now it felt like sludge against me, sticking to my soul, weighing me down.

The heavy mire pushed against me as I waded through it, straining to see the tent further, my heart rate picking up at the sight of the guard who stood before the narrow opening, his hands holding a gun tightly against his chest. A gun?

Trpaslíks don't use guns. Magical people do not use guns.

I tensed as I looked into the nervous apprehension on the Trpaslík guard's face. He was miles away from us, with no reason to face battle, and yet he was nervous.

The other Trpaslíks that were in the camp sat around a small fire. They were laughing, excited for the battle, for the bloodshed. Something was still off; their backs were stiff, the laughter forced, their eyes continually darting toward that same tent.

My heart beat quicker as I looked back toward the tent, my need to know what was behind the burlap swallowing me. I sped my magic toward the tent, my body and magic weakening the closer I got until the image of the tent began to dim. I pushed through it, ignoring the burn in my chest until my vision faded to black, a sharp pain exploding inside my skull as my head made contact with the cold stones of the floor.

"Joclyn!" I heard everyone exclaim at my collapse, different levels of worry all moving together into one confusing sound that expanded the pressure in my head.

"Is she okay?" Wyn asked from somewhere far away, the alarm in her voice drifting down to where I lay on the floor.

I felt the heat of Ilyan's hands against my ankle as he tried to hide the touch, his worry so paramount I found myself crying from his emotions alone. Ilyan's magic flooded into me as I writhed in pain on the floor, while flashes of the Trpaslíks' fear ignited in the black of my eyes, the panic in their faces alerting me to something much more dangerous.

They were scared of a weapon they meant to use against us.

"You can't go that way!" I shouted the words through my labored breathing, my panic making it impossible for me to control my decibel level.

"Joclyn?" Ilyan asked, his worry smothering his regality for the moment.

I pushed my way off the floor in a desperate attempt to reach the table. Everyone around me moved away as if I had caught fire. Ilyan reached out to me in an attempt to keep me down, but I only broke through his hold, my fingers clawing at the smooth wood in an effort to warn them.

"Joclyn, what it is?" Ilyan asked, his voice strong as he moved behind me, his unquenchable need to hold me consuming.

I said nothing; I only clung to the side of the table as I stretched my hand over the ink that had returned to the surface of the map. My fingers were shaking as I reached toward the empty space on the map, my heart still thundering at the oppressiveness of the tent.

Something is here, I sent into Ilyan's mind, my voice quivering inside of him. "Something bad."

"Do you know what it is?" he asked, the fear he held for me turning into something deeper, something that scared me.

I can't see; something is blocking me... I can't get too close.

"What is going on, Ilyan?" Thom asked in irritation from behind us. Ilyan paid him no mind as he leaned down to me, his hand a brief, forbidden touch before it was gone.

"If you use my magic, can you show me?" he whispered,

his face moving closer in an attempt to keep his words hidden, something that I wasn't sure had worked. I was sure Ryland had heard and understood my failure, my weakness.

I tensed at the thought of using Ilyan's magic, of needing help, of being as weak as Ryland had told me, as Edmund had made me. Just like Atlas.

Except Atlas wasn't weak, only a fool; and I wasn't Atlas. Not anymore.

My eyes darted to Thom at the thought, his eyes hooded as he tried desperately to keep his emotions hidden. Even through the tough-guy look, I could still see his worry for me, for what was happening.

I pushed aside my pride and held onto Ilyan's hand, knowing I would need it for what was coming.

"Yes." I closed my eyes as I leaned against the table, pulling Ilyan's magic into me as I stretched the combined power away from us.

The murmurings of confusion hummed through the kitchen, the sound distancing as I pulled my mind away. I could hear Ilyan try to explain what was going on, but his voice was tinny and hollow, the sound lost over the sound of the birds that filled the trees around me. Everyone else was too far away now.

I was too far away.

I could still feel the warmth of Ilyan's hand around mine as my consciousness sped through the trees and over the camps until it reached the tense encampment that surrounded the burlap tent. Until I felt the magic that was dead in the air.

The air was stagnated with oppression, but I did not feel the same weakness as I had before. Ilyan's magic strengthened as he supported me, looking through my eyes, moving forward with me. The guard shook a bit as we approached, obviously affected by the same magic that was smothering us. His fingers were white as they held the gun, his grip so tight I was afraid the thing might snap in half.

I tried not to let the guard's fear fuel my own as I watched the flap of the tent snap in the wind as if it, too, feared what it was hiding. My heart rattled in my chest as my magic moved through the stiff fabric, bringing us face to face with a terror we hadn't expected.

"Vilỳs," Ilyan yelled, the echo of his voice sounding clear in my ears before the distant murmuring took over, everyone's questions sounding like angry waves in my ears.

I looked around the tent through my mind's eye, my heartbeat speeding up as I tried to make sense of what I was seeing.

Everyone had spoken of Vilỳs as fun-loving sprites, magical creatures who helped man and were gentle and kind. I had seen that idea mirrored back to me in Ryland's drawing in the Tõuha, in the sights I had seen. I had expected winged creatures no taller than the length of my arm with odd, sphinx-like faces and brightly colored skin. However, these creatures looked nothing like what I had seen; these beasts were terrifying.

From floor to ceiling, rows of dented, metal shelving lined the fabric walls of the tent, every inch crammed with the large, shackled creatures. The mutated, infected things were folded and contorted in an effort to pack as many of them in as possible, the mania on their faces clear as they screamed and yelled. The once bright hues of their skin were brown and diseased, large gashes littering their bodies from clawing at the ones who sat next to them.

They screamed as they fought against the tiny shackles that bound them, their faces turned up at me, almost as if they could sense my magic amongst them. Even from so far away their magic was so strong I could barely breathe.

Ilyan's fingers dug into my hand as his own fear gripped him, our heartbeats speeding up in time.

I gasped and pulled my magic away from the contagious hatred that filled me, my eyes snapping open to the dimly lit room. I wanted to say that I was safe, that I had left the putrid magic behind, but I could still feel it. I could still feel the panic wind through my frayed nerves.

"How many more of the tents are there?" Ilyan asked of me, his body shaking in fear as he moved to mark the tent we had just seen on the map.

I did not want to feel the poisoned magic, but I had no other choice. I closed my eyes and sent my magic back through the forest that surrounded us, the glinting tendrils floating through the trees as I counted the tents. My eyes snapped open as I felt the last of them, my palm tensing against the table as I tried to control the fear.

There were ten tents.

Ten weapons.

I stared blankly over the surface of the map as ink spread from my fingertips. It flowed over the surface of the map, forming small, black boxes where each one lay. I stared at them as they darkened the paper, my breathing still trying to regulate from the smothering sickness that had infiltrated me.

"All those are Vilÿs? I thought Edmund had killed them all," Wyn asked, her voice shaking as the fear in the room seeped into her.

Ilyan said nothing; he only nodded as he watched the last box appear, his lips a hard line as the plan he had formulated crumbled to the ground.

"My Lord," Sain said, his voice tentative as he broke the silence. "Were they infected?"

My head snapped up at his question, my teeth grinding together in fear. I could see everyone else turn toward Ilyan in question, different levels of fear clear on each of their faces, but I couldn't look away from my father. I couldn't look away from an answer I was terrified to hear.

"What do you know, Sain?" Ilyan asked, his jaw hardening as he glared at him.

"I am unsure, My Lord," Sain replied. "I only saw one, in the beginning, after I made sure the birthstone was delivered to my daughter. They captured me and forced the water into me. I didn't know what I was seeing at first as I did not know who I was, but I saw it in that sight, a Vil ̀y. It was sitting on Edmund's dresser, like a prized bird."

"Edmund's dresser," Ilyan repeated, his voice suddenly monotone. I looked at him in question, sucking in breath at the weird, distanced look in his eyes. "Was it next to his bed?"

"Yes." The word shattered through the room in waves of terror.

Ryland's eyes darted to Sain in shock while Wyn looked like she was ready to explode.

Ilyan groaned beside me, his hand dragging through his hair as he moved away from the table, his steps heavy in frustration. His muscles tensed as he paced in the darkness away from us with mumbled Czech on his lips.

I looked from Ilyan to Thom, to Wyn, desperate for some form of explanation, but no one was looking at me.

"He found a way to strengthen himself," Wyn said, her voice strangely odd and distanced, like she was repeating something she had heard before. "You don't think it is the same, Ilyan?"

"I do," Ilyan replied from behind me, his strong voice echoing around the elongated room.

"But Cail never said anything about a mutation." My legs almost buckled at the use of his name. I had no idea what they were talking about, but right then, I didn't care. I could already feel the fear creep in, see the mortar in the wall turn to blood.

I looked to Ryland unwillingly as my body began to shake in fear—his dark eyes meeting mine—and I cringed, the anger pulsing, screaming at me to attack him, to kill him. I gasped as I tried to push the emotion away, my ears filling with the beat of my heart as I gulped in air.

"Cail never spoke of many things, Wynifred," Ilyan growled, the repeated use of the name like a blunt blade gashing me open. My fingers dug into the wooden edge of the ancient table as I attempted to steady myself, my knees trying their hardest to buckle underneath me.

"Ilyan, you know that he would—" Wyn's voice was sugary sweet again, and I cringed at the unfamiliarity of it.

"Do not use your prowess on me, Wynifred. This is hardly the time." The loud snap of Ilyan's voice ripped through the thin layer of my serenity, my torso folding over as I fought to hold onto my sanity.

"Yes, My Lord."

"He has obviously done something to them, but what? And why?" Ilyan's voice was softer now, the volume coming right down on top of me from where I lay over the table. I almost expected his hand to press against my skin, his comforting magic to fill me, but that never came.

"They will turn you mad," Ryland said out of nowhere, the hard edge of his voice increasing the lack of stability I was experiencing.

I saw nothing other than the blackness behind my eyes

as my fingers dug into the map, Ryland's necklace digging into my chest as I struggled to control my emotions. I could already tell it was a lost cause.

Everything picked up as the voices washed over me, one after another they came. I couldn't focus beyond the fear, past the way my magic sped through my bloodstream. Everything blended together so perfectly that I wasn't sure who was speaking or even what they were saying.

"He has scores of them. I don't know what he has done to them, but if they bite you, you'll go mad. If they bite a human... well..."

"Edmund will have an army."

I tried to focus on the voice as it echoed through the tunnel of my mind, to make sense of it, but everything only spun violently through me.

"Hovno, if he builds an army out of the humans, he will be able to end everything."

"We can't wait; we have to fight him."

"Joclyn can't possibly fight these."

"The sight has shown that she will be ready... Joclyn...? Joclyn?"

I was vaguely aware that Ilyan was calling my name, that he was scared. I could hear the fear in his voice, feel the waves of it in my mind, yet I couldn't grasp it enough to pull me back. I couldn't see behind it. All I could see was red, the flame of an ember washing over my eyes as I drifted into the fluid awareness of sight.

Except this time was different than any other sight I had been given before. This sight felt hollow, open, as if I stood before a wide valley, ready to swallow the world.

It felt powerful.

The ember burn in my eyes drifted into black before a red-roofed skyline I had never seen before came into view.

The roofs were tinted in gold as the sun set around them, the beauty of an unknown city covering my eyes before a fountain of black shot through the sun. The spout of brown, muddy water faded into faces of horror as hundreds of mortals ran through cobblestoned streets, their hands and faces covered with blood as they yelled and cried in a desperate attempt to find safety from whatever had attacked them.

My mouth opened as the sight shifted, the air filling with the hollow tones of my own voice, the sound of the sight echoing in my ears.

"The death will come; the sky will fall."

The sight flipped again to a group of people huddled in an alley, screaming and crying as the small winged creatures I had seen in the tent flew down from the mass of brown in the sky, their teeth bared as they prepared to attack.

"Smrt přijde, nebesa se zhroutí," a deep, unfamiliar voice spoke through the sight, the man's voice hollow and distorted.

The vision flashed from the alley to a foreign river, the wide, winding brown sludge turning red as I watched.

"The war begins in the dark of night," my voice rang out as I watched myself run into a solid cliff face, the stone carved with a man atop a horse. I ran through the stone like it was little more than air, Ilyan and more than a dozen others following me.

My sight flashed from the ornate carving to one of Ilyan holding me against a wall, his arm strong as he protected me, his face hard as he faced an enemy I couldn't see.

"Válka začíná v temnotě noci," the same male voice echoed around us, the sight changing to those same red roofs, bathed in firelight as they burned away, the long tongues of fire reaching into the dark night sky.

"With hell behind and hell before," my voice spoke on its own as the fire left my sight only to see myself standing on a burning rooftop, draped in the same long cloak I had been wearing in the last image.

"S peklem zezadu a peklem vepředu," the voice spoke again, and this time I understood what was happening. My magic had connected to my father's, the sight opening between us as he experienced this sight as I did, hand in hand.

"One must fall before the light," I said as blood flowed down the dark cave floor. It trailed through the bodies of men I had never seen, the amount of bloodshed twisting my stomach even through the dampened emotions the sight gave me.

"Jeden musí padnout před světlem," he spoke the words as the blood continued to run over the stone before the sight fell on the loosely curled fingers of a hand, a hand I was sure to be dead. I waited for it to continue, to show me who was to die, but the vision faded to nothing, leaving me in the glowing red embers again.

"Je rozděleno," we said together, our voices perfectly matched in the darkness of my sight as I spoke words aloud that I did not understand.

The sight left me just as my breathing picked up, my eyes still drifting in and out of focus. I gripped the table as I waited for the strobe in my vision to slow, to recover from the intensity of the joint sight I had been infused with.

Ilyan moved my hair aside as he pressed his cool hand against my neck, my Drak blood so sensitive that with his touch I was flooded with his words and thoughts, the images of his thoughts coming so fast they flashed in a blur of color.

"Where?" I asked, my voice so strained and elongated it almost didn't sound like me.

"Where what?" I heard Ilyan ask in alarm, the roofline of the city flashing in my mind, the screams of the people echoing in my ears.

I groaned in physical pain as the recall left, leaving me heaving as I tried to fight through the dizziness that still felt like it was trying to move into me.

"Where... is that?"

"Prague."

Ilyan's emotions spiked through me as Sain's answer sent him into a panic. His demand for knowledge came quickly, the context easily understood, even though he spoke in Czech.

The images of his home flowed from him so fast I couldn't stop them. The memories of his life matched up with the sight until all that was left was a jumble of fear and happiness.

Edmund is going to use the Vilÿs to attack Prague. To use the humans to create an army, a magical race that only he can control. I sent the words into Ilyan's mind as I looked into him, his wide eyes boring into me.

"When?"

Soon, I wanted to answer him, to send the words to him, but I couldn't.

The time table made no sense. Edmund was due to arrive in Rioseco at any time, to fight in the battle that the sight had shown would be his end. When I would kill him.

Which could mean one of two things.

I would either fail and give Edmund a chance to build his army, or the attack against Ilyan's beloved home had already begun.

Ilyan's eyes were desperate as I looked into him, his pained need for knowledge breaking my heart. I couldn't tell him.

"It's too late," Sain answered for me. "It has already begun."

Ilyan's eyes widened as his jaw clenched, the look in his eyes almost haunting. I could feel his anger and feel the pain over the knowledge that he could do nothing.

I grasped Ilyan's hand, desperate to give him the calm he needed—desperate to help him find clarity—when a yell broke out from somewhere in the abbey. A deep, masculine scream that echoed through the stone hallways of the abbey before it reached us.

My blood sped at the sound. My hand wound tightly around Ilyan's as the sound came again, Ilyan's fear at a possible battle flooding into me.

Not yet. I wasn't ready yet.

I sent my magic away from me in a tidal wave that crashed over the abbey, filling every nook and cranny until I felt the source of the scream, the answer freezing my blood.

It wasn't the battle.

I had thought I had failed.

Thanks to the fight Ryland and I had gotten ourselves into, no one except Ilyan and I knew what I had tried to do.

What had apparently worked.

Dramin had woken up.

16

_____

DRAMIN.

I spoke the word into Ilyan's mind before I bolted away from the table, my red shoes slipping on the stone as I ran away from the kitchen toward the faint pull of magic that throbbed and pulsed as Dramin tossed in his bed.

I focused on him as I ran, my stomach dropping in alarm as his magic ebbed a bit. The weakening strain worried me that he was slipping away again. I needed to get there before that happened.

I had made it down one hall before voices and footsteps erupted behind me, the thunderous tumult making it obvious that everyone was following me. I picked up my pace as I turned the last corner, my feet slipping on the rubble from where I had thrown Ryland into the wall. I could see the wide door just ahead, the wooden slab inset in the stone.

I took the last few steps at what felt like a snail's pace, though I knew I was running; the door swung open as the flare from my magic pushed it. When I slid into the door frame with a loud grunt, Dramin turned toward me, his green eyes hooded and tired.

Everything stopped as our eyes met, my face heating and burning as I looked into the bright sheen in his eyes. I had thought I hadn't been able to heal him; I had thought I had failed. I couldn't have been happier to be wrong.

"Uncle."

"Silnỳ." His voice broke and cracked as his weak body tried to push himself to sitting.

I couldn't help the smile that spread across my face, my joy at seeing him awake temporarily trumping the guilt I felt at putting him there. I entered the room at a dead run, my arms wrapping around Dramin as I tackled him, pushing him right back down onto the bed.

He grunted at the impact, his arms stiff before they came to wrap around me, his touch calm and hesitant. I felt the soft touch on my back, and I snapped, my guilt and sadness tumbling together until they ran down my cheeks in warm streams.

"I am so sorry," I sobbed into him, my voice breaking as my chest heaved, everything in me tightening in despair. "I d-didn't mean to. I am s...sorry."

I pushed the words out the best I could, hating when the stutter came back yet pushing past it. I needed to tell him. I needed him to know that it had been an accident. I needed him to understand.

"Silnỳ," Dramin said in my ear, his voice so soft I could barely hear him. "Dear child, you did nothing other than what the sight had shown, nothing other than what was in your heart, and I do not fault you for that. I never could."

His arms wrapped tighter around me, his words digging into my soul as the tears came faster. The weight that had hidden itself in the deep pit of my heart vanished, taking a tiny bit of the stress I had harbored with it. I gasped for breath as my body relaxed, the now joyful tears that slid down my face increasing as I felt the others enter the room.

"Dramin," Ilyan gasped from the door, his voice a wave of awe that washed over us. His quick gait pounded through the surprised silence, his hand landing lightly on my hip as he came up beside us.

"You are well, my friend," Ilyan whispered, the emotion choking his voice away.

Dramin looked toward him and chuckled, the sound that I had grown so used to—the sound I had missed so much—warming me. I had almost expected never to hear it again. Hearing it lifted the fear that had lived in my heart and warmed the chill that had dwelled in this room. It was its own form of magic.

"You're alive."

The irritation that was so normal in Thom's voice was choked by his joy, his face pale from where he stood in the doorway. I moved to the side as Thom rushed to his friend, embracing him as a brother. The two men clung to one another as Wyn and Sain helped Ryland into the room, his agitation obviously growing alongside the heightened emotions that surrounded him.

They moved in slowly until Sain caught sight of the scene in front of him. He froze in place, the deep emotion that I had wanted so desperately to see over the past few days glistening down his cheeks.

"Můj syn," he whispered, and although I didn't understand the words, I caught the meaning, the joy at seeing his son alive.

Sain rushed forward before the echo of his voice had fully faded, his feet stumbling over themselves in his desperate need to reach his son.

"Tatí," Dramin whispered, the break in his voice making it clear that he, too, was weeping, but I didn't see that.

All I saw were his hands wrapped around my father's. His father's.

All I saw was the greeting that I had so desperately wanted, the love behind it one that I wasn't so sure I hadn't pushed away.

Jealousy rocked through me, green and bitter in my veins. I stumbled away from Ilyan's side, fighting the need to run away and destroy something, to scream, to mourn what I had lost when Cail had murdered my mother.

A family.

The realization rocked through me, my heart clenching as it felt what I had been trying so hard to ignore. I think a large part of me had healed Dramin because it was the right thing to do. However, another, much smaller part had broken my father's rule in desperation to gain back the closest thing that had felt like family.

To prove that I didn't need him.

"My boy, my boy," Sain said as tears streaked down his cheeks, his words adding yet another stabbing pain to my heart. "You're alive. After so long…" Sain's voice trailed off into Czech as he clung to Dramin's hand.

My heart seized with want as I watched them, pain moving through me as it tried to drum up the anger that I was working so hard to hide. I couldn't stay here. I let the shaking sadness out and moved toward the door, staying in the shadow and as close to the shelved wall as I could in an attempt to go unnoticed.

"I don't understand," Sain said, "Joclyn saw your death. How is this possible?"

I froze in place at the sound of my name, my eyes shifting toward them as I pressed my back into the high shelving. For the first time since Sain had come to him, Dramin looked up to me, his eyes widening at where I stood, waiting for the reprimand to come. I looked into my brother, but instead of frustration, I saw the pride that he had looked at my father with a few minutes before. My chest loosened with that look, my heartbeat steadying with the hope of being welcomed.

"Joclyn healed me, Tatínek."

To me the words were a calm, comforting cloud of acceptance, however my father heard anything but. His focus snapped to me, the pride in his green eyes vanishing.

"You healed him? After I commanded you not to?" Sain asked, the disgust in his voice catching me off guard, and I flinched, wishing I could hide myself into the shadows for one breath of a second before the girl I had become came shining through, leaving the girl my father had abandoned behind.

"Commanded me?" I asked, unable to keep the scoff out of my voice. "You wanted me to let him die."

"It was what your sight guided you to do."

"The sight was wrong."

Sain's eyes widened at my words, his anger strong before it slid from his face, leaving him blank. I knew I should have felt bad for saying that, to deny something that I knew he revered, but I couldn't stop the words. I couldn't lie to him just to try to win his affection. It was not who I was. Not anymore.

"The sight was wrong? How can you say such things? No Drak would say such things."

"Then maybe I am not a Drak, *Sain*," I said, snapping his name out in disgust. "Letting someone I love die is wrong."

My words were hard; I knew it. I knew it, and I didn't care. This wasn't like the fight with Ilyan—when I had said things that I didn't mean—because I meant these. I needed him to understand me.

I stepped closer, my eyes pinned on Sain, knowing that if I looked anywhere else, my resolve would weaken.

"Do not deny the gift the earth... the mud has given you..." Sain said, his voice finally moving above that calm tone to rumble through the air around us.

"What gift?" I interrupted him, the screech in my voice hitting a level I hadn't heard since before Santé Fe. "You make it feel like a curse. A curse I want nothing to do with. I do not want to die. I do not want him to die. Not every sight can be true, Sain."

"You speak of things you do not understand," Sain hissed, the sound as quick and painful as if someone had slapped me.

"I can't understand what I don't know," I snapped back, hating how my defenses had gone up just by looking at him. "I can feel the power of the sights in my bones, but even with that, how can I walk into battle knowing that I am going to die? How can I let Dramin die if my magic begs me to heal him?"

I extended my hands toward him in hope of an answer —almost pleading with him to tell me—but he stood still, the hard glaze in his eyes boring a line of pain right to my heart.

I dropped my hands as I forced myself to look away from him, my eyes darting around the room as I tried to process the denial I had just experienced. Wyn stood by the door, her lips a hard line as she watched, the confusion on her face as clear as I was sure it was on mine. Thom's joy had been temporarily trumped by his standby scowl as he tried to make sense of the anger that had taken over such a joyous moment.

Ilyan stood a few feet away from me, his arms folded across his chest as he towered over all of us, watching me. He didn't flinch when I looked at him, making it clear he was not going to step into this verbal assault I had gotten myself into. His eyes met mine and his lip twitched into a small smile, the love that shone through his eyes seeming to recharge the control over my madness that my father's disappointment had weakened.

"Tell me why, Sain."

"You healed him because of your own fear, Silnỳ, because of your regret at what you did to him. You acted on a selfish, mortal desire, nothing more."

A selfish, mortal desire. No. It was so much more than that. I attempted to keep the anger I had so recently controlled in check, but I already knew it was a lost cause. It boiled inside of me, looking for a way out.

"I saved my brother's life. I did what was right," I said in a growl. I did not need to explain myself, not to him.

"No. You have changed the forces of the sights with a childish choice. You have destroyed us."

I had wanted an answer, but instead I only got more questions, and judging by the way everyone's eyes narrowed toward Sain, I could tell that I wasn't the only one.

"What are you saying?" Wyn's voice shook from where she stood by the door, her query putting voice to what everyone else was thinking.

"You change the sights, you change the world. Is it that hard to understand?" Sain spoke to everyone around us before glaring back at me as if I was the one who had asked the question, the one who had changed the world.

"Why haven't I been told of this before?" Ilyan asked, his voice rumbling in anger.

"Not all the knowledge that the Drak possess is meant for you, Ilyan."

"So I am noticing." Ilyan's anger washed through me as he scowled at Dramin before his eyes glanced back to Sain. "I am king of this people, Sain. I should know..."

"And I am of the first! I will keep from you what I deem."

"You will keep nothing from me!" Ilyan roared, the defiant glare that Sain had born into him melting away.

"The sights of my people are infallible; it is the choices of others that burn them away."

"Are you meaning to say that we could fail? That the fight, that all of this... is for nothing?" Ilyan's voice roared through the room, his anger so volatile that I flinched.

"Anything is possible now, My Lord," Sain said, the glare of his eyes darting toward me again. "If this is to be one of the Zlomený, there will be a sign that it has broken, but for now all is still in place."

"That really doesn't comfort me, Sain," Ilyan growled as he moved closer to me, his hand pressing against mine for the briefest of moments before it was gone.

Ilyan's rancid anger remained heavy in me as he moved away. I fought the urge to reach out and hold him, to push my magic into him and calm him, but Ryland's head had jerked up at Ilyan's close proximity to me, his supposed ownership flashing in his eyes. It was better not to try his patience right now—the emotions in the room were high enough as it was.

"I am sorry, My Lord, but I cannot control the foolish changes others would make." The timber in Sain's voice changed as he spoke, his eyes burning right back toward me. "Their magic should have told them as much."

"My magic told me to heal him!"

"No Drak magic would do such a thing."

"What do you want from me?" I screamed as I rushed toward him.

I didn't know what he expected of me. I wasn't even sure what I expected of him, but it wasn't this. It wasn't this man, who looked so much like my father and spoke in that calm determination that cut through me. It wasn't this Drak who expected impossible things from me.

"I expect you to do as my bloodline demands of you!" Sain yelled, his voice darkening as his eyes did, the green fading to the black of sight. I cringed against it, not wanting to hear what was coming. "In the end, when the sky rains fire, a new life will rise as another falls, and in your hands is our salvation."

My breath caught in my chest as his eyes lightened. I could feel my magic grasp at the sight he had just given, desperate to understand it. I held it back though, *I* didn't care. Not right then. I don't think I would have cared if the sight had told me exactly how to kill Edmund. I didn't want to hear it. Not from him.

"It is your destiny."

"I will decide my own destiny," I growled through gritted teeth, my eyes digging dangerously into his before I turned away, unwilling to see any more.

"Is that why you are treating her like a pariah, Tatínek? Because it is her destiny?" Dramin's voice was soft from behind me.

"She should know of our ways, accept them, and become better than us. If she is to become all that I have seen, then it is the only way," Sain growled. I could tell just by listening to the tone in his voice that he believed that. That he doubted nothing.

I couldn't.

In the sights, I had seen the amazing things that were

expected of me, but it wasn't until Ilyan held me—until Ilyan supported me—that I had felt even a sliver of possibility of being the girl I had seen. If Ilyan had taught me anything, it was to do what was right.

I couldn't deny that.

"You must let her become who she is, not who you saw, Tatínek. The rest will come," Dramin said with the deep parental wisdom I had expected from him.

"I have never believed in such trifles, my son. I expect more of those who hold my blood."

"I know this, Tati, but she does not. Perhaps it is time that you think of what needs she has of you," Dramin said softly as his hand reached toward mine, pulling me to him. "I have seen her overcome amazing trials, accept herself for who she is, and accept her title..."

"But it is not enough," Sain interrupted him with a growl. His words made everything feel like such an oppressive weight against my heart that I could barely breathe.

I looked toward Ilyan, his eyes soft as he looked into me, the pride I had sought for during the past few minutes so strong within him that it caught in my chest, my heart swelling comfortably as Ilyan gave me what I had so desperately been looking for.

A family.

My body seemed to swell in a white light at the realization, the fight that raged around me meaning nothing now.

"Stop, Tatínek," Dramin rumbled, his harsh words making his own father stop in his tracks. "You are speaking like an old man kept too long in the dark. Do not let Edmund's poison infiltrate your soul. Even you know that your sight told us—that only her Protector can make her strong enough. It is only Ilyan who can make her who she needs to be."

I saw Ryland flinch out of the corner of my eye at the use of Ilyan's name in connection to me, yet I couldn't look away from Ilyan. Dramin's strong grip on my hand was the only thing keeping me from running to him.

"Ilyan has been with her through all, training her, protecting her, keeping her safe even at night when the nightmares plagued her. When Cail stole her mind, he held her," Dramin said as he pleaded with our father, begging him to see what everyone else had seen all along.

"Is this true?"

"Yes. It is my birthright, my desire, to protect her, and I will do all in my power to see that happen," Ilyan said, the royal tone in his voice catching me off guard after the gentle look I had just seen in his eyes. He broke the spell he had trapped me under as he looked toward my father.

"You have held her through all of it?" Sain asked, his voice strangely soft and accepting after the rejection I had been plagued with.

"Always," Ilyan's voice was so soft, so calm, as he walked up to me, his body so close I could feel the heat of his skin against my bare arms.

I looked toward him, sure that the message was more to me than to Sain. My hands shook with need as I reached toward him, desperate to feel the pulse of his magic, the warmth of his skin, and to have our souls move back to where they belonged.

Ilyan's eyes captured me as he answered my call, his hand pulling me into him as his magic plunged into me at the touch. I pulled his magic into me, our souls relaxing as they moved together. I sighed at the contact, my head moving to rest against his chest.

"Get your hands off her!" Ryland's rabid scream broke the peace that had consumed me. The walls rocked as his magic exploded along with my own fear and anger.

The room filled with the loud crack of wood as the mugs full of Black Water on the shelf behind us tumbled from the now broken shelf. I clung to Ilyan on instinct, a shield erupting from me as Black Water rained down on us, the strong barrier keeping the acidic water away from Ilyan.

"Don't tell him what to do!" I roared as my magic crackled between my fingers, the silver sparks casting long shadows through the dim room.

I stepped toward him in a fury, my hands raising just as Ilyan wrapped his arms around me, pulling me into his chest. I fought the hold as my anger sparked, my magic erupting from me as the room began to shift beneath our feet.

"No, my love," he whispered into my ear as he tried to calm me, the warmth of his magic tunneling through me in desperation.

I tried to move past his tight hold as Wyn pushed Ryland to the ground, Sain and Thom rushing to her aide. His howls of anger lessoned, whereas mine only grew. My soul ached as I kept Ilyan away from me, the anger growing.

"I am safe, my love, you saved me," Ilyan whispered, the gentle reminder rumbling through my fury.

He was safe.

I pressed myself into Ilyan while I kept the shield strong, his arms keeping me against him as I steadied my breathing, as I pushed the anger away.

"I'm sorry, Ilyan. I didn't mean...I just lost track..." Ryland whimpered as he calmed. His body relaxed as he leaned against the wall with Wyn and Sain surrounding him.

"It is all right, brother," Ilyan said as he loosened his tight grip. "I understand."

Ryland only nodded as he looked away, his curls bobbing as he hit his head against the wall in pained desperation.

"I'm sorry," I whispered as Ilyan moved me into the darkened corner of the room, not knowing who my words were meant for.

"Are you all right?" Ilyan whispered down to me as his fingers trailed over my skin.

"Yes," I sighed as Ilyan's magic continued to flood me. I knew I didn't need his power to calm me anymore, but the warmth was so familiar, so comforting, that I wasn't about to push him away yet.

"I am proud of you, my love," Ilyan whispered, his hand pressing against my cheek, my heart moving to beat in time with his.

For not trying to kill anyone?

"That, too. But more for confronting your father, for showing him your strength." His accent was thick as he looked down to me, his eyes brimming with so much emotion it was all I could do not to lean forward and hold him. So I held onto his hand tighter, the warmth of his skin intoxicating.

"You can help next time," I said with a smile, unable to stop the playful chuckle from leaving my voice as I stepped closer to him.

"Kill someone?"

"No, battle with my father."

"No, my love, some battles are meant for you alone, and this is one. He is your father, and as much as I would have loved to step in, to protect you from the pain I am sure you feel in your heart, this moment may come to define who you are. I want you to discover that for yourself."

I knew he was right. I already felt my shattered relationship with my father becoming a deeper vein of who I was. Before, his abandonment had destroyed me, turned me into a scared little girl who would rather hide than become who I felt inside. Now, his distance was somehow making me stronger, making me want to prove to him that I was better than he saw me.

I wanted to show him that.

I nodded once as I moved into Ilyan, not really caring if Ryland saw. My eyes darted toward him on instinct, but instead of Ryland huddling against the door, I saw the forest miles away, my magic pulling me to the camp where Edmund's guard stood. I saw Ovailia laughing at a letter, her smile wide as she instructed the dozens of men that surrounded her. They stood, miles away from us, their focus on a large map almost identical to the one we had in the kitchen.

Fear rippled through me until every muscle felt bound and useless. I clung to Ilyan as Ovailia looked up—almost as if she could see me—before the vision passed, my brain screaming at me what I already knew. This was not a sight, this was now.

Ovailia was preparing her battle plan with instructions from Edmund in her hand, and that could only mean one thing.

We had run out of time.

17

"Ovailia has received her instructions from Edmund." I spoke the words louder than I had anticipated, my voice hollow and dead.

The noises that had filled the room stopped abruptly at my words; even Ryland's mumbled sobs slowed and morphed into whimpers. A powerful surge of determination rumbled my bones as Ilyan stiffened beneath me.

I looked up to Ilyan, the corners of his mouth twitching beneath the powerful mask that he tried to hide behind. His eyes glowed with power as he looked into the darkness of the room, the depth of his eyes showing me things I knew I couldn't possibly understand.

My heart restarted at seeing that look, my nerves supercharging at Ilyan's sudden eagerness to fight. I only wished I felt the same.

"Where is she?" Thom growled with a loathing I had never seen from him before, the hatred stronger than what I had even seen in the cave.

The air around Thom rippled as his muscles tensed and

flexed while he silently pleaded with me for an answer, something in the way he looked at me ringing true, the look hauntingly familiar.

"Where the forward guard is," I said, careful to keep my voice level. The traumatic edge of Thom's magic swelled in the air.

Even though Thom was looking at me, I could tell he didn't see me. He was looking at something far away, or maybe even far behind. I waited for him to say something, for his anger to bubble out of him, but he stayed silent before he turned toward the door, ready to take on Ovailia himself.

My arms dropped from Ilyan as he rushed toward his brother's retreating back, my feet planted in place.

Thom tried to make it out of Dramin's room before Wyn intercepted him, her arms wrapping around his waist as she pulled him back. I felt the heat of her magic surge in the air, and Thom yelled in pain as Wyn's magic dropped him to the ground.

I cringed as Thom continued to fight her, Ilyan meeting them in the middle of the room in a tangle of arms and hair, grunts and yells.

"Let me go, Wynifred!" Thom growled as he swung toward Ilyan, a bright blue flame sparking off his skin.

"Put him out, Wynifred!" Ilyan yelled as he blocked the attack, only to have Thom fire another, even though he knew he could never fight Ilyan and hope to win.

Thunder rocked through the room as their screams increased, the room erupting in ear-splitting sound that slithered through me. The noise ignited my fears as it did Ryland's, his fingers clawing in his hair as he rocked and moaned on the floor, grey sparks flaring in the air with his mania.

My own fragile sanity tried to take me down the same path that Ryland had spiraled down. The screams grew along with the streaks of Thom and Ilyan's magic as they continued to fill the room. I howled as a shelf to my right exploded in splinters of wood, my feet pulling me toward Dramin on instinct. The wizened man struggled to sit up and grasp my hand, giving me the contact I required.

The room was moments away from implosion when Sain reached Ryland and Ilyan grabbed Thom's arms, restraining Thom against him. Thom balled his fists against his thighs as he gave into Ilyan's hold, knowing he couldn't break free from him.

"Thomas," Wyn pleaded, her hand soft against his face as she tried to get his attention.

Thom's head snapped to her at the touch, the oppressiveness of his anger beginning to lift. I could feel the iron bands around my chest loosen as the waves of his magic left.

"You cannot do this, not now." Wyn's voice was calm, and deeper than what I was used to as she pleaded with him, but the panic was still clear in his eyes. I cringed at the look, clinging to Dramin's hand as I tried to push away the trembling fear.

"Wynifred, please." Thom's desperation filtered through the silence in a low rumble that hindered Ryland's recovery, leaving him shuddering against the wall.

"Not now. I want them to pay, too, but not now." Wyn kept her hand flushed against Thom's cheek as he weakly fought against Ilyan's hold while she looked into his eyes.

She looked at him as if she knew him, spoke to him as if she knew exactly what he was talking about. Spoke about him as if she understood him.

It didn't make any sense.

I had heard Thom comfort her when she was dying. I had seen him hold her as he calmed her, soothed her pain. Right then, she was doing the same to him. I was obviously missing something; it was distressing not knowing what. I looked toward Dramin in question, but he only shook his head, obviously unwilling to enlighten me.

Ilyan dropped his hold as Thom turned to him, his dreads swinging with the quick movement. "Ilyan, brother, he is so close. Please."

A streak of lightning lit the room as the earth shook beneath us, illuminating Thom and Ilyan as they stood still in the light of the storm. Ilyan's lips were a hard line as he pressed his hand against Thom's shoulder. Ryland's arm wrapped around Thom's as he, too, came up behind him.

The three brothers stood side by side in the dim light of the room, the silent comfort they offered each other speaking for them. Their father was coming. Edmund. A father that had harmed each of them, a father who had attempted to destroy each of them, one by one. Even though they all desired his end, they wouldn't let Thom do this on his own. They understood him.

"I know, Thom, but now is not the time, and it is not your place."

"Then when, Ilyan?" Thom asked in little more than a whisper as he glared at Ilyan from behind the thick dreads of his hair.

"Soon," Ilyan said as he stepped away from Thom, a golden glow emanating from his hand as he moved it over the room. The furniture shook as the light he held cast over them, the power he controlled causing the chairs, dressers and tables to slide across the floor and slam against the walls. Dramin's hand was ripped from mine as his bed skated away from me, pressing itself against a table and chairs that Ilyan had already cast aside. The furniture shook against the walls as a massive table sped through the door, the large slab of wood hovering unsupported in the middle of the now cleared space.

I took a hesitant step forward, my heart banging in my chest as Ilyan rushed toward the large map that still lay on the surface. His jaw was a line of steel as he placed a large star next to the 'O' that was already surrounded by half a dozen guards.

I could tell at once that this was different. This wasn't the possible 'what-if' planning everyone had been arguing over before. This was the final stage; this was real.

This was the end.

"When will my father arrive, Sain?" Ilyan asked, his eyes unwavering from the map in front of him.

"The sun will be in the sky." Sain's voice had lowered to the tone of a sight, but his eyes had remained green, his vision focused on the large map that covered the table in front of us, making me wonder if what he had said was sight or knowledge.

"It will begin tomorrow," Ilyan announced, the dread seeping out of his words until they felt like lead and poison in the very pit of my heart.

Angry voices erupted at Ilyan's proclamation, their questions coming in Czech and English so fast that I probably wouldn't have been able to understand what was happening even if I had been able to focus on it.

I couldn't focus on it, however, because the earth had shattered. The air that I was sure I had been breathing a minute ago had vanished, leaving my lungs feeling strangely pained and heavy, like lead weights had somehow been secured around my neck to drag me down.

I had known it would be soon, but to know with

absolute certainty that it was hours away—that I had hours to live—was terrifying.

The dread that had settled in my stomach grew as images of that first sight crashed through my mind, the visions of me strong and powerful, bravely fighting. I saw my face as I fought, Ilyan by my side as he kissed me before he held my body in agony.

Before I died.

I had been trained to fight; Ilyan had showed me how to find who I really was. Part of me still believed I was that person, still had faith that I could do what was needed of me. However, another part of me tensed in fear and saw blood drip down the walls.

Part of me still thought I was weak and imprisoned, the way that Edmund had made me, breaking me down so that I could no longer rise to what I was supposed to be.

Who I wanted to be, though I just wasn't sure I *could* be.

I wasn't sure I could willingly walk into my death.

The fear that had been trying to snake through me won out and my hand shot forward, my shaking fingers wrapping around Ilyan's arm in desperation to find something to steady me.

My fingers pressed into the warmth of his skin, his magic flooding me at the contact, unprompted by him. I could feel his warmth, my nerves calming just with the knowledge that I wasn't alone in this.

I forced the weakling Edmund had created out of me, leaving me with who I really was.

"Umlčet!" Ilyan roared, and I flinched, the heavy magical restraint in his voice catching me off guard. It washed through the air and over my nerves, freezing me in place as the strength of the magic numbed the anxiety.

My gaze darted over the table, to the other stone figures in front of me before the magic released us, freeing us from our prisons, and pushing my emotions back into me with a sting.

"Sorry, My Lord," everyone's mumbled apology came at once.

Ilyan nodded once in acceptance before his focus dropped to the map, ready to lay out the battle plan that was now only hours away.

"The four of you will travel along this path here." Ilyan dragged his finger near the same path he had outlined earlier, deviating enough to avoid the tent full of poisoned Vilÿs this time.

My heart thudded loudly against my chest as I watched the red glitter trail from his finger until it dragged off the map in a line of sparkling light that shot through the darkened room before it fell to the ground and disappeared.

"You will take this path toward the cave at Vitoria. Once you clear this line, take to the air." Ilyan's fingers intersected with the red line he had just made, putting a blue streak through it. Thunder rumbled as his finger dragged over the paper, the flashes of lightning that filtered in through the windows casting odd shadows of the map we all stood around.

"Wynifred, you will need to burn the trail here and here," Ilyan continued, his finger swiping over the map as line after line appeared on the paper.

"How do you wish me to burn it, My Lord?" she asked, her face filled with the same excited frenzy she had had in the LaRue mansion last June, her eyes alight with the anticipation of battle. It was the same look I had seen in Ilyan's eyes, except hers was more of madness than control and power. The look rippled through my spine, and I fought the need to step away from her.

"Slow. Burn the undergrowth and let it linger, you need to keep the Vilÿs off your trail if they escape that tent."

I cringed at the memory of the rabid look in the Vilÿs eyes, their brutality as they descended upon that beautiful city in my sight. My stomach tightened as the vision flashed before me, my confusion at what it meant growing.

I didn't want to think of that city under siege as we stood here. I did not want to think of the army Edmund was creating, and us, helpless to stop it.

"So, begin with the earth, burn the trees and then take to the air." Wyn's eyes glossed over as Ilyan's voice deepened, his eyes boring into her as he leaned across the table, his magic binding Wyn to his command.

"Yes, My Lord," Wyn said, her voice monotone and dead as Ilyan's magic took hold.

I was in awe of the control he demanded, the resounding respect they all held for him. No one moved as Ilyan told them how to lay out their magic, how to fight, how to transport Dramin and Ryland without problem. His confidence radiated over everyone, and even with what we were facing, none of the others looked like they might go hide in the corner and empty the contents of their stomachs.

Only me.

"Joclyn and I will let ourselves be seen here and here, drawing the armies away from this line before we begin the main battle at this camp by destroying the Vilÿs tent and drawing Ovailia's attention." I jumped when Ilyan said my name, my knees threatening to buckle as he detailed my role in the fight.

I watched his hands move over the map, a green trail leaving the tip of his finger in swirls and circles. It was only a shadow of a movement and sound, a faded memory of color. I knew I was looking at it, however, my brain was unable to focus, the rapid pulse of my heart making it impossible to control my breathing.

I wasn't sure if everything was slowing down or speeding up.

"We will begin an hour before dawn," Ilyan announced, the loud echo of his words bringing me back from my panic as his hand pressed against my back, the faint whispers of his worry moving through my mind. My skin warmed underneath his touch, the fabric of my shirt keeping his magic from trailing into me. I gasped at the pressure, knowing that even though his focus was on the map and the plan in front of him, he had heard my panic, and he was worried.

I swallowed hard as his touch left, his voice an echo in my ears as I pushed my fear away, my nerves still wiggling as the map came into focus.

"Spend the next twelve hours to prepare and rest. We will begin before dawn." Ilyan hit his hand against the map, his palm making a loud smack that echoed through the stone room. His fingers were stretched wide as he lifted his hand above the paper; the glittering trails of magic he had made mirroring the movement until hand and lines hovered inches above the map.

His hand froze as the lines glimmered in the dim light, his magic expanding until he flexed his fingers, the pulse of movement sending the glimmering specks of color soaring through the air into each of our minds as Ilyan's magic infiltrated us.

Even though I had barely heard the strategy through my stress, one look at the image that had been placed in my mind's eye and I knew exactly what to do. I saw it in detail as everyone's part was laid before me, I understood it, and I knew that it was going to work.

"The wells of Imdalind will follow you, and bring you peace in life or in death," Ilyan said, his voice strangely sad as the map rolled up in front of us without anyone so much as touching it.

"And to you as well, My Lord, may the wells of Imdalind follow you," everyone said in a whisper, their voices blending together in deep respect.

I looked away from the bare table top to Ilyan just as his hand moved up my back to skim over my bare neck.

"Are you all right?" he asked, his voice soft as he whispered to me, the powerful look in his eyes softening.

"You have been asking that a lot lately," I said, the humor I had hoped to convey swallowed up by nerves.

Ilyan's lip twitched at my attempt to break the strain in the room, his concern burning through me while I tried to find words, tried to come up with something—anything—to tell him, for once wishing he could sense my thoughts as I could his.

Because nothing was coming.

We stared at each other, somehow knowing that was enough. That just standing near each other was enough. And even though nothing felt okay, somehow everything was.

"My Lord?" Sain said from somewhere beside me.

I heard Ilyan's thoughts shift at the call, his features stiffening as the king in him came to life so quickly that I knew he wouldn't be able to ignore it.

"I will be right back," he said, his promise a quick whisper into my soul before he left me.

I stood still, staring into nothing before a slim arm

snaked through mine, Wyn's familiar smile meeting me as I jumped.

"Come on, Jos," Wyn said, a smile on her face even though the situation really could call for anything other than that. "Let's go have a final drink before we all plunge into certain death tomorrow."

I cringed at her words. I could tell they were meant in jest, however, I was sure she had no idea of what they really meant to me. Of how true they really were.

She pulled me away from the table and dragged me— half-tripping, half-walking—across the room. I fought against her lead, my eyes darting to where Ilyan stood with his hands wrapped around Ryland's as he mumbled something I couldn't hear.

"Don't worry about your boyfriend." My head snapped to her at the term, the familiarity of it almost catching me off guard, but she only smiled with that wide smile of hers, making it clear she had chosen that word on purpose. "He will catch up, I promise. If anything, this will get him out of the room quicker." She laughed at her own joke.

I let myself fall in step beside her as we weaved our way through the disheveled furniture and out into the hall. The door closed behind us with a bang that sounded like a cannon, and I flinched, my muscles and joints tightening painfully as my anxiety lit itself into an aggressive fire. I fell against the stone wall next to the door as I tried to control it —tried to push it away—yet it didn't seem to be helping and the openly worried look that Wyn was giving me was not exactly helping me to win the emotional battle I was waging.

"I'm fine," I grumbled in answer to the unasked question, glad when her face relaxed, giving me a chance to calm the firestorm of nerves that was waging within me.

I kept my breathing even as I pushed the last of my anxiety away, the uncontrollable emotions leaving until all I was left with was the panic of what would come tomorrow. I knew I couldn't push that away, however, even if I wanted to. That panic was different than what Cail had given me; it didn't turn my world upside down, it only made me more aware, and I kind of liked that. I would take 'aware' over 'psychotic break' any day.

"I'm fine," I repeated as I pushed off the wall, moving away from her in what I hoped was going to be the right direction.

"So..." Wyn said, the way she lengthened her vowels, making me worried for what was coming. As long as she didn't mention my inability to manage my emotions, I think we would be good. "Speaking of boyfriend..."

Or not.

"We weren't," I let my voice growl, desperately hoping she would drop the subject, even though I knew she wouldn't.

She didn't, and the mischievous grin on her face grew before the most embarrassing phrase known to man tumbled off her tongue. "Is Ilyan a good kisser?"

"What?" I practically shrieked, knowing right away that my frantic outburst had given me away. Even though she had figured it all out before, there was no way I could get out of her demanding a full play-by-play now.

"I knew it," she cooed, causing every single blood vessel in my body to freeze in place. "Spill."

I exhaled, knowing that I wouldn't tell her anything. It wasn't a conversation I wanted to have.

"No," I said, my voice distorted as I ground my teeth in embarrassment.

"Oh, come on! It's not like it's a secret or anything.

Although why you want him to kiss you, I have no idea." She said it just like she always had and my head spun toward her at the familiarity.

Now she talked about him like she was grossed out by him, like she had before when Ilyan had trained me at the motel. Not like this morning, not like earlier when Ilyan had laid out the plan. It was like the many faces of Wyn. I thought I had known her, but now I just couldn't keep up. I narrowed my eyes at her, almost willing my sight to come so I could figure out what she was playing at.

"What?" she asked, obviously confused by the look I was giving her.

"You didn't seem so adverse to the idea this morning," I said, my eyebrows arching as I waited for an explanation. She, however, looked at me like I was crazy. "You came to our room, and looked at him like you wanted to eat him. Not like he was disgusting."

"Now you are sounding a tad bit jealous."

"No, I'm just confused. Last I heard, you didn't like him and wouldn't try to hit on him like you did this morning."

"Hit on him?" she asked, her eye roll so exaggerated that I knew she was hiding something. "Whatever."

She scoffed like it was some big joke, like I had just imagined it. I didn't know why, but it cut through me. Who knew, maybe I *was* being a bit jealous. Jealous or not, it didn't change the pain I saw in her eyes, the way she avoided me. It didn't change that somehow, I got the idea she had become a different person when Edmund had captured her.

"I know what I saw, Wyn," I said as I pushed into her shoulder a bit, hoping that the somewhat playful gesture would thaw the ice that had encased her.

Instead, it had the opposite effect, and she stopped, her jaw tightening as she held her breath. I didn't know why, but

I almost expected her to attack me. Right then, she felt dangerous. My pace slowed to a stop as I turned toward her, the dim light of the hallway making the valleys of her face darker. The hairs on the back of my neck prickled with fear for the briefest of breaths before her jaw loosened and her eyes softened.

"I just have trouble knowing who I am sometimes."

"What?" I asked, the one word seeming to break the spell that I had somehow put over her, and her head jerked up, her face twisted into a mischievous grin.

"You tell me how good of a kisser Ilyan is, and I'll spill."

Even if I wanted to respond, I had no idea what to say. I had no idea how to explain what it felt like when Ilyan's lips pressed against mine, when his hands pressed me against him. When everything became light, and the world stopped spinning. Every time, it felt like magic before I had known that magic was real, and I could feel the power of the world rejoice as if it was celebrating our union. It was perfect.

The words were in my head, but I knew they would never find a way out.

She knew it, too. She also knew I wouldn't give in. I just stood there, my jaw working mechanically as the thunder from the storm continued to crash around us.

"Just what I thought," Wyn said dreamily, a knowing smile on her face as she turned a corner into another dimly lit section of hall.

I fell into step beside her and she laughed, the sound claiming her supposed victory before she shoved me playfully into the wall next to her, her hand hot like fire against my skin.

With one touch, an inferno burned away the tendons in my hand. I screamed as pain spread through me, the sight of my fingers twisting into weird, broken angles only making the scream that much louder. I pulled my hand away as I tried to stifle my screams and control the nightmare that was threatening to take over.

I stumbled against the wall as the fire moved up my arm, my fingers clawing at the heated skin while the muscles continued to cramp and bend. I could hear the clanging of pipes in my ears, the madness getting closer. I couldn't focus beyond the pain to chase it away, the loud scream that ripped from me only seemed to be bring it on faster.

I bit my lip until I could taste the blood in an attempt to stifle the scream, to keep the insanity from taking over. I felt my magic rush through me, trailing the burn with ice as it attempted to heal me.

Wyn jerked up to me when I yelled, the fear in her eyes almost as painful as the heat that surged through my hand. I expected her to apologize, but she only stared at me, her eyes wide as if she was trying to figure out why I had reacted the way I had.

I shook my hand as my magic extinguished the branding iron that had ignited inside of me, glad when the fire lessened to nothing more than an exaggerated heat and I could focus on keeping my mind intact. I gasped as the ice chilled me, keeping my eyes away from the blood-drenched wall across from me.

"That hurt," I gasped as I closed my eyes, bringing back Ilyan's dream in an attempt to keep the madness away.

"My magic hurt you?" Wyn said, the confusion I had seen on her face even more defined in her voice.

"Burned me more like," I grumbled as I brought my hand up to eye level, almost expecting the skin to be charred away, yet it was smooth, like nothing had happened. Wyn ducked down in an attempt to see better, but didn't say anything, her heart-shaped face screwed up in confusion.

"What happened? Your magic was so cold before."

"It's never done that, moved like that..." She spoke to my hand, her focus a million miles away.

"What has never done that before?" I was trying not to panic, but Wyn's obvious lack of knowledge was not good for my nerves. That was, if I had any left. She may have just burned them all off.

I waited for a response, but none came, so I pulled my hand into my chest in an attempt to get her to stop looking at it.

I don't know what it was about the way she was staring, but she looked lost in thought, her dark eyes haunted by horrors I had never seen before. Something was definitely up, and it worried me.

"Wyn?" I asked when she didn't look away, the blank stare starting to bother me again.

"Sorry," she said sheepishly as her eyes finally shifted back to me. "It's probably just the Drak magic, my Trpaslík blood and all that. Maybe my magic hates you."

Her voice was light, as though she was trying to make a joke, but the sound did not reach her eyes, and I flinched a bit, waiting for whatever was going to come next to jump out and slap me in the face.

"Are you saying we are enemies now?" I asked, unable to help the way my voice cracked in the echoing hallway. I stepped away from her out of habit; that one word seeming to awaken a wild animal, the raw emotion expecting an attack. I knew she hadn't meant it that way, but I couldn't help the way my magic flared. Whether it was in preparation of attack or to run for my life, I wasn't sure. My anxiety was almost too raw for me to control after my last panic attack.

"Well, aren't we? Technically, I mean," Wyn said with an

exaggerated roll of her eyes before she turned and continued down the stone hallways. "Not like I would ever actually attack you."

Her voice echoed back to me as she waved her hand through the air. Her actions made it clear that she hadn't meant it at all the way I had perceived it.

"No!" I yelled as I ran to catch up with her, the loud slaps of my red shoes sounding twice as loud as they really were in the seemingly endless, stone hallway that stretched before us. The large, wooden slabs of the doors were set so perfectly that, if it weren't for the color, I wouldn't have been able to tell they were there at all.

"What?" she asked as she laughed at me. For some reason she obviously didn't believe that I didn't view us as enemies. It seemed like such a weird thought to me, though. She was my best friend. Why would I want to attack her? And yet, somehow she seemed to feel like it was expected that I would try.

"Trpaslík, Drak, Skřítek. Human. Chosen Child. It doesn't mean anything to me," I said as I fell into step next to her.

"Spoken like a true human," she said in a ridiculous baby voice as she patted my head. I batted her hand away, fully prepared to scowl at her, but she only laughed.

"Half-human," I corrected her, unable to stop the smile that spread over my face with the memory of Vienna sausages.

"Whatever. You are kind of everything," she said with a smile, yet the words only wiped out my temporarily good mood.

"So I have been told."

She was right after all. I was kind of everything. Ilyan may be half-Chosen, but he was also half Skřítek. He knew what he was. However, my father was a Drak, my mother a human, and my neck held that mark that had given me every other kind of magic. I *was* a little bit of everything.

"What's it like?" she asked softly, her voice loud in my ear as she leaned in close and wove her arm through mine again. I only groaned at her question, fully expecting her to guilt me into a step-by-step kissing documentary. Instead she pulled me to a stop before one of the many doors that lined these hallways, this one bearing the same handprints I had seen on her door at the motel except now it looked like someone had tried to scrub off the larger handprint with a scouring brush.

My heart clenched together at the faded paint—at her heartbreak—knowing I should look away, but unable to make myself do so.

"What's what like?" I asked, my voice dead.

"Seeing the future?"

I cringed at her question; no part of me wanted to answer it, not after what had just happened with my father. I wasn't even sure why she wanted to know. After all, she had stood there, watching my father berate me for being a useless Drak only minutes after sharing a sight with him. I guess that didn't really answer her question, though, unless she wanted to know what it was like not to follow sights.

Because that seemed to be all I was good for.

"I dunno; it's fine unless you talk to my father..." I said, a little more bitterly than I had meant to, wishing she would drop the subject.

"Sain is only trying to—" Obviously not.

"Can we talk about something else?" I snapped. I really didn't want to hear the rest of that comment.

"You mean like the day after tomorrow?"

I looked at her in alarm only to be met with a wide smile

that I tried very hard to return, although it didn't quite want to take. My face felt like it had suddenly become devoid of blood, my heart pumping madly against the lead I had been filled with. She knew what tomorrow was, and she knew that there might not be a day after.

"You're scared about tomorrow, aren't you?" Wyn asked, making it evident that my fear was as clear on my face as it felt. I just looked at her without knowing what to say. If I should even talk about the sight; if I even believed it.

Wyn shook her head at me like I was the most pathetic thing she had ever seen, and I guess that in some ways that's exactly what I was. I looked away from her sheepishly, suddenly feeling that old, introverted part of me coming on strong. Wyn pushed off from the door she was leaning against, her arm reaching up to drape around my shoulders. She almost looked like she was going to impart a secret wisdom passed down for generations, but instead, she did what Wyn did best.

She pulled out the Styx.

"*I know you feel these are the worst of times....*"

"Wyn, don't..." I begged, but she only smiled wider and sang louder, her horribly off-pitch voice echoing off the stone and rippling back to us, bringing the laugh out whether I wanted it to or not.

"*The best of times!*" She stepped away from me to dance through the hallway, her movements crazed and wild.

She spun and danced before making one last spin and ending up in front of me, her hand extended like a microphone, obviously expecting me to provide the last word.

I restrained the last of my laugh as I stared at the microphone, knowing there was no way she would let me off the hook.

"Paradise," I said, knowing I had totally rained on her parade.

She, however, only smiled wider before grabbing my hand and dragging me into her room.

"Close enough."

18
_____

I COULD TELL THAT, at some point, Wyn's room at Rioseco had looked closer to the room I had seen at the motel. One wall was painted neon green, and the bed had been pushed up against another wall where several large rectangles of stone appeared to be cleaner than the rest. Shelves were emptied, carpets rolled up and put aside, and the garbage overflowed with band t-shirts and the posters that had once graced the walls. The bed had been stripped bare, the old, stuffed mattress instead covered with a single woven blanket that looked oddly similar to the one that had hung over Thom's bunk in the cave in Italy.

Her room was a window into the heartbreak she was feeling, and looking at it made me feel filthy and somehow unworthy to be here. Not ten minutes before, we had walked down the hall, her suffering showing as she spoke of not knowing who she was. I should have pressed her, found a way to help her, but instead of sharing with her one thing, I had shut her down.

It made me feel sick to my stomach.

"I would ask you if you wanted something to eat, but I

just cleaned the floors," Wyn's voice floated to me from somewhere within the depth of the room. I turned toward it, expecting her to emerge, but I faced nothing other than more destroyed remains of her life. I stood still, waiting for her to return while I tried not to let the fear that standing in the open, unfamiliar space was giving me.

"Funny," I said into the empty room, knowing my voice wasn't loud enough for her to hear.

Wyn appeared a minute later from what I could only assume was a kitchenette, her hands full of tall, clear glasses and an archaic looking bottle. She smiled brightly as she bounded over to me before setting her bounty on the low coffee table I stood next to.

"I can't drink that, either," I said matter-of-factly.

"You wouldn't want to," she said as she carefully organized the glasses. "It's a two thousand year old whiskey. It'll make your hair fall out."

My eyes widened at her words, and although I wanted to say she was joking, one look at that bottle had me wondering. The bottle was brown and so dust covered that it looked like Wyn had dragged it out of some long forgotten attic, rather than a prized collection. Most of the label had long since disintegrated and what little was left was written in what I was sure was Czech.

"Lovely," I said, suddenly glad I had a reason to casually decline. I wasn't sure what was in there, and it kind of worried me that she would even trust it enough to try. At least my body would rebel against anything I put in it.

"Did you raid some ancient catacombs to get this?" I asked as I grabbed it from off the table, the bottle heavier than I had assumed. The glass was strangely gritty, not like dust, but more like dried fungus.

I was just turning the bottle to see the label when Wyn

snatched it away, her eyes narrowed at me as she set it back down.

"No," she practically snapped, her face hard and frightening.

My eyes widened in confusion at the expression on her face, at the way her eyes dimmed within seconds of the word escaping her lips. My muscles rippled at the darkness behind her eyes, part of me screaming to attack while the other pleaded with me to cry, to scream.

I begged my mind not to view Wyn as a threat, to stop seeing enemies where only friends remained, however, my agitation wasn't sure it wanted to listen. I exhaled shakily as I tried to take control of the fear, hoping that Wyn wouldn't notice any immediate change in me.

"This is the last of the abbey's stock of Slivovica. For the last night."

"The last night?" I asked, my voice trembling before the remainder of my foolish anxieties melted away.

"It's what we call the toast before battle, Jos." Her face was hooded and tensed, a million thoughts and memories weighing her down as she casually touched the ancient cork that had plugged the bottle for longer than I cared to think about.

The cork popped out easily at her touch, leaving the top of the bottle smoking slightly. A heavy smell of fermentation filled the room, rotten fruit and cat vomit mixing together as it hit my nose. The stuff smelled terrible, worse than any of the wine that my mother had served to Edmund for all those years—and I thought that stuff had been foul. I scrunched my face up in a foolish attempt to block the smell while trying to be polite and not run gasping out of the room.

Add another reason why I would never put that stuff in

my mouth.

If only I had brought a mug with me, then at least I could drink of the Black Water and drown out the smell with my water's strong aroma.

"We call it the last night because it is the last night for many of us. Not only for this battle, but for all of them. And this war has been going for quite a while," Wyn said softly, the calm sadness of her voice pulling my mind off the smell and right into her words.

My heart pumped faster, the pain moving through me so fast that I was barely able to fight the sob that tried to seep out. She was right; it was the last night for many of us. Not only me.

It was my last night.

Strangely, seeing the sadness on her face—thinking of the thousands who had lost their lives before me—had numbed the fear. It's not that it wasn't there anymore—because it was—it just didn't bother me as much as it had only minutes ago. The mind-numbing fear had disappeared, leaving me with a sadness for what I was going to lose; for the short time I had been given to experience it.

"Oh." It was the only word I could manage. I didn't know what to say after that. I wasn't sure I could trust myself to say anything.

"Don't worry," Wyn said as she turned to face me again, her glass now full of a foggy red liquid. "I am sure Ilyan will be fine. I don't think he is capable of dying."

I gasped at her words, at the misplaced worry so startling my chest tightened under the pressure.

"Wyn?" I started, my pulse quickening as I fought the need to tell her, to tell her everything. I wanted to tell her of the sight, of what was coming for me, of what was expected. However, part of me said she already knew, and even if she didn't, I wasn't quite sure how I would begin to have that conversation. I wasn't sure I was ready to say goodbye.

She had already lost so much.

"I—" I tried again, part of me grateful when she interrupted me.

"I didn't mean it that way, Jos." She said it with the obvious intention to put me out of my misery. *I* didn't mean it that way, though; not in the way that she had taken it. Not in the way that her voice cried toward me.

I looked away from her to the green wall, to the garbage can by the door overflowing with things that had made Wyn who she was: band t-shirts, feather earrings, posters. I stared at the pieces of her broken heart, crumpled and tossed away, my heart breaking right alongside her.

A deep rumble of thunder vibrated through the abbey, this one bigger than the others had been, and my focus pulled from what I had been saying to what I needed to say. What I needed to help her with.

"I know," I said, my voice soft as my heart rumbled painfully with what I was about to say.

I breathed in and closed my eyes, my magic stretching away to make sure I still had time before Ilyan and Thom arrived, only to sense them stalled a few feet before the door. I needed to make this quick.

"When Ilyan kisses me, I feel like my whole soul is going to fly away into Heaven. His touch is like a numbing fire; his passion is so encompassing that I don't feel like anything could drag him away from me, that even death couldn't take away the way I feel for him."

I had begun with the intention of speaking very fast—of giving in to her request in the hopes that she would give in to mine—but the moment I opened my mouth, the memory of Ilyan's touch, the feel of his lips on mine, pushed through the embarrassment and my voice slowed, my eyes lost in the depth of my memories.

"Wow," Wyn said as dead-panned as she could possibly manage, her glass perched in her hand as she stared at me. "Thanks for sharing."

"Wyn," I practically whined as I stared into her, trying my hardest not to stomp my foot in indignation.

I wasn't going to let her get away from me that easily. I could tell by the look in her eyes that she knew exactly why I had said what I had.

I scowled at her as she stared at me, her eyes softening bit by bit until she groaned and set her glass down on the table. Her fingers remained pressed against the condensed surface as she looked into it and her breathing slowed.

I wanted to help her, but I was suddenly beginning to wonder if, instead, I had only caused her more pain.

"I felt the same way. I *feel* the same way," she said softly, her focus still on the glass that the tips of her fingers ran over, the soft touch leaving glistening trails on the glass. "But it's half. One half gone and the other half confused as to whether I ever felt that way in the first place. As to which love was real, or if either of them were."

"What do you mean?"

"Sometimes, I think it possible to love too much, to hurt too much. To live too many lives. I thought I was all right, but Thom has only confused me more."

"Wyn?" I stood still as I watched her fingers on the glass, waiting for her to continue, to make sense of the small insight she had granted me.

She never did. She just looked down, her magic ebbing until I couldn't feel it in the air around me like before. She brought it into her as she broke apart, a feeling I knew all too well.

"Is that why you tore apart your room?" I asked, my soft voice sounding strangely loud in the broken pieces of her heart that the room had trapped around us.

"I don't know where I fit anymore."

"Without Talon?" I asked, my tongue tripping over his name, fully aware he had been the elephant in the room until I let it slip from my tongue.

Sure enough, her body tensed, her eyes darting to look away from me to the door on the other side of the room, almost as if she expected Thom and Ilyan to burst through, but they hadn't moved since I had last felt them.

I could see the pain she still held from her loss in the way she held her body, the sadness and confusion that hid behind her eyes. I wished I could take that loss away; I wished I could make her feel like she wasn't alone.

The hardest part was that I knew I could. I could take away her pain. I wanted to.

I just wished that she hadn't hated what I had to say.

"I can still feel his magic inside of you, you know," I said, careful to speak slowly as I tested the waters for what I had to tell her. "Deep down."

"You can?" she asked, her eyes widening with a deep desperation that rocked through me.

I nodded, keeping my eyes on hers, begging her to understand; to know I was telling the truth. "You do fit."

"I don't," she said, her focus dropping back down to the glass again. She grabbed it, bringing the foul-smelling liquid to her mouth before she drained it in one gulp, a soft bang echoing through the room as she slammed the cup back down to the table. "It's complicated."

"You can tell me. I can get some ice cream." I plastered a wide smile on my face, even though it felt out of place. I wanted her to smile; I wanted her to feel comfortable enough to tell me. To let me help.

It did the trick; she smiled, and a small laugh escaped her as I repeated the words she had given me. She laughed as I did, the sound of our artificial joy evaporating much faster than I would have liked.

"You're one of the first friends I have ever had, Jos." The last of her laugh faded into nothing as she reached forward, wrapping her hand around mine. I held onto her hand tightly, my heart clenching at her words, at the memory of that first day, and of every day since.

"Mine, too."

"I know," she whispered, her grip on my hand tightening, "so do me a favor. If you really feel that way about Ilyan, don't let him get away, even if you both are going to die tomorrow. One day of promise would be worth it. It's better than having none. You'll regret it if you don't."

The smile that had lingered on my face faded as ice washed over me. I knew what she was talking about. I didn't need it spelled out because I had heard my heart plead the same words to me. I had held them safe, not really trusting myself to agree.

"What are you talking about?" I asked, even though I knew. Even though I could feel my heart rate increase, even though I could feel each push of blood through my body. I knew.

The earth seemed to spin faster as I looked at her right as the door swung open soundlessly behind her, and Thom and Ilyan walked in. Ilyan's face smoothed at seeing me, his eyes lighting up. My heart rate relaxed as unabashed joy spread through my joints. I felt it rock through me in a pleasant ocean of happiness.

That was, until Wyn spoke, and the words that came out

of her mouth sent my joy into a wave of nerves and embarrassment.

"Bond yourself to Ilyan, Jos," she said, oblivious to the boys behind her. The blood drained from my face, the look of shock and embarrassment mirrored in Ilyan's face as my vision focused on him—my nerves unable to respond—even though I begged them to look away.

"Don't wait," Wyn continued.

My eyes widened as her hands gripped around my forearms, bringing my attention back to her and away from the way all the blood had drained from Ilyan's face.

"If I had known I only had a day, only an hour. If I had known everything when I had made the choice," Wyn's voice broke as she looked into me, her eyes shining with the emotion she had tried so hard to keep away, "I would still do it again in a heartbeat."

"That is awfully deep for you, Wynifred," Thom barked as he strode into the room, his deep voice only increasing the uncomfortable, smothering blanket that had covered me. He laughed as his hand slid over Wyn's shoulder, causing her to freeze in place, her eyes widening in as much fearful embarrassment that had been raging through me for the past few minutes.

Her jaw dropped slightly before she recovered, her mouth shutting with a snap as she turned to glare at Thom.

"Yes, well, what can I say? I am a shallow pool of misery, Thom." Wyn dropped my arms as she spoke, her body quick to turn and grab one of the other glasses she had filled minutes before.

She said nothing else as she drained the glass in one gulp, slamming it on the table as she had with the last one before she walked toward Ilyan, her face screwing itself up into a mischievous grin.

"Do yourself a favor, Ilyan. Think of yourself every once in a while. It's what Talon always said. He worked so hard for you because he wanted you to have something for yourself. You can't think of everyone else all the time. Find your own happiness." Wyn said it all very quickly, her sass seeping out like some sort of poison as her words slurred together.

I stiffened at her bluntness, the way she spoke to Ilyan more shocking than what she had said. I swallowed as I forced myself to look away from the rebuttal that I was sure Ilyan was going to dish out.

Nothing came.

"Thank you, Wynifred."

I would have expected Wyn to shy away from the acid in his voice, yet she stood still, her body swaying slightly as the over-potent alcohol began to take effect.

Ilyan looked down at her briefly before he moved away, walking right up to me and wrapping his arm around my shoulders. He said nothing as he held me against him before his hand slid down my arm, his fingers intertwining with mine.

I could feel that his body was somehow warmer than it had been before. Everything felt heavier just knowing he had heard what Wyn had said. At his touch, my heart rate sped to match the quick drum that lay in Ilyan's chest. I almost cringed at the nervous pressure that had built up inside of him, a shadow of it moving into me as his skin slid against mine. I let my magic flow into him, desperate to hear even a shadow of what he had heard—what he had thought—only to be met by a dark wall of Ilyan's magic.

He had blocked me out.

I could feel his mind, his emotion. I knew they were

there, but what he was thinking—what he was guarding—was kept from me.

Ilyan? I sent to him in my panic. He didn't so much as look at me. He only leaned down and grabbed the last full glass, his eyes focused on the blood-colored liquid in his hands.

"Where did you find the Slivovica?" he asked as his hand tightened around mine. "I had thought we had used the last before we burned the manor in Brno."

I kept my eyes on him as he spoke, waiting for him to look down at me as he always did, but he stayed straight and tall, his frame elongated against me until I felt shorter than I knew I actually was.

Ilyan? I tried again, my heart rate picking up when he once again ignored me. I almost wondered if he could hear me, but I felt his heartbeat pick up as I said his name, his nerves almost setting me on edge. Ilyan was nervous. The simplicity of the thought piqued my own nerves and I shivered, trying not to let my worry take over.

"I found this bottle when I was going through some stuff," Wyn said as she moved to refill the other two glasses that she had already drained. "It's the last one."

Her tone was soft and sad as she overfilled the glasses, causing the liquid to pour down the side and onto the table.

Don't block me out, I pleaded, careful to use the same words he had used with me before. This time I knew he had heard me. His lips turned up ever so slightly as he turned to look at me, the hungry look in his eyes catching me on fire.

My breath caught in my chest as I gazed at him, his smile increasing until he leaned toward me, his lips pressing against the hollow of my ear. I stifled a gasp at the warmth of his lips against my skin, his hand tightening around mine as he pulled me into him.

"I need to speak to you," he whispered, my spine tingling as his breath ran over my skin.

Then talk, I pleaded, not trusting my voice to form cognitive words.

"Not here," he whispered before he pulled away, the grip on my hand loosening until he was gone.

His body was still close enough that I could feel the heat of him; it would only take one short movement to reach out and touch him. Still, that distance could have been a football field. I don't know why, but those two words had somehow closed me off from him. My worry about what was on his mind increased until it was a tight, little ball in my chest.

"The timing couldn't be better." Thom leaned down and grabbed one of the now-filled glasses, his voice pulling me out of the revelry Ilyan had trapped me in.

I stepped toward the table cautiously, not sure where I fit.

"Na zdraví," Ilyan announced, his voice deep and regal as he lifted his glass toward the ceiling.

"Na zdraví," Thom and Wyn repeated in unison as they followed suit, all of the glasses held above their head before they lowered them, draining the contents in one swallow.

The room filled with the thump of the glasses against the table, the sound sending a jolt through me. They stood in silence, their eyes closing as each of their faces turned down in a solemn reverence that I did not quite understand. Watching them—watching a tradition that reached back before much of what I had retained in history class—was awe inspiring.

And lonely.

I felt like I was intruding on something beautiful, something I wasn't quite sure I would ever understand. Wyn silently moved to refill the glasses, none of them speaking before they raised their glasses again.

"To Talon," Ilyan said, his voice breaking on the word, the name of the friend he had lost.

That everyone had lost.

"To Talon," Thom's voice rang clear, but Wyn's stuck in her throat. Even though I saw her mouth move, no sound escaped.

Their hands stayed above their heads before they again drained their glasses, dropping them back to the table. Once again they looked down, their faces masked in pain and regret before Wyn moved to refill her empty cup.

"For my brother, who gave up everything," she said as she filled the one she had just drained, the liquid pouring over the side as her hand began to shake.

She handed the bottle to Ilyan who took it steadily and filled his glass right to the brim.

"For Talon. Goodbye, my friend," he said, his eyes still focused on the glass on the table below him.

I couldn't help it; even though the tight knot of nerves still sat in my heart, I heard the pain in his voice, and my heart reacted. I closed the football-field-sized gap and wrapped my arm around his waist, my fingers curling into the fabric of his shirt as I came to stand next to him. I heard his breath catch as his arm moved over my shoulders, his lips pressing against the top of my head.

Ilyan passed the bottle to me, the glass heavy and uncomfortable in my hands. I looked up to Ilyan, sure he had made a mistake, but he only looked at me, a single nod of his head prompting me to continue.

A shaky breath fled from my chest as I looked at the bottle. I knew what I was supposed to do; I knew who I had lost, who my heart still longed for.

"For my mom," I said as I partially filled the glass, the pressure in my chest growing as wet tears began to cloud my vision. Ilyan's arm tightened around me in support as I passed the bottle to Thom, his hand already shaking as he took it from me.

"For Rosaline. Your life was not in vain, my child." Thom's voice broke as he poured, the glass overfilling before the bottle came clattering to the ground. Wyn gasped at the sound, tears falling in rivers down her cheeks as she moved to wrap her arms around Thom, their bodies pressed close together as they cried into each other.

My heart clenched as his words sunk in, the admission of what each of them had lost in the war sounding louder than a million battle cries. It echoed through my soul, louder than a million cannon booms. I stood still as I watched their faces, the way that Wyn and Thom clung to each other, and my heart broke.

I loved the people in this room, and to see their loss, feel their pain...

I didn't want that to happen, not anymore.

We had all lost someone—someone precious—all at the hands of a man who had built an army, who had declared our end.

I wouldn't let him take anything more from us.

I might still be plagued by the demons Cail had infected me with; I might fear the sights I had been given, the prophecy of my death.

But I was also infected with strength, and with power, and with a reason to fight.

"To happiness," Ilyan said loudly before he pulled me toward the door, leaving the full glasses on Wyn's table.

Leaving them in hopes that our own names wouldn't join them.

19

——————

ILYAN'S ARM was tight around me as we walked down the hall, and even with the awkwardness of our position, we still walked smoothly, his hand steadying me as he held me against him. The way he held me, so soft and gentle, calmed the knot in my chest. Almost. I continued to feel it, the fear of what he wanted to talk about still strong. It was numbed by the calm that being next to him gave me, though.

He hadn't spoken a word since we left Wyn's room. I wanted to know what I had just witnessed—know if he was all right after walking in on Wyn's strange proclamation—but he stayed silent. His face was an expressionless mask as we walked through the dim light from the dilapidated torches that lined the halls, each one casting odd, flickering shadows of light and dark over the stones.

The brightness of the magical light covered the smooth lines of Ilyan's face, giving him dark valleys that made him more intense, more desirable. I refused to look away from him as he led me down the halls, my heart caught between fear and expectation. Even though I was sure he knew I was staring at him, he didn't seem fazed. He just continued to move us forward, staring straight ahead.

"Can we talk now?" I whispered when I couldn't wait anymore, my soft voice pulling him out of a trance as he looked down at me and pulled us to a stop.

I followed his lead, unable to make any other choice as his eyes held me captive. His hand reached up to caress the skin of my jawline as I looked at him, my breath catching at the look in his eyes, the way his touch sent fire and lightning into my spine, the jagged jolts of electricity rushing through me.

I could tell right then that something was different—his gaze was different, his touch was different. Something had changed. I searched him as he held me, his face giving no more clues than the undying love that I already knew he felt. The eternity behind his eyes opened into me as a million words and hopes and memories passed through the depths of our connection before he leaned toward me, his eyes holding mine as his breath blew warm against my face while his nose ran the length of mine. The touch pulsed through me as his ragged breathing flowed over my lips, making me forget how to breathe. The warmth of his touch ravaged any hope of logical sense I had.

I gasped for air before he pressed his lips against mine, the pressure desperate as the warmth of him spread through me. A storm of rejoicing power erupted as our magic met and mingled, the tiny little lights that had become so familiar to us popping and sparkling in the chilled air around us.

Ilyan pulled away before I was ready, his soft touch leaving me reeling, gasping for breath as my soul hungered for more.

Ilyan? I asked, not trusting myself enough to speak

aloud, unable to keep the confusion inside any longer. My question filled his mind and he smiled, his fingers fluttering against my chin as his hands shook, his eyes opening to meet mine again.

"I think Wyn is right," he said softly, his voice moving over my skin and sending chills down my arms, a hundred goosebumps growing to speckle over the skin.

"What do you mean?" I asked breathlessly, my heart thundering in my chest as my heart put possibilities of his meaning into place, possibilities that I couldn't help letting tie my stomach into knots.

Ilyan smiled at my question, his lips twitching playfully as his fingers ran down my neck then over the collar of my shirt until they came to a stop right over my heart, his touch gentle. The treacherous organ beat so fast I was sure he could feel the frantic movement through his fingers, the echo of it inside of him as his own tried to keep time. He smiled wider as the bass beat of it moved through him, the look of pleasure on his face heating my blood.

I tried to control my reactions, foolishly waiting for Ilyan's answer before he wrapped his arm around me and carried me down the hall, his pace quick as he held me against him. Our feet were soft against the lowrumble of thunder that filled the halls, the sound lost in the deep patter of the rain.

Ilyan turned a corner at full speed—a corner I was sure did not take us to his room—before he ducked into the tiny alcove we had tucked ourselves into once before, the closeness of the stone plunging us into almost complete darkness.

I gasped as the darkness moved into me, my heart rate increasing for a completely different reason. Then Ilyan's hand pressed against my neck, his magic plunging into me while his lips crashed against mine. The pressure of them was startling as his hands moved over my back, pulling me against him.

I lost all sense of fear at the touch of his hand against me, the feel of his fingers in my hair before I wrapped my arms around him, my tongue darting over his lips as I clung to him, my lungs forgetting to breathe, my heart too preoccupied to beat. I hungered for him as my magic reacted, filling air and space at his touch, the lights popping in the air until the darkness we had been surrounded by became as bright as day.

I pressed my lips into his, parting them just enough to breathe him in before he pulled away, his forehead warm and strong against mine. I opened my eyes at the change, my chest heaving for breath as the twinkling lights of our joined magic faded into the black.

Ilyan held still against me as he panted, his eyes closed as his skin pressed against mine, my heart thumping wildly in desperation for him to come back to me.

"Bond yourself to me," he gasped through his strained breaths, his voice so soft I wasn't even sure I had heard it right.

"Ilyan?" I asked, my voice shaking in nerves and fear as I tried to process what he had just said.

"My entire life, I have waited for you. I have searched for you. I have worked to become someone worthy of you. And tomorrow, if the sight is true, I will lose you."

He opened his eyes as he spoke, the blue so light they were the color of warm ice, the color freezing me beneath the touch of his warm hands.

I couldn't deny the way my heart beat faster, the way my magic seemed lighter. I wanted this, and I could tell by the look in his eyes that he did, too. As much as my heart rejoiced—as much as my magic swelled and my mind swam in the dangers of what I held inside of me—the words that Ilyan had said days before still pounded in my ears.

"But you said-" I began, my words cutting themselves off as he shook his head, his fingers pressing softly against my lips.

"I know, mi lasko. I know what I said," he interrupted smoothly, "and I was wrong. Wyn was right; Talon was right. For a thousand years, I have done what others have needed of me. All my life, I have served my people, protected those in need of me. I never wanted... I have never asked of anything for me. I never sought after my heart's desires. But tonight," he whispered, his fingers moving off my lips as they ran over my cheek, "tonight I am."

I stood still under his touch, my body unwilling to move or look away. I stood transfixed as I stared into his eyes, my heart thumping in fear and excitement of what he was about to say to me.

"Will you bond yourself to me? Do you wish it?" His voice was soft, the whispers rushing over me.

"Yes," I breathed, my voice a feather over his skin. My heart caught at the desire and joy that rocked through me.

Ilyan closed his eyes, and a wide smile spread across his face as he threw his head back, his lips moving in quick Czech as he spoke to the sky. His words left as he gathered me up, lifting me off the floor as he crushed me into him, his eyes boring into me before his lips brushed against mine, the touch the softest of pressures before it was gone.

"I love you, my Joclyn," he whispered in Czech, his heart translating the words as his emotions came crashing into me, his joy so strong I could barely breathe through it.

"I love you, Ilyan," I said, the words the truest I had ever spoken.

I had barely gotten the words out before he leaned into me, his cheek pressing against mine as his magic flooded me.

At the feeling of his warmth, the pressure of his magic, I gasped. I expected the touch—expected the movement of my magic as it met with his—however, the touch continued to deepen, and my nerves rose in confusion. I snapped my eyes shut, waiting for the pressure I had felt before, for the electric fusion of a bonding, but nothing came before Ilyan lowered me down to the ground. I opened my eyes to the stormy sky right outside the window of our room, and the gentle taps of rain as it fell over the stonework on our balcony.

I looked around in confusion, confusion I knew I should not feel at Ilyan using the Stutter to move us across the abbey. He kissed my forehead before moving away, leaving me standing alone in the middle of the room we had shared for the past few nights, the room we had fought in, the room I had kissed him in.

"This was my mother's." Ilyan's voice was reverent as he walked back to me, his hands wrapped around a small, golden box. He held it out to me, the carving on the top rattling through me.

I gasped as my hands flew to my chest, my stomach tightening in surprise.

Ilyan held in his hands the box I had seen not once, but twice. First in the nightmare that had woken me before I went to heal Dramin and then in the sight that had come to me after our fight. I stared at the box as I tried to make sense of it, as I tried to understand what this box meant and why my magic had shown it to me so many times. My hand shook as I reached toward the golden surface of it, trying to determine if it was wood or gold, but right then, it didn't matter.

"I have seen this before," I whispered as my fingers ran over the lid, tracing the faces of the two bears, one on either side with a wreath of roses held between them.

I touched the delicate carving as the image of the sight came back clearly; the two of us sitting on our bed, the box on the bed beside us, Ilyan wearing the same shirt he was now, sitting behind me as he braided my hair.

I gasped as the realization hit me so strong my head spun, my Drak blood reacting to the closure of a sight, the magic promising me of its fruition.

"He will tear us apart," I gasped as I replayed the images again.

"If you wish to see the end, give me your heart," we finished together, my eyes widening in shock as his voice joined mine.

"How did you know that?" I asked, my hand jumping off the box as if I had been shocked. I narrowed my eyes at him in fear, the emotion twisting through me as layers of confusion joined in.

"You have told me before," he said as his eyes dug into me, the amazement clear on his face as it numbed the fear that was trying to move into me.

Ilyan placed the box on the bed, his eyes never leaving mine before he came to stand before me, his hand moving to lift the sleeve of his shirt. He turned toward me then, his bare forearm staring at me, and the scar I had seen before glistened against his lean muscle.

"When you were trapped, Dramin and I gave you water in hopes to wake you," he said, his voice tense as I looked at the mark, my fingers rising as my heart called for me to touch it, to heal it. "You spoke those words while you were still trapped after some splashed onto my skin."

I pressed the tips of my fingers against the raised skin that I was sure was just as sensitive as the scar that lined the palm of his hand.

"Give me your heart," I whispered as his hand covered mine, pressing it into the scar.

I tore my eyes away from his arm at the words, the burn in my chest growing. He had heard the words before I had even awakened. No wonder they had felt so familiar. They had happened before, and now the sight would be fulfilled.

I cringed at the realization, the joy that had been raging through me wavering uncomfortably. This sight was coming to pass, just as the one tomorrow would, just as they all would. I had so ruthlessly questioned them, attacked my father with them, and now I stood, the pulse of the one I loved on my fingers—the strength of his love flowing through my mind—and I knew.

The sight had been correct.

The magic of a Drak was correct.

And tonight, I couldn't ask for anything more.

"You already have it." Ilyan barely got the words out, his throat closing with emotion as the burning behind my eyes grew.

Ilyan said nothing more as he led me over to the bed, his touch gentle as he sat down, placing me before him.

I sat down, too, his chest pressing against my back as our intertwined hands moved me into him. He held me against him, his magic flowing into me before he released me, the loss of contact taking the comforting swell of his magic with it. My hands dropped into my lap as he moved away, my heart clenching in nerves as the clouds rumbled. I felt my heartbeat heighten then heard labored breathing from behind me.

I didn't dare move; I didn't trust myself to do so. So I held still and watched Ilyan pull the ornate box toward us, his fingers gentle as he lifted the lid, revealing strands of faded ribbons, vials of oils, and nestled in the middle, a simple golden hair brush.

I could tell just by looking that the brush was made of gold. Ilyan reached toward the box, his shaking fingers hesitating in the air as if he were afraid to touch it.

His nerves tensed as he paused, his thoughts a rampage of doubt and love and confusion. My breath caught as I felt it, the emotions so human that I would never have expected them from him.

I turned from where I sat, my hand extending to wrap around his from where it hovered above the box. I intertwined my fingers with his as I plunged my magic into him, letting it pulse into him as I warmed him, soothing his heart. He froze at the touch, his eyes still locked onto the box that sat beside us, the open lid beckoning him.

"It's okay," I whispered. His eyes darted to mine as I spoke, the rivers of wet that seeped from them catching me off guard.

"It's okay," I repeated. "I'm here. I'm not going anywhere," I whispered.

His emotions peaked, and before I knew it, I was crying right along with him.

He had waited so long, watched so many others find their happiness, and now it was his turn. After so long. I couldn't help the joy I felt for him, the excitement that I knew was hidden under his doubt. He didn't need to feel that, not right now.

I dropped his hand from mine, my movement slow as I

reached up to touch his face, resting my palm against his cheek as I pushed my magic into him. I kept my palm against his skin as his nerves faded and his breathing leveled, as his fear of losing me swelled before it, too, faded.

"I am staying right here," I whispered before I reached up and pressed my lips against his, the soft touch enough to pulse through him, to promise him of the truth of my words.

His eyes lightened as I looked into him, his heart calming before I turned, settling back against him just as the thunder rumbled through the abbey, a lightning strike firing closer than it had before.

The lightning dissipated as I felt Ilyan's hand on the crown of my head, his touch gentle as he ran the golden brush through my hair, the strokes long and even as he moved from top to bottom, over and over. The last of my nerves melted away at his touch. The slow, steady strokes matched the beat of our hearts, the pulse of our souls.

Before I was ready, he replaced the brush in the box, his long fingers digging through the contents to produce a long, white ribbon, the fibers old and worn enough that I was sure it had been a different color at one point.

"For this ribbon, I give you my heart, for every beat is yours," he whispered, his voice shaking as his fingers began moving deftly through my hair, his touch gentle as he weaved the ribbon through the strands, his movements quick and practiced before he reached down, grabbing another ribbon, this one just as light and almost appearing longer than the first.

"For this ribbon, I give you my soul, the other half to your perfect match." My breath caught as he spoke, the vow almost seeming too perfect given the way our souls had fused together.

Ilyan had barely gotten the words out before he went

back to work, his fingers careful and slow as they moved through my hair. Even though I knew this braid to be intricate, I never felt a pull, he never moved my head. His touch was soft, the pressure of his fingers against my head bringing small pulses of magic into me.

I held still as he pulled another ribbon from the box, this one shorter and a darker color than the other two.

"For this ribbon, I proclaim my love, my dedication, and my passion for you."

Ilyan's fingertips brushed over my hairline as he pulled more hair into the intricate braid, the touch soft against my neck. Each press of his fingers against my skin set my heart on fire, my chest burning as I tried to regulate my breathing.

He reached over to the box, grabbing another ribbon and pulling it out until all that was left in the box was the hairbrush, a small vial of oil, and a silky, golden ribbon longer than my arm.

"For this ribbon, I give you all that I possess, for in this moment, my life becomes yours."

My life becomes yours.

I couldn't stop the words from repeating themselves, the true meaning rumbling through me until my eyes began to burn.

My hair moved as his fingers pulled through it; all the hair was off my neck now as he continued to work. Part of me wanted to see, to close my eyes and sneak a peek, but I couldn't ignore the way my heart beat, the way that Ilyan's magic moved deeper into me with each movement. It wasn't my place to see, not yet.

The movement in my hair paused as Ilyan leaned over, his fingers pulling the last ribbon out of the box; the long, silky snake of gold flowing over the palm of Ilyan's hand as he, too, treasured it. His emotions flared with memories as he treasured the ribbon. His thoughts of the way his mother had worn this very ribbon in her hair until the day she died flooded me.

My heart seized at the realization, my heart breaking for Ilyan as he paused, his hand hovering over me, letting the golden ribbon fall in front of me, the silken thread soft against my face.

"For this ribbon," he began, his accent thick as his emotion broke through, "I crown you my queen, and the Queen of my people."

I gasped at the words, the realization of all that this meant slamming into me until it was hard to breathe. His emotion washed over me as he spoke, his joy rumbling through me as I felt his happiness at no longer being alone, that he didn't have to be.

I stared straight into the storm that raged around us as his fingers moved, my heart rumbling as the thunder did. I didn't dare look anywhere else. I watched the storm as I focused on my breathing and began to accept the reality of his last few words.

I felt his touch slow, the ribbon winding around the end as he finished, his hands gentle as he placed the long braid against my back. I was frozen in place as the weight dropped against me, my body still trying to remember how to breathe as his fingers trailed over the braid, the touch extending down my back until it vanished. His hand moved to grab the small, clear vial that was now the only thing beside the brush that sat in the box.

My heart rate increased as Ilyan's did until I felt his chest against my back, the pulse of his heart thundering against my skin as mine matched the beat, the pulses beating against our skin as he placed his heart over mine.

His palms pressed against my skin as his hands ran

down my arms, his touch soft as he brought my hands together, forming a small bowl in my lap. His fingertips caressed my skin as his hands moved away, leaving me still as my heart pulsed, as my magic surged.

I stared into my hands, watching as Ilyan poured the oil into them, his hands coming to cup my own as he rested his chin against my shoulder. I couldn't take my eyes off the oil as his breath moved over my skin while his cheek pressed against mine, the wetness of his tears cold against my face. I inhaled at the touch, my breath shaky through my own tears, through my nerves that still raged.

"Můj majetek se proto rozšířila tento den dní, moje srdce roste v zemi a způsobu. Pozemky jsem chodil, se navždy vázané na můj kamarád přede mnou." He whispered the words as he began to massage the oil into my hands, his magic seeping into me with the touch. The strength of his magic shocked me, the headiness I had never felt rocking into me as the oil magnified it.

His hands stopped moving as he pressed my hands together before he cupped his hands in my lap, his motions making it clear what I was supposed to do.

I reached toward the box, my hands shaking as I grabbed the small vial, pouring what was left into Ilyan's hands, my nerves so strong that I was sure I wouldn't be able to rub the oil into his hands as well.

"My property has hence expanded this day of days, my heart increasing in ground and way. The lands I walk shall forever be bound to my mate in front of me," I repeated the words as he had guided me. My tongue stumbled over words I hadn't said since I first learned to talk.

Ilyan never laughed; he never smiled in jest. He only watched as I moved the oil into his skin, his heartbeat steadying mine as I pushed my magic into him, filling him as he had me.

Ilyan wrapped his arms around me as I dropped his hands, his arms strong as he moved me to face him until I could see the streaks of tears on his face, the golden light in his eyes stronger than I had ever seen before.

"Budu tě opatrovat až do dne zemřete," he whispered— the meaning hidden from me—before he pressed his lips to mine, the pressure soft, hesitant.

I could taste the sweetness of him on my lips, smell the scent of his magic in my hair. I pressed into him, needing him.

His arms wrapped around me as I called for him, his touch strong as his magic flooded me at the same time as mine flooded him. It was a sensation of electricity and fire as everything melded together; as his hands pressed me to him, as his lips pressed into me, as his tears fell onto my nose.

"Ilyan," I gasped as his magic pressed further, the pressure consuming me. The heat grew to be more than when he had placed the Štít, more than when he had protected me.

It grew until that was all I felt and my own scream filled my ears before everything went black.

20

————

I HAD NEVER BEEN on a beach before; I had never felt the warm sand beneath my fingers, the sun against my body.

I definitely felt the sand now and ran my fingers through it, the gritty texture new and yet somehow familiar. My fingers dug into the tiny granules until I reached a colder underside that I hadn't expected. The chill from the sand was a nice opposite to the sun that beat against my face.

I sunk into it, letting the dream take me away, wanting to linger in the peace of it if only for a little longer. The sand enveloped me as I breathed in the salty air until the call of a gull echoed in my ears and I jumped to sitting, my eyes flying open to the burn of the sun in confusion.

My eyes snapped shut again in an attempt to stifle the pain, the gulls continuing to call around me, heightening my confusion. My dreams never had sound, and if they did, it was distorted and frightening. This sound, though, was clear, crisp—perfect.

I opened my eyes again, careful to control the burn, only to have them widen at the long stretch of white sand and the endless length of blue water that filled the world in front of me.

It was a world I had never seen before.

It wasn't a dream; everything was too perfect to be a dream.

It didn't make any sense. Nothing about this made any sense. I had just been sitting in my room with Ilyan, his fingers soft as he braided my hair. I could still smell the oil on my hands, hear his voice as he spoke to me in Czech, feel the pressure of his magic as it fused with mine.

Ilyan's magic.

The Zělství.

The bond must be complete.

The sun seemed to warm at the thought, my body heating as my magic bubbled along with the sun. It was silly that I hadn't thought of it sooner—that I hadn't put it all together—but now I knew.

This was a Tŏuha.

Our Tŏuha.

I had never seen anything so beautiful as the place I stood in at that moment; I had never known something like this was possible within the Tŏuha. This was not the white-walled spaces and tormented hell I had experienced before. This was paradise.

The beach was lined by endless stretches of water that lapped and kissed the length of the white sand I sat on. My toes dug into the sand as I turned, the beauty of the beach increasing as the waves crashed and exploded against the brown rocks off in the distance. White foam from the breaking waves sprayed into the air and toward the large manor house that was nestled into the trees just behind.

I stared at the house, my heart relaxing at the beauty

and perfection of this place I found myself in. It wasn't complete, though, because I was alone.

My heart called desperately for my other half, fear building that I hadn't seen him yet.

He had to be here somewhere.

"Ilyan?" I called toward the house, knowing my voice wasn't strong enough to carry over the sound of the waves and the gulls.

I watched the house as another wave broke over the rocks, almost expecting him to walk out the front door toward me. I knew he was over there; I could feel it. I could feel his magic, living inside of me, swell and pull me in that direction.

I had felt the sensation before with Ryland, but then, it had been cast in fear and had been unwanted. This time, as the warmth moved through me, my magic responded joyfully. It pulled at me as my bare feet slipped through the slick sand, making it hard to keep my balance. I had never walked in sand before, and now I was wondering how all those old people in denture cream commercials did it. My leg muscles were on fire as I pushed myself forward, my need for him growing with each step.

Why Ilyan had brought me to the south of France, of all places, I had no idea.

I stopped in place as the idea hit me, the battering ram of a thought strong and unexplainable.

The south of France.

I didn't know where the thought had come from, or why I would even think that this unfamiliar beach would be there. The only time I had ever spoken to anyone about France was in that tiny room in that farmhouse when Ilyan had told me about his house.

His house.

The frantic beating of my heart increased as I looked up to the large manor. It was a little more than the 'little house' that Ilyan had spoken of at the time, but right then, I didn't care.

I sped into a run in an attempt to reach the house, my feet slipping and arms flailing as I tried to keep my balance, tried to find any sort of speed. The sand gave me neither.

"Ilyan!" I yelled as my feet slipped out from under me, my knees crashing to the sand as I lost my balance.

I stared toward the house as I tried to catch my breath, my chest rising and falling as the salty air moved into me, the humidity bringing me little relief. I didn't even know why I was breathing so hard; my body didn't really feel like I needed it.

I pushed myself to standing, ready to make a new attempt at a run when my magic pulled at me with a warm tug that took my breath away. I gasped at the sensation, my eyes narrowing toward the pull just as Ilyan made his way down the stone steps of the house. The wide smile on his face was an electric shock through my system.

"Ilyan," I gasped as I took off, my feet moving before my body received the message. Arms flailed as feet moved, the uncoordinated movement sending me crashing down hard enough that I was sure I had looked like a wet fish that time.

"Careful, my love," Ilyan laughed as he crouched beside me. "It is not easy to run in sand."

"So I've noticed," I grumbled as I rolled onto my back. I didn't think I had the strength to get up again, not like I wanted to. Ilyan was here now. I had nowhere else I wanted to be.

Ilyan had perched himself next to me, his face soft and welcoming as he smiled at me, the warmth in his eyes turning me to the equivalent of warm jelly—warm jelly that was melting under the heat of the French sun.

The thought was as ridiculous as it was perfect; as perfect as everything was right in that one joyful moment. It was a feeling I hadn't felt in months, a peace I had been seeking since the day I had run from Ryland's house. Somehow, I had finally found it. I wasn't sure what to do with such joy as a smile didn't seem like it was enough, so I began to laugh, the sound fresh and elated as it echoed through the air, the gulls chatting along as if my happiness was contagious.

"I don't think I have ever seen you this free, Můj Navždy," Ilyan whispered as he sat down beside me, his arm propping up his weight as he leaned over me.

His side pressed against mine as his arm enclosed me under him. The warmth that radiated off him seeped into me, my body pulling at it as if I couldn't get enough, as if I wouldn't be able to live without it.

The sun framed him from behind as he leaned toward me, his hair glowing in that weird, ethereal light that should be reserved for bad romance movies, yet somehow, right here it fit him.

"Můj navždy?" I asked, the awe leaving my face as confusion took its place.

"It means 'my forever,' Joclyn."

"My forever. Můj navždy," I repeated the words as accurately as I could, getting used to them on my lips, in my heart.

I smiled as my stomach fluttered, the gold flecks in Ilyan's eyes shining brightly.

"Yes," Ilyan whispered, his hand moving from the sand to my face, the usual, soft touch tingling over my skin. I closed my eyes as my body heated and cooled with the pleasure of his touch. The sensation was stronger than anything I had ever felt before, making it hard to control my breathing. I gasped as the feeling swelled, at the way my toes tensed and my magic popped in sparks of heat inside my body.

Ilyan's fingers ran the length of my jawbone before the touch left, the supercharged sensations trailing away as his fingers did. My eyes snapped open as his hand withdrew, shock still running through me only to see him gazing down at me, a knowing smile on his face.

"What was that?" I gasped, the words barely able to find their way out of the pressure in my chest.

"The sensation that a Zělství gives you, mi lasko. A true Zělství. One forged in honesty and commitment. It is your body reacting to mine, your soul to mine, your heart to mine. I never thought it would be this strong. I never thought..." His voice broke as he looked away, the movement of his head casting his features in shadows.

Even though I couldn't see the lines of his face, I knew what had come over him. I could feel it within me as his heart swelled, the thankfulness he felt for the gift we had been given. It was as strong as the waves of the ocean that crashed over the rocks.

I lifted my hand from where it lay until my fingers touched the side of his jaw. I could feel the stubble on his chin—the warmth of his skin—but it was the way our magic reacted—the way the sensation rocked through me—that affected me the most, that sent Ilyan's breathing to shallow pants of desire.

I didn't stop, even though it was hard to focus, even though my hand shook. I ran my fingers over the smooth lines of his face, across his hair line, and down his neck until my shaking hand fell into the sand, taking the supercharged sensations with it.

"Is it all you hoped for?" I asked, my voice shaking with nerves as I asked him.

I didn't know why I was so nervous. I wasn't even sure why I had asked in the first place. I could feel his contentment, hear his soul rejoice as he found pleasure in what he had been waiting for his entire life. Maybe it was my own insecurities, my own worries that had brought the words out.

Ilyan turned toward me as he lowered his body to the sand, his tall frame parallel to mine as we lay side by side. I was barely able to turn toward him before his hand wrapped around my waist, dragging me through the sand until I was an inch away from him.

I could feel his breath against my face, the warmth of his hand against my back, and I didn't want to move away. I lay still beside him, the words in his mind projecting through the light in his eyes before the love shown through, and he finally put voice to his feelings.

"All and more, mi lasko," he whispered, his voice so soft and tender that any nerves I had faded into oblivion. "I am here with the woman I love, the woman I would die for, in a place I have created for us. My heart could not be more content."

Ilyan's hand left my back, his touch like a feather as it moved up my spine and over to the skin of my arms. I gasped as his skin came into contact with mine, a wide smile spreading over his face at the reaction. I knew I shouldn't have been embarrassed by the way he looked at me, but I couldn't help the way my stomach tightened. I looked away in a foolish attempt to fight the blush.

"So that is your house, then?" I asked, inclining my head toward the giant manor nestled into the rocks behind him.

Ilyan didn't even turn toward it, he just smiled, his fingers continuing to trail up and down my arms

"Mmmhmmm," he sighed as I looked back toward him, his eyes capturing mine. "I told you about it, remember?"

"So it is real, then?"

"Yes, it stands just outside a city by the name of Giens. I built it for you, for us, about a hundred years after I first received the sight."

"No wonder it's a little run down," I said as I reached forward and poked him playfully, only to keep my hand against him, resting lightly on his side.

"It is yours now, my love," he whispered as his fingers moved off my arm, the soft touch moving up my neck and over my face. I closed my eyes at the calming pressure, my focus on the feel of his fingers against my skin as well as the way his free hand moved to wrap around mine, his magic settling in joy.

"Thank you, Ilyan," I said, my mind so relaxed I wasn't even sure if I had spoken the words aloud.

"Anything, my love."

Ilyan caressed my arm, my jaw, the bridge of my nose as we lay in the sand, the waves crashing by our feet—the water splashing over our toes as the tide came closer—but I didn't move. I didn't want to. He looked into me so passionately that I was sure I was going to get lost in his eyes —lost in the way he held me, lost in the feel of his touch. I didn't care; I wanted to be lost.

Ilyan smiled as he began to sing to me, our song gentle and calming as it rose and fell with the rhythm of the waves. He shared the words he had written for me all those years ago. Words I was beginning to finally understand.

Hush now, child. Be still, be calm. The world will change at the new dawn. And when it does, you will see, just how you and I were meant to be.

He sang over and over, my lips moving along until I began to sing as well, my voice shaky as my breath washed over his chest.

We sang together until the ocean left and the rumble of low thunderheads crashed through our room in the abbey, jerking me awake as Ilyan's arm tightened around me, pulling me into his bare chest.

His tension swelled into me, the fear rumbling through me with the same power that the thunder surrounding us did.

It was time.

I intertwined my fingers with his as I leaned back into him, his hold on me increasing until I could feel his heart beat against my back, his magic that would now forever live inside of me bubbling around to protect me, to calm me.

It was weird to feel so connected to him; the power of the Zělství so strong that it shocked me. Before, with only our souls fused together, I had felt some of his emotions, I had heard some of his thoughts. It was nothing compared to what I was experiencing right then.

In that moment, I felt things I had never felt before, heard things that I knew were just for me, and even some things that I knew were not. I felt my magic within Ilyan, the same way I was sure he felt his within me. The presence was so pleasant I never wanted to lose it.

I spun in Ilyan's arms until I faced him, my face burrowing into his chest as he held me. His lips pressed softly onto the top of my head.

I'm scared, I sent into his mind, my voice quaking as my body did.

His arms tightened around me as the warmth of his magic spread, the hot water warmth soothing my nerves.

Do not be afraid, my love. Know that I will be here.

My eyes widened at the clarity of the thought that moved into me, Ilyan's voice echoing inside of my head clear enough that I wasn't sure if I had just missed his lips move.

I had heard him.

His forehead knit together as he looked at me, obviously concerned about my response. He either didn't know, or being able to hear him after a Zĕlství was so normal I should have expected it. Except it wasn't normal. They had told me as much when I spoke into Ilyan's mind for the first time, and now he was speaking into mine.

"Do not be afraid, my love," I repeated his words out loud, my voice soft as his eyes widened in shock.

"You heard me?"

I did.

You can hear me? he asked, the smile on his face spreading as his eyes lit up.

I nodded once and his smile grew, his arms wrapping around me as he pressed me into him, the warmth of our body heat trapped in the heavy blanket we lay under.

You can hear me.

I felt his rapture at this new development, his joy at being able to be so close to me, even if it was only for a precious few moments. His joy filled me and I smiled, letting his warmth run over me as the thunder rumbled, the lightning brightening our room. I let his joy build in me, my body snuggling into his until a loud knock sounded against the door, causing our arms to tighten around each other.

"It's time, My Lord," Sain said as his voice drifted toward us, the sound loud and unwanted in my ears.

"Thank you, Sain," Ilyan called back as he dismissed him.

The warmth of the bed suddenly felt cold and brittle against me.

The air seemed heavy as we lay there, looking between us without seeing, the reality of what we were about to walk into so unwanted that neither of us dared to put voice to it. Ilyan said nothing before his lips pressed against my forehead, the pressure warm and needed before he was gone.

I followed his lead, my legs swinging over the side of the bed as a flash of white filled the room, bringing in the light of day before it was gone and thunder took its place.

The flashes and rumbles were so close together that the sky could barely breathe before the next strike came. I watched them, knowing what they meant, my heart breaking as they came closer. As my time grew shorter. The earth knew what was coming, and she was preparing the way.

I listened to the grinding of wood as Ilyan pulled clothes out of the dresser—the sound almost as loud as the thunder—and still I did not move. I wasn't in any hurry, anyway. It wasn't like I had many choices of what to wear anyway. What does one wear to the day they die?

My love, Ilyan whispered internally as he kneeled down before me, his glistening eyes hooded as they swallowed me whole. He set a small pile of clothes beside me before gathering my hands in his, his magic warming through me as my skin prickled with the touch. While not as strong as it had been in the Tòuha, it was still more than it had been before the bonding—more than I had ever felt—and I smiled at the contact, even though my heart beat irregularly in fear.

"I won't let anything happen to you," Ilyan promised, the impossible words like ash against my soul.

"Please don't, Ilyan," I begged, my voice dragging as I looked down to our intertwined hands. I couldn't hear him say something like this. I couldn't let the false hope into my heart.

"Don't say things that you can't control."

"I may not be able to guarantee your life, but I will protect you. I promise you this with my very breath."

I looked up to him. The promise that he would do what he had trained for—what he had been born for—threatened to shatter me into millions of tiny fragments.

"This morning, I hold the hands of my mate in mine. I hold her heart inside of me, and I vow to protect her. To protect you. To keep you safe, and alive, at all costs. I will follow my heart, and keep my mate safe. Because it is right."

Ilyan repeated the words that I had battled with my father over for the past few days. It was more than that, though. He had made a vow that could very well break the sight, if it hadn't been broken already. The unspoken support rang through me, the promise of what we could lose, of what we did not want to lose.

What I didn't want to lose.

I didn't want to lose the feel of his touch; I didn't want to lose his smile. I didn't want to lose the way he had helped me through the biggest trials in my life. I didn't want to lose him. I just didn't know if it was possible, not anymore. After last night, after seeing that box and feeling my magic flare with knowledge, I knew. The magic inside of me knew. We couldn't change it.

No matter what my father had said.

Right then, looking into his eyes, I wanted to change it. I wanted to break the sight and experience an eternity with him, experience life, have the future that the sight told me I could never have. I knew, right then, I would give anything to change it.

I nodded once, not knowing what else to say, as he pressed his lips to my hands.

He said no more. His kiss left as he stood, leaving me alone as he walked into the bathroom, the pile of clothes by my side. I heard the click of the door and stood, stripping off Ilyan's lightweight pajamas that I had been wearing for what felt like days to replace them with what I recognized at once as what I had worn in the sight.

I pulled on the dark washed jeans Ilyan had brought, almost afraid he would come back before I had the chance to change. The chill of the diamond shocked me as I stripped off my shirt, the necklace cold and hard against my chest. I had forgotten that Ilyan had put it on me. I didn't know why, but it almost seemed fitting that I would be wearing it when everything ended. I pulled my shirt over the necklace, keeping it under the fabric where it would be safe; where it would stay with me.

The white shirt seemed like a weird choice given the full scale battle I was expected to go into. I didn't question it, though; I only pulled it over my head, careful not to disrupt the braid, and then pulled as much of the long golden ribbon that trailed through my shirt as I could. I slipped my shoes on and stood in front of the bed, my eyes focused on the wad of fabric that still lay on the comforter as I heard the bathroom door open.

My fingers wrapped around the heavy fabric of the hoodie as I lifted it up. It seemed weird to be holding this in my hands, to be rebelling against putting it on.

I had hidden behind one of these almost my whole life, scared to really find myself, but I *had* found myself. I had cast the hoodies aside, moved beyond them. Even when I was trapped in Cail's mind as well as after Ilyan had pulled me out, I had never really wanted to hide again. I had merely wanted to become stronger than what haunted me.

I was stronger than it now.

"A hoodie?"

"Yes," Ilyan said softly as he came up beside me, taking the fabric from my hands.

"I can hear what is on your mind, my love. I can feel your strength, I know that you do not need this."

"Then why give it to me?"

"Because it is cold outside," he said as he gathered up the material, ready to help me into it. I pursed my lips as he held it up to me. I knew that wasn't his only reason. I could hear the secret in his voice, see the caution behind his eyes.

I sighed and lowered my head as he moved the fabric around the braid, careful not to disrupt any of his artwork as he placed the sweater over my head.

"Why else?" I asked as I emerged from the mass of fabric, unsurprised to see the corner of Ilyan's lips turn up, his eyes still avoiding mine.

"This braid is my gift to you, my Joclyn. It is a piece of my heart and soul, and meant only for you. The hood will help you keep that sacred until the time is right to tell the world." His eyes ran over the braid before meeting mine, the softness of the blue like a billowing cloud that I found myself getting lost in.

I nodded my head once in understanding, knowing that he was right. Right now, this moment was just between us.

"I will be with you, my love."

"Until the end," I whispered as the mischievous light from his eyes seeped into me.

He pulled the braid from the neckline, the long string of

golden ribbon sliding up my back as he pulled out the full length. I had thought I had gotten it all when I had changed shirts, but apparently not; the strand stretched all the way to the floor.

I pulled at the long, golden ribbon, the texture soft as it flowed over the palm of my hand, like feathers and wind, the golden surface glinting as it came in contact with my magic.

"That is the délka vedení královského," Ilyan whispered, his hand moving to run the length of the ribbon right along mine.

"The what?"

"Come here," Ilyan whispered, his hand wrapping around mine as he led me to the bathroom where the large, ornate mirrors stood above the sink. He turned me around, tilting one of the mirrors enough that I could see the braid that Ilyan had placed in my hair, my jaw dropping in disbelief at what I was seeing.

My hair had been turned into a bouquet of roses. Rose buds of woven hair shot off from the braid, the ribbons winding together to make each delicate flower, and the golden ribbon intertwined through all of them, the string touching every part of the braid he had given me.

"It's beautiful," I gasped, knowing that the word was not enough to convey what I truly saw.

"Each flower is my vow to you," he said, his finger trailing over each one, his fingers soft as if he was touching antique china, which I guess in some ways he was.

"My heart," he said as he brushed the first rose. "My soul," he said as his fingers moved to the next one. "My devotion, my life," he finished as his fingers touched each one before moving to the golden ribbon that moved through my hair so completely I wasn't sure how he had gotten it into the intricate braid.

"And the délka vedení královského—the length of the royal line. This ribbon is one of two, wound from fibers of gold mined below Prague. It is the sign of your position of power. What you now mean to me and to my people." His fingers continually moved over the ribbon, his touch so soft I could barely feel it.

"The king and queen are to wear the délka vedení královského every day, and I will bind it in your hair every morning... so that everyone will know," his arms wrapped around my waist as his fingers left the braid, pulling me against him as our eyes met through the mirror, "that you are my queen. My life."

My heart thumped wildly in my chest at the thought as the deep reality of what had happened hit me. Queen. The thought was like ice and adrenaline, the combination sending my heart into palpitations so fast that I was sure Ilyan would notice.

I stared at him through the mirror, the light in his eyes calming me as the love I felt for him flared.

I had bound myself to Ilyan, and I would do it again because I loved him. I had not bound myself to his title, however, his title was an integral part of him, and I loved that side of him as much as I loved the side that he only showed to me. I would take this on me because it was worth it, because he was worth it. Because I loved him.

"Where is yours?" I asked, my voice shaking as the last of my anxiety left me. "Your délka vedení královskéh," I said, knowing I messed up the pronunciation somehow.

Ilyan's lips twitched through the mirror before he kneeled down behind me, his fingers unwinding the long string from where he had concealed it around his ankle.

He held the mass of golden ribbon out to me as he stood. The ribbon tangled and crinkled in places, making it obvious that he had hidden it there for centuries. I knew at once why; it was the same as when he had cut his hair. He had been hiding something that he wasn't sure he would ever have. Except he had it now.

I looked at it carefully, my fingers fluttering above the ribbon before I took it in my hand, the length still warm from being against his skin.

I said nothing as I grabbed his hand, my grip light as I led him to the bed, my eyes pleading with him before he sat, his hair growing in anticipation of what I was about to do.

I crawled over the bed to kneel behind him, the golden ribbon held tightly in my hand as I leaned against his back.

Don't expect anything spectacular, I whispered to him, my voice soft within his mind.

I expect only what you have to give me, he returned. My heart soared at the sound of his voice in my head.

My fingers searched through the nest of gold until I found the end, the frayed edges soft like goose feathers. I pulled at the end until it came free, my chest quivering with nerves as I exhaled, willing my stress away.

Everything in me shook as I ran my fingers through his hair, knowing I would barely be able to manage a simple French braid if I was lucky.

I kept the ribbon tight in his silky hair as I weaved the strands together. The knuckles on my fingers shook as I tried to keep the tension right, knowing I was pulling too hard at times. Without the amazing skill that Ilyan had, my simple braid was done quickly, my fingers wrapping the golden length around his hair from the base of his neck, surrounding the braid as I tightened the string, praying that it would be enough to keep it in place.

I knew it wasn't as good as it could have been; my shaking fingers had made it a little bit off center, but it was done. Sloppiness and all, it was probably the most treasured thing I had ever done.

I ran my fingers down the braid I had given him, my lips pressing against his lavender-scented hair as I sealed my gift to him. He reached back as my hand grazed over the skin of his neck, capturing my hand in his as he brought it to his lips.

"Thank you, my forever, for giving me this gift."

I stared into his eyes, unsure how to answer; his breath was soft and warm as it ran over my hand. He kept it there, holding me in place as his thoughts and worries floated over me, his mind full of the image from the sight—the way he held my limp body, the way he howled to the sky. I flinched as the image burned into my mind, my heart tightening uncomfortably with the pressure.

"It will be all right, my love," Ilyan whispered, his hand finally releasing mine from his grasp.

He opened his mouth to say something more when a loud, frantic knock sounded on the door, the surprising sound sending my heart into matching frantic palpitations that Ilyan's magic soothed at once.

We both had stiffened at the sound, Ilyan's eyes closing as mine lifted to the heavy door, another knock coming soon after the first.

"My Lord," Sain's voice came through the wood, causing my shoulders to knit together. "We are in need of your assistance."

I looked away from the door to Ilyan who was now staring at me, his hands wrapping around mine as he pulled me toward him. His fingers traced over the skin of my neck, and I tensed, expecting his fingers to brush over my neck to touch my mark, but they never did. The softness of his fingers skimmed around the edges, careful not to touch it.

"Are you ready?" he asked, but I could only stare at him.

I knew I never would be. How do you walk into what is sure to be certain death? I don't think there is a way to. Not without tears. Not without fear. I could feel both, but there was a difference. I was stronger than my panic. Stronger than the girl who had been thrown out the window; stronger than the girl who had run from Ryland.

I might not be able to defeat death, yet I could meet it head on.

I pushed the tears away and squared my jaw as I faced Ilyan, pulling the hood over my head as we walked to the door, making sure that the flowers in my hair were concealed, guarding the commitment I had bound myself in. I could feel the intricate braid through the fabric, felt his warmth within me, and I knew that Wyn had been right.

I had known there was only a day, and I would gladly make the choice all over again.

Because it was worth it.

21

———

Ilyan led us toward the kitchen, one hand wrapped around mine and the other carrying the large duffle bag that I could only assume held all of his belongings. The hallway seemed darker as we walked; the old, grey stones looked black in the dim light of the hall that stretched on forever.

I tried to keep my breathing even in order to stop the fearful shake that seized through my torso, but it came anyway. The panic was just enough to keep me aware while I fought to keep the demons away.

The kitchen door was a tall slab of wood like all the others, but it might as well have been iron bars for how it felt against my soul. I let out one last shaking breath as we stopped before it, Ilyan's grip on my hand tightening.

We just stood, staring at the door, knowing what it meant. Ilyan's terrors ran through my head as I was sure mine did to him.

This was it.

Ilyan exhaled into the silence, his hand running over my back and pressing me into him, his lips pressing against mine in one hard, desperate line. Pressure and desire ran through me with that kiss, his need for me growing as I pressed myself into him.

I felt all his love in that instant, all his worry and sadness. I felt every promise and every vow. I felt it all in one tick of a clock before it was gone from me. His golden eyes devoured me as his fingers trailed over my jaw, lighting me on fire. He swallowed my soul with that look before he turned from me, his back straight as he towered before me with the long ribbon of gold hanging down his back and to the floor. His chest rose and fell as he stood. Once, twice he breathed, and then he opened the door and led us into the dimly-lit room.

I made my way into the room, the door shutting behind me with a loud snap that made my nerves jump.

The room was full of desperate whispers and the scraping of forks as the few who had to eat scarfed down the last of the food Ilyan had brought a few days before. Everyone was seated together at one of the large tables on the other side of the room. While Thom and Wyn had mostly cleared their plates, Ryland just sat between them with a plate of untouched food before him, rocking back and forth as Sain stood over him. The majority of the mumbles I heard came from Ryland's lips.

Ilyan took one look at what was happening and rushed toward them, his intent to block Ryland's memories echoing back through his thoughts.

Is he all right? I asked, unable to take my eyes off my friend. The clarity of my mind that Ilyan's magic had given me took away the monster that Cail had created for a moment. Right then, I only saw my friend, and my heart pulsed in worry. I reached toward the diamond that hung around my neck, knowing I needed to do something.

I was one step away from moving toward Ryland when he looked up at me.

My heart turned into a dark, painful fist at the look in his black eyes, at the hatred and pain that poured through him. In that one look, the veil of clarity vanished, leaving me face to face with the monster that still terrified me. I froze in place, my fingers still pressing the cold stone into my chest, unable to look away. Unable to move away from the raw hatred that stared back at me.

My voice curled and moaned as I forced my eyes down to the floor, the strange emotion leaving just as Ilyan's words flitted into my mind.

His soul is destroyed, my love. I will help him. I promise you.

I nodded once at his words, even though I knew he couldn't see me, and turned from them, needing to get away. Dramin sat at the table behind me, his hands wrapped around a large, earthen mug, another one at his side. He smiled as I caught sight of him, his head inclining toward the space next to him and to the mug I could only assume was for me.

"You always forget," he said as I slid into the chair beside him, "so I came prepared."

"Thank you." I was unable to stop the smile that lit up my face, but it wasn't for the mug. No matter how much my stomach turned in need of it, my smile was at seeing him, sitting on his own beside me.

"You're okay." It was a statement, not a question, my awed voice making me sound a little bit more like an amazed child than I had meant it to.

"Thanks to you, child," Dramin said with his usual chipper tone as he lifted his cup to me, his eyes twinkling in a wink.

I wanted to smile at how familiar he was. I wanted to

laugh and drink the Black Water, but I couldn't, so I sat still, my smile fading somewhat as I looked into him. The question I knew I needed to ask felt like lead on my tongue.

"Are you mad at me?"

"I could never question your choices, child," he said as he patted his hand against my arm, his motions slow and controlled. I raised my head to look at his green eyes that matched my father's, and had matched mine many years ago, smiling brightly at me. "I might be very mad, however, if you don't actually drink what I have given you."

I smiled at Dramin and placed my hands over the rim of the cup, the warm steam of the liquid heating the palm of my hand as it filled. The warm aroma of honey drifted through the air, and I sighed, letting the scent warm me before the water did. I had just pressed the rim of my mug to my lips when Ryland yelled out, making my body jump and tense at the sound. I cringed and grabbed hold of the table, my knuckles turning white in expectation of him lunging across the room toward me.

Ryland hadn't moved, however, he only sat, crying into Ilyan's shoulder. Ilyan held his brother as he calmed him, his voice soft as he soothed him. Even though I could feel Ilyan's anticipation of battle and the tense nature of his emotions, his demeanor remained calm as he held Ryland, working to soothe him. Wyn and Thom dutifully helped Ilyan as he pacified his brother while Sain... Sain stared at me.

My father's eyes bored into me with a painful pressure that made me uncomfortable, his forehead wrinkled and I looked away, not really wanting to see the disappointment that would be there.

"Do not let him under your skin, Silnỳ," Dramin said, the tone making it obvious he had witnessed the quick exchange between myself and Sain. "He is not 'mad' at you, as you say. Father just expects more from his children than most."

I tried not to bristle at his words, but emotions pulsed and my head shot up, my eyes narrowing dangerously.

"Ha!" I said, the humor that I didn't feel pushing itself into my voice. "I don't see him telling you to buck up and go save the world."

"And yet, here I sit."

I jolted a bit at his words, the meaning as clear as day. Dramin had woken only last night, yet he sat before me, ready to run into the forest, ready to face what might be his certain death as well. While I knew Dramin was stubborn, I was aware that he wasn't *that* stubborn. He probably wouldn't be here if it weren't for Sain.

I didn't know how to react to that. Heck, I didn't even know what to expect from a father. I had memories of scraped knees and bedtime stories, not of an immortal who would do anything to push his children toward their true potential.

I sighed and smoothed the lines that had taken up residence on my forehead, trying to ignore the truth that lay behind Dramin's words.

"Trust your heart, Silný. Your magic will guide you. Whether it be to heal me, to run from a fight, or to learn underwater basket weaving. Trust in who you really are. Tatínek will, too."

I nodded once at his words, desperately wanting him to be right. This was not just about my father coming to accept me; I wanted him to be right about trusting myself and trusting my magic.

Silence stretched between us as Ryland's whimpers increased, the sound of his pain as heart-wrenching as the nervous fear that lay heavy in the air. I took another deep drink of Black Water, attempting to drain the mug and push away the fear.

"How does it feel to be a married woman?" Dramin asked out of nowhere, his voice conspiratorially low as he leaned toward me. His voice had been soft, but to me it was like the boom of a cannon, and I jumped, the Black Water trickling down my hands and over the table.

I knew I hadn't heard him wrong. I was certain because I could still hear it echo in my mind over and over. The world felt twice as heavy as I turned toward him, shock lining my face. He didn't seem deterred, however. He just smiled wider, chuckling deeply as if he had found a great joke.

"Is that not what they call it amongst the humans? Marriage?"

Joclyn? Ilyan's voice rumbled through my head, his distress peaking as the fear that gripped me moved right into him.

Dramin knows. About our bonding, I returned, my eyes still glued to the man in question, my face a mask of shock that I knew gave me away.

My eyes darted to where Ilyan sat with Ryland. Ilyan's face and body were calm even though I could feel the pulse of worry in him, but he showed no outward signs of the silent conversation he was absorbed in with me.

Of course he does, Ilyan sent back to me, his voice lined with such a heavy joy I was surprised it wasn't plastered on his face. Instead, he stayed still, his hands wrapped around Ryland's as he whispered to him.

"How did you know?" My tongue stumbled though the words as my heart moved into my throat, the sensation making it hard to breathe, let alone swallow.

"I know everything,"

"Did you see?"

"No, my dear," Dramin said, his voice almost sad as he took another drink of Black Water. "It is much simpler than that. Ilyan has not worn that ribbon where it could be seen since the 1400s."

The golden ribbon Ilyan wore glinted in the light as it fell over his shoulder, the sign of his royalty available for everyone to see. Ilyan didn't seem too plagued by it as he calmed his brother, but Thom and Sain kept looking at it curiously, the looks on their faces making it clear that they knew exactly what it was. Wyn, on the other hand, looked right at me, her face torn between awe and confusion. I was one hundred percent sure she knew what it was, and what it meant for me.

"I guess he should have covered his hair, too." I tried very hard to keep the groan out of my voice as I folded myself over the table, my forehead pressing into the smooth wood of the ancient surface.

"Don't you worry." Dramin's smile stretched the width of his face as he patted my hand comfortingly, his happiness almost infectious. Almost. I felt more embarrassed than anything right then. "Those who know will be happy for you. A bonding as treasured as this should never be a secret, My Lady."

"My Lady?" I asked as I turned my head to face him, not ready to lift my head off the table yet.

"I suppose Ilyan has woven the length of the royal line through your hair as well?"

I didn't say anything, I just sat up as my stomach threatened to turn out its contents. I wasn't quite sure how to answer him; a simple yes would have worked wonders, but a part of me still wanted to keep it all sacred, as Ilyan had said.

I didn't need to worry. Dramin's grin increased at the look on my face, the wide smile obviously enough to answer my question.

"Then now you are My Lady, and my Queen. I think it suits you." Dramin's voice was soft in my ear as he leaned toward me, his tone deeper, almost respectful. The sound sent a shiver of pleasure and nerves up my spine.

"And how does a true bonding feel, My Lady?" he asked with the same deep voice, his head inclined toward me as if we were involved in some kind of wonderful secret. I guess, in a way, we were.

"Free. Perfect," I said, my eyes focused on Ilyan as I spoke.

"As it should be. You will find the peace you seek, Silnỳ."

"I hope you are right, Dramin."

"I usually am."

The need to laugh at Dramin's comment left as a loud bang echoed through the long hall. The sound of Ryland hitting his head was a loud, steady beat as everyone tried to grab his hands. I cringed against the sound, against the agony of his moans as everyone tried to stop him from hurting himself, and Ilyan turned to speak to Sain in an urgent whisper.

I hated watching this. I hated seeing Ryland so broken and Wyn so sad. I wanted them to be whole, and I wanted them to find peace, just as I had.

"I hope you are. I hope we all find what we are looking for," I whispered, the words truer than I had expected them to be.

They all turned to Sain as Ryland began to cry. Sain's lips moved as his eyes glossed over with the blackness of sight. My pulse sped at the dark embers in his eyes, my magic flaring so abruptly I jumped.

"You should try to see what he sees, My Lady," Dramin said as my head whipped toward him in shock.

"Is that possible?"

Dramin had told me of sights received by the group. I had seen them in the sight with Ilyan, and I had felt one with Sain yesterday, but to plug myself into someone else's sight, like some sort of circuit breaker—I didn't think I could do that.

"Yes, the Water will let you. The Drak are all connected through the wells of Imdalind, through the water. I am sure your blood felt the connection the moment the sight filled our Tatínek."

I stifled my gasp as I turned toward the other side of the room, my magic still a gentle current of electricity through me. Although Sain's eyes had returned to their usual green, I could still feel the pull of my magic, just as Dramin had said.

"Something to work on, eh?" Dramin asked as he drank from his mug, yet I could only nod as Thom slid into the seat beside me, his face stretching as he yawned. Everything about him looked more haggard and angry than usual. I wondered how much longer the drinking had gone on last night, or at the very least, how long they had been trying to calm Ryland down this morning.

"If Ilyan can't get Ryland under control, we may miss the deadline. If we leave after the sun comes up, it's going to put us all in danger," Thom said matter-of-factly as he wound a leather cord around his long brown dreads, placing the clumps in a low ponytail.

"Is that what Father saw?"

Thom nodded at Dramin's question, his magic surging as he brought the can of artichoke hearts he had been snacking on over to him.

"What's wrong with Ryland?" I asked, even though I

already knew. I felt so many of the same things when I fought my own insanity, felt the same anger pull at me when my emotions surged. When wicked magic got too close.

"Edmund is getting closer, Silný. Ryland can feel it in the air, and it's affecting his madness the same as it is for you. Same as for everyone. The earth has been screaming for days." Thom waved the speared artichoke heart toward the never-ending thunderstorm that surrounded us as he spoke.

I cringed. I had felt the pulsing anger for days, and although it had run through me and heightened my agitation, Ryland's actions seemed more like someone else was pulling the strings. I didn't want to think of it that way, though, of what else Edmund could be doing to him.

"Although you seem to be coping well. Did you sleep well last night?" Thom's statement snapped me right back from my reverie, my heart rate picking up as I narrowed my eyes at him.

"What does that mean?" I asked, my voice hard as I glared into him. Thom didn't seem to care, however. He grunted, looked away, and plopped another artichoke in his mouth. I narrowed my eyes at him in expectation of an answer, but he dutifully ignored me.

It was probably best he didn't answer me; it was just as Dramin had said, everyone had seen the ribbon in Ilyan's hair. They already knew, and Thom was just as good as anyone at pointing out things he shouldn't.

I sighed grumpily and looked away from him, my eyes pulling me right back to Ilyan who now had his eyes closed, his hand placed over Ryland's temples.

"You seem to really care for Ryland," Dramin whispered, his voice low. I didn't even turn to look at him. I kept my focus on Ilyan, knowing that Dramin's worry was misplaced.

"He was my best friend, Dramin," I said, the truth of the

word 'was' painful on my tongue. "Beyond that—anything we had before—those feelings are gone."

Ilyan's hands dropped from the sides of Ryland's head as he finished binding his emotions and memories. Ryland's eyes opened as he shook his sagging curls, his body seeming somewhat limp and deflated. Sain and Wyn moved right up to him, helping Ry to stand before they swept him from the room, their departure a silent signal, the last knoll before we plunged into the forest to fight our way out.

Ilyan stood as they did and walked toward us, his face dark and stoic. My nerves cringed against what I knew was coming, the words he was preparing already circulating through my head. He walked up right behind me, his magic that lived within me warming the closer he got until it sparked into a pleasant fire at the pressure of his hand against my shoulder. I sighed at the contact, hating the hoodie that dampened the warmth I was so used to feeling.

"Are you well enough to travel, Dramin?" Ilyan asked, his voice deep as it spread through the room.

"I can walk, if that's what you are asking," Dramin chuckled as he drained his mug before placing it in a large knapsack he had set on the floor beside him. "Although for how long, and how fast, has yet to be seen."

"I will help him, Ilyan." Thom shoved his hands into his pockets as he stood, accusation and humor shining behind his eyes as he looked at me, though he stayed silent. It was probably best; with Thom his comments were either overly sharp or terribly rude. Neither of which were needed this close to fleeing the abbey and facing the armies that lay in wait.

When Dramin wobbled as he leaned against Thom, my heart bumped so hard against my chest that it was a pain that shot through me. He was so weak, I wasn't even sure he could walk, let alone fight. Or escape. My throat closed up at the thought.

"Congratulations, may the wells of Imdalind follow your union," Dramin whispered, nodding his head reverently toward us before he turned to go, Thom careful to lead him away.

"My Lord. My Lady," Thom said, his voice deep as they walked out the door toward stage one of the plan that Ilyan had burned into my mind.

"Why am I not surprised?" Ilyan chuckled into the silence of the empty room as I pulled myself to standing.

You should have hidden your hair.

"And wear a hoodie? Not for me."

"I'm sure I could find a magazine that would tell you otherwise."

"Hmmm, Spanish magazines were never my forte," Ilyan sighed as his arm wrapped around me, guiding me from the room.

I walked by Ilyan's side as we made our way down the hall, Sain supporting Ryland just in front of us. We had only walked down one hall before we turned into a large courtyard, the shadows of light and dark that filled the open space as haunting as the forks of fire that lit up the sky while the thunder shook the earth.

One of the trees just within the forest line caught fire as the lightening hit it, the dried wood bursting into flames as the earth greeted us. The fire spread in a wall of rampant energy, my vision flashing as more fire infiltrated my thoughts. I shook my head to clear the sight and watched the trees burn, the omen of what was to come burning through my blood.

"We will part here," Ilyan announced, his arms still enclosed around me as everyone turned at our arrival, their faces as hard and stressed as the blood that flowed through my veins.

Thom nodded toward us before continuing to lead Dramin into the forest, his goodbyes already said, and even if they weren't, I had an idea that he wouldn't have said anything more anyway. Sain moved toward me, his pace slow after having helped Ryland to sit on one of the many benches that littered the large courtyard.

"I hope this choice you two have made does not affect the outcome of the sight." The timbre of Sain's voice changed as he looked at me, disapproval bleeding with disgust as his eyes glared into me.

Ilyan's muscles rippled underneath me as he looked at my father. I could feel his stress roll through me, my own matching it as I narrowed my eyes at him, my back stiffening as I made to step toward him. I didn't know if I wanted to yell, or scream, or berate him until he vanished to smoke. I just couldn't handle this, not anymore. If he wasn't going to support me then I didn't want him around.

Ilyan's arm wound around my waist before I could make my move, his strong grip keeping me against him, knowing what I had in mind. My frustrations didn't lessen at Ilyan's touch, however. If anything, they only heightened, Ilyan's own irritation fueling it.

"We have made this choice of our own accord, Sain," Ilyan rumbled, his voice growing dangerous as he stood his ground. "As her father, we request your respect for her choice, and your blessing if you would give it."

I would have expected Sain to stand down—to wilt under the power of Ilyan's voice—but he stayed straight, his chin rising as his eyes darkened. I wanted to cringe away from the look in his eyes, knowing what was coming, but I couldn't move, and my anger wouldn't let me look away.

"I will not," Sain spat. "The length of the royal line was not in the sight, Ilyan."

My blood froze as my sight flashed, image after image shooting through the darkness of my vision. They were sights that I had seen before, that I had seen too many times over the last few days, and in not one of them was my hair braided. In not one was Ilyan wearing his ribbon.

He was right; there were no ribbons, but last night... I had received that sight as well. I had seen Ilyan place the ribbons in my hair; I had received a sight of our bonding. I had felt the power of that sight last night as I lay wrapped in Ilyan's arms. The sights should match up. If everything Sain said was right, they should match up.

Something was missing. The sights were scattered and broken, just as Sain had warned. I just didn't understand why.

What does it mean, Ilyan, I sent him as I glared into my father, my distrust of him keeping my glare in place.

I do not know.

"I warned you," Sain said, the words that could have so easily been a threat sounding more desperate, as if he feared the end of the world.

Sain said no more before he walked back to Ryland who had fallen asleep against the bench Sain had left him on.

"What are we going to do?" I asked once Sain was out of earshot, my hand tightening around Ilyan's.

"Follow the plan," Ilyan almost growled. "We have to trust that all the sights are correct. You saw our bonding. Sain saw your victory. Both will come to pass."

He spoke like he believed it, but I knew he didn't, not anymore. I could hear the doubt and fear wind through him, his mind working tirelessly through the thousands of other options and commands he could give.

None of which he would.

I grit my teeth and looked away from him, knowing now was not the time to question him.

Wyn stood just across the courtyard from me, her body stiff as she watched me. She jerked forward like she wanted to run to me, like she needed to say something, anything. Neither of us moved, our words trapped deep inside. Her focus lingered on me as she removed her shoes and placed them in her backpack, the large, dark orbs of her eyes saying what I didn't want to hear, what she couldn't say.

What I couldn't say.

I couldn't bring myself to say the words that would come next; to say goodbye.

When we had charged into Ryland's manor, we had been outnumbered, but not to this extent, and there was something in the air that made everything feel more final.

More like the end.

I pinched my eyes shut at the thought, blocking Wyn from view as I pulled at my recall, the visions from the sight filling me, image after image of Ilyan fighting by my side, Ilyan screaming as he held my body, the stones of the abbey in the background.

My chest heaved and stuttered as I tried to breathe, my eyes opening to the empty courtyard, ready to face what was ahead of me.

"Are you ready?" Ilyan asked, his voice a powerful torrent of faith and confidence.

I nodded once and straightened my shoulders, letting the map Ilyan had placed in my mind flood me. The plan was so well laid out that my confidence shifted and grew with the knowledge of what was to come.

"Yes."

Ilyan's warm hand wrapped around mine, although I

didn't turn to face him. I stared straight ahead, the dark legs of the trees against the flickering fire a beacon of what was to come.

I squeezed Ilyan's hand back once, his pride and power pulsing in return before our legs pumped in unison, taking us toward our first destination; toward whatever was to come.

Together.

22
___

THE LIGHTNING ERUPTED a few feet from us as we flew through the trees, the thunder shaking my bones at the exact moment that the trees erupted in light. I jumped at the sound, the temporary daylight illuminating just enough of the camps below us that I felt my skin crawl.

I chanced a glance at them before darting back up into the thicker growth of tree limbs and their shadows. I gripped one scratchy limb after another as I pulled myself through the trees, the soft, dewy leaves brushing against my face as I sped past them.

A jagged razor of light cut through the forest a few seconds after the first, the storm seeming to follow us through the trees as we made our way to our final destination. I could see the camp we were headed toward just ahead, my mind circling the land with a ring of glittering green as it compelled me forward. Our target was about two miles from the camp that Ovailia and Edmund's guard occupied—the camp where Edmund would be within a few short hours if Sain's sight was correct.

I could hear the words repeat over and over in Ilyan's

mind, the sight mixing seamlessly with the plan he had given us. For hundreds of years Ilyan had fought this war and prepared for this battle, and suddenly, it had come. The moment that it had, however, he had begun to question everything that he had prepared for. His determination to protect me and to defeat his father cycled through with his need to keep me alive. Every possibility his mind created rotated around the conflicting sights that we were now being faced with.

I grabbed hold of a large branch as I swung to a stop, my grip tight as I hung precariously over the forest floor far below me. The air buzzed with electricity as a lightning bolt struck behind us, the jagged bolt lighting up the large camp that Ilyan had specified for our first attack.

The Trpaslíks were already awake and moving about in worried aggression, their magic prickling in the anger of the storm, of the final battle they believed to be hours away. My face fell at seeing the numbers of them, the attack that Ilyan had hoped to begin before they even awoke already spoiled. We would have our work cut out for us if we wanted to come out of this unscathed.

The heavy thunder shook through me as a jagged bolt of light came down on top of us, my muscles tensing as I fought my nerves. I expected rain to start falling at any minute, to soak the world and put out the fires that had already begun. I knew better, this storm was not for the tears of the earth. This storm was in anger.

I looked up at Ilyan from the large branch where I hung, his jaw tight as he glared into the camp, his eyes dark and trembling. I could already see the raw power burn into the world around him, feel his magic peak within and around me as he prepared to fight. His excitement burned into me, and I almost smiled.

Make sure Ovailia and the guard are where they need to be.

I could only nod at his request, the deep voice I almost never heard directed at me, detailing the severity of our situation. My magic soared through the trees and away from me as I closed my eyes to see, cringing as the rotten magic from the tent below us hit me, my stomach tightening in disgust before I sped past it in search of my prey.

I couldn't help but revel in the brilliancy of Ilyan's plan. Ovailia was close enough that once she heard of our arrival, she wouldn't be able to stay away. Yet, thanks to the density of the trees that separated us from them, they wouldn't know we had arrived right away.

It didn't take me long to locate Ovailia, her magic surging in expectation as she sat in the larger camp just beyond the gentle rise of the forest.

She paced along the edge, her eyes constantly darting up to the large field beside her where I was sure she expected Edmund to arrive from, and judging by her behavior, he was already late.

She's there. We don't have much time, I said, my voice shaking as much as my hands were.

Ilyan caught my nerves, his magic flaring as he jumped over the few branches that separated us to land right above me. His magic kindled as he lifted me up to him, his power a soft caress against my body as I flew into the tight grip of his arms.

We stood against each other as the sky cut apart, his soft hand running over my cheek as my magic reacted, sending warm vibrations into me. The strength of our magic moved together, our power ready for what we were about to plunge ourselves into.

"I have trained you for this; you are ready," he promised,

his voice a whisper as he leaned forward, pressing his lips against my forehead.

The warmth from the kiss seeped through me, lighting me on fire and supercharging my magic until I could feel it buzz into my blood stream. I nodded once at him in understanding, his answering smile illuminating the maniacal light that was in his eyes.

I didn't need him to say anything to understand what that look meant. I smiled as the warmth in his hand grew, his fingertips soft as they traced the line of my jaw before his touch was gone and the last precious beat of our time was over.

I closed my eyes as my magic stretched and I exhaled, stepping away from Ilyan's hold, off the branch and into the open air below me.

The air rushed passed me as my magic stretched away, my hand stretching forward to wrap around the strong branch that extended from the tree. I swung from branch to branch as I had so many times before. Adrenaline beat through me as I felt the tree warning me of what was coming, guiding me through the correct path of limbs, thunder covering our descent.

It was as natural as breathing.

I dropped to the ground before Ilyan did, my red shoes silent against the forest floor as I landed. My magic prickled in excitement as I stood, Ilyan landing right beside me just as another flash of light cut through the sky.

The garden of tents that we had landed in sprouted up like weeds, the filthy white canvases casting shadows and creating dangers that we hadn't really planned for. We had expected them to be asleep, but now they could be anywhere, a wrong turn could easily end in our failure.

I stretched my magic through the tents from where I

stood, seeking out the location of each of our enemies. My magic pulsed the information right into Ilyan without me having to focus on it. I saw him nod once from where he stood, his excitement flaring as the precise plan of what was going to happen fell into place. Ilyan's hand trailed up my back as he stepped in front of me, his muscles tensing under his t-shirt as he led the way.

We darted through the darkness between the tents, hiding among the canvas city with each lightning strike. Every few tents, Ilyan's magic would prickle, the air shimmering as he placed a shield over one of the many filthy tents, blocking the inhabitants from sound and sealing them inside. Ilyan's intent to save as many lives as he could was clear.

Part of me wished he wouldn't, that we could just wipe them out and finish this war in one clean fight. I knew better, though. Ilyan wasn't only King of the Skříteks, but of the Trpaslíks as well, and even if they didn't recognize that, Ilyan still held the same respect for them as he did for all of his other subjects.

Our subjects.

I shook the thought from my mind as we moved around another tent. My magic flared in caution and I reached toward Ilyan on instinct, the painful warning coming a second too late. My fingers wrapped around Ilyan's arm just as a Trpaslík came to face us, his eyes widening in confusion before the light of anger clicked in understanding. The Trpaslík's brain moved far too slow to grant him an escape, however; his mouth opened in warning just as the ground began to shake with Ilyan's magic, the dirt shifting as it swallowed him whole. A wave of dirt sealed itself over him, leaving only a small salad plate-sized patch of hair visible, the small spot almost indistinguishable amongst the dirt.

The man had disappeared before any sound had escaped him, the whole process moving so fast that I didn't fully understand what I had seen.

I stood still as I stared at the ground in awe, my body moving forward only when Ilyan grabbed my hand and led me off in the opposite direction. We had only darted down another dark trail of the maze when voices yelling about earthquakes sounded through the jungle of tents, the voices drowned out by yet another rumble of fire in the sky.

Stay close to me, my love, Ilyan pleaded, his hand warming against mine before he released it.

He didn't need to tell me twice, I could already feel the magic of the enemies that surrounded us awaken; the sharp, angry points of their terror and want of blood shaking through me until I fought the need to vomit. Their magic had changed from apprehension to the bubbling torrent of a blood hungry war. I could almost hear their teeth gnash together as they scattered, darting between tents. Searching for us.

They are coming, I said to Ilyan.

The muscles in his back rippled as his magic did, his excitement flaring aggressively just as a small Trpaslík darted between the tents before us. I jumped at his appearance, but Ilyan wasted no time. He spun on the spot, grabbing the man's head between his hands as he jerked it to the side, his magic severing the man's tendons as his hands broke his bones.

The Trpaslík crumbled to the ground like a rag doll, my eyes widening at the now lifeless man that Ilyan had dropped at my feet.

"Come on," Ilyan growled, his hand wrapping around mine as he pulled me after him, our feet taking us closer to our destination. Toward the center of the camp and the large fire that most of the Trpaslíks had gathered around. I could feel it just ahead of us.

I dropped Ilyan's hand as I ran behind him through the maze of dirty canvas, the dead leaves crunching beneath my feet in loud slaps. I could smell the rot of the food, the smoke of a fire, but I heard nothing except thunder. My heart growled with a quick, painful pulse as we darted through the horrifying blindness the tents had created, sure our enemy was behind the next turn. And the next.

Another Trpaslík jumped in front of us as we ran, his face wide with a grin as he found his bounty, obviously expecting to do us in and win a great honor.

He didn't even get a chance to try. Ilyan stuttered the moment he saw him, his body vanishing from between me and the Trpaslík. My jaw grit in determined fear as Ilyan left me exposed, my fists clenching as I tried to convince myself I was ready to fight. The Trpaslík grinned at the change, his yellow teeth flashing before I felt Ilyan's magic surge, his tall body reappearing unseen behind the Trpaslík who faced me.

A giant line of glittering black extended from Ilyan's hand as it cut through the air, moving through the solid flesh of the Trpaslík as he cut him in half. I could see the look of pain in the Trpaslík's eyes, his mouth opening in a scream only to have blood seep from his mouth as he tumbled to the ground, his fingers twitching in death.

My heart thundered painfully as I watched the Trpaslík collapse into a heap, just as another one darted through the tents, a battle cry on his lips. He attempted to ram Ilyan but Ilyan's hands stopped the tiny man's progress before he made it even half way. I was frozen in place as our enemy's screams were silenced with a simple movement of Ilyan's hand.

It was too late, though. With that one scream, he had given away our position, and I could already feel them closing in on us.

The aggressive warning of my magic rocked through me and I turned just as two husky Trpaslíks burst through the tent behind me, the canvas tearing to shreds as they ripped it apart in their fury.

White hot dread tightened through me as I saw them, the feeling of terror gripping me in an iron fist as my two attackers smiled, their wide grins snapping through me.

I stood frozen in fear, staring into the smile of death, my death. I could stand and die, or fight. Ilyan had trained me for only one thing.

And I was ready.

My fear vanished at the blood thirsty look in their eyes. The filthy touch of their magic ignited something else, something that I hadn't felt before. A mad power rippled and warmed through me in a dangerous energy—energy that promised I could do anything.

I smiled as they approached me, my magic erupting as I sent a wave of electricity toward them, knocking them off their feet. They shook with the mild pulse before I clapped my hands together. A straight path of lightning shot from my fingers, the crackling white light digging into their chests and frying their nervous systems. They couldn't even have moved if they tried.

My heart clenched with the knowledge of what I had done, the fear and regret growing before another Trpaslík darted behind me, his quick attack catching me off guard and burning through my shield. I screamed as fire spread through my bones, folding my body together painfully before my magic fought it, the burn leaving as my powerful magic counteracted what I was sure was supposed to have been a death blow.

I rose to face him, but Ilyan had already dropped my attacker to the ground in his panic to protect me. His eyes were wide in fear as he looked to me.

My breaths came in deep pants as I attempted to rebalance. My magic and my body felt jittery as adrenaline and fear ran rampant through my blood stream.

Ilyan said nothing as he stepped over the bodies between us. He didn't need to; I could feel it all, the heart-stopping fear as he had heard my scream repeating through his mind, the loss and devastation that still shook him. His warm hand wound around mine as he led me away, closer to the center of camp and the tent that was our target.

I just hoped we had enough time. If the Trpaslíks were seeking us out, there was no guarantee that Ovailia wouldn't already know of our arrival.

I could hear the heavy footfalls as our enemies closed in, their magic growing and flaring from all sides as they surrounded us. I clenched onto Ilyan's hand, sure he felt it, too, just as we moved through the final ring of tents, breaking free of the horrifying labyrinth, to face hundreds of Trpaslíks who stood around the red and purple fire, waiting for us.

They all looked up at our arrival, wicked smiles illuminating their eyes with a maniacal light that seemed to scream of our death. I could tell by the way they licked their lips—the way their fingers crackled and pulsed with power —that they thought this would be a quick end to the man they had hunted for so long.

They were wrong.

I smiled at the looks on their faces, smiled because they thought they had the upper hand. I could see the canvas walls of the Vilỳ's tent just beyond the crowd, the whole thing vibrating from the diseased creatures that had been restrained inside. That was where we needed to get to, the first major step in Ilyan's plan. By the look of fury in the Trpaslíks' eyes, though, they were going to make this harder than I would have liked.

My magic prickled as I pushed it away from me, my mind creating a map of the exact placement of every Trpaslík that surrounded us. The surge of their anger influenced my magic until it prickled under my skin. The power ran through me, the anger that Cail had infused me with finding an outlet, and I smiled, eager to begin.

My fingers sparked as I stepped in front of Ilyan, my hands spreading wide as I showed them the power that was waiting to escape, the magic that wanted to end this as much as I did.

The power continued to swell as I held it inside of me, the heat of my attack pressing against my skin, ready to explode. I saw the fear in the eyes of the Trpaslíks closest to us as their understanding peaked, yet it was too late.

My magic exploded in a rush of air and fire that spread away with the strength of a bomb. It burned through the fabric of the tents, and through the bodies of those who were closest to me. It washed over the entire camp as the smiles and jeers of a hopeful victory turned to yells and screams of agony and death.

Lines of men that had surrounded us fell, their screams evaporating into the air as their bodies hit the ground, never to rise again. The screams spread through the circle as the attack broadened, the sounds rippling away as more and more of them began to understand what was happening, the weak running away while the strong stepped forward, ready to face us.

To face me.

I was sure Ovailia had heard the screams, had seen the fire light the sky, and felt the residual waves of the attack. If she hadn't been aware that we were coming for her already, she was now, and we hadn't even blown the tent yet. Time was not on our side.

I only hoped Edmund had not arrived yet.

Get the tent, I ordered, hoping that Ilyan wouldn't second guess a command given by me as I rushed away from him toward the survivors who were charging me, their battle cry loud in my ears.

Ilyan rushed through the remaining army as I did, his movements quick as he took to the air, flying toward the tent in a streak of gold. I wasted no time and ran into the fray, my magic pulsing as two Trpaslíks found their feet, their faces hard as they rushed me, their magic sparking in preparation to kill.

I smiled at them, my hand pressing away from my chest as I pushed with an aggressive wall of magic that picked them up and sent them high above the trees. Their flight was illuminated by the lightning that littered the sky.

I had no time to watch them or to bask in any success before my magic flared in alarm and I spun on the spot, a swipe of my hand sending a flame of red through the air, the act removing the hand of the Trpaslík who had stood behind me, his hand placed for a final blow. He screamed in agony as he dropped to his knees, the fire of my attack sealing the flesh of his now dismembered arm.

I left him screaming as I took two steps back, a stream of black soaring through the air I had just vacated. I turned toward the attacker and pressed my hands against him, the pressure of the air working against me as if it was a brick wall. I pushed against the pressure, my magic exploding as it worked past it, sending the tiny man away from me and into a tree that stood twenty feet away.

I turned and ran as the loud crack of breaking wood filled the clearing, my feet skidding against dead leaves as I worked to make it toward Ilyan. My feet pumped forward as I jumped over the lifeless bodies that surrounded me, only to be stopped by a pulse as strong as a jackhammer against my spine.

I screamed at the impact, my spine contorting into a weird angle as I fell to the ground, my muscles seizing and flaring as I pushed myself onto my back, desperate to find a way to escape the pain, to fight the Trpaslík with the blood-stained eyes who looked down on me.

Joclyn!

I howled in agony as I fought the pain, the warmth of Ilyan's magic flooded me as I silently pleaded with him not to come to my aide, even though I could hear the desperate need in his mind.

I looked into the blood tinged teeth of my attacker as he laughed above me, and I screamed louder. The pain in my back fell away until all I felt was Ilyan's warmth, but I didn't stop screaming. I let my throat crack and bleed in my supposed pain, my magic prickling with awareness as more and more Trpaslíks surrounded me.

My heart broke as I continued to feel Ilyan's unfounded worry, his agony so broken that I almost lost hold of my erroneous scream, of my plan. I held on, though, my determination surging as my scream did.

More Trpaslíks looked down at me as they sneered and laughed at their supposed success. Their magic flared in victory, mine growing along with it.

I stopped screaming.

Silence rent the air as I smiled at them, their confusion

plastered on their faces before I pressed my hand against the dirt I lay against. My magic flooded the earth in a violent pulse, the power causing a rumble that shook the world. The ground shifted beneath me as the earth groaned and broke apart; dirt, rocks, and burning logs exploded into the air in a wide circle of destruction. Fire and rubble lifted from the ground in a spectacular blast that spread away from me like the ripples of a pond, the ground opening up as it prepared to swallow everyone in its path.

I watched the men's faces change from curiosity to fear as the stable ground they had stood on disappeared into a wide cavern that was ready to swallow them whole. The ground shifted beneath me and I rolled onto my hands and knees before I took off running, my muscles pumping fast in an attempt to escape the chaos I had just created.

I jumped and dodged the shifting ground as the dirt continued to explode around me, little pops of my magic acting like grenades against the forest floor. Each explosion showered me in dirt before I jumped into the air, the wind catching me when it took me away from the fray, past the screams and the open maw of earth that would swallow them all. The wind caught my hood as I flew, ripping it from my head as my braid fell free from its confines.

I had just cleared the line of dirt when the sky opened up in a pillar of fire, the blaze of power exploding from the tent of Vilÿs as Ilyan's magic ignited it in an explosion so powerful the trees that surrounded me swayed and shimmied in the wake. The sky glowed red as the eruption grew, the screams of the Trpaslíks below me faded out, replaced by the high pitched screams of the Vilÿs as they burned from within Ilyan's blaze.

Goodbye, my friends. I felt Ilyan's regret flood me as I

landed beside him, my feet stumbling as the strong wind that had supported me attempted to blow me over.

The powerful wind picked up the endings of the long, golden ribbons that bound our hair, the long strands tangling together as they hovered in the wind that surrounded us. I watched the blaze as my ribbon danced alongside Ilyan's, the long strands winding around each other as the red light reflected off the glittering surface.

Magic I had never wanted to feel again rocked through me, the waves of hatred and despair rising so quickly I couldn't stop the anxiety, no matter how hard Ilyan's magic worked to counteract it. I clung to Ilyan as the magic infiltrated me. The earth shook under the horrifying weight of the oppressive magic, and the red flames of the explosion turned the long, slender trunks of the trees into streaks of blood. I clung to Ilyan as the fear filled me, my legs unable to support my weight.

"Cail," I gasped the name, knowing it was wrong, knowing it couldn't be true.

Cail was dead. I had killed him. Besides, this magic was so much more than what had filled Cail's mind, more than the guards that had come before. This magic was the source, the pure hatred that had fueled Cail, that had fueled my fear and my tortures. I was feeling it in its unfiltered form, and the sensation was crippling.

It wasn't Cail I should be afraid of; it never had been because it had never been Cail who had held the cards, never Cail who had trapped me.

It was Edmund.

Edmund who had captured me. Edmund who had controlled Cail. Edmund who would kill us all.

I fought the scream as the realization hit me and my body fought a fight I wasn't sure I could win.

Edmund is here, I sent the words to Ilyan, knowing I couldn't possibly grasp enough oxygen to speak.

Ilyan's magic sparked violently as my words filled his mind, the anxiety growing as I clawed at the warm threads of Ilyan's power and weaved it with mine. I felt my magic peak at the added warmth, my Drak blood flaring as it pulled my mind through the fire-licked forest. Ilyan's mind moved right alongside me until Edmund's face came into view, the red tinge of the burning fire lighting his eyes.

I gasped as I realized how close he was, my breath coming in heavy spurts as my lungs fought what they so desperately needed.

I pulled my magic back as the vision faded from me, Ilyan's hand wrapping around my waist as he took off into the air away from Edmund. I felt the strong grip of Ilyan's arm as well as the wind that bellowed through my hair, but I couldn't focus beyond the panic that seeing his face, that feeling his magic, had given me.

"Fight it, my love," Ilyan whispered as the ash-tinged air flew over us. "Focus on my heartbeat. On our heartbeats. You are stronger than it."

I gasped for air as he held me to him, trying to focus on the steady thrum as our hearts beat in time, allowing the sound to calm me. It just wasn't working, the power of Edmund's magic seemed to be following us, to be growing.

I opened my mouth to scream, to warn Ilyan that Edmund was here just as our bodies crumpled against a stone barrier we could not see. Ilyan's magic left the air, the wind that had supported us falling from the sky, sending us tumbling to the ground.

We dropped like rocks through the air, Ilyan's arms leaving mine as we fell into a large branch, the bark scraping against my skin as I slid against it.

My fingers clawed at the smooth texture of the bark, trying to grab on, but my body continued to fall. Just like before, when I had been thrown from the window. I screamed at the memory; at the impact I knew was coming. My agonized voice ran through the forest as I fell into yet another branch, my back impacting into the solid surface before I slid away and fell to the ground in a painful jolt.

A loud grunt escaped me as a wave of pain moved through my bones. I froze in fear and pain as I tried to figure out what had happened, and if I could even move.

I wasn't sure I could. The pain was everywhere. Even without the pain, Edmund's magic continued to cripple me, my body winding itself in knots as I tried to move past it, to stay stronger than it.

My hearing peaked, waiting for another soft thud, but none came. I was the only one who had landed.

Ilyan? I asked, my voice panicked as I felt his mind rush, his magic surge.

I could sense Ilyan's magic rush through me, feel the pull of his heart. I fought my demons as I sought him out, my mind knowing where he was without so much as trying. I could feel him, surrounded by a circle of Trpaslíks just on the other side of the thick line of trees that surrounded me.

Joclyn! Ilyan yelled to me, his mind panicked for me while I felt the surge of excitement as he prepared to face battle. I needed to get to him, to help him.

I shifted my weight as I tried to stand, my body aching as I attempted to move fast, my broken ribs protesting against the movement as my magic frantically moved to heal them.

I looked through the trees as his battle cry rent the air, my magic pulsing with such a maniacal energy that I wasn't quite sure whether it belonged to me or him.

I prepared to take off into the air, knowing my aching

body would take too long to run, when the reason for our fall suddenly became clear. A magical pulse I hadn't felt in months swelled behind me just as the sound of crunching leaves met my ears. I cringed as I felt her, cursing myself for not paying better attention to my surroundings. For being so focused on the fear of Edmund's magic and my need to get to Ilyan. It had been a mistake I wouldn't repeat twice. I turned toward her, my eyes narrowing as her magic solidified.

"Well, well, well," Ovailia said, her voice hard and sweet as she made her way into the small clearing. "What a pleasant surprise. I had expected to capture my brother, but you as well? It must be my lucky day."

I said nothing as she moved closer to me, even though I could feel the anxiety slip away, the fear replaced by an angry pulse that sped through me. I just looked at her and let the emotions run over me, but the prickle of my animosity wasn't what I was focused on.

I narrowed my eyes at her as my magic surged through Ilyan, my power moving through his blood stream as I felt him fight, his heartbeat erratic as he realized who I was facing. My magic pulsed through his heart as mine sped up, his beating in time with mine.

Focus, my love. Ilyan's voice came strong as his magic pulsed in an attack, his mind moving as he sped to his next opponent.

I said nothing in reply; I didn't dare. I just stayed still, not daring to let my eyes leave Ovailia's, to give her the upper hand that I could tell she had been hoping to obtain.

Ovailia inched her way closer, her icy eyes digging into mine. This wasn't like with Cail, when I had feigned strength to give myself the upper hand. I had strength now, and I wanted her to know it. I wanted her to fear it. I narrowed my eyes as my fingertips sparked, her lips peaking in excitement.

She walked steadily with her long, blonde hair looking strangely out of place against the elegant black outfit she wore. She looked like she was dressed for a club, not a fight, right down to her cherry red stilettos. I wanted to smile at the image, yet kept it inside, knowing exactly what Ovailia had planned. She wasn't here to fight me; she was here to break me.

I was already cracked; they had seen to that. What they didn't know was that my crack was healing, and I was going to fight against it.

"What? Not going to say hello?"

"Hello." I let the darkness that was in my heart seep into that one word, hatred and malice fueling the heavy tone as I smiled. The wicked line of my grin spread over my face and she flinched ever so slightly, her feet stopping her in place as her eyes trailed over my small frame. Her eyes widened at the long, golden ribbon that trailed over my shoulder.

"You little bitch," she snapped, "cheating on Ryland like that. Just wait until he finds out, he's going to track you down, hunt you. He will kill you."

I flinched at her words, my heart rate increasing so fast I could barely control it, but I could. I would.

I grit my teeth and snapped my fingers as I brought my magic to me, a wall of power soaring away from me and right into Ovailia, sending her tumbling away.

She screamed as she slammed into a large tree, her face shocked as the attack she hadn't been expecting carried her away.

Her head snapped up to me as her magic surged, her eyes blazing in an angry heat of malice. The emotion was stronger than I had ever seen from her.

I knew the look was meant as a threat; I could see the warning behind her eyes, however, it didn't faze me. I just matched it, my eyes narrowing as I waited. Waited for her to fight back, knowing that if she didn't, I would finish her anyway.

She jumped to a standing position as my eyes met hers, the scorn on her face making it clear she wouldn't hold back.

That was good because neither would I.

23

OVAILIA RUSHED me as she screamed, her hair a streak of white light behind her as her magic pushed her forward.

I took one look at the anger in her eyes and exploded into the air, knowing I couldn't face her head on. I soared through the smoky air until I was high above her, my magic changing directions as I slammed myself down on top of her. I landed in a rush of wind and magic, pushing her into the hard ground as a bolt of lightning struck only feet from where we had collided.

The earth vibrated with the power, the air prickling with the electricity that lingered in the air. I felt the heat of it against my skin, almost like it was trying to find a way inside of me.

My teeth grit in anger as I pressed my hand against Ovailia's neck, my palm heating and pulsing as my bones tensed, my pressure against her wind pipe increasing. She began to choke and laugh underneath my hold, her snide glare boring into me and I hesitated, giving her just enough time to slam her hands into my chest with a hot wall of force.

I called out as the pulse of her attack rippled through me, the violent magic sending me hurdling through the air away from her. The slow burn of her magic flooded through me only to be extinguished by my power as I fell.

Air and ash swirled around me, the long, golden ribbon whipping about before I brought a strong gust of air against me, the strength of my magic aligning my flailing body before I even hit the ground. I glowered into the stoic blonde before me as I dug my heels into the dirt. The grind of dirt and rocks rumbled through the small clearing as I skidded to a stop, the sky opened up in a deafening groan.

A sharp crack of lightning erupted behind me, the clearing illuminating with a blinding light. I didn't dare take my eyes off Ovailia from where she stood before me, my heart thudding in my chest as I looked into the icy blue that was so different from her brothers.

The golden ribbon that was bound in my hair glowed as the long end trailed softly to the ground in front of me. I watched the delicate ribbon glide toward the ground while my eyes remained trained on Ovailia as she stood, her hands balled into fists. The ribbon landed against the dirt between us and I jumped into action, my feet pounding as I rushed her, my fist a hard rock as it intercepted with her stomach.

She yelled at the impact before shoving me away, the powerful jolt of her magic increasing the force, but not as much as she would have liked. I let my determination rip from my throat in a yell as I rushed back at her, my magic speeding behind my fist as I punched her hard in the jaw, sending her and her ridiculous stilettos skidding through the dead leaves of the forest floor.

"I don't know why you are even trying to fight me," she taunted as she wiped the blood from her lip, her voice the same acidic tone I had always heard from her. "There is no way you can defeat me."

I said nothing, I only glared into her, a small smile playing on my lips as I panted, waiting for my fear and anger to settle into something I hoped I could manage.

Ovailia's hands fanned out, her fingers stretching as sparks of fire spread between them, the rainbow of colors flashing violently. Her eyes flared with a wicked gleam before she brought her hands together, the colors and magic colliding in a bang that echoed through the forest.

I cringed at the sound, my anxiety sparking as a wall of fire and smoke erupted from her hands. It stretched across the entire length of the clearing, the height of it kissing the top of the lightning strewn sky. My teeth clenched as I watched it grow, watched the flames flow and swim through the barrier that was now sneaking toward me.

The fire Ovailia had sent at me deepened to a blood red as the earth rumbled and lightning sliced through the air on either side of me, the two giant forks framing me as I faced Ovailia, who stood hidden behind the attack that would devour me.

The jolt of electricity sped through the earth, and pressed against my body, seeping into me as it electrified the frantic energy that pulsed through me. I felt my magic bubble in reaction; I felt it crush against me as it tried to race out of me. I pressed my hands forward, letting the earth's magic swell through me and out of my fingers. The stream of crackling power collided with Ovailia's wall in an explosion of air and fire before it melted to the ground, leaving her hard, hatred-lined face glaring into me.

I dropped my hands as the last of the liquid fire seeped into the ground around me, the useless attack turning to little more than ash. I was unable to stop the fiendish smile that spread over my face, the gleam now a stark contrast to the fear that was seeping through Ovailia's eyes. I said nothing as I stared into her, knowing full well that she had just sent her best weapon my way, and I had demolished it.

"I am going to destroy you!" Ovailia screamed as she rushed me, her intent clear. If magic didn't work, she would do her best to rip me apart with her bare hands. Good thing I didn't mind playing dirty.

My heart thudded with adrenaline lined fear as I ran at her. Ready to meet her head on, ready to finish this.

We met in the middle of the clearing, our magical pulses colliding in sparks of black and grey as fists met skin. Ovailia threw frantic punches as she screamed, my own retaliation serving more as a block while I tried to claw and scrape at her in any way I could. I reached forward blindly, winding my fingers around her long hair before I took two wide steps forward, pulling her by the long strands as I whipped her around behind me. My hand slammed into the small of her back as my muscles pulsed with a maniacal energy. I threw her through the air, sending her hurdling away from me.

"You are not who I am meant to fight," I screamed in frustration, hating the way my voice deepened, how my sight fueled the words and told me they were true. Even if they were true, I didn't want them to be; I didn't want the words to escape me.

My muscles tensed and flexed as I faced her, the strength that I did not know I had engulfing me. Ilyan's magic surged as I screamed, my magic stretching toward him, pressing into him, his pride for me surging as Ovailia ran back to me, a long snake of an attack dripping like tar from her fingers before she sent it through the air at me.

"Do you really think you can fight Edmund? That you can defeat him?"

My heart thudded at her words, at the meaning behind them. Everything in me tightened as she rushed me, my anger rippling over me as I pressed my hand toward her attempted attack, one pulse of my magic turning it into smoke.

"I know I can!"

"And stay alive?" she taunted, her tactic changing as she tried to pull out the madness that they had implanted in me.

I swallowed as I tried to control my panic and narrowed my eyes, fighting the fear that tried to pull into me, desperately fighting against her games.

My magic moved, unbidden, to Ilyan as I focused on her, the spaces of each Trpaslík laid out as Ilyan twisted and turned in his fight with them. As soon as he felled one, another one would stream through the trees toward him. One after another I could feel them as they ran toward him. I could feel them cut him, feel his blood drip over his skin. He needed help. I needed to get over there, but with Ovailia breathing down my neck, I knew there was no way.

I didn't pull my scowl off Ovailia as I let my magic surge into Ilyan, pulsing through him as his attacks grew in strength and exploded out of him as he wielded my power, taking down several with one simple attack.

That's my girl, Ilyan's voice filled my head, and I fought the smile that wanted to seep over me.

"Didn't think so," Ovailia said, pulling my mind right back to her, only to see her move from my line of sight.

She moved so fast I barely saw her, her body right in front of me one minute and behind me the next. My body tensed in fear as her hand wrapped around my braid as she pulled it down, my back arching uncomfortably at the forced movement.

"You might as well give up now," she grunted in my ear as the smell of burning hair met my nose. "Die now, die later, what does it matter?"

Her voice ground between her teeth, her words a taunt that hit more in fact than in fiction. She just didn't need to know it, and right then, it didn't matter.

I screamed as she pulled me down further, my back aching as the fragile bones bent unnaturally. The smell of the beautiful braid as it burned beneath her fingers hit my nose, the heart-wrenching aroma growing as she destroyed the most precious thing that anyone had ever given me.

I screamed louder at the smell, my heart ripping open at what she was doing. My magic surged in my frenzy, the air prickling as my magic exploded in a flame of white light, the pulse of energy releasing my hair from her grip as she fell away from me.

I had wanted to fight her, to defeat her. But now, smelling the charred remains of Ilyan's gift, it became more than that. It became an angry flame that wanted to destroy her. I lunged at her as she stumbled away from me, my legs locking around her waist, pinning her beneath me as I compacted her into the dirt. I pressed my hands against her face, my fingers clawing into her as I kept her in place, the fire of my magic working through her body as the earth attempted to swallow her.

The earth beneath us rippled like quicksand as I screamed in anger. The dirt swallowed her body as the ferocity of my magic led it on. My body ached as my heart thundered against my chest, my blood heating as I stared into her, watching her fear seep through her eyes before the movement stopped, her own magic beginning to fight back.

The dirt that had been engulfing her began to shake, small explosions popping around us as Ovailia screamed against my hands, sending an explosion of earth right into my face. I fell away from her as the pulse threw me to the ground, the simple weapon blinding me as I scooted away from her over the piles of dirt I was now surrounded by.

I wiped the dirt from my face in a panic, my chest heaving in fear as I tried to regain my vision, knowing she wouldn't wait. I wiped the dirt from my eyes when her fist made contact with my stomach. I could taste blood and bile on my tongue as lightning struck into a tree right behind her, sending it into a blaze, the dried leaves that covered the ground catching and spreading the fire as it moved to surround us.

The rumble of the earth's energy roared through me as Ovailia's hands moved to wrap around my face. She clenched her fingers into my cheeks, pressing against the gentle bones before her hands lunged forward, sending my face into the hard surface of her knee. I screamed in agony as the pain rippled over my face and down my spine, the bones snapping as my nose broke. Blood flowed freely down my face as my magic swelled to heal it, but I knew it wouldn't be fast enough.

I knew it would be foolish to wait.

My head spun as the blood flowed, a sight I knew would kill me threatening to break through. I fought it, knowing that if I were to black out for even a moment, Ovailia would end me. I couldn't let that happen, even if I were to survive it; I couldn't risk Edmund finding out that I was a Drak.

I was beginning to understand why Drak's did not have offensive magic.

The fearful pressure in my chest ached as I spit the blood out of my mouth and pushed the sight away with a gasp, my blood-covered hands jutting forward as I pulled at Ovailia's slender legs. The action was unexpected and she tumbled to the ground in a heap right onto the already smoldering leaves. She screamed as the fire surrounded her, rolling away from it as she extinguished her now-singed clothes.

I shuffled away from her just as the air prickled with the storm, the magic of the earth screaming into my heart, crying through my fear and telling me what to do.

I wasn't one to question it.

My breath heaved as I stood, lifting my hands to the sky just as it broke apart, the bolt of lightning cutting through the dark clouds to strike against the palms of my hands. A pulse of steel surged through my body in a million volts of pain and fire. I screamed as it hit me, as it moved through me—moved into me—until everything that I was had turned into heat and agony. My ears filled with the sound of thunder, with my own scream, and with Ilyan's yells of terror as he registered what had happened to me.

I heard them; I felt them, but ignored them all. I let the energy move into me, let it rock through me before I moved my hands, pointing right into Ovailia as my body redirected the power that had just filled me. The air snapped with a rumble of thunder that moved out from me as the lightening erupted from my hands, shooting right into Ovailia's chest and sending her flying away from me. Her body crumpled against the large trunk I had sent her into before. The flaming tree broke apart easily as her body continued on, speeding through the dark forest until it swallowed her and I could no longer see her.

I panted as she disappeared, wishing that it would be the end of her, but somehow knowing that it never would be. That she would be back.

I sunk to my knees as Ilyan's magic flooded me, the warmth welcome. My lungs pulled in desperate gasps of air in an attempt to find my footing, to find calm.

I breathed in deep spurts as Ilyan broke away from the thinning Trpaslíks he still fought, most running in the other direction after the explosion I was sure they had just witnessed.

That I had just witnessed.

I had seen it, felt it. I could still feel it, feel the rumble of electricity that surged through me, and yet I had no idea how I had accomplished such a thing.

I stared at the darkened patch Ovailia had disappeared through, twigs snapping as Ilyan broke through the trees, his movements quick as he rushed to my side, gathering me into his arms. His hands were warm against my skin as he pulled me into him, his worry so strong it almost scared me.

"You're okay?" I asked as I turned to look at him, my heart fluttering at seeing him there, at the wide blood stain that spread over his shirt.

I reached my hands up shakily, almost afraid that the lightning I could still feel buzzing through my veins would seep into him. I held my hand above his skin, the warmth of his body radiating into me before my hand pressed against his face, the skin soft and calming, the lightning still restrained within my body.

"Thanks to you," he gasped, his voice broken and soft in emotion.

I smiled before I turned toward where Ovailia had disappeared, almost expecting her to come strolling from the darkness, ready to continue the battle.

Ilyan's hand wrapped round my waist as he lifted me to standing, his pace slower with the extra work. I pushed my magic into him, warming him as I moved to heal him, feeling his skin already knit together from the deep cut he had received, the bone he had broken already bound and repairing.

"We need to finish this," I said as I clung to him, my heart beating in fear and excitement at what I had just said. I let the words flow, hard and strong, as the truth rocked me. I knew I didn't have another choice; it wasn't true that I ever had.

I grit my teeth as Ilyan's acceptance filled me, his pride strong as he wrapped his hand around my destroyed braid, his magic sparking as he repaired the damage that Ovailia had done.

"I will follow you wherever. You are my forever," Ilyan whispered as we turned toward the abbey, the flickering fire that was far ahead of us a shining beacon of where the building sat.

It was there, just beyond those trees, that I would find my destiny. That my life would define the fate and future of all those that I held dear.

I clung to Ilyan as I heard my own words repeated back to me, my thoughts moving through him as his so often did through me. There was no stopping this anymore; that much was clear. The only thing left was to face it.

"Where is my father?" Ilyan asked, his voice hard as he moved forward, his magic flaring through me as our bodies lost contact.

My magic surged as I followed him, the electric tendrils of my power laying out the map of the land that surrounded us. My eyes closed at the image of the Trpaslíks who swarmed through the forest, most on their way to us, others running through the abbey or standing guard outside. There, in one of the rooms at the center of the large abbey, tucked near the back, was Edmund.

"In the abbey, in a room near the bell tower," I answered, my eyes snapping open to the long, golden ribbon that trailed down Ilyan's back.

Ilyan nodded once as he began to move, and my heart thumped at the thought of the hundreds of Trpaslíks who separated us from Edmund. I moved to meet Ilyan, my fingers weaving through his as I pulled him to a stop, turning him to face me.

"Let's go right to Edmund, Ilyan. Let me finish this." I clung to his hand as I begged him, knowing he could feel the need, feel the power that coursed through me.

I needed to finish Edmund, and right then, I knew that I could.

I wanted to.

"How? When the abbey is swarming with his guard?" Ilyan asked, his nerves fluttering at what was to come.

"A Stutter."

Ilyan's eyes widened at my request, his mind going into overdrive as he thought through every option of the plan, every possibility. I felt them rumble through me as I tried to understand, but with the mixture of Czech and English and the quick flashes of his thoughts, it only confused me more.

"We cannot Stutter," Ilyan said, his thought slowing down as the depth of his voice grew. "Not this close to him. He will be able to feel us coming; he will know right where we will appear. I have run into this problem before. I do not want you to get lost in the blackness between worlds."

Ilyan leaned closer to me as he pressed his hands against my face, his touch soft as he looked into me, the desperate need that had taken over him seeping into me. Edmund was stronger than I had assumed. Being able to feel a Stutter? The thought sent ice into me and I nodded, the strong confidence I had felt before ebbing.

"Then what do we do?" I asked.

Ilyan's eyes burned into mine as his hands trailed down the side of my face, his fingertips brushing over my neck. I shuddered at the touch, my magic warming and reacting to the connection as Ilyan pulled the hood over my head again, tucking the braid and the ribbon carefully away.

"You tell me, my love," Ilyan said, his smile feeling strangely out of place. Then I understood. I understood the question and the meaning behind it.

I could see what was ahead.

I nodded once and closed my eyes, my chest heaving as I caught my breath, pulling at the dizziness I had pushed away before. It rumbled through me as Ilyan held me, his hands warm against my skin and my blood reacted to it. It boiled through me as my vision burned red, the blackness flashing before the images came, flashes of fighting that moved through my vision in a strobe.

I gasped at the images, the flashes of Ilyan fighting through fire, the stones of the abbey surrounding us as the maniacal light hit his eyes. My body tightened uncomfortably as the images slowed and the words Ilyan sought seeped from my lips.

"Take the fire and find your strength. The last moment is yours."

The words faded as the image did, my confusion growing at the nonsensical words which had seeped from my mouth, leaving me to replace them with ones I could understand.

"We fight."

"Then we fight," he repeated, his hand wrapping around mine as together we ran through the forest. Our speed spiked as his magic surged, the power moving right through me while we ran. We didn't stop as we approached the burning tree line, Ilyan's magic surrounding us in a shield that kept the flames from burning our skin.

We came to a halt just before the large pasture that surrounded the abbey, my heart falling to see fire erupting from many of the windows. The flames licked at the stone, sending billows of smoke into the already darkening sky. The grounds in front of us were filled with dozens of Trpaslíks; rows of an army, all at attention. All ready to fight. The scene before us was laid out so perfectly I could feel my stomach clench together in warning.

Edmund had set a trap even though he did not know all the contents of the sight. He had made his plan, hoping he could assume enough to give him the upper hand.

Ilyan clenched my hand as we prepared to move, his body bouncing in excitement before a pain shot through his arm with an intensity so sharp that I could feel the shadow of it in my own body. I gasped at the pressure, my hand clamping over my arm as the surge faded, the sharp pain disappearing into nothing.

"What was that?" I hissed, unable to keep the frustration out of my voice, the memory of the pain too fresh.

It felt like I had been stabbed, and even though the pain was gone, I almost expected the culprit to remain, my arm to be drenched in blood, yet nothing was there.

"Something has happened. Wyn has deviated from the plan," Ilyan almost growled, his eyes narrowing as he glared through the abbey grounds and toward the forest on the opposite side that had been the escape route for the others.

I looked through the fires and the armies as he did, my magic taking my sight away from me and through the trees until I found them. The others walked forward in a quick pace that none of them seemed capable of maintaining. Thom supported Dramin while Sain practically dragged

Ryland. They followed Wyn as she led them, her face haggard and blood-covered.

If they had followed the plan, they would have been flying; instead, they stumbled and limped through the forest. They had been attacked, and what was more, more of our enemies were heading right for them. I could feel the deep, angry pulses as the Trpaslíks ran to surround them.

"They are headed into an ambush; they can't fly as you commanded them." My voice sounded distant as I kept my vision on what was happening several miles away from us.

Ilyan's muscles tensed, the same pain shooting up his arm as his magic again warned him of the break in his plan. His eyes stayed focused on the coming massacre that he could not see, his heart a thundering pulse in his chest as his jaw clenched and unclenched.

I could feel Ilyan's need to help them, the same need pulsing within me. My friends were about to come under attack; they were about to die. I needed to help them. I needed to rush there and fight for them, not stay on this foolish mission that would only end in my death.

I could save them.

But I couldn't, because this mission wasn't foolish. It was needed, and I was the only one who could finish the job.

They are on their own, I spoke the words into Ilyan's mind, my heart breaking as Ilyan's did, too. The foolish hope that maybe we could still get there in time raged through him like wildfire.

"We need to get to my father."

I nodded in agreement, Ilyan's hand tightening around mine as our magic met between us. We burst through the trees in our desperation to reach the abbey, the wind at our backs as the thunder rumbled overhead, blocking our movements from view and our sounds from our enemies' ears.

Our hands broke free from each other as Ilyan continued to shield me from within, our pace quickening as we ran to meet the first row of Trpaslíks. Their faces were hard as they stared into the tree line expecting our arrival, oblivious to the fact that we were already there.

Kill as many as you can; move straight through, Ilyan's voice rumbled through me, my heart stuttering at the word *kill*, my soul fighting against it.

My muscles tensed before I continued on, knowing I didn't have another choice. Not anymore.

I met the first line of the army, my hands pressing against two men's chests as I sent a line of fire right into their hearts, stopping them on contact. I burned their magic to nothing with the one touch, their eyes rolling back as they fell to the ground, just as three more dropped dead a few feet away from me. The movement caught the attention of those who surrounded them, yells of fear and anger rising around us as they rushed to help and turned to face their invisible foe.

I ran forward in an attempt to get away from the now blindly fighting Trpaslíks, pressing my hand into one chest after another, my arms wrapping around heads as I twisted necks. Men dropped to the ground like stones as I kept pace with Ilyan, the lifeless bodies dropping before us.

It didn't take the Trpaslíks long to figure out what was going on, to pinpoint where we were and where we were headed. A wall of fire erupted in front of us as the army herded their prey, hatred discoloring their features and fueling their magic.

It was then that I understood why Ilyan had asked me to

kill, and not just injure. We were cornered, and there weren't as many to fight now.

A ripple of nerves overtook me as I came to a stop in the exact place the Trpaslíks had predicted, Ilyan halting only steps away from me.

I pressed my back against his as I faced our attackers. Ilyan reached back and clasped my hand, the shield dropping away. Shouts of glee and dark excitement surrounded us as we came into view, bloodthirsty grins flashing around us.

I stared into them as my fear grew, the confidence I held before seeming to vanish at the sheer numbers that surrounded us.

I could feel Edmund just within the walls that were now within touching distance. I could get there. I could end this.

My chest heaved as the sky cut with lightning and the flickering of the fire that consumed the abbey lit the faces of those who surrounded us. The tongues of light and dark turned them into the menacing monsters that they had become inside. The group came closer, my eyes hardening as Ilyan's did. He wasn't going to give up, and neither would I.

"Use my magic," he whispered to me as his magic flooded into me, a lightning storm of energy rippling through my body.

I pulled the energy into me, stretching it alongside my own as it grew, my power expanding, the lightning that still raged within me sparking. I held onto Ilyan's hand as I pulled him around, a green fire shooting from my hand as it spit through the air toward the circle of demons that wished to take our lives. I let the wicked flames flow from me, the fire strong as it caught those who would kill us, their clothes and skin catching fire in the impermeable blaze as their screams rang in my ears.

I had only made it halfway around the hoard before I erupted into the air, my arms clinging to Ilyan as I took him with me. We soared away from the screams and the angry calls, only to land in the nearby courtyard of the abbey, the enemy I had hoped to escape only feet from us.

The heat from the fire I had created seeped into me as the screaming continued, the agony of those I had cursed to a slow death twisting my insides. I didn't look back to see what I had done; I pushed the regret away, turned, and ran, my red shoes making a hollow sound against the stone as Ilyan followed me.

I pulled us into the closest entry I could find, the stone entry collapsing behind us as we entered the building, trapping us inside. The fire that had engulfed the building cast long shadows as we raced through the stone hallways, the heat from the fire growing the further into the belly of the building we moved.

Closer.

Closer.

Edmund was so close that I could hear his laugh echo in my head. My breathing picked up as his magic grew, the fear that had been misplaced for so long surging violently through me. I pushed the fear away, knowing I had no choice other than to continue, to face him and the insanity that he had controlled me with.

We ran up a small flight of stairs to emerge into what should have been another hallway, but instead was now only open air.

Happy laughter met my ears as a small group of Trpaslíks who had been destroying the space turned, the joy in their voices fading into a menacing growl as they caught sight of us.

I stepped forward, ready to fight my way past them just as more than a dozen came streaming in behind them, their eyes lit in hatred as they ran at us with the others, ready to destroy us.

I squared my shoulders, ready to attack, but Ilyan pulled me away, his muscles tense as we ran toward the pulse of Edmund's magic, searching for a way to break through the lines of guards Edmund had set for us.

Ilyan pulled me down the elevated hallways as ash flowed around us, the waves of destroyed stone rising and falling beside us, letting pools of firelight cover the floor and the angry crackle of the flames fill my ears. Ilyan's hand was tight around mine as Edmund's magic grew the closer we got to him.

The icy chill of his magic ran down my spine, writhed through my stomach. My fear and anxiety grew the nearer we came. I fought my mania, my anxiety; I wasn't sure how much longer I would last.

I tried to push beyond my broken emotions, I knew I needed to. It was my destiny to beat him, to defeat him. I just wasn't sure I was strong enough to keep the terrors away. Even with Ilyan's magic running through me, Edmund's magic awakened something that was proving to be bigger than me.

I panted as we ran, my breath breaking as the flames seemed to grow, the red of the fire dripping over the stones in streaks of blood. Ilyan stopped abruptly as we came head on with at least ten of Edmund's men. Their battle cries raged over the fire, sparking at the anxiety that was already threatening to drown me. They were ready for us, just as we were ready for them.

I pushed away my mania, a deep scream ripping from my lips as I rushed them, Ilyan by my side as flashes of fire and smoke and light and dark surrounded us. I fought from one to another, desperate to make it through, to fight just as Edmund's magic flared, the power so strong I knew he was only a few steps away.

I screamed in terror as my insanity blended in my eyes, the few stone walls that surrounded us bleeding red rivers as my scream continued. Edmund's magic pulsed into me like a hot knife that cut into me. It was pain and heat and agony and I screamed more, the pain rushing into me so quickly that I knew it wasn't my insanity that brought the pain. It wasn't my nightmares that caused the blood to flow over my stomach.

My body seized in agony as a Trpaslík's sword that I hadn't seen, a weapon I hadn't expected, sliced through my stomach, an acidic magic plunging into me.

Ilyan spun as my scream rent the air, his eyes wide in fear as he watched the sword pull from my stomach, watched my blood spray over the man who had attacked me, and watched it flood out of me.

My scream grew as Ilyan disappeared from sight only to feel his magic pulse behind me, the life of the Trpaslík who had injured me leaving with only a pulse of Ilyan's magic. I gasped as life left my attacker, my body falling as his did. I screamed as my bones split and shattered, my skin burned as I fell. I was falling, endlessly falling. I waited for the impact, for my back to break only to have Ilyan's strong hands catch me, pulling me into him. I tried to reach to him, but everything was pain as my body tried to turn itself inside out. All I could focus on was my pain, on keeping my hands against me, desperate to stop the blood from flowing.

Ilyan's magic pulsed into me as my own sped to my belly,

my stomach attempting to knit itself back together before it was too late. My mind screamed in fear, telling me that it already was. I could feel the Trpaslík's venomous magic burn off my magic's attempts to heal me, the blood flow only increasing.

Ilyan's magic grew in a pulse of tight, cold pressure as we moved between worlds, but all I could focus on was the pain.

"Ilyan?" I moaned as he began to run, his movement quick and smooth, the motion so similar to when he had found me behind the dumpster. When I had broken my back, when the flame of fire had crippled me, and when I had wanted to die. Everything about this was so similar except that, this time, I didn't want to die.

"It's all right, my love. You are going to be all right." His words were desperate as his feet moved more quickly, the fear of what he had just done outweighing my healing injury.

Ilyan had Stuttered.

He hadn't dared to go far from what the sight had shown, to put too much strain on the magic that was trying to heal me, and so we remained in the abbey, the smell of fire surrounding us. Trapped and unable to Stutter again.

Ilyan held me close to him as he ran, his magic trying to numb the agonizing pain that split through my bones. I clawed at the wound, pressing myself into Ilyan's chest as his worry washed over me, his need to keep me alive screaming at him, trying to convince him that he shouldn't follow the path that sight had given us. To defeat Edmund.

I could already feel him rushing toward us, Ilyan's Stutter showing Edmund exactly where we were.

Everything tensed as I felt him move closer, and I gasped in pain. Ilyan's magic enveloped me as I coughed, the warmth of my blood spreading over my chin, the taste of dirt and iron spreading over my tongue.

"He is coming," I gasped, my voice deep and strained as Ilyan's grip on me tightened.

I wanted to say that we could still fight—that we could get out of here alive—but I was no longer so sure, and judging by the internal war that raged through Ilyan, I knew he felt the same.

Ilyan's feet slowed as we came to a small alcove, the light from the fire flickering against the rock as well as us. It illuminated the stormy dusk with eerie shadows, and dark slivers of fear.

Ilyan leaned me against a large portion of rubble, the slab of wall slanted just enough that it could support my weight. His hands were soft as he lowered me down, making sure I was stable before he released me.

His fingertips lifted the shards of the shirt and hoodie to reveal the deep gash. I cringed as I saw it, my blood seeping out of large gaping gash as my magic tried to knit it back together before my eyes.

"Oheň z pekla," Ilyan said, his teeth grinding together as he ran his hand over the injury, coating his already burned palm in my blood. "A cursed blade, one that is meant to kill on contact. Your magic appears to be stronger than it, however. You should survive it."

I shook my head, although I wasn't quite sure I understood. A cursed blade sounded much more dangerous than Ilyan was making it sound, and the word 'should' was anything other than calming.

Especially given where we were.

I bit my lip as he carefully placed what was left of the hoodie back over my stomach, leaving his hand against the gash in my skin underneath.

"Can you stand?" he asked, his palm still flat against the open wound as he pushed his magic into it.

"Yeah." I nodded my head as I let Ilyan pull me up. My stomach felt like it was being torn apart, the open wound pulsing angrily as I stretched it in ways I knew I shouldn't be.

I wanted to lie down and sleep, not stand and fight, but it wasn't like I had much of a choice.

I could hear Ilyan tracking everyone's movements in his own mind. I could feel Edmund as he ran right toward us. I could sense the fear in Ilyan's mind, the desperation to end this. I could also hear his fear that I was injured, that I wasn't strong enough to fight. I was little more than a sitting duck with my hunter steps away, his gun already drawn.

I leaned against the wall behind me as I tried to find my strength, Ilyan's arm wrapping around my back as he supported me. I gasped at the pressure, the pain leaving as Ilyan held me. I looked into the golden blue of his eyes, the light so bright that I almost forgot that we were being pursued. I forgot that we were moments away from death.

I forgot that I had failed.

"I love you, my Joclyn," Ilyan whispered, tears building in his eyes as he reached up to press against my face, his touch soft and gentle. I cried alongside him, my heartbeat racing.

I heard the words, knew of their truth, but I also felt the words behind them, heard the pained goodbye that screamed from Ilyan's heart.

"I love you, my Ilyan," I said, my voice breaking, and he smiled, his joy a bright light behind his pain.

He moved closer to me, his lips brushing against mine before he stopped, his heartbeat fluttering so fast that my own froze in confusion.

Ilyan moved away from me, the image of the sight flashing through his mind: the broken image of Ilyan holding me against the wall as the abbey burned and we cried in each other's arms. I replayed the sight of the moment we had shared, letting it flash through me as he dwelled on it, as his fear peaked. I knew at once what he had seen; I knew what was wrong.

"This is the wrong wall," I gasped. Ilyan's head whipped around as he searched for the right wall, his mind moving fast as he tried to place sense against what had just happened.

"This is wrong. The sight... it's wrong." His deep voice affected me more than I would have assumed. My father's warning was loud and angry in my ears. The sight had been broken, and now nothing was seen; nothing was guaranteed. My Drak magic heated me as it affirmed this, the power of the realization scaring me.

"I can't beat him," I said just as the screams of the Trpaslíks who descended on us reached my ears, Edmund's roar of anger rippling through them.

They were coming, the sounds warning us of how little time we had left.

"I don't know anymore. I don't know what is going to happen now," Ilyan said, his fear at his lack of knowledge startling.

This whole fight, all of Ilyan's life, had relied on that one sight, and now we stood on the wrong wall with everything shattered before us.

I felt Ilyan's determination—his readiness to die for me —but today was not my day to die, nor was it Ilyan's. I would see to that.

"I'm going to get us out of here!"

"How, Jolcyn? A Stutter could kill you right now."

"It'll be okay." I yelled the words over the rumble of fire and thunder that moved over us, the screams for blood mixing in with them until they broke through the thunder.

The vision from the sight I had a few minutes ago broke through me, my magic screaming at me, telling me what to do.

"Take the fire," I repeated the words from my sight as I held Ilyan against me, my blood burning as the lightning shot through it in answer.

My spine straightened as my magic sped through me, the trapped energy ready to do what the earth had designed it for.

Destroy.

My eyes shot to Ilyan's as he looked down at me in confusion, a wide smile spreading over my lips as I stretched onto the tips of my toes, my breath running over his lips as I extended up to meet them.

I could hear the screams of our pursuers and felt the rumble of the earth. I saw the battle as the others screamed, and I knew we needed to get there, knew I didn't have another choice. I was perfectly aware that the destiny everyone had laid out for me was wrong.

I pressed my lips against Ilyan's as the lightning inside of me sped up. The power was strong as Ilyan kissed me back, his touch desperate as his arm wound over my back, pressing me into him at the same time his tongue parted my lips. I let him into me, breathing him in as I felt his passion, the love growing without regret as the kiss deepened, my hands clawing at his sides in an attempt to bring him into me.

The fire in my stomach grew, my skin sealing itself together as Ilyan's hand trailed up my back, his touch soft against my neck as his finger made contact with my mark.

I screamed at the contact, at the way the lightning fought its way through me. It was the first time he had touched the small brand since our bonding, and our magic reacted, rocking through us with an aggressive force more powerful than I had ever felt before. His scream joined mine, an eruption of power and lightning streaking through the air as the Trpaslíks who surrounded us evaporated into smoke and ash, as the building we stood in rumbled and rocked with the power until I was sure it could not stand.

I gasped for air as my eyes opened, Ilyan's dark blue eyes staring into me as he tried to control his own breathing to regulate the power that still jolted through him. I looked into his eyes until the walls around us shifted, making it clear that the abbey was falling apart below us.

My eyes darted away as the wall moved, the silver of my eyes coming into contact with Edmund's for the first time in months and I smiled. I smiled because I knew there was nothing he could do to stop us, and while I would not kill him today, his day was coming.

I continued to smile as I clung to Ilyan, my eyes locked with Edmund's as my magic pulsed, as I sent the army that surrounded us away.

Fire ripped away from us as Ilyan's magic pulsed alongside mine, my body tightening against Ilyan's as he took us away.

Into the black void between worlds.

Into a place Edmund could not follow.

24

I CLUNG to Ilyan as the world re-emerged around us, ash and soot filling my lungs while the sound of fighting met my ears. My eyes shot open as I turned from Ilyan to the battle that still raged in front of us. It wasn't the battle we had just escaped from, however. This fight was a perfectly planned execution.

One that I would make sure would fail.

Sain and Dramin sat, huddled into each other not thirty feet from where we had emerged, their weak, defensive magic serving as no more than a shield around them. Wyn and Thom stayed as close to them as they could, their magic surging as they fought the Trpaslíks who streamed through the trees like a slow-flowing ketchup bottle.

Amongst them all was Ryland. A Ryland who screamed, and yelled, and cried. A Ryland who was attacking everyone.

Light and fire erupted from him as he screamed, his attacks firing at everyone with no regard for what side they might be on, or if they had already been attacked or not. He moved from screaming to crying so fast that it looked like someone had punched him. He cried as he turned to Wyn, his wails ringing through the trees as he fired a stream of golden knives at her.

The sharp blades glinted in the dim light before Wyn deflected them in one glance, her magic sending them to the ground before her hand pressed away from her. A line of dark ink shot from her palm, right to a Trpaslík who had just exploded from the trees, dropping him to the ground.

I'll stop Ryland, Ilyan said urgently, my mind buzzing with the strength of his magic as he pushed the words into me. *You get everyone to the cave.* Ilyan pushed a flash of our destination into my mind, the path perfectly laid out as he ran to his brother's aide.

I rushed toward Wyn as her magic surged, burning the two attackers in front of her to ash right before my eyes. They were frozen in screams before what remained of their bodies floated into the wind, adding to the mass amount of ash the burning forest had already surrounded us with.

Wyn's face lit up as I met them, the smile on her face chilling.

"Did you kill Edmund?" she asked in mad excitement, her hands flicking just as a tree to the right of her caught fire. Thom lifted it from the ground from where he stood, throwing it into a line of Trpaslíks running toward us.

"We have to get out of here!" I yelled back, purposefully avoiding her question. I didn't even know where to begin with an answer.

I stretched my magic out, my heart falling at the wave of attackers that were headed in our direction. We hadn't even begun to see the end of this; our only hope now was to run.

Wyn looked at me like she was going to press for information before she thought better of it and nodded once. Her jawline tightened as she turned to where Thom fought behind her, his magic strained as he tried to keep up with the battle that had surrounded them.

"Thom, you take the Draks with Jos. I can stop them all long enough to give us a good start, but you all have got to be ahead of me."

Thom nodded at Wyn's instructions at the same time that Dramin and Sain pulled themselves to standing. Thom moved closer, ready to whisk them away toward the cave that stood just beyond the next clump of trees.

Thom had just begun to get away as a woman with wild hair broke through the tree line right behind them, blocking their path. Her hands rose as I felt her magic surge toward Thom's exposed back, and my heart raced as I witnessed the underhanded attack take place.

My magic surged at seeing her there, the power reacting without me having to so much as move. The powerful pulse I sent toward her slammed into her heavy frame, sending her right into a large tree trunk, which promptly broke apart into slivers at the impact.

The three men jumped at hearing the wild woman scream, seeing the flash of light that had flown right over their heads. Their faces turned up to me in panic, but I only stood still, my chest heaving as I waited for my heart rate to stabilize after witnessing an attack on my family so close to me. Thom nodded toward me in thanks before he helped the two men into the forest, the Draks' tired bodies making their movement slow.

Ice raced through my blood as Wyn's scream rent the air behind me, the name on her lips igniting my fear "Ilyan!"

My magic surged toward him as I turned, almost expecting Ilyan to be writhing on the ground in agony. Instead he stood, his hand on Ryland as he put him to sleep, throwing his limp body over his shoulder before he turned to push the enemy that surrounded him back, their bodies crumpling to the ground.

"Ilyan!" Wyn screamed again, realization dawning on me. She wasn't scared for his life, she needed him to move.

Ilyan, run. You need to be ahead of Wyn. Run, I rambled. His fear heightened as he heard me, his confusion at what was going to happen running wild.

Run! I yelled to him, pleased when he turned, ready to make his escape. I didn't have time to explain.

"He's coming," I said to Wyn before turning to run after Thom, only to find him just beyond the clearing as he fought through a line of Trpaslíks who had hidden in the trees.

My magic surged as I threw one of the Trpaslíks to the ground, severing his spine as I pushed another away.

Ilyan ran up beside me, one swipe of his hand sending the remaining few ahead of us into the burning fire we stood beside, clearing the way for our escape. I lifted Dramin from where he had curled up on the ground, slinging his arm over my shoulder as I supported him, pulling him toward what I hoped would be security.

Our feet crashed through the undergrowth, heaving breaths and groans of pain sounding alongside the cracking of the fire that raged through the forest. I pushed ahead blindly, moving through a wall of smoke only to feel the earth begin to shake, the heat of Wyn's magic surging through the ground as it rippled under us. I felt it move through the earth, a wave that heated the soil only to shoot through my feet and up my legs in a wave of fire.

I let out a gasp, my eyes darting to Ilyan in fear as I ran. The burn boiled through my bones, continuing up my spine in an uncomfortable pain that made it hard to move. I opened my mouth in horror before the pain lessened, just as

Wyn came streaking behind us, a maniacal laugh on her lips.

"Run!" she yelled joyfully, as the heat in my feet sizzled in tiny points of pain and pressure.

I heard the screams behind us, and I didn't dare turn to see what Wyn had done. I only ran, my feet picking up as I helped Dramin through the forest, toward the dark jaw of the earth, the jagged teeth of the ancient rocks welcoming us in.

Our breaths heaved in exhaustion as we moved, the opening growing wider and wider the closer we got until the blackness swallowed us up, leaving the flames of fire and the screams of pain behind us.

My chest ached, my stomach twisting in agony as it tried to rip open again. I ignored it all. I didn't stop running.

Magic sparked around me in a multitude of colors that bounced off us and lit the way into what appeared to be an endless stretch of tunnel. The colors flickered against stone, the mixtures giving off rainbows of light that in any other situation might have been beautiful, yet right then, they were horrifying.

The sounds of our pounding feet echoed off the cave walls as the light did, our breaths coming in pants and spurts and grunts as we pushed ourselves beyond what our physical bodies would allow. My magic pulsed through me as I ran, but I could already feel my energy lessening, the power straining as I pushed. I didn't dare stop, not yet; I could still feel the Trpaslíks, their pursuit resuming just behind us, their magic surging as whatever Wyn had done wore off.

"Does it strike anyone else as funny that I am in the same cave, running to the exact same city I escaped from less than a month ago?" Wyn asked, her voice coming in spurts as she panted in her exhaustion.

"Shut up and run, Wynifred," Thom snapped, the red light he held in his hand flashing in his agitation. "At least you wanted to be here in the first place."

"Through Germany or through Italy?" Wyn asked from ahead, obviously ignoring Thom's outburst.

I looked ahead, part of me desperately hoping to see the end—to see something ahead that would mean some rest—but instead I saw a wall of rock with two smaller openings, each leading in an opposite direction.

One to Italy, one to Germany, just as Wyn had said. I couldn't tear my eyes from the darkness of the caves, the endless pits desperately wishing to swallow us up, however, it was more than that. I had seen this somewhere before.

My feet kept pumping as my vision flashed to black, the recall of the sight I had right after I had healed Wyn blocking my vision in a spark of light before it was gone, leaving the same two caves I had seen in front of me.

"Take the left!" I yelled, everyone in front of me turning toward the left tunnel without question.

I had barely turned my feet toward the new destination before my vision blacked out again, my body only able to keep my feet moving forward as my mind filled with another sight: Edmund and his men digging away at a wall of rock at the right tunnel while leaving the left tunnel untouched.

I watched them dig, Edmund yelling, the slight shimmer over the other tunnel giving me all that I needed to know.

"Collapse the other tunnel," I panted. Thom's face whipped around to look at me in confusion. I just ignored him, keeping my face straight ahead as I screamed, "Do it!"

Ilyan's magic flared as he sent one pulse through the

rock, a giant crack moving through the ceiling as rocks began to fall, blocking the other tunnel.

Everyone ran through the dark opening of the left cave, the lights they held in their hands flickering against the dirt and stone as the tiny opening drew us in.

Keep running, I panted into Ilyan's mind, my feet sliding against stone as I slid to a stop, a plume of dust and pebbles flying around me.

I watched Ilyan, Dramin and the others continue to run into the endless dark. The light they held dimmed until I stood alone in the darkness, my breath heaving in my chest. My body ached as I watched the black before me, my magic pulling me after Ilyan, while my heart pumped in expectation of what I needed to do.

I ran back to the opening, my legs screaming in agony as I continued to push them. My chest shook as I inhaled, raising my hands into the air. My palms were flat as I pushed them against the space in the opening of the cave, and the wide wall that I was going to create in an attempt to keep Edmund from pursuing us. My magic surged as my fingers stretched, a shimmering smoke seeping from my fingertips. The smoke was like liquid against oil as it spun and danced in the air, moving and swirling and fanning out as it crept from me.

Light oozed from my hands as the shield grew and spread. A weak glow floated around me as it licked against the air. The smoke stretched over the opening like a net, the light touching every bit of space before the opening was sealed. The light of my magic decreased as it solidified, creating a seemingly solid wall of rock. To the cave beyond my wall, the barrier was now just an expanse of stone, another stretch of wall, the same as it was surrounded by. To me, it was a window that tinted everything brown and red until the light seeped from the surface, leaving me in the ebony pitch.

I stood still in the dark, my breathing a heavy pant as I tried to get my body to relax, my attempts forgotten as more than a dozen Trpaslíks ran through the main tunnel, their own lights held in front of them. My breath tightened in my chest as they ran into the space, my body frozen as I tried to convince myself that they couldn't see me. They screamed in anger, their pace slowing as they faced the caved-in tunnel before them, unaware that I stood only feet away.

The lights they held flickered as they looked around in question, each of them yelling in a language I didn't understand before they ran at the collapsed cave, their fingers clawing at the rocks that blocked the opening while their magic surged and began to blast the rock away.

I didn't need to see any more. I turned and ran, a light of pure gold erupting in my hand as my magic pulsed. I moved as fast as I could, my legs protesting every step, my muscles aching and throbbing. I pushed myself until the burn left, unable to ignore the desperate call of my heart to meet back up with the others. With Ilyan.

Are you okay? I asked Ilyan as I ran, hoping that he could still hear me.

That he wasn't too far away.

Yes, his deep, worried voice pulsed into my head, giving me a little bit of relief. *Is it safe?*

Yes. It worked. They can't see our cave. They should be working on your collapse for a while.

You are amazing, my love. I smiled at his words, not knowing what to say to them. I slowed my pace as my heart swelled, the calm I felt moving right into him. Our hearts slowed in unison, my soul calming as his did.

We are going to stop and make camp. They can't go on much

longer, he said, and I could already feel his body slow, the pulse of his magic growing stronger as he stopped. They weren't that far ahead of me; it should take me about ten minutes to walk there.

My agitation calmed at the thought, and I quickened my pace a bit, desperate to get back to Ilyan as fast as I could.

I'll be there soon, I whispered.

I'll be waiting.

I smiled at the tenderness in his voice, the calm that he pushed into my heart, and I continued walking. The golden light I held in my hand pulsed against the crevices of stone I was surrounded by, making it look like I had inadvertently walked into a cave of gold and diamonds. It was beautiful.

I fought the urge to reach my hand out and touch the glittery surface, not wanting the illusion to be destroyed. The golden light looked so pure, so perfect. I wanted to share the light with everyone.

I smiled at the thought just as my magic pulsed, the signature of Wyn's magic flying right toward me. Her power seemed heightened as she ran at me, the strong heat setting me on edge.

Wyn is coming to you, Ilyan spoke into my mind, the tone of his voice adding to the worry her magic had given me

Yes, I can feel her.

She knows. His voice was simple, but it ran through me like ice. I knew she did, I had seen that look in her eyes in the kitchen before, but I could already tell that this visit wasn't going to be congratulatory.

Is she mad? I asked, her magic flaring the closer she came. Ilyan's agitation washed over me, his memory rushing into me as it repeated the quick conversation he had with her.

I could see her prod for answers, her demeanor more of

that confusing adult persona that had been flashing through her lately. Ilyan had laughed at her demand, unwilling to give her the answers, and so she stormed out, right to me.

I guess I'll find out. I cringed when a blob of orange light flared ahead of me as she grew closer, the aggressive flare of anxiety running through me. I pushed it away as best I could before she came into view.

"So when exactly were you going to tell me?" she snapped the moment she came into view, the orange light she held mixing with my gold to make the cave look like molded cheese sauce.

I already missed the gold.

I watched her come, letting her words wash over me, determined to keep my face as impassable as possible, knowing she would see through it anyway. As much as I wanted to tell her, I was still apprehensive, and her full blown accusation wasn't helping much.

"Tell you what?" I asked, my voice higher than it should have been for such a simple question. I guessed I wasn't going to be able to make her fight for it as much as I wanted.

Sure enough, she rolled her eyes, her jaw clenching and unclenching in agitation.

"Oh, don't play coy," she grumbled as she came right up to me, forcing me to come to a full stop. "I can read you like an open book. You walking around like a goon wearing a hoodie, Ilyan binding his hair with the délka vedení královského again, and obviously Ilyan can read your mind or some nonsense. It's not like you guys really hid it or anything."

I knew we hadn't; we had foolishly tried, and I supposed to anyone else it might have worked, but not to Wyn, not to Dramin, and certainly not to Ryland.

I swallowed the lump that had built in my throat and

tried to come up with some form of response, but none came, so I held still and waited for the police-force-style questioning to continue, knowing full-well I had to answer her. Judging by the smile trying to creep onto her face, she knew, too. Although, I wasn't sure if she was going to erupt into giggles or hysterics.

"When?" she asked, her voice hard even though I could still see the smile trying to escape.

I exhaled deeply and looked away; I knew I couldn't leave her completely hanging.

"Last night. After we left your room," I whispered, my voice breaking as if I was letting her in on some dirty secret.

"Obviously," Wyn said as she rolled her eyes again, the action so over-exaggerated that I couldn't help but smile. "Well, at least whatever I said worked."

"I knew it."

It was a lie; I hadn't really known it so to speak, but looking back on it now, it made perfect sense. Silly, meddling Wyn just wouldn't leave well enough alone; she never did. I should have caught onto her game sooner, however, at the time, I had been too embarrassed at having been caught in such a conversation.

Wyn smiled, breaking through the angry mask she had given herself and prancing a bit through the darkened cave, her joy at having been caught in her game infectious.

"I couldn't let Ilyan ruin this for himself. He's been waiting so long." Wyn laughed as she pleaded her case, but she didn't need to; I agreed with her

"I know."

"I am happy for you," she squealed in my ear as she rushed at me, the bone-crushing hug wrapped so tightly around me I was having trouble breathing, yet I didn't care. I clung to her as she did me, the wide, goofy grin plastered to my face.

"You seem so much stronger, calm. I don't know how to explain it, but something has changed."

"Thank you," I gasped, the words barely coming out.

Wyn pulled away, finally realizing I couldn't breathe, her body practically bouncing with excitement before me.

"So are you going to let me see it?" I stiffened at her question, my nerves prickling in fear. I had no idea what she was talking about. My confusion must have been clear on my face because Wyn rolled her eyes as she pulled at the hood that was still placed on my head.

"The braid," she clarified, her voice showing exaggerated irritation. "I am assuming Ilyan did it the right way this time."

Her voice had gotten soft, the whisper almost pulling me back into the ceremony—the beauty of it, the feel of Ilyan's fingers in my hair. I could still feel that secrecy, that need to keep something so beautiful hidden, something for Ilyan and me to treasure. Strangely, part of me wanted to show her, though, like a secret that you just couldn't keep to yourself.

My heart thumped as my stomach turned, my hands lifting to remove the hood that Ilyan had so gently placed over his masterpiece. I felt the weight on my head change as I released the braid, the long, golden ribbon untangling itself to fall down my back and snake to the floor. Wyn said nothing as she stepped around me, her breath catching. I waited for an explanation, anything, but she stayed silent.

"Is it good?" I asked when I couldn't take it any longer; her silence was too much. My hands wound around each other in agitation as I waited, her fingers pressing against the soft strands of hair.

"I have never seen one so perfect before," she finally said, her voice unbelievably awed. "The lines... nothing is out of place. And the roses, I have never seen the ribbons bound into roses."

The soft pressure I had felt left as I felt a gentle tug, certain she was letting her hands run down the délka vedení královského.

"Did it hurt? He must have had to pull to get it so right."

"I barely felt anything," I whispered, my heart beating faster as the memory swelled, the strangely intimate moment affecting me more than I would have thought.

"Really?" Wyn asked, her voice echoing around us as she shrieked, her shock causing me to smile more. "Talon gave me a bruise, right here."

Wyn pressed gently against my head, right above my left ear, and I couldn't help grinning. I had felt nothing except the touch of Ilyan's fingertips and the gentle pressure of his lips against my head.

"You are blessed, My Lady. I cannot think of anyone more perfect than you to take that role." My insides tightened as she spoke. For some reason, my new title hadn't bothered me so much with Dramin, but with Wyn, it felt foreign and unwanted.

"Don't call me that," I said, the snap coming out of my voice no matter how much I tried to ignore it. I spun to face her, my sudden movement shocking her, and she froze with her eyes wide, her hand still lifted awkwardly in the air.

"My Lady?" She looked at me with those wide eyes before her features softened, her hand dropping to perch indignantly on her hip. It was already obvious that she was going to fight me on this, something I really wasn't interested in.

I exhaled deeply and walked away from her, following

my magic as it pulled me toward Ilyan. My golden light followed me as I moved, the bouncing of it matching my gait almost perfectly.

"You wear the délka vedení královského," Wyn said as she ran up to me. My heart fell that she was going to push it so soon. "It's kind of a requirement, Jos."

"Don't give me that." I turned toward her as I walked, my voice a little harder than I had intended it to be. "You barely call Ilyan My Lord; you can break the rule for me."

I knew I was pleading, begging, and I knew it shouldn't mean anything, but it did.

I pulled out the full, pouty lip at her as we walked, knowing I needed to break out the big guns. Thankfully, she only laughed, lacing her arm through mine.

"Well, if it's for you," she said with a smile just as the bright light of the campfire ahead flickered into view. "I am still happy it's you, My Lady."

I glared at her, but she only smiled brightly at me.

"Now that I have shown you my secret, you need to tell me yours." I kept my voice low, hoping to prompt her into being honest about whatever was going on with her and Thom, and how she was coping with Talon's death.

Her smile faded for a second as she sucked in breath, her chest heaving as she looked away from me toward the glow of the campfire that continued to grow closer, her face lighting again almost immediately.

"I guess I owe you that, don't I?" she said, her voice brightening. "Tomorrow."

Wyn smiled broadly at me as she walked away from me and into camp. My nerves prickled in agitation, but I guess I couldn't get too mad; this time I had a feeling she was actually going to talk to me. Either that or I would force it out of her.

I shook my head as I followed her into the circle of light where everyone had made camp, the warmth of the fire moving over me. The fire glowed a brilliant yellow, the blaze peeking out from a pile of rocks as if the rocks themselves were on fire. Everyone sat close enough to the fire that they were bathed in its light, most leaning against the side of the narrow tunnel as they tried to find comfort. Their bodies were spent and exhausted after what we had just gone through.

Sain was handing Dramin a large mug from where he sat, his magic throbbing dully with exhaustion. Ilyan stood up from where he had been hunched over Ryland's sleeping body at our arrival, his face tense, almost apprehensive at how things had gone between Wyn and me.

Are you all right, my love? he asked silently, his eyes capturing mine the closer I walked to him.

I nodded my head once as Wyn smiled at me. Her knowing glare sent my stomach squirming until she left me, walking over to where Thom sat, his body sprawled out as if he was sleeping. I knew better, though; he was far too still to be sleeping.

Sain turned toward us as Ilyan came to my side, but I didn't move my eyes from Ilyan's. My magic rocked through me as Ilyan grabbed my hand, lifting it to press it against his face.

"Are you sure?" he asked, his tone deep as his magic flared, moving right to my abdomen and where the large opening had been minutes before. Through everything, I had almost forgotten what had happened.

My face tightened as the memory flashed through me. Ilyan's hand left mine as he pulled the hood back over my head, carefully making sure everything was hidden.

Ilyan said nothing as he led me back into the darkness of

the cave away from everyone else. His shield moved around us to block us from view as we walked. We didn't move far, only far enough that we were out of earshot, where the only light was the faded glow of the fire. Everything around us was chilled and cast in shadow.

"Did Ilyan leave?" Thom suddenly said from behind us, his gruff voice filled with exaggerated mocking. "I really wanted him to tuck me in, too."

My head spun around at his voice just in time to see Wyn smack him upside the head while Dramin chuckled from the other side of the tunnel. I couldn't help but smile at the exchange, something about it so normal and familiar even though I could feel Ilyan's frustration usurp the humor in it.

"Does everyone know?" I whispered, my nerves flying rapidly through me as I asked the question.

Ilyan smiled, his joy streaming through me as he moved me against the wall. I leaned against the cold rock as his hand rested against the cave wall right next to my head, his body moving closer to me until I was trapped with only an inch of air between us.

"Everyone knows," he said, his smiling eyes meeting mine before his lips twitched and he lowered himself to inspect the blood-stained gash on the hoodie, and the mutilated flesh underneath.

"We need to take this off." Ilyan didn't wait for me to answer; he just balled the thick fabric as he lifted the heavy hoodie over my head, his movements careful as he worked to keep my shirt in place and the braid untouched.

I closed my eyes as the fabric passed overhead, only opening them at the touch of Ilyan's hand against my shoulder, the sound of fabric against stone as he dropped the hoodie to the ground.

Ilyan wasn't looking at me, though; his eyes were focused on the massive red stain on the shirt. The glistening patches of my own blood appearing twice as bad in the dim light of the cave. Ilyan's hands dragged down my bare arms as he kneeled before me again, his hands squeezing mine before he let me go, his eyes focused intently on my abdomen.

He lifted my shirt as his hands brushed against my stomach, revealing the layer of blood that had dried against me.

The warmth of his breath ran over me as his fingers moved over my abdomen, his chest tight in worry. He said nothing as he grabbed the hoodie off the ground, pressing it against my bare stomach as his magic surged through the fabric. The fabric warmed against my skin as he pulled the water out of the air and into it, giving him a chance to clean the blood that covered me.

His movements were slow and gentle as he cleaned me until all that was left was a long, raised brown scar the stretched over my navel and down toward my hipbone, right where the Trpaslík's blade had cut through me.

Ilyan sucked in a pained breath as he saw the ugly scar, his fingertips tracing along the long, dark line as I held my breath. His touch was soft as his heartbeat faltered, his regret flooding into me. I could see it in his eyes and hear the thoughts of failure as my stomach tightened.

I reached forward and ran my hand over the soft feathers of his hair before he looked up to me, his eyes wide as he pled for forgiveness.

"You didn't fail me, Ilyan," I whispered. "You healed me; you got me out alive. This is not failure."

He said nothing as he looked at me before he closed his eyes, his regret melting away. He looked down, leaning forward until his lips pressed against the long, ugly scar that I knew I would always have. His magic surged through me at the touch, my stomach tightening as the intimate touch jolted through me.

His lips lingered as his magic flowed to check for any internal injuries he might have missed. I moved down carefully to kneel in front of him, my knees digging into the hard stone as I met him eye to eye in the darkness of the cave.

I could still see the regret, feel his worry. It hurt that I couldn't take away that feeling of failure. It was more than just my injury that was bothering me, though; it was failure of another kind.

"I will kill him, Ilyan," I whispered, my voice hard with the conviction I knew he shared. "I know the sight has changed, but I will find a way."

"I know you will. I will fight alongside you," he said, his voice soft as his hand moved over my shoulder and down to my elbow. "Let's just hope we can get to Prague before the Vilỳs do too much damage and the city is lost."

After everything that had happened, I had almost forgotten about everything that I had seen in the sight that I had shared with Sain before Dramin had awakened. Just hearing Ilyan speak about it—feeling his worry for his home—brought the images into my mind along with Sain's promise that the sight had already happened.

But it hadn't already happened. Dramin had told me that past sights were always dimmed, the pictures and voices echoed. These were clear as day. What was more, I had been in them. I had been running into the rock wall; I had been sitting on the rooftop.

I don't know why Sain would have said they had already happened; why he would have lied. I had watched as the sky

375

rained with Vilÿs. I had seen a small child screaming amongst the rubble...

"I don't think that attack has begun," I said, my voice deep as my Drak blood flared.

Ilyan's eyes widened as I spoke, his confusion clear as the grip against my elbow increased. My magic ignited right along his, the uncertainty rumbling through me.

"What are you saying?" Ilyan asked, his voice deep.

I swallowed, my eyes darting away as I tried to figure out what to say to him. I wasn't quite sure if explaining the way the images weren't dimmed would be clear enough. Besides, it was more than just the images; it was a feeling. Something that my blood promised was still to come.

"In my sight, it felt like it was *coming*," I explained, hoping it was enough.

It was. Ilyan's jaw clenched, a feral growl rumbling through his chest as he understood.

"You mean we could be heading into a trap?"

He said the words and my blood sped up as if in answer. We were walking into a trap. Somehow, the sights had been broken even before we had run into the forest, perhaps even before I had healed Dramin. Something had changed and the fate of our future had been manipulated. I wasn't sure how, but I knew one thing: Nothing was guaranteed anymore.

"Yes," I gasped as I reached toward him, my fingers winding around the fabric of his shirt in desperation.

"But you had that sight before the battle."

"I know," I gasped. "And the caves? I saw those after I healed Wyn. Before I even healed Dramin; before our bonding. Why am I seeing things before the sight was broken; things that happen after I was supposed to die?"

"I don't know. Sain will know."

"I don't trust him, Ilyan. I feel like he isn't telling me something." I had expected Ilyan to fight me on my statement, to try to convince me that I was wrong, but he stayed still, his head nodding slightly in understanding. Almost as if he agreed with me.

"We will figure this out and find a way to end this together." Ilyan's hand moved from my elbow to the exposed skin of my hip as he spoke, the promise so clear in his eyes that it took my breath away.

I knew we would because, even though so much of the sight had come to pass, there was much more still hidden from us. And if there was one thing that boiled in my blood and promised me of its fruition, it was that I would be the one to kill Edmund.

"I will defeat Edmund, Ilyan. I was born to do so, and even though the sight has changed, I know that I will with you by my side."

"I know you will," he said, his thumb running over the raised skin of my scar, the movement heating my sensitive blood, the need for his touch sparking deep.

I reached up and ran my fingers over his lips as his eyes met mine, the fire in them hot and dangerous. I smiled at the look, my hand sliding around his neck as I pulled him to me, his lips meeting mine for the first time in what felt like days.

I sighed at the pressure, at the way our magic flared and heated. He wrapped his arm around my waist as he pulled me against him, his hand a wide fan against my back.

I groaned at the pressure, the sound coming out much louder than I had expected it to be in the stillness of the cave. It echoed around us only to have the laugh of the camp echo back, Thom's joyous taunt following the echo.

"Sound barrier, Brother!" he yelled.

Everything froze in me, and I pulled away, suddenly wishing I could find a way to hide.

Ilyan, however, smiled, his arms pulling me back into him as he kissed me again. I smiled at the contact, moving to stand when he did. Our hesitant feet took us back to the fire, Ilyan's shield dropping from us once we were bathed in the light of the fire.

Thankfully, when we returned, Thom and Wyn seemed occupied in some form of heated conversation while Sain kneeled over Ryland, leaving Dramin and his wide smile to greet us. A shock of embarrassed pleasure moved up my spine at the look Dramin gave me, and I turned into Ilyan, his hand wrapping around my waist on instinct. It was that touch that flared in me, and I turned my eyes, squinting through the dark in search of the hoodie we had left behind.

"Be proud, my love," Ilyan whispered in my ear, obviously picking up on my alarm. I looked up at him only to be met by his sweet smile. He kissed me once on the cheek before moving away toward where Sain was crowded over Ryland.

I remained still after he left me, feeling very out of place standing in the middle of everyone, fully aware that Thom could see the braid from where he sat behind me. I looked around in confusion until Dramin met my eyes, his face wide and happy as he lifted a mug toward me.

I couldn't help grinning at the action, happy to have somewhere to go and not to stand like a loon for much longer. I slid down the wall next to him, Dramin handing me the mug in silence before he turned back to where Sain and Ilyan gathered around Ryland, the steam from his water floating through the air.

We sat in silence as we drank, the quiet feeling

comfortable and almost needed. After all, there wasn't anything that needed to be said. I could feel Dramin's comfort at making it through the battle alive, and in a lot of ways I felt the same way. I could have asked him about the sights, but I knew he already knew, and nothing we said about it now would change anything; there was always tomorrow.

I rested my head back against the stone wall, and for the first time in what felt like days, I wanted to find rest. Thanks to the Drak blood that flowed through my veins, I wasn't tired, but my body was exhausted.

I leaned against the rock wall as Sain stepped away from Ryland, leaving Ilyan alone with his brother as he came to join us. He didn't take his eyes off me as he sat on the other side of Dramin, the intensity of his stare making me uncomfortable. I could tell at once he had something to say, some sort of blame for our failure, for the broken sights. For anything.

I didn't want to hear it.

My jaw stiffened uncomfortably as I looked stubbornly into the fire, then at the grey rock that surrounded us, anywhere other than at the potent look he had fixed me with.

"Joclyn," Sain began, his voice softer than it had been, almost a whisper.

I could tell he wanted me to turn to him, but I wasn't going to give him that. So I stayed still, letting the whisper of what came next wash over me.

"I am so sorry for treating you the way I have. After waiting so long to have you return..." He paused, his head hanging down as his shoulders rose and fell.

I waited, waited for more to come.

Wishing I could block him out in some way.

"I'm sorry," he repeated. "I should not expect so much of you. I am glad to see you alive."

I jerked toward him, my jaw working as I let his words seep into me. I just stared at him, not trusting his words, not wanting to believe them. He had told me hours before that he would celebrate my death, and now he was grateful for my life.

I didn't really think he felt either of those.

I nodded once, not trusting myself to say anything. Sain's face fell ever so slightly before he moved away from me and leaned against the wall.

I turned away from him just as Ilyan moved away from Ryland to Thom and Wyn, who already looked to be half asleep. Wyn had her head resting on Thom's shoulder and didn't even move as he approached. Thom only nodded in feigned sleep at whatever Ilyan said before Ilyan moved over to us.

"We are going to rest for five hours before we move again. We need to get to the safe house above the clock before night falls tomorrow, so the earlier start we get, the better." Dramin nodded his head at Ilyan's words, and I had a sinking sensation that he had already known what Ilyan was going to say.

"Sain has said we will be safe while we sleep, so I suggest everyone rest," Ilyan continued, the deep presence of the king heavy in the darkness of the cave.

Sain and Dramin both nodded their heads before closing their eyes, their bodies already relaxing in feigned sleep. I wasn't sure the Drak would let them sleep.

Come, my love, Ilyan whispered into my mind, his hand extended toward me. I set Dramin's mug down as Ilyan pulled me to standing. His fingers weaved through mine as I followed him to the other side of the fire where the last open space sat across from where Ryland slept. Everyone else was laid before us like the spokes of the wheel. I could see them all. I don't know why, but for some reason the thought made me calm.

I slid down onto the rock as I tried to get comfortable, careful to keep my braid from touching the rough rock behind me.

"Are you tired?" Ilyan asked as he sat beside me, his voice soft in my ear as he leaned toward me.

"No," I whispered, my spine shivering at the feeling of Ilyan's breath against my neck.

I turned my head toward him, pressing my lips against his forehead as I leaned into him. I could feel the exhaustion in his body. I could sense his heart rate slowing as my magic flowed into him.

"Go to sleep," I whispered against him as I pressed him down into my lap.

His body settled into me as I moved the hair that had come free of my haphazard braid out of his face. I ran my fingers over the stubble on his jawline, the bridge of his nose, then the soft skin over his eyes. I traced the lines of his face as he relaxed, moving closer to sleep at the contact. He looked up at me as my finger ran over his neck, his bright eyes blazing.

I love you, Můj kamarád, he whispered into my mind as his eyes closed, his body relaxing against me as his arm moved to wind around my legs.

I sat still underneath him as I continued to touch him, his body still under my caress, relaxing further with each touch as his breathing lengthened and I was sure he was asleep.

I sat in the dark as I listened to Ilyan's breathing—the deep, calming tempo of everyone's breathing relaxing—but it was Ilyan's that moved through me, that rocked me. I could feel the calming pulse of his heart. I could hear the sleepy fragments of his thoughts as his dreams flowed through me. I heard our song in his mind as he slept, my lips humming through the silence as I joined him, my heart swelling at the depth of the connection we shared.

I had never felt so calm. Nothing had ever felt so right.

I closed my eyes as I finished the song, letting the warmth of the fire that still blazed among the rocks kiss my face.

"Does he make you happy?" The voice came out of nowhere. It was so familiar that it should have been calming, yet it only had the opposite effect.

My spine stiffened as my eyes snapped toward Ryland, his body so still he could have been sleeping, but I had heard his voice, and I would know it anywhere.

Waves of impregnated fear washed over me, the emotions strong as I pushed them away, knowing that now was not the time for a fight, and agitating Ryland would only end in disaster.

"Yes," I answered, my voice tight as I tried to keep my anger at bay.

"I can tell," Ryland said, his voice just as relaxed as before. He sighed and turned onto his back, his body flopping over as his eyes stayed focused above him into the hard, black of the roof of the cave. I was glad he didn't look at me; I didn't think that either of our emotional instabilities could handle that right now.

I looked away from him, careful to keep my focus on the fire, even though I could still see him, just in front of me through the flames. I just looked, not knowing what else to say, secretly hoping that he would fall back to sleep.

"The way you look at him, the way he looks at you, it's

different than with us. It's better." Ryland's voice remained calm. He spoke casually and the fear that had stiffened my spine relaxed, the tone of his voice giving me hope that maybe we could share a real conversation; that maybe things could get better. "He's made you better."

"Is that a good thing?" I whispered. Even though I knew better than to egg him on, right then I couldn't help it. It seemed so natural, so much like how it used to be all those months ago.

"Yeah," he said, the smile clear in his voice, and I couldn't help it; I looked.

My eyes shot over to him just as his lips turned up, his eyes darting over to mine before returning to the ceiling, obviously worried that looking at me would ignite his monster. I understood the fear, I felt the same way. I looked away as fast as he did, my heartbeat accelerating as I tried desperately to calm it.

I focused on the beat, on slowing it down as the silence stretched between us. I could feel the thump, the fear, until it left, leaving a silence that made me wonder if we had somehow ruined our chance.

As much as I wanted to sit with him the way we used to, we still weren't there. Not yet.

"You remember how your mom's rolls were too bitter until Metta came along and showed her how to do it right?" He continued speaking as if nothing had happened, as if his eyes hadn't turned black at seeing me, as if I hadn't felt the need to kill him rise up in me. As if the silence hadn't stretched between us for the past few minutes. "That's how it is with you two."

"Are you saying I'm bitter?" I asked, my voice snapping as the last of my fear and anger left me. Ryland didn't seem to notice, however. He only laughed.

"No, I am saying that Ilyan has made you sweet. Perfect."

"Do you mean that, or are you going to turn around and try to attack me?"

"I mean it." His voice was so honest that it almost broke me into pieces, scattering me and my emotions across the cave floor.

I stiffened at the realization, at hearing him admit to something that had worried me so much. I knew I should have given him thanks—said anything—but I couldn't. My shock had frozen all capable speech, and I looked toward him, careful to keep my breathing even as his eyes met mine.

My breath caught as his did, neither of us looking away, lost in each other's eyes as we both battled the demons that lived inside of us. As I tried to ignore the scream to kill him that was echoing in my mind.

I swallowed and forced my eyes away, not trusting myself to push it even further.

"I won't attack you, not right now," he whispered, his voice even.

My fingers wrapped around Ilyan's hand subconsciously, even though his fingers were limp in sleep. His magic responded to the contact, warming me, helping me.

"What changed?" I asked, my voice a gasp as my nerves swallowed it up.

"My father is too far away. The soul's blade is too far away. He's been using it against me, manipulating me."

"Manipulating your soul?" I asked, my insides tangling in physical pain, the memory of how my soul had ached by being separated from Ilyan.

I had given him back his heart, but it hadn't been enough.

"I'll fix this, Ry." My voice was hard as I spoke, my words

more of a vow than a promise. I felt the conviction deep down inside, my need to help my friend a burning that I was determined to heal.

I looked at him, waiting for him to turn, but he stayed still, his eyes focused above as his lips turned up.

"See, that's what I mean. You're better," he whispered, and I couldn't help it, I smiled.

"I like seeing you smile. Your smile... it never used to hit your eyes; it never used to make the diamonds sparkle, not like it does now. I saw it first this morning. I saw them shine."

I was unable to look away from him, my smile fading as his words began to sink in. I didn't understand what he meant. No, that was wrong, I didn't want to understand because even I felt the difference in me. It wasn't just strength; it was something more, something that I wasn't even sure I understood yet.

"I am happy for you, my diamond girl." His voice drifted away as he turned away from me, the familiar phrase sounding somewhat foreign to me now.

I couldn't look away from his back as his broad chest rose and fell, the rhythm slowing as he fell back to sleep. I sat still as his breathing joined the others, my heart caught between happiness and confusion.

I couldn't be sure, but I thought that Ryland had given me his blessing. That he really was happy for me. Somehow, that made everything in my life seem a little more perfect, a little less hopeless.

I sighed and leaned back against the rock as I looked away from Ryland, away from the fire toward the heavy black of the cave that stretched far ahead of us. The black tunnel that would serpentine through Europe until we found Prague, the city I had never seen with my own eyes.

But I had seen it.

I had seen it in my sights, in my vision of the trap that was ahead of us.

Somewhere, beyond the black in front of me was a battle that waited for me.

And tomorrow, I would meet it.

ALSO BY REBECCA ETHINGTON

THE WORLD OF IMDALIND

THE IMDALIND SERIES

KISS OF FIRE, IMDALIND #1

EYES OF EMBER, IMDALIND #2

SCORCHED TREACHERY, IMDALIND #3

SOUL OF FLAME, IMDALIND #4

BURNT DEVOTION, IMDALIND #5

BRAND OF BETRAYAL, IMDALIND #6

DAWN OF ASH, IMDALIND #7

CROWN OF CINDERS, IMDALIND #8

ILYAN, IMDALIND #9

THE KING OF IMDALIND SERIES

SPARK OF VENGEANCE, BOOK 1

FLARE OF VILLAINY, BOOK 2 (COMING 2019)

BOOKS 3-6 TBA

THE CIRCUS OF SHIFTERS

THE PHOENIX'S ASHES SERIES

RISE OF THE WITCH, BOOK ONE

FALL OF THE DRAGON, BOOK TWO

FLIGHT OF THE KING, BOOK THREE

Flame of the Phoenix, Book Four

The Dragon Queen Series

Rising Flame (coming March 2019)

Books 2-4 TBA

THE OTHER WORLDS

The Through Glass Series

Book One: The Dark

Book Two: The Blue

Book Three: The Rose

Book Four: The Cut

Book Five: The Light (Coming 2019)

Book Six: The Ascended (Coming 2019)

Of River and Raynn, The Series

The Catalyst: Act One (Rereleases 2019)

The Requisite: Act Two (Coming 2019)

ABOUT THE AUTHOR

Rebecca Ethington is an internationally bestselling author with almost 700,000 books sold. Her breakout debut, The Imdalind Series, has been featured on bestseller lists since its debut in 2012, reaching thousands of adoring fans worldwide and cited as "Interesting and Intense" by *USA Today's Happily Ever After Blog*.

From writing horror to romance and creating every sort of magical creature in between, Rebecca's imagination weaves vibrant worlds that transport readers into the pages of her books. Her writing has been described as fresh, original, and groundbreaking, with stories that bend genres and create fantastical worlds.

Born and raised under the lights of a stage, Rebecca has written stories by the ghost light, told them in whispers in dark corridors, and never stopped creating within the pages of a notebook.

Find me online
www.rebeccaethington.com
contact@rebeccaethington.com

ACKNOWLEDGMENTS

Sometimes there are not enough words to convey the thanks
you feel to all the people who supported you.

This is one of those times.

I love you all.

THE IMDALIND SERIES, BOOK 5
FULL SERIES AVAILABLE NOW